Death's Dream Kingdom

Being the first Volume of

THE REDGLASS TRILOGY

There is no happinesse within this circle of flesh,

nor is it in the opticks of these eyes to behold felicity;

the first day of our jubilee is death.

Sir Thomas Browne, *Religio Medici*

First publication: Clickworks Press, 2015.
Release: CP‑RGT1‑INT‑P.IS‑1.1

ISBN‑10: 1‑943383‑18‑9
ISBN‑13: 978‑1‑943383‑18‑4

For the gentlemen of Pints and Prose,
in gratitude for their remarkable artistic good sense,
and their tolerance in sitting through this work
so many times.

A faithful friend is a strong defense:
and he that hath found such an one, hath found a treasure.
Nothing doth counteruail a faithful friend,
and his excellency is vnualuable.
—Wisdom of Sirach VI.14-15

Editor's Preface

This volume contains a redacted reproduction of the first volume of the well-known *Diaries* of Miss Marie Redglass, once thought to have been lost or destroyed. The *Diaries* provide an invaluable, direct insight into the vampire society of the nineteenth and twentieth centuries, and do appear to be one of the few sources on the subject penned by an eyewitness, rather than a mere recorder of testimony.

It is, to the best of my ability, a faithful version. Some editing was required: chiefly for the purposes of formatting, expanding some of the authoress' often cryptic shorthand, limited rearrangements of the text in the interests of comprehensibility, and the inclusion of some related material from the few surviving records and letters of this fascinating aspect of London's history. I have also appended an index of foreign language passages (both Miss Redglass and her original audience, being acquainted with Latin and French as a matter of course and with Italian, Greek, and German not infrequently, naturally composed no such guide), and a list of the persons mentioned in the book, with some of the more significant facts about them, so far as I have been able to research them. As a rule, excellencies should be presumed to be Miss Redglass' own, and mistakes, mine.

I was at first reluctant to publish this account, which I had thus assembled chiefly for my own convenience, owing to its aforementioned redactions. However, a number of my colleagues, particularly the illustrious Professor N. W. Clerk of Miskatonic University, Arkham, and Dr Nemo Aucun of St Udemia Hall, Cambridge (whose *Encyclopædia of Pneumatological History* has proven invaluable to me), ultimately convinced me to make this work available to the general public—if only for the sake of those undergraduates and bachelors of pneumatology whose means do not permit the rather expensive and international hobby of vampirological science, and who would therefore benefit most from a concise and affordable resource.

Like so many students of vampirology whether professional or amateur, I owe them both my profuse thanks for the tireless work that has made the contemporary state of that science possible. My special thanks also H. Sparrow Dobbs (PhD Ontography, Crandular Univ), Basil Fitzgerald (PhD Pneumatology, St Cedd Coll), Jacob Cinnamome (PhD Prohibited Mss, St Isaac Leibowitz Coll), Sylvester Paris (PhD of Antinecrology, St Udemia Hall), Fr Forrest Saint-Etienne (PhD Paradoxical History, Miskatonic Univ), River Levi (PhD Recherchic Actuality, Miskatonic Univ), Belteshazzar Aquino (PhD Incomprehensible Mss, Delmarva A&M), Mary Therese Coleman (PhD Metahistory, Delmarva A&M), and Roberta Plummer (PhD Prohibited Metaphysics, Miskatonic Univ) for their assistance and support, especially in making the resources of the Bodleian, Crandular, and Miskatonic Libraries so readily available to me. Each of them has assisted me in the making of this—to quote the motto inscribed over the entrance to the bright Georgian interior of the enchanting Miskatonic archives—my *Sacrificillum Scientiæ*.

Table of Contents

Chapter I

Descent Into Hell

Desire with loathing strangely mixed
On wild or hateful objects fixed.
Fantastic passions! maddening brawl!
And shame and terror over all!
Deeds to be hid which were not hid,
Which all confused I could not know,
Whether I suffered, or I did:
For all seemed guilt, remorse or woe,
My own or others still the same,
Life-stifling fear, soul-stifling shame.

— Samuel Taylor Coleridge, *The Pains of Sleep*

Quick footsteps echoed through the quiet, fog-obscured street. Not a soul was present to see the figure making the rapid *clack-clack* on the cobblestones, but even if there had been, no one could have recognized her in the night. The street lamps were suffocated by the November mist.

The dark shape paused at a cross-roads. Glossy black ringlets spilled from beneath her hat, and black gloves of delicate, tightly-fitted lace showed a hint of ivory skin where they abutted the sleeves of her gown. A high, close collar of deep heliotrope purple surmounted the throat, half obscured by the fastenings of the figure's mantle; a minutely embroidered bodice pulled in at the waist, and then threw generous folds of black out over an old-fashioned crinoline, so that the whole outline vaguely resembled a bell. The face was a little different: she wore a thick veil that hid the eyes, but it was drawn only halfway down, so that white skin and a vivid red mouth were exposed.

She moved her head to look down each road in turn. Her left hand drifted upwards of its own accord, the tips of her slender fingers massaging her throat—then, abruptly, the hand was jerked back, as if from a sudden sting. The young woman raised her chin and clenched her hands; then she took the left-hand way and cantered on through the darkness.

Spheres of lamplight hovered above her course, like living gold suspended in the swirling fog. Above the low-lying clouds, where no eye could pierce, a waxing crescent of silver hung in the heavens.

Number Four, Ramshead Place[1], was well-kept in spite of its venerable age, the wrought-iron railings free of rust, the dragon's-head knocker smartly polished. The woman darted up the steps, rapped the knocker sharply several times, and waited. A strange unease was coming over her. She wondered whether it was worry over her father's reaction to her lateness … no, it was not that; he would coo and fuss and not be angry, because he was never angry. Yet a sensation of exposure was mounting in her brain. Too quickly, she reached up and knocked again.

Instantly the door opened. A man of fifty stood on the other side, in shirtsleeves and wire-rimmed reading glasses, with an untidy crown of grey-flecked brown hair. 'Marie!' he exclaimed.

'Papa!' she cried at the same moment, equally surprised. 'I should have expected that Harker—'

'I sent all the servants to bed at one. I don't mind waiting up for you, though I must say I was beginning to worry.'

'I am sorry, papa, truly,' Marie began.

'Oh, never mind that. Come inside. You are safe and sound, that is the vital thing.' He took her hand affectionately and lifted her over the doorstep into the house. Her sense of agoraphobia diminished immediately. She lifted the veil from her face, revealing a pair of striking violet eyes. Her father embraced her.

---

[1] Though unmarked on most contemporary maps, Ramshead Place ran between Belvedere Road and York Road just south of Vine Street, in the general neighborhood of Lambeth Palace. The street has since been razed and filled in.

'Your skin is like ice,' he tutted. 'And why on earth are you dressed like that? You look as if you were in deep mourning. Goodness sake, the blood has gone clean out of your face, child. Anybody would suppose that you ran across London to get here. Come and warm yourself by the fire.' He took her cloak from her and threw it over a chair just inside the drawing room. 'Ravenhurst Manor?'

'Yes,' she admitted. 'But Lady fitzUrse was there as chaperon.'

'I wish you would not stay there till all hours like this, Marie. Viscount Ravenhurst may be a charming man, but he has a reputation as a Spiritualist medium, and I am not, I confess, altogether certain I trust his morals. I have no wish to be a detractor or a slanderer. But people could talk about you too, and I should hate to see your reputation tarnished for the sake of someone else's.'

'I know, papa.' She twisted her hands uncomfortably in front of her; her father, leading the way, saw nothing.

'Your mother,' he went on, 'disapproved heartily. Such a pious woman, far more than I ever could be. I know I ought to be, as a Redglass: old recusant family and all that. I think I am overly Oxonian about it, too merely literary. She was always the devoted one. I loved her for that, among other things. Though you seem to have wedded the contrasting features quite successfully,' he added with pride.

They reached the door to the study at the back of the house, and he strode in. 'There, all things bright and beautiful.' He moved aside, so that she could get a view of the glowing hearth.

The room fell to pieces to all Marie's senses at once. The firelight overwhelmed and fractured her vision, and the merry crackling of the logs beneath her father's voice became a cacophonous roar. No discursive consciousness remained: only an overpowering urge to escape. Someone was shrieking. Strong band-like things were entangling her—she swiped at them savagely—there was a hideous cry, and a bizarre, liquid sensation on her fingers, together with a nauseating smell. A rhythmical thudding followed, and then a blast of icy air, and her vision was plunged back into soothing darkness, like a cold cloth placed over the forehead of one in delirium.

The front door of Number Four, Ramshead Place, yawned behind her as Marie's black gown billowed in her rushing wake. The veil fell from the brim of her hat back over her face as she ran, and the wind pulled it taut against her eyes.

Meanwhile, on the floor of the study, his arms and chest lacerated and a rib broken by his fall, her father, Baron James Redglass, was choking and coughing up blood.

When her wits returned, Marie found herself in a part of London she did not even recognize. Though she had run the whole way, there was no stitch in her side, nor perspiration on her forehead. She was not even panting for breath. Lord Ravenhurst's words tried to force themselves back into her mind, but she repulsed the notion with the vigor of hysteria. *It cannot be. There are no such things.*

A strange aroma, at once repugnant and intoxicating, wafted up to her nostrils. She looked down at her gloves: they were sticky and wet. Convulsively, she snatched them off, to find both hands and gloves damp with slowly gumming blood.

Awareness was swallowed up again. After an indistinguishable period of time, Marie recollected herself. Her hands were once again white, and dry as bone. But there was a foreign object in her mouth, something clingy and web-like. She reached up to remove it, and found that it was both her gloves; she was still eagerly sucking the last drops of blood from the black lace. A vague memory of her lips and tongue, sucking horribly at the skin of her hands, seemed to form in her mind.

She removed the gloves and lowered them from her lips. The faintness and nausea that she had expected and hoped to feel were stubbornly absent. The rising panic at being out in the open, however, had returned, and she knew why now; or rather, she was now admitting the explanation that she had refused hitherto. The sun would be rising soon. No such things as vampires?

She looked around; she did recognize where she was now. In her panic, she had run all the way to Cavendish Square—nearly halfway back to Ravenhurst Manor, the residence of the notorious Spiritualist, Augustus Fairfax, its lord. His figure rose in her imagination, and she snarled aloud with hatred: he had lied to her— could it be, really killed her? Perhaps even damned her. The notion of going back for revenge seemed for a moment to be extremely attractive, but she had no idea how she could exact it. And in any case, she had to hide from the sunlight, and where else could she go? She could hardly explain the situation to a friend, who would merely assume she had gone mad. Unless perhaps William—but that thought was immediately thrust away like white-hot iron. He could never, ever know of this. To return to Ravenhurst for *haven* was infuriating and humiliating even to contemplate; the possibility of simply letting herself be caught by the sun appeared to her thoughts, but that was too frightening. The desperate, blind appetite of survival asserted itself. Between Lord Ravenhurst—though depraved and unearthly—and certain death, she would, with deep resent, take Lord Ravenhurst.

Somewhere not far off, Marie heard a bell tolling the first Mass of the day. The sound shot through her head like a railway spike, and she clapped her hands over her ears. She turned north up Chandos Street, away from the sound.

But it is not a choice between Augustus Fairfax and death at all, said a disturbing voice in her mind. *You are already dead.*

The manor and its grounds lay north of the city, east of Hampstead Ponds, with Primrose Hill looming to its south out of the greyness. It was, as Lord Ravenhurst had once explained to Marie over sherry and biscuits at one of the little literary salons he held at his house, the ancestral seat of the Fairfax family, of which he was the last surviving member. Not, he noted, to be confused with the Scottish Fairfaxes of Roxburgh: it was rather a curious corruption of the Norman *fer-face*, presumably in reference to a Mediæval helm. As for Mediævalism, Ravenhurst had as much of that as any Pre-Raphaëlite could have wished: the manor was more castle than house, with spires and embattled parapets thrown up against the sky like jagged stone teeth, a weird and gigantic tower looming out of the unseen center of the edifice, and an age-blackened *façade* that frowned out of a mass of ivy, pierced by thin, pointed windows heavily draped against the daylight.

Marie had only ever seen it by night before, when the curtains were drawn back and the light of lamps and candles and chandeliers made every window look like a magic lantern, the uglier features being concealed or softened by the dark. Now, as the forerunning light of dawn crept through the late autumnal fog, she wondered briefly whether she would ever have gone near the place, had she first seen it in better light. But this was no time for metaphysical speculations. Having left the road some time ago, she had to pick her path inconveniently over the railway line, and, once she had cleared it, she lifted her skirts and broke into a run.

It did not take her nearly as long as she had expected. It was a furlong or more from the railway to the front door of Ravenhurst Manor, yet she had traversed the distance in less than a minute. Ignoring this puzzle, she turned to the great front door, with its large brass knocker in the shape of a lion's head with bared fangs. She tapped it and waited, wishing miserably that she could be anywhere else in England. An owl hooted somewhere nearby, and was promptly contradicted by the chirrup of a sparrow.

The door was opened by the grey-mustached butler, Godalming. 'Good day to you, Mademoiselle Redglass,' he said colorlessly, as though he had not witnessed the volatile parting of a few hours before.

'Let me in,' she replied urgently, with no pretense at good manners.

'One moment, ma'm'selle. I shall ascertain whether his lordship is—'

'Please, Godalming, you know me, you know he knows me—'

'Forgive me,' he said, now becoming a little stiff in his manner. 'I have no power to invite you over the threshold. Excuse me.'

He left her on the doorstep. Marie tangled her fingers together nervously and untangled them again a few times, looking out at the grounds (where the fog was turning from grey to pearl at every moment) like a bird scanning the sky for predators.

'Ah, my dear,' interrupted a *basso cantante* voice. She turned quickly back. There stood the master of the house himself, Augustus Fairfax, wearing an indecently triumphant smile. 'This is a thoroughly expected pleasure. Though admittedly, I wondered, when last you left, whether you realized you would be imparting it; I believe you said you never wanted to see me again as long as you lived?—words to that effect.'

Marie lowered her eyes a little from his. 'Please, Lord Ravenhurst; I am sorry—'

'I dare say you are.'

'Please shelter me. I beg you.'

He tutted and stood back. 'Come in.'

She lifted her skirts and stepped over the threshold. 'Thank you,' she said to him quietly.

The aristocrat made no reply, but ordered her to follow with a gesture. Goldaming came over and shut and bolted the door; the sound was loud yet stifled, more like the shutting of a box than of a door. They went to the library, whose windows, like all the others, were thickly curtained to keep out the lethal sun. Augustus' pale shirtsleeves flashed on either side of his emerald waistcoat in the semi-darkness as he turned up a few of the gas-lamps at the edges of the room, and then crossed to one of the chairs near its center, a finely carved ebony thing with cushions in Paris green. Standing behind it, resting his elbows on its back, gazing at Marie as she stood still near the door of the room, he was the very image of leonine, indolent contempt. He sniffed ostentatiously.

'Dead?' he asked.

She stared, uncomprehending. 'What?'

'Is he dead?' the vampire expanded; and then, with a touch of impatience, he clarified, 'The man whose blood you drank. You are positively reeking of him, there is no use prevaricating. Did you kill him? Most fledgling vampires are more reluctant than that at first—'

'I didn't! Man whose—how dare you!'

Augustus' eyes flashed. 'Manners, Mademoiselle Redglass. I speak to you thus because I am your sire. My authority over you henceforward is, as it were, *paternal*. Accustom yourself.'

Outrage choked her. Helpless to act, dependent and bewildered as she was, she took a few aimless steps about her corner of the room and was still again. Her host watched her, making no attempt to hide his malicious amusement. After a few moments, he turned his gaze to the small circular table beside the chair he was leaning upon. On it stood a jade-green glass vase, about two feet tall, minutely adorned with silver filigree.

'I purchased that in Venice, eighty-six years ago, on the centenary of the deposition of King James the Second,' said Augustus, a little dreamily. 'Such a dismal summer that was! But once or twice, when the weather did manage to get hot, then even at night the Adriatic was like a blue oriflamme, billowing out to the southeast. And outdoors or within, the fragrances of the wines, the perfumes, the scents of grapes and rosemary and pomegranate blossoms … Have you ever been to Venice, my dear?'

Marie was stonily silent. The amused look on Augustus' face increased for a moment, then faded: he was unnaturally still, his eyes fixed on the vase. Suddenly it exploded, shards of costly glass flying outwards with violence. She started and cried out. Then she noticed that the vampire's hand was extended, not in a fist but spread out flat, into the space that had a moment before been where the center of the vase was. He had broken it with a mere flick of his hand. He stared at the fragments silently for a long while, and then turned back to Marie and spoke.

'It was the wrong color,' he explained placidly. 'I take my time deciding.' He circled the chair, brushed a few bits of glass out of it, and seated himself, transfixing Marie with his eye.

'You have nowhere else to go. Your family, your friends—they are incapable of understanding the change that has taken place in your nature, and incapable twice over of accepting it; more importantly, their company is beneath you now. As for other vampires, I shall say simply that our kind, while capable of accepting strangers, is more inclined to hang them upside down by hooks in darkened cellars if they find their hospitality presumed upon. You reside beneath my roof; or, you face the dawn. Do I make myself clear?'

A dry silence intervened. 'Yes, Lord Ravenhurst,' Marie whispered at last.

This answer seemed to satisfy the other vampire. He rose and walked over to a small black cord on the wall and pulled it; the muffled sound of a silver bell was just distinguishable as he did so. Walking back to the chair and seating himself again, his fingers tented, he said, 'We do little, as a rule, during the day. The sun tends to make the appetites sluggish. Personally I prefer solitude for a few hours about this time. Godalming' (here the butler entered) 'will show you to your room; in my absence or seclusion, you may amuse yourself there, or wherever else in the house it suits you, except where the doors are locked, where of course you will not wish to go. If you wish any alterations to be made to your room, simply tell Godalming and it shall be seen to. Oh, and Godalming, if you would have this mess swept up and put in the usual place.' The butler assented, and the viscount turned his attention back to Marie. 'Good morning, mademoiselle.' He inclined his head.

'Good morning, Lord Ravenhurst,' she answered, dropping a half-curtsey.

'If ma'm'selle would follow me, please,' Goldaming told her quietly.

Soon, the butler was ascending the large mahogany staircase that led to the second floor, with Marie in tow. Though she had been in this part of the manor a number of times before, everything looked different now—partly because the drawn curtains, combined with the fact that the lamps were extinguished, left everything extremely dim. This did not appear to bother Godalming, whether owing to sharp eyesight or long familiarity with the place. They came upon the first wide landing, where the path of the stairs ran level, clinging to the wall of the entrance hall about two-thirds of the way up. In the center of the landing's course there was a semicircular balcony, with a white marble sculpture on display, mounted so that it could be seen over the balustrade from the floor below. It was a copy of Bernini's *Apollo and Daphne*, executed in the same exquisiteness as the original: every laurel leaf on the nymph' fingers, every strand in each lock of hair, was as minutely picked out by the sculptor as if the whole work had been done solely to produce that single element.

'Ma'm'selle,' prompted the butler.

Marie shook herself, realizing by the sound of the clock that she had been staring at the sculpture for a solid minute. She crossed the remainder of the landing and began following Godalming again as he mounted the hidden part of the staircase. Their footfalls made no sound on the thick Persian rugs.

At last, after a passage that Marie judged from its windows must run along the topmost edge of one of the battlemented outer walls, Godalming stopped and opened a door on the right. 'His lordship directed that this room be set aside for you, Mademoiselle Redglass. The window, naturally, has been secured, and those few effects which you left here have been arranged in the vanity. You have been expected for some little time—his lordship voiced some concern when you did not return as swiftly as he had anticipated.'

Marie blinked. The thought of a creature like Augustus worrying about her was rather repellent than comforting. After a moment's hesitation, she went in and looked about the room.

It was spacious, painted in a muted shade of rose, with a curtained four-poster on one side of the opposite wall. A deep bay window (forming a curious architectural contrast to the neo-Mediæval *façade*), with dark green cushions in the seat, took up most of the rest of the wall. Between the bed and the bay was a slender wooden pillar, topped by a platform that displayed a miniature copy of Canova's *Psyche Revived by Cupid's Kiss*, executed in onyx. On the left wall was a large wardrobe; on the right, an ornate vanity inlaid with tortoiseshell.

'If you need anything, simply ring for it' (here he gestured to the black cord connected to the serving bell) 'and your maid will fetch it for you; her name is Hyacinth.'

'Good,' she replied vaguely. 'What time in the—evening ought I to go down?'

'It is up to your discretion, ma'm'selle. His lordship likes to rise early, generally between six and seven p.m.'

'All right. Thank you. Good morning, Godalming.'

'Good morning, ma'm'selle.'

He withdrew, leaving Marie to the unalloyed silence of her room. She sat down on the bed, not really seeing her surroundings, trying to pacify the thoughts that were battling one another in her brain: hatred of Augustus, fear of the outside, the vertiginous realization that the nightmare was real, and the brute fact of thirst, contended within her for the mastery. If only she could sleep. Could vampires sleep? *To sleep, perchance to dream—ah, there's the rub! For in that sleep of death, what dreams may come When we have shuffled off this mortal coil Must give us pause*, she thought irresistibly. She shook her head, as if to dislodge an insect.

Abruptly, her sire's words rose to her memory: *Is he dead? You are positively reeking of him.* Whose could the blood have been that was clinging to her gloves?

There was only one answer, of course. Marie wished bitterly that she could have found some way of evading the matter; but it could only have been her father's blood. There was no one else she had seen or spoken to—she must have hurt him, badly, when she panicked at the sight of the fire. Unless she had cut herself somehow or other? Augustus had said *he*, but Augustus need not know everything—he had not been there. She crossed to the vanity to examine herself for wounds. A moment later, she screamed.

There were the black gown with the violet piping in the mirror, the lace gloves, the hat with the half-drawn veil. But in the center there was no one. The clothes appeared to be suspended in a void.

She looked down at her hands: one of them was crushing the delicate gloves that, she now remembered, she had never actually put back on; the other was rubbing its opposite shoulder nervously, as if trying to warm it or bathe it. There was her body before her eyes, yet when she lifted an arm to the mirror, with a crawling sensation, no part of her was reflected in it.

She sat down sharply, throwing the gloves down on the table and setting her hat on top of them. Of course, she thought acidly: all of the stories and novels said that vampires had no reflections and cast no shadows. According to the traditional superstition, it was because they had no souls—but Marie's mind recoiled from that idea. What had she come over here for again? Oh, yes, to check for wounds. What a pleasant change of topic. In any event, the mirror being of no use to her, the only thing to do now was to search by hand where she could not see.

Her hands were immaculate. She felt all about her throat, which seemed to be quite unmarked, save for two faint, all but healed puncture wounds—*no, don't think of that.* She unlaced her boots and kicked them off, rose, and began struggling with the array of buttons and cords that secured her gown and the retrograde crinoline beneath. It crossed her mind to summon the maid for assistance, but she dismissed the thought the instant it came to her, desiring no witnesses to this affair. Layers of bombazine and linen came off, until she was stripped bare.

Marie carefully studied every inch of skin that she could see as though it were a paper covered in coded writing. Wherever she could not see, she stretched her fingers over her body as far as they would go. Her flesh was as smooth and lily-white as the day she was born.

She seated herself again, staring unseeingly into the mirror. Every drop, then, had been her father's. And a man in his health—a man with health twice as good as his—could not expect to survive a wound that bled like that.

The tears did not come. She tried to force them. A tiny drop of liquid did collect in each eye, and she rifled through the drawers for a handkerchief. When she raised it to each eye to clear them, it came away looking like a consumptive's, with a rosy stain in the center.

Marie's mind seemed to distend itself, gently seeping out of discursive functions and into mere semiconscious awareness. Awareness of nothing in particular, except each moment remorselessly succeeding its predecessor. One of her last thoughts for several hours—she could not be sure when she thought it—was to wonder whether she were falling asleep; and then, to recollect a Gospel text she had heard, once or a hundred times: *Howbeit Jesus spake of death; but they thought that he had spoken of taking rest in sleep.*

CHAPTER II

THE BANQUET OF THE GODS

Sweeter than honey from the rock,
Stronger than man-rejoicing wine,
Clearer than water flowed that juice;
She never tasted such before,
How should it cloy with length of use?
She sucked and sucked and sucked the more
Fruits which that unknown orchard bore;
She sucked until her lips were sore;
Then flung the emptied rinds away
But gathered up one kernel-stone,
And knew not was it night or day
As she turned home alone.

— CHRISTINA ROSSETTI, *GOBLIN MARKET*

After hours of a strange stillness that seemed to be neither sleep nor waking, Marie shook herself a little and stood up. She resumed her chemise and corset and put her gown back on, struggling unassisted with the crinoline—practically an antique, but the black gown required it. She turned to leave the room, with a half-formed notion of visiting the library, which she knew from previous visits to be well stocked, but was arrested by the sight of a large painting, on the wall beside the door, which she had not hitherto noticed. She went over and examined it.

It was a masterful piece, executed in the style of the later seventeenth century (Lord Ravenhurst seemed to have a great affection for the baroque). Marie studied it. Five figures were depicted, two priests, two monks, and a nun, in a vast basilica. A massive pillar in warm brown stood just off-center in the background, with a billowing, impossibly expansive length of crimson velvet falling down and around it, as if coming out of Heaven. It descended from the same side as the altar, and curled about the pillar toward the nun. Far behind, a wide, white arch could be distinguished, and a patch of blue that might be sky lay beyond it.

Of the five humans depicted, only the nun's face could be clearly seen: she was kneeling, habited in white with a black mantilla, and holding a smaller piece of blue cloth in her left hand, with her right laid gently against her breast. One of the priests was holding out the Blessed Sacrament to her, and she was gazing at it, transfixed, her lips slightly parted. The priest's own face, though a nimbus glowed around his head, was in obscurity, and the other priest, also starting to kneel, was facing away from the viewer toward the Host; but both, as if their persons were effaced for the exaltation of their office, had their vestments picked out in flawless detail: translucent albs surmounted by stiff, sumptuous chasubles in gold and scarlet. A rich carpet in the same colors lay between the second priest and the nun, disordered and pushed up, as if the movements to adore had been abrupt and impassioned. The nun, the kneeling priest, and one of the monks, who was facing the Host but reaching out towards the nun, all had thin haloes painted over their heads—she wondered whether the artist had simply changed his mind about how he wanted to depict haloes. The second monk was mostly concealed by the ministering priest, and appeared to be looking at the altar rather than the Sacrament. And there in the center of the painting was the Eucharist Itself, a little white disc in the priest's hand, putting forth a shining aureole of golden light.

Marie moved closer, peering at a brass nameplate mounted on the bottom of the frame. *The Holy Communion of Saint Teresa of Ávila or of Jesus. Claudio Coello. Copied by Augustus Fairfax, Viscount Ravenhurst, 1745.*

So Augustus painted. But what on earth had possessed him to copy this? It matched his taste, displayed throughout the house; but there was no shortage of classical and historical subjects in art, whether for him to copy or create his own, and in the previous year of their acquaintance she had never known him to express any interest in Christianity; so why choose this picture? And, come to that, how had he managed it? Vampires were supposed to be vulnerable to sacred things. Or was that only superstition? She thought suddenly of the liturgical bell she had heard on her way to the manor; no, that myth was most likely fact. Which left this painting a mystery.

She left her room for the library.

Marie floated down the staircase, her fingertips brushing the glossy banister. As she alighted on the ground floor, the grandfather clock in the hall struck six. Evening at last.

She turned to the right, passing through the hall and into the panelled corridor that led to the library. The doorway had a triangular pediment over it, containing a neoclassical relief of Minerva and Pluto, supported by slender false columns: it had the look of a little temple. Within, every wall was concealed by oaken bookcases. Even the windows had smaller shelves running beneath the sills. A large table had books, open and shut, strewn over a third of its surface, and the assortment of end tables that stood by the armchairs each had at least one or two more lying upon it, along with some curio or statuette, these latter sometimes built into the structure of the table.

Marie surprised herself with the realization that she had examined almost none of the titles hitherto. Before, she had always come for the evenings of witty conversation and artistic criticism—and, she guiltily acknowledged, for the *séances* that Augustus sometimes deigned to grant to special favorites, though those of course were held in the upper room of the tower.

She walked along the shelves, examining the books. They displayed a remarkable variety: age-yellowed pages abounded, and some volumes clearly predated the printing press. The English, French, and Latin languages were to be expected; Greek, German, and Italian showed their owner to be respectably well-educated; Spanish and (she presumed) Russian were rather more unusual; but here was a whole shelf of Arabic volumes, another filled with Hebrew, a third in the bewildering script that she had learnt to associate with Hindoo volumes, and yet another that bore titles in the sinuously beautiful lettering of the Chinese. Some bore planetary or alchemical signs instead of letters. Still less familiar scripts and symbols presented themselves, many of whose provenance she could hardly guess. She was suddenly overcome with the thought of how much, known and unknown to mortal history, must be preserved by this deathless race.

Shaking herself slightly from her reverie, Marie scanned the shelves with greater care, trying to find the organizing principle. The works were not arranged alphabetically, either by author or by title; neither were they arranged in order of publication. She did observe a curious series of letters, carved directly into the shelves at irregular intervals—F, A, A, J, E, L, Y, R, H, G, A. She could make nothing of these; eventually, on finding Donne's *Songs and Sonnets*, she gave up on trying to discover the indexing structure of the library, pulled the long-beloved work from its shelf, and settled herself into a chair with it. Beside her was a table on which lay a miniaturized copy of a sculpture she suddenly recognized, from sketches done by a cousin of hers who had spent two years in Italy: it depicted Diana transfiguring Actæon into a stag, and his hounds leaping upon him. This copy was in soapstone, executed in the minutest detail—

She caught herself again. This was the third time in a matter of a few hours that she had become so entranced with some piece of artwork that she had lost all sense of purpose, in the middle of doing something. Marie opened the book with firm hands, holding it away from the little tabletop piece rather pointedly, and began to read.

She did not enjoy it as much as she expected, partly because she was wondering why she had become so distractible; and partly also because Donne's themes were, well—*Hee swallows us, and never chawes: By him, as by chain'd shot, whole ranks doe dye, He is the tyran Pike, our hearts the Frye*—that suited Ravenhurst's behavior a little too perfectly. And one could hardly expect to find distraction from distraction in *A Valediction: Forbidden Mourning*. After a score or so of pages, she impatiently slapped the book onto the end table, with a resentful glance at the soapstone rendition of Actæon's tragic death.

'Utterly brutal,' said a voice from the doorway. 'Women are wickeder than men.'

Marie looked up. Augustus was there, looking at the statuette and smiling, in only his shirtsleeves, without a waistcoat or even a collar on. His left arm was up against one of the slender pillars as he leaned on the doorframe, while the fingers of his right hand seemed to caress his breastbone. He looked the very portrait of indolent pride.

'Good evening, Lord Ravenhurst,' she whispered.

'Oh, come, come,' he said more breezily, 'it is surely idle to treat one another like strangers, *ma fleurette*.' (She bristled at the endearment, but said nothing.) 'We have transgressed, transcended that state.'

'Is that why you have chosen to parade yourself in this stripped fashion?'

His eyes flashed and were still. 'The gong will be struck for breakfast in a few minutes. Do you remember the way to the dining room from here?'

She nodded, her face as cold as the carven Diana beside her.

'Very well; that is all I wanted to know. I'll see you shortly.' He left.

She sat uncomfortably in her chair for several seconds, feeling unable to pick up her book again. Finally she rose and followed him.

The dining room was unusual to the point of eccentricity: high and rather narrow, it was neither papered nor painted, but hung in emerald-green charmeuse silk, descending from a central point in the ceiling around the oval room. It had the feel of a pavilion, lit by a chandelier suspended from its apex. There were no windows—at least, none that could be seen—but a few rifts in the silk formed alcove-like framings of several paintings that encircled the room.

Augustus was seated already at the head of the table, if *seated* is the right word; his leonine carelessness made every pose look more like a lounge than a posture. Marie came in, and he nodded and smiled, more broadly than before, showing his fangs. The eerie light was scattered by the prisms and jewel ornament of the chandelier and glowed, here dull, here keen, upon the silken hangings.

Since the lord of the manor plainly was not about to rise to draw a chair out for her, she turned to do so herself, and gave a brief cry of shock as Godalming appeared out of thin air, and drew her chair back from the table. A moment later she realized that he had simply been standing at the edge of the room. She slowly lowered herself into the chair, looking warily at Augustus. He seemed to be enjoying her discomfort immensely.

'Godalming, would you go and fetch me a waistcoat and collar and some cuffs? I fear my current state of undress leaves the *demoiselle* somewhat scandalized.'

'Yes, my lord.'

'Have Howard bring them in.'

'As you wish, my lord.'

The butler departed. Augustus continued smiling. Marie kept her hands folded in her lap, staring awkwardly at the chandelier and saying nothing.

'And what do you fancy for your first glass of the night, *ma fille*?'

A dark flame leapt up in her face, and she met his eyes. 'I am *not* your daughter—'

'Silence,' he said, with perilous restraint. 'In this world I am your sire and I shall address you accordingly, as often as the fit takes me. I counsel you to accustom yourself.'

His expression slid back toward its previous cruel flippancy. 'So what would you like? A whole world of vintages is before you, every one of them fresh to your palate. I like to have something small but rich in the early hours of the evening: a demitasse of Provençal or Aragonese, for instance, or even Sicilian. But a beginner such as yourself might prefer something milder, yet substantial; say, a glass of Flemish, or something homier like a Shropshire …'

It took Marie a few moments to realize that he was talking about blood. She recoiled.

'Have you any—er—ordinary—I mean, is there human food in the house?'

'The servants eat it,' her sire replied. 'Why?'

She found herself unable to articulate her request, but it was obvious from the viscount's face that he swiftly divined her meaning. A mixture of incredulity, amusement, and contempt formed there. 'You cannot be serious.'

'I'd prefer it. Please.'

He stared; then, with a gesture as of one who gives someone up to uncleanness through the lusts of their hearts, he replied, 'Well. I shall have it seen to. Ah, Howard,' he added, as a young footman entered.

The servant was perhaps fifteen, and quite good-looking, with a long face and a sturdy frame. He was holding a silvern tray in his right hand, on which lay two collars and three sets of cuffs, and his right arm bore two silk waistcoats, one in pale grey, and a figured one in burgundy, displaying a pattern of white cherry blossoms on slender black branches. Augustus took the tray from him and selected a wing collar and portofino cuffs, and then indicated the burgundy waistcoat; the servant set the remaining articles on a chair.

The aristocrat rose, extending his arms and raising his chin, doll-like, to be dressed. Howard picked up the cuffs and began fastening them to the sleeves of his master's shirt. The latter made a great false wince as the former worked upon the cuff-links, saying, 'Be gentle, Howard; those cuffs are extremely stiff.' He then cast a glance in Marie's direction and leaned his head back, showing the servant his throat, and said, 'Put on the collar.'

'But my lord, this cuff isn't done—'

'Put on the collar, I say.'

Howard nodded and picked up the collar, white and starched to rigidity. As he reached around the vampire's neck, Augustus closed his eyes lazily and let out a faint moan. The young man blushed unhappily. He fumbled a little over the studs, and Augustus quickly placed his fingers on the servant's. 'No—like this'; and he slowly guided Howard's fingers, brushing them against his own throat and sighing heavily. He looked over at Marie again, who was unable to prevent her face from contorting in disgust.

'Now the waistcoat,' he said, smiling. He turned around. Howard picked up the embroidered silk, which shimmered under the light of the chandelier. Backing far too close, almost into his servant, Augustus let each of his arms be pulled into it, letting out more sighs, and then caressingly took Howard's hands in his own and pulled them across his stomach, buttoning the waistcoat from the top downwards, while he leaned his head back again, grazing their ears together. With each button, Howard's expression became more humiliated and repelled; at the last one, Augustus moaned yet again, and gripped Howard's hands hard by the wrists, as if he would force them still further down. Howard shut his eyes tightly.

'You may go,' said the vampire suddenly, releasing him, 'for the present. Tell the cook to prepare two Champagne flutes of the Artesian, and also a pot of tea with a soft-boiled egg and a toasted muffin.'

'My lord?'

'Just do it.'

'Very good, my lord,' answered the servant quickly, and quickly exited.

'Nice boy, young Howard,' said Augustus as he left, settling into his chair again. 'I hope you feel at ease now that I am more fully dressed.'

'That was revolting,' Marie spat.

His expression softened. 'Perhaps you are right. I would value your opinion on the subject—if you think the figured waistcoat is too lavish, I'll send for Howard again and change into the grey.'

Marie gave him a poisonous glare. 'The poor fellow seems decent enough. It is quite intolerable that you should abuse your power over him that way.'

'If he dislikes my little game, he is perfectly free to seek other employment.'

'As if you would let him! I can see the likes of *you* giving a servant decent references!'

'There is no need to be insolent. Anyway, I have done,' said Augustus mildly. '*Ma fleurette*, do you suppose I keep my servants trapped here permanently?

Except for cooks, whose skills in this world must be somewhat specialized, I replace most of my servants every thirty years at the outside.'

'But—you just let them go? Knowing what they know?'

'How much do they know?' he asked, smiling crookedly. 'Vampiric mental powers (of which more in a moment, my dear, calm yourself) can muddy that a great deal. And anyway, who would believe them, in the modern, enlightened cosmopolis of the Victorian Empire? No. We are quite safe as far as that goes. And while I take my pleasures as I find them, I am no Marquis de Sade or Theresa Berkley; the infliction of pain, merely as such, bores me, without some great beauty involved in the experience to provide a striking contrast. Howard is beautiful for his type, but he does not suit my taste so neatly as some others. I shall very likely allow him to seek other employment within a decade.'

Marie gazed at her fingers, which she had unconsciously tangled together in her lap. She was struck by a bizarre urge to laugh. The depravity, the luxury, the terror, it was all so unsupportably preposterous. It was obviously a dream; she would wake at any moment. Unless—the thought came to her that she had simply come unhinged. Her interlaced fingers gripped one another tightly.

'Do you sing, Marie?'

'Do—what?'

'Do you sing?' Ravenhurst repeated. 'Funny—having known you, what, a year now, I've never thought to inquire before. I have always supposed that you did. Your voice has a certain mellifluous quality that suggests some talent for music.'

'Yes, I do,' she replied. 'Father saw to it that my brothers and I were thoroughly educated musically.' She lapsed into silence, thinking of her family, worrying.

'Come along, my dear,' came the vampire's voice from across the table, 'you can do better than that. There is no good being stilted and uneasy here, you know: the castle is your home now. I sired you for your company, to which I have taken something of a liking, but if you prefer to spoil that company I can find others'; and that could make an awkwardness for you.'

Sired for company, Marie thought. How trivial. She had been murdered in cold blood to round out a dinner party. And now, it appeared, she was being subtly threatened with expulsion on the grounds that she was not rounding it out particularly well. She felt terribly small.

'Sing for your supper,' Augustus said to her mockingly. 'I should like to hear your voice.'

She looked up. 'What shall I sing?'

The monster at the far end of the table laid his hand on his chin, gazing wistfully into space for a few moments, and then began himself, accenting the words as one who had learnt them three hundred years before.

'Alas, my love, ye do me wrong
To cast me off discurteously:
And I have lovèd you so long,
Delighting in your companie.'

He gestured, and Marie joined in on the refrain and the second verse, doing her best to intone the vowels in the bygone manner of the sixteenth century; she kept the melody, and he began to sing a lilting, melancholy harmony:

'Greensleeves was my delight,
Greensleeves was all my joy,
Greensleeves was my hart of gold,
And who but Ladie Greensleeves.
I have been ready at your hand
To grant what ever ye would crave.
I have both wagèd life and land,
Your love and good will for to have.'

'Very good,' Lord Ravenhurst said judicially as they closed strangely on a fourth, 'yes indeed. You make a fine light soprano—your voice has a hint of the *soubrette*, which I think will mature into the more lyrical variety. You would make a taking *Colombina*. Have you ever studied opera?'

From there the conversation turned to Gluck and Mozart, soothingly reminiscent of the salons that Marie had attended in the past. She even found herself enjoying it a little.

After a few minutes, Godalming re-entered, with Howard and another footman in tow: Howard brought another tray, with two tall, narrow glasses containing a thick red liquid, while the other bore a larger tray, with a tea service, an egg cup, and a small plate on which lay a freshly toasted muffin. The tea service itself was lovely: the kettle was Italian silver; the teapot, saucers, and cups were made of bone-white Chinese porcelain, delicately lacquered in jade green and glossy black, depicting phoenixes, cranes, and dragons. Between the pot and the cup upon its saucer were nestled a cruet of milk, a little bowl of sugar lumps, and a dish with a pat of butter. Marie looked to Augustus.

'Ladies first,' he told her with a hospitable wave.

She reached out for the kettle, and then stopped, suspecting treachery. 'Doesn't silver scald vampires?'

'Oh, no. Gold does—hence my sparing use of it in the ornamentation of my house, except for the grandfather clock. Silver merely fails to reflect us, whence the apotropaic usefulness of mirrors.'

Marie nodded, and gingerly took hold of the kettle, and sure enough it produced no unpleasant result. Feeling more assured, she poured some water into the teapot, with a twinge of delight at the music of its bubbling and steaming. She picked up the teapot, poured herself a cup, and added in a lump of sugar. The spoon clinked familiarly against the cup as she stirred. She picked it up and took a sip.

'Aaah!' Sharp, scalding pain filled her mouth, as though she had swallowed acid. A little tea trickled down her throat and into her stomach, and the burning pain went with it. Instinctively, she spat out the rest, drenching both the cup and the pot. 'What's wrong with it?' she cried desperately, massaging her lips with one hand and snatching up her napkin with the other.

Lord Ravenhurst laughed. 'Nothing. I think you have forgotten that your body is about forty degrees cooler now than it was the last time you had a cup of tea; you might have anticipated the difference of effect, had you given your mind to the question.'

Throwing the bitterest glance of rage she could in his direction, Marie dried her chin and mopped up the tray a bit. She turned to the muffin—then she suddenly realized that it was probably not much cooler. Suppressing a grimace of frustration, she took the knife and knocked open the egg, then picked up her spoon and extracted a mouthful.

Almost before she had spat this out, too, Augustus had begun to laugh again, his head thrown back, each pulse of scorn visible in his throat. The soft-boiled egg tasted like nothing at all; it felt on her tongue like a rubbery ball of slime. The egg cup and the muffin were drenched in it. Sputtering, Marie reached automatically for her teacup, but had hardly touched it when she remembered that it was scalding and released it at just the wrong moment, so that it fell with a clatter onto the edge of its native saucer, spattering tea everywhere again and chipping the base of the cup. In an attempt to avoid the spray, she leapt in her chair, but this too was miscalculated, and she found herself toppling sideways out of it, so that her body slammed itself upon the floor. And through the whole performance, her sire's chimes of laughter had become more and more pronounced, until he seemed ready to fall to the floor himself.

Godalming helped her back up again, and pulled her chair out to re-seat her. He nodded to the second footman, who advanced, silently removed the disaster-laden tray, and departed with it. Augustus' peals of laughter slowly subsided.

'Why?' rasped Marie.

'Ah, my poor, petulant pigsnie. Vampires are not made to live off human food, any more than humans are made to subsist on dirt like earthworms. To abuse the language of Professor Darwin, we have evolved via unnatural selection into a new order of being. In consequence' (he waved a hand at her place,) 'that which once was *good for food and pleasant to the eyes* is now a tasteless mess. The temperature and the texture are still perceptible, hence the pain and disgust that particular attempt at a meal provoked—I expect you never really thought about soft-boiled eggs up to now, did you, *mon petit chou?*—but the savor is irrelevant to your palate, and likewise the nutrients to your stomach. They will only respond to blood now.'

Augustus nodded. The gloved hands of Godalming picked up one of the champagne flutes and brought it to the other end of the table, setting it directly before Marie. The blood shone with a faint fire beneath the chandelier. She stared at it, wide-eyed, gripping the table.

'I shan't,' she said, trembling.

'*Ma fleurette*, I think it has been made sufficiently plain that you have no choice.'

She shut her eyes, she opened them, she looked about the room. Augustus picked up his own glass and inhaled the aroma, his eyes rolling as if in an ecstasy.

Her fingers touched the stem of the glass gently. Without warning, the fragrance met her: savory as the choicest cut of venison, rich as an Armagnac, delicate and subtle as a Viennese pastry. She clenched her left hand into a fist, shut her eyes tightly, and raised the glass to her lips and sipped.

The taste was hypnotizing; what had been a sip became a mouthful. The room swam. The blood both sated and strengthened her thirst as she drank, and she could feel her skin flush and a heavy, irregular thudding in her breast; every point in her body was individually present to her consciousness, as if all were a single nerve; her senses became as keen as rapiers, and as the experience disentangled itself in her brain, she was able to pick out Augustus' scent, and the smell of the candles in the chandelier above, and of the tiniest traces of sulphur from the matchsticks that had lit them, and the particles of dust that had settled into the silken canopy overhead. She opened her eyes, and every color in the lavishly furnished chamber was more violent than mortal eyes would have borne: the drapes were greener than envy, the burgundy waistcoat more livid than wrath.

Several seconds went by, and the sensory Bacchanalia gradually subsided. Augustus' face split into a leer, cunning and voluptuous. 'Delicious, isn't she?'

Marie looked back into her glass, and was only half-surprised to see that she had been frenzied enough by the taste to finish it in one go. 'Who was she?' she quietly asked.

'Is, not was. We rarely kill prey' (Marie's heart leapt, and she narrowly avoided crying out with relief); 'it is superfluous, and can attract notice. Besides, it is more elegant to obtain blood from the living than to extract it from the dead: more of a challenge; in addition to tasting markedly better. And of course, when taken from the dead (aside from fellow vampires), there is scarcely any vitality in it: you would need a quart of the stuff before you got as much out of it as you'd get from a teaspoon taken from the living. Blood drawn from the dead is, compared to the vivacious girl upon whom we have breakfasted, a stale mouthful of pumpernickel bread set beside a tray of *chouquettes* fresh from the oven.

'But I digress. To answer your question, this particular young lady is the only daughter of a wealthy industrialist—half-Belgian by her mother, hence that touch of smokiness to the flavor, which I dare say you did not notice this time, but you will as you learn to appreciate varieties of blood. She and her father were guests of mine a few nights ago. Rather a rebelling little thing, too much accustomed to getting her own way; and she believes that she got her own way here as well, which is not altogether untrue,' her sire said with a soft laugh. 'She is a great beauty. I must have taken about three pints from her before they left—rather a lot, bordering on the conspicuous, but she put her exhaustion down to my other talents.'

'Do you—did you hypnotize her?'

Augustus scoffed. 'Hypnotism is a crude, human picture of vampiric powers. One can make suggestions telepathically, and even manipulate thoughts to a limited extent: encourage this impulse, distort that memory, and so forth. But one cannot simply override the other person entirely. Of course, some people beg to be ridden upon more than others do, which makes the work easier. But ultimately—' he fixed her with his eye—'every victim lets it happen.'

She bared her teeth and hissed, 'How dare you.'

'Deny it,' he replied quietly.

Marie started up from her chair, as if to leave the room, in an access of rage too powerful to focus into a single aim. She made a few paces around the emeraldine chamber, trying to steady her nerves. Augustus' eyes followed her, gleaming with spite and amusement. At last, she seated herself again. Feeling that there was no adequate answer to his insolence, she elected to change the subject, and raised a question that had been troubling her.

'What does one … do, as a vampire?'

The thing in the lavish evening dress at the other end of the table smiled and spread its hands out as if overshadowing all the kingdoms of the world and the glory of them. 'What one pleases. *Usque ad futurum sæculum non desinam, et in habitatione sancta coram ipso minitabar,*' he blasphemed. Then he picked up his glass, bowed to her slightly, and drained it.

CHAPTER III

WONDERS OF THE INVISIBLE WORLD

The Worldly Hope men set their Hearts upon
Turns Ashes—or it prospers; and anon
  Like Snow upon the Desert's dusty Face
Lighting a little Hour or two—is gone.

Think, in this batter'd Caravanserai
Whose Doorways are alternate Night and Day,
  How Sultán after Sultán with his Pomp
Abode his Hour or two, and went his way.

— The *Rubáiyát* of Omar Khayyám

A short while prior to midnight, Marie was sitting in her room again, having brought with her Donne's *Songs and Sonnets* and the first volume of Gibbon's *Decline and Fall*. She had never enjoyed Gibbon before, but she thought the time might be ripe for a fresh attack upon him. Augustus she had left downstairs, poring over a copy of *Les Fleurs du Mal* signed by the infamous Baudelaire himself—she was given to understand that he had spent several agreeable weeks in Paris in the company of the poet about ten years before.

There was a knock at the door. Suppressing a cry of frustration at the intrusion on her privacy, she called out, 'Come in.'

A plain girl in her late teens entered, clad in the black of a lady's maid. She curtseyed to Marie.

'Who are you?'

'Hyacinth,' said the other timidly. She spoke with a pronounced Cockney that grated Marie's nerves still further. 'Your maid.'

'What is it?'

'I thought I'd akse if you needed anything, me lady. Only 'tis the usual time.'

The usual time? she wondered. Aloud, she replied, firmly and distinctly, 'No thank you.'

'Very good, me lady,' the girl quavered at her, and scuttled out of the room. The silence within became intense; the ungentle tick of the grandfather clock on the ground floor could be made out, echoing through the entrance hall.

Marie turned back to her book, but, after the third realization that she had just reread the same line of *Loves Alchymie*, she accepted that she could not concentrate. She rose and wandered over to the window, seating herself among the cushions and pulling back one of the drapes so that she could look out at the stars. She knew relatively little about astronomy—that was more her brother Henry's line—but she loved looking up at the heavens. She smiled, thinking back to some fable her father had told her once, that the Mediævals believed the stars themselves to be punctures in the great sphere encasing the universe, through which the light of the Empyrean, the realm of the being of God Himself, shone: unimaginably distant, yet unaltered.

That, she thought, was where her mother was. Her original acquaintance with Augustus had been innocent enough, since they both were of a poetic bent: her father had sent her to Mount Holyoke in America to study, and Augustus cut a fashionable figure among the more esoteric intelligentsia with his periodic literary and philosophical salons. But when she had discovered he was a Spiritualist medium, the hunger for secret knowledge had awoken. Marie tried her best to be a faithful Catholic; but her mother's long absence—she had died giving birth to Henry, sixteen years before—had been bitterly trying, and she could not help wanting to know what her mother thought of her now, especially of her efforts to be there for her younger brother, whose maternal influences were so few. Before long Marie's visits had come to be punctuated by occult attempts to commune with the dead.

Her mind drifted to Henry and James. She knew could guess how they were handling her disappearance: Henry, hotheaded and mercurial, demanding that something be done instantly, preferably by themselves; James, methodical, a little pompous, strict with others and stricter with himself, insisting that everything should be left to the metropolitan police because That Is How Things Are Done. And her father would be caught in the middle of them—

Her father. Was he alright? *Could* he be alive? If he had been found quickly enough, a blood transfusion might have been essayed; admittedly a desperate chance, given the unreliable nature of the procedure, but by no means impossible. She could think of no way of finding out, save by going back to Ramshead Place, and after her last disastrous appearance she did not dare risk others' safety by doing that.

Unless … A newspaper might have an obituary notice. If he *were* dead. It would be horrible to find out for certain that way, but worse still to wonder and not know. The Redglass household were faithful subscribers to the *Times*, and in fact her father had contributed a few articles to them—it could probably be relied upon. She got up and rang briskly for the maid.

After a few moments, Hyacinth appeared. 'Yes, me lady?'

'Is there a copy of the *Times* in the house? The one from the second?'

The girl blinked uncertainly. 'A railway time-table, you mean?'

Marie compressed her lips and inhaled sharply through her nose, before remembering that she did not need to. 'No. *The London Times.* The newspaper.'

'Oh! Oh, er, I believe so, me lady. Shall I fetch it you?'

'Do, please.'

She turned and went. Marie paced the room slowly, casting occasional glances at the *Holy Communion.* A few minutes later, Hyacinth came back, paper in hand, and gave it to her. She thanked the maid carelessly and dismissed her, then sat at the vanity, looking firmly away from the mirror, and began to search.

After a few minutes, an uncannily familiar quality about this particular newspaper emerged in her mind. What was it, she wondered. She had scanned the obituaries carefully and found no mention of Baron James Redglass, which was comforting enough, but something was not quite right. Surely she had seen that notice before, for instance. She flipped back to the front page of the paper and checked the date. It was from the second, certainly: of September, now just over two months ago.

Seething, she ignored the bell for her maid, and went to find Godalming to acquire a fresh newspaper.

Marie encountered the butler drawing the bolt of an unfamiliar door with a large, antique painted panel hung upon it—perhaps it was a passage into the servants' quarters.

'Excuse me, Godalming, can you bring me a paper from the second of this month, please?'

'Certainly, ma'm'selle. Have you any preference?'

'The *Times*.'

'Very good, ma'm'selle. Peter!'

A slightly grubby boy appeared from a plain door. Godalming tutted.

'Do you call that taking better care of your uniform? Go and get Mademoiselle Redglass a copy of the *Times*.' He dropped a few pence into the boy's outstretched hand. 'Be quick about it.'

'Yes, sir.' He scurried off.

'Thank you, Godalming.'

The butler nodded, and departed through the door that Peter had entered through. That would be the servants' door, then. But—then what was this door that he had been locking up? She drew closer to it. The painting was of St Clare (perhaps Augustus had an affinity for Catholic symbolism), executed in tempera in the style of late Sienese Gothic. A slight aroma of myrrh clung to it. The door itself was very plain, without varnish, both bolted and locked. She took off a glove and felt it: its surface was surprisingly cool. Perhaps it led into a cellar. A faint scent of earth seemed to come from underneath it. After a moment, she shrugged to herself and wandered towards the library again.

Miles south and east, past Primrose Hill and over the Thames, James Redglass III—now Baron, and the patriarch of the London branch of the family—was sitting in the study of Number Four, Ramshead Place. His dark, meticulously kept hair was slightly disordered, and his spectacles had a neglected look. His eyes were sliding over a line in his book: he kept realizing that he had not actually grasped its content, going back to reread it, and realizing the same thing again afterwards. Too tired for the energy of impatience to enliven him, at last he lay the book on the table beside his armchair and blotted out his unfinished cigar in the ashtray. He stared at the dimming fire.

The door opened softly, and his brother Henry came in. Fairly tall for a sixteen-year-old, he had their mother's golden hair and sea-green eyes. Like the elder, he was in his shirtsleeves.

'You cannot sleep either?' he asked.

James looked over at him, then back at the fire.

Henry walked further into the room and found a chair. 'When will Marie come back, do you think?'

'Don't know.'

'She is coming back. I feel sure of it.'

Silence.

'When is father's funeral?'

'On the ninth.'

'Oh. Why so late?'

'To give the Cornwall branch of the family time to arrive,' said James.

'They won't come.'

'They are family. They might.'

Henry looked into the fire for a few moments too. 'Has anybody spoken to William?'

'I sent him a telegram. Henry, it's late. Go to bed.'

'I cannot sleep. I've said.'

'Go to bed,' James snapped.

His younger brother sat still for a few seconds; then he rose and exited. James picked up the poker and struck the burning logs sourly.

The grandfather clock in the entrance hall of Ravenhurst chimed one. Marie laid down the talentless commentary on *Hamlet* that she had been reading—this particular one was as mad as the prince. She was homesick for her own books; she had only recently acquired a copy of St Theresa's autobiography, and had hardly read more than the first few pages. Small chance of finishing it now.

Peter reappeared. His uniform was a little smarter than before—evidently he had taken the butler's rebuke seriously. He proffered the large newspaper.

'A copy o' the *Times* for you, me lady.'

'Thank you.' She snatched it from him and began searching the headlines with care. After several seconds, she became aware that the boy was still standing there, wringing his cap.

'What is it?'

'Only, was there anything else you wan'ed, me lady?'

She stared. 'No. Thank you, Peter.'

'All righ' den,' he said in a rush, and darted from the room.

She went back to the paper. Another diplomatic upset between the infant Kingdom of Italy and the Vatican. Ongoing economic depression in much of Europe, and as far afield as America, owing to the fluctuations of the silver trade. Another series of imprisonments of bishops in Prussia due to the nationalist policies of von Bismarck. She flipped a few pages sharply. A ponderous review of Max Müller's *Introduction to the Science of Religion*. Some ludicrously out-of-date republican cartoon, dredging up the old, foolish rumors about Her Majesty's supposed secret marriage to one of her devoted servants—probably drawn by a disgruntled MP with much time and little sense at his disposal.

And then she saw it. A small headline, buried in one of the inner pages, reporting the death of a minor nobleman in his townhouse in Lambeth, and the disappearance of his daughter. Baron Redglass had tragically bled to death, owing to horrifying lacerations on his body perpetrated by an unknown assailant, in the wee hours of the morning on the second of November. His daughter, Marie, was nowhere to be found; she had last been seen leaving the house the previous evening by one of the servants. The metropolitan police were conducting a search, and soliciting information regarding her whereabouts and safety.

Marie dropped the newspaper listlessly and stared at nothing. It was confirmed. Her father was dead. She had killed her father.

Miles away, she could hear the front door opening, Godalming making some politely pointless remark, Augustus tossing a careless *bon mot* back at him. She sank into a chair, mute, powerless, still. Out of the force of habit she took out a handkerchief, then grimaced and replaced it. She could hear him, out in the hall, singing bits of a Mozartean aria in his clear, lyrical bass: '*O, poverini, per femmina giocare …*'

He entered the library, peeling elegant kidskin gloves from his fingers. 'Ah, Marie. *Bonsoir, ma douce fille.*'

A red shroud passed over her eyes, and she raised herself to her full height, shaking with anger. Clawing at the paper, she thrust it into his hand, folded open to the ghastly article. 'Did you know about this?'

He gazed at the paper dispassionately. 'No, but I assumed, correctly. Why?'

'Why? *Why?* You—you callous—' She sputtered with wrath and shock.

'He was not going to live forever,' Augustus told her in a be-sensible tone.

'How *dare* you!'

'Don't you blame *me*. Face facts. I told you what you were, and you refused to believe me. I warned you not to go home, and you disobeyed me. Venting your spleen upon me will do no good.'

'*I killed him!*' she screamed.

His face softened a little. 'I know you did. The first one is always the most difficult—'

'Don't speak to me that way! Don't ever speak to me again, Ravenhurst! I am leaving!'

Marie picked up her skirts and swept through the hall, not even pausing to grab a cloak, and flung the front doors open. They crashed against the walls like gongs—

Blackness.

A rosy something or other above her swam into focus by degrees. The ceiling of her bedroom, partly obscured by the four-poster on which she found herself to be lying. Augustus was sitting close beside her. He had drawn the chair from the vanity toward the bed, and was watching her attentively. He spoke as she began to stir.

'*Quand on dîne avec le diable, il faut se munir d'une longue cuilleur.* Drink this, my dear.'

Obediently, she took the cup from his hand and swallowed. Her senses burned momentarily and subsided. She was alarmed for a split second when she noticed that it was a teacup, but then realized that it must contain blood, or it would not have revived her. Yes, there was the smell, and the color. Marie sat up gingerly, and noticed that the lights were dim and the drapes had been drawn shut.

'It'll be sunrise in about forty minutes,' said her sire. 'How are you feeling?'

'All right, I suppose,' she muttered. She looked at her fingers, tangling them together in her lap.

'There was a real danger of your bolting from Ravenhurst, you see. I had to stop you. If you were to leave, you would kill again, and be caught, and be killed yourself—how could you avoid it, without proper training in technique and stealth and manipulation? You must remain here, Marie.'

She nodded miserably. 'What did you do?'

'I knocked you out. Don't worry, it is quite harmless. A bit embarrassing, I know, but I had the advantage—I am an experienced and powerful vampire, and your sire what is more. Not everyone will be able to exert such force upon you, and as you gain in skill and knowledge under my instruction, your defenses will improve. Before long I can make you as competent as many vampires that are decades your seniors or more.'

He seemed to run out of things to say in this vein, for his speech became less and less enthusiastic and finally petered out. Marie was still staring into space.

'The sun is nearly up,' he said several minutes later. 'Will you take the daylight hours in seclusion?'

'Yes—thank you.'

He nodded and rose, replacing the chair before the mirror. At the door, he bowed to her slightly and said, '*Bonjour, mademoiselle.*'

She laid herself back upon the bed, wishing she could sleep.

Interminable hours of daylight drifted past. Marie watched a tiny sliver of light travel along the uppermost edge of the wall, from one side of the room to the other, as she lay motionless upon the four-poster. She heard the grandfather clock at whiles, rooms away beneath her in the entrance hall, tolling and tolling again: seven; a quarter past seven; half past; a quarter to eight; eight; a quarter past eight …

Nightfall came at last. She rose slowly from the bed into a sitting position again. None of the lamps were lit. Even with her unnaturally enhanced vision, she could hardly distinguish anything in the gloom, save for a pale line above the drapes that suggested starlight. The curious painting loomed opposite her, a patch of irregular bright and dark shapes on the wall.

She went to the window and pulled open the curtains to look out onto the grounds. Trees, statues, topiary, and a fountain were laid out below, all looking skeletal and grey in the moon. It struck her again how vast Ravenhurst really was, and how little of it she was acquainted with; even taking the other inhabitants of the manor into account, it was a labyrinthine and solitary place.

Marie left her room to find Augustus. He was in the library, slowly swirling blood around in a brandy snifter and reading an ashen-colored book titled *Theatrum Chemicum.*

'Good evening,' she said.

He looked up. '*Ah, bonsoir, ma mignardise. Comme-es tu?*'

'*Bien, merci.*'

He stood up, setting his book on the table. 'Well. Would you care for some breakfast?'

She looked away from him. 'No.'

He shrugged. 'Please yourself.'

'Lord—Augustus?'

'Hmm?'

'I was wondering,' she said, realizing as she spoke that she was really talking because anything sounded better than silence in that ghastly house, and seized on the first question that entered her head—'are vampires unique? I mean, other creatures from fairy-stories and so forth, are they real as well?'

'Yes,' said Augustus simply. 'Many of them.'

'Werewolves?'

'Few in England. Which is just as well, they're frightfully dull, you know.'

'Dragons?'

'Extinct. That is, in the British Isles; some places still have them.'

'Church grims?'

'All too numerous, I'm afraid, *ma chèrie.*'

'Pixies?'

'Don't be ridiculous.'

Marie glowered. Her sire smiled charmingly, and promptly took command of the conversation. 'I was at the court of the Duke of London yesternight—'

'What? There is no Duke of London.'

'Do not interrupt me. There is a Duke of London among us; his name is von Orlok, and he has been preëminent among English vampires for, oh, about two hundred years. He wishes to meet you.'

'Why?'

'His Grace prefers an exact and unmediated knowledge of everyone whom he governs. He is accustomed, too, to being obeyed. And you would have to have some sort of *début* in any case.'

'This Duke sounds Mediæval.'

'Hardly; he was sired in 1605,' Augustus replied. 'That aside. I have spoken informally on your behalf, as is customary, and you will be presented to His Grace the Duke on the night of the ninth, at the Manticore Palace—his residence.'

Marie thought. 'Just less than a week.'

'Yes. So you have plenty of time to prepare.'

'Prepare? Prepare what?' she asked, with a flutter of alarm.

He chuckled. 'Nothing heroic. Chiefly I mean mental preparation, *ma fleurette*. The etiquette of the place will be unfamiliar to you in certain respects; mind your *Your Ladyship*'s and *Your Grace*'s, of course, but there are a great many conventions of which you could have no knowledge as a mortal, unless you had become a courtesan.'

She grimaced. 'There will be prostitutes at the court?'

'Not as you mean the term. Courtesans in this peculiar *malebolgia* offer their blood, not their flesh (at least, not necessarily), and their compensation consists chiefly in the thrill of being hunted, as well as a certain amount of accidental knowledge of this grand, secret world.'

Marie shook her head in disgust. 'Even in a society as virtuous and upstanding as Queen Victoria's Great Britain, some people simply will not control themselves.'

Augustus scoffed. 'In a society as virtuous and upstanding as Queen Victoria's Great Britain, the magnetic attraction of perversity is all the stronger behind the *façade*. Suppressing one's darker desires does not kill them, it only leaves them starving, and willing to take increasingly rank nourishment in consequence; they, like us, live indefinitely. Some of the most polished and respectable specimens of our own era and those before us have been courtesans—Sir Robert Peel, for example, and Archbishop Tait.'

'Sweet heaven,' she breathed.

'Evidently not,' he replied. 'Tait has a particularly bitter, musty aftertaste, in fact. Anyhow. The first necessity in all this is that you learn to drink like a normal person' (his lip curled slightly in pronouncing the word *normal*), 'and not to be extravagantly shocked by things every five minutes, as you seem so fond of doing. In addition, there are certain people whom you must be specially careful to defer to, as you are in their debt.'

'How can I be in anyone's debt?' she said plaintively. 'I have only been here for two days.'

'*Nights*,' he corrected her. 'Watch that—it's the sort of slip that marks you out as a dragonet. Of course, everybody *knows* you are, but every habit maintained from mortal life, especially in one's manner of speaking, is an invitation to be mocked for the fact. As for how you can be in debt to anybody, I have had to make particular mention of you to a few figures in the court. His Grace does not like new vampires; he is domineering and jealous. I had to smooth things out with some people to ensure that your *début* would be altogether dignified. They shall be expecting suitable demonstrations of gratitude on your part.

'First of all—and do keep in mind, please, that our titles do not consistently overlap with those of mortals—there is the Marchioness of Bath and Wells, Livilla Thackeray. She is a great favorite of the Duke's, on account of her beauty, which is admittedly formidable; moreover, being an empty-headed parasite, she poses no threat to his control.'

Marie was taken aback by the forthright insults, especially on the heels of his cautions about etiquette. 'You are very, er, frank, my lord.'

'I can afford to be. I am sufficiently talented in the arts of telepathy to keep my thoughts private, and in any case, I am saying nothing about Lady Livilla Thackeray that is not already well-known to everyone aside from Lady Livilla Thackeray. There are, I confess, wheels within wheels, and vampires that I cannot afford to offend, but she is not one of them.' He motioned to Marie to take a chair, and she did so. He continued.

'Now. Lord Nigel Carroll, the Earl of Richmond, is another vital figure. He is the Lord Chief Justice, and has, how shall I put it, a sort of self-appointed following among younger vampires—those sired since about 1700.'

'What is their ideal?'

'His followers? Pure anarchical claptrap. They've taken in these ideas of constitutions and democracy and so forth, which are debatable even among humans and stark raving among ourselves, and run with them. Lord Richmond is not a fool, but there is a sense in which he cannot be held responsible for his disciples—except perhaps for Monsieur Chastelard, of whom I will tell you more in a moment.

'The Judiciary Council, of which Carroll is head, reviews all cases and resolves those which fall under its own purview; some judgments are reserved to the Duke alone, and difficult cases are traditionally referred to him, even if only in an advisory capacity. Disputes over territory, for hunting and for selecting servants and courtesans, are the main matter of its examinations, together with occasional reports of irreligion.'

'Irreligion, a crime among vampires?' she said incredulously. 'But surely—'

'There shall be time for questions later, *ma fille*; permit me to continue. You ought to know that approval to sire a new vampire is one of the cases reserved to the Duke, and that your own siring was not authorized. The judgment of the matter is, strictly, in the Duke's own claws, but I have asked Richmond to intercede for you and for me as far as possible. You are therefore more indebted, probably, to him than to any other single vampire save myself. Do not forget it.'

'I won't,' she said quietly.

Lord Ravenhurst smiled. 'A rather pleasanter figure with whom you will have cause to deal is an old friend of mine, and in fact another of my children, Paul Chastelard. I sired him about a hundred years ago now. He is Lord Richmond's lover, and—oh, don't *squirm* so,' he said testily. 'Sodomite affairs have been carried on since the dawn of time. I have had several myself, with Monsieur Chastelard for instance. The only difference between vampire society and human society in modern England is that *we* are not duplicitous hypocrites about it. That aside … Chastelard and I, as I was saying, are old friends; he has participated in several of my *séances*, though I do not believe you have met him more than once. He was a Frenchman in life, and delights in good theatre. He is a decadent, dissolute, irresponsible narcissist, so naturally everybody adores him. His personal lack of interest in politics will be significant in the Duke's eyes, in that it will help to prevent your siring appear to have been a political ploy if Chastelard is in favor of welcoming you. He is well known to be a personal connection of mine, of course, but equally, he would never pretend to like anyone or anything if he didn't—if only because there would be more fun to be had by mocking it.'

A disquieting thought occurred to her. ' *Was* my siring a political ploy?'

'Certainly not. Nothing bores me like intrigue, and anyway you are no use, though your *naïve* vanity is rather touching.'

'Er … thank you,' said Marie. 'Is there anyone else I ought to thank?'

Her sire gave her a stern look. 'I hope you shall do no such thing. You are to *demonstrate* your gratitude, not to state it in so many words. It is tacitly understood that anything said at court is a well-mannered lie, except negotiations of terms to borrow someone else's courtesan.'

'Oh.'

'But, as to other important figures ...' Augustus mused. 'There is the Reverend Doctor Tinsmith. I believe and hope that he shall not be in attendance: he is a frightfully religious bore. Thankfully he despises the frivolity and license of the court, and rarely appears there. If the cult needs to be represented, he will generally send Canon Glover along to do it for him, who is marginally more agreeable.'

'How is it a vampire can be frightfully religious?'

'Can you imagine a vampire's religion being anything other than frightful? As for his specific flavor of terror, he was an English Calvinist in life, and was sired around the time that Cromwell took power. I don't think he has altogether got over the Restoration. But the cult, though still important, is less powerful than it was. Younger vampires enter its orders less frequently: its particular brand of hellfire is not as fashionable as it was in the seventeenth century. Nevertheless, officially, it is the religious organ of our society, and lip service is paid to it by all respectable vampires.

'The only other figure who springs to mind is the Duchess of Ely, Carmilla Borgia. She is remarkable chiefly for her age—she is older than the Duke, older even than myself, but a nonentity; she has become one of Lady Bath's hangers-on. I suppose if you find Livilla indispensable to your sense of well-being, you are welcome to cultivate Lady Ely for leverage.

'Now, you will in all likelihood be called upon to speak for yourself before the Duke when you are presented. He was a Prussian, so be prompt, clear, and exact in your replies, and exhibit the deportment of a subject—but don't grovel, or speak to him as if to a tyrant. He is fearfully sensitive about being made to look despotic; he knows well enough that the Anglo-French vampires of London would not stand for that. Lord Richmond, who has more of a sense of humor, you will want to approach with just a *soupçon* of charming impertinence mixed in with flattery. Lady Bath you can merely flatter. Monsieur Chastelard is already an admirer of your beauty, but will be most impressed by an air of slightly jaded epicureanism. Are you certain you will not sup?'

'I am certain,' she said, a little too loudly.

Augustus smirked at her. Rising, he summoned her to the dining room with a gesture.

'Something fresher tonight, I think, Godalming,' said the vampire to the butler as he seated himself.

'Very good, my lord. August, or Howard?' The footmen on either side of him both became very still.

'Mmm, neither. My breakfast was a little too rankly male—throw out the rest of that bottle of Welshman, by the way. Something feminine.'

'Yes, my lord. I shall instruct the cook.' The servants exited.

'There is something I have been wondering about, since yesterday—er, yesternight,' Marie said diffidently, and Augustus smiled and nodded to indicate that her rephrasing was correct. 'About the blood. How was it still liquid? You said that it was taken from a woman who had been at Ravenhurst weeks ago.'

'The cook does very little cooking,' Augustus said. 'Her primary function is precisely to keep human blood in its liquid and vital state. It could be partially done through refrigeration, but that renders the taste bland and unpleasant, and anyhow it is a fairly recent invention. We have a long tradition of sanguine cookery, necessity being the mother of invention. Some vampires experimented with magic and alchemy in the Dark Ages and the earlier Mediæval period; around the tenth century, in Mahometan Spain, alchemists stumbled upon techniques that preserved blood outside the body to be fit for vampiric consumption. Up until that time, we had relied very largely upon herds of slaves and upon courtesans. Many of them were taken through witches' sabbaths: some of us sometimes acted the part of the Devil at their meetings, which made things a great deal more convenient—hunting, though a necessary skill (and one in which I shall train you before long), is most often a bore. But I am losing my subject. The alchemical techniques spread through the Mediterranean and northward over the next century, and by the time Abælard was teaching in Paris, vampires as far afield as Kiev and the Faroes were drinking of the scarlet nectars of Sicilians and Egyptians.'

'You speak as though you remember it,' she said, her curiosity aroused.

'That original era, I confess, I do not. But I am closely acquainted with vampires whose memory reaches deep into the mists of time: vampires who were already living their deaths when Arthur routed the Saxons at Badon Hill, when the Byzantines stole the secret of silk-making from the people of Cathay, and when Saint Jerome choked in the Holy Land for the sack of Rome. Though I am not young even by our standards, my own unlife goes only as far back as the advent of the Black Death, under the extinct Plantagenets.'

As he finished pontificating, a heavyset woman entered. She looked nearer fifty than forty, and was dressed in the black and iron-grey uniform of the household; her hair crowned her head with a neat bun, all already pure white. She curtseyed without expression. It was the cook.

'Ah, the cup that cheers,' said Augustus. He motioned her over. Marie supposed that he was going to give her special instructions about the blood, though in that case it was odd that he did not simply relay them through Godalming as he had done before. He reached up and began undoing the cuff of the cook's sleeve; for a moment, Marie was bewildered, and then he struck.

As her master's teeth sank into her flesh, and his tongue and lips began to suck up her blood, the cook barely winced. Not a drop escaped him; it would have been possible to suppose he was merely kissing her, if not for the obscene noise. The air curdled around them. Marie gripped the arms of her chair, aghast, yet desperately hungry, waiting for the hideous spectacle to stop. After what could only have been a few seconds, Augustus withdrew, licking the horrible red-black wounds, which glistened wetly.

'Do excuse me,' he said in his most urbane tones, 'being so loud at meat. And look, how thoughtless of me, too—I have served myself before the lady. That will do for me, Mrs Cassilda. Marie, will you have some?'

The cook's empty face turned to her. Marie clutched the table and mouthed a wordless refusal. She turned away, yet she could sense the spiritless servant looming beside her—could hear, with the dreadful precision of undead senses, the sounds of a ribbon being untied and a cuff pushed up to the elbow.

'A different vintage, maybe? I could send for Howard if you prefer, or young Peter.'

'No!' Marie cried in a strangled voice.

She could practically hear Augustus roll his eyes. Mrs Cassilda was dismissed; she exhaled heavily, curtseyed, and left the room. Marie turned miserably back to her sire, forcing blood-tinged tears into her eyes.

'Can't we drink from animals?'

'Don't be disgusting.'

CHAPTER IV

HE THAT SITS UPON THE THRONE [2]

Unreal City,
Under the brown fog of a winter dawn,
A crowd flowed over London Bridge, so many,
I had not thought death had undone so many.
Sighs, short and infrequent, were exhaled,
And each man fixed his eyes before his feet,
Flowed up the hill and down King William Street,
To where Saint Mary Woolnoth kept the hours
With a dead sound on the final stroke of nine.

— THOMAS STEARNS ELIOT, *THE WASTE LAND*

The evening of the ninth of November was frigid, even for a London autumn, but clear. St John the Divine Roman Catholic Church glowed through the dusk above Mr William Vavasour, the *fiancé* of the deceased's daughter—or putative *fiancé*, as no one now knew Marie's whereabouts. The requiem had begun at six, so that he was already several minutes late.

He pulled the great scarlet door open as quietly as he could, pausing at the stoup to dip his fingers into the holy water and cross himself. The cærulean Gothic Revival vaults brooded above him; the vast and dimly illuminated space of the nave passed overhead as an unminded cloud. A blaze of light shone out from the

---

[2] This chapter contains some Latin quotations not annotated in the index, as they are translated in the body of the text at later points.

mass of candles in the sanctuary through generous openings in the rood screen, the images of the saints on its lower register all but eclipsed. At the peak of the screen stood the rood itself: a crucifix with trefoiled arms holding up the naked, bleeding Savior, flanked on one side by the Mother of Sorrows and on the other by St John, the church's patron. Before the great door, directly in line with the black-veiled tabernacle, was the catafalque, surmounted by the shrouded coffin. The Gradual was being chanted from the loft behind and above the congregation, where the pipe organ and the choir were concealed: '*De profundis clamo ad te Domine,*' *Out of the depths I cry unto thee, O Lord.*

William tried to keep his footsteps quiet on his frostbitten way into a seat behind the Redglass brothers. Near them, but separated by a space, were three strangers: a brown-haired girl and two grim-faced, tall men; relatives, he guessed, from the Cornwall branch of the Redglasses, from whom the Londoners had been largely estranged for a solid century, owing to the stubbornly Jacobite sympathies of the westerners. Still, here they were; family and faith were cords not easily broken, even by the weight of crowns.

A tenor out of the choir began to intone the Sequence:

'Dies iræ, dies illa,
Solvet sæclum in favilla,
Teste David cum Sibylla.
Quantus tremor est futurus,
Quando Judex est venturus,
Cuncta stricte discussurus.'

A day of wrath that day shall be, The world dissolved in ash will be, David and Sibyl testify, William mentally versified; *The future shaking, ah, how great, When that Judge shall descend in state, A-sudden every thing to break.* The voice raised the chant heavenward as something pure, solitary, angelic. He closed his eyes.

The pastor of the parish, Fr Weld, vested in a shining black chasuble with the dull sleeves of the alb beneath showing, crossed the altar, genuflected before the tabernacle, and came to the Book of the Gospels. The congregants rose. He crossed his forehead, lips, and heart with his thumb, intoning clearly, '*Continuatio Evangelii sancti secundum Joannem sanctum. In illo tempore, venit itaque Jesus et invenit eum quattuor dies jam in monumento habentem. Erat autem Bethania juxta ...*'

William's mind could not help but drift, lulled by the familiar polysyllables of the Latin. He tried not to think about Marie. He studied the chief mourners in the pew in front of him, though it was difficult to read their faces from the small fractions he could see. James—now himself Baron Redglass—all the way on the left, his face stony. Henry to his right, his eyes downcast and listless, not at all his usual pious self. The Cornish girl, directly in front of William, unreadable. Her dark curls of hair were a little like—no. One of the male relatives, tall and wearing a scowl, whether of dislike or sorrow. The other, politely attentive to the reading, though William had noticed that he had inscribed the sign of the cross on himself a beat behind the rest of the congregants, hastily, like a *noveau riche* at a dinner party who must eye his hostess to make sure he uses the right fork. But that was uncharitable. Perhaps he was a recent convert, unaccustomed to the Mass.

'*Resurget frater tuus. Dicit eo Martha, Scio quia resurget in resurrectione in novissima die. Dixit ei Jesus, Ego sum resurrectio et vita. Qui credit in me et si mortuus …*'

William gave in and began to wonder where Marie was. No one had seen even her shadow since the night of her father's death. Could the murderer have made an attempt on her life as well, which she fought off? Was she kidnapped? What? What?

Fr Weld passed out of the rood screen's wide door to the outer lectern, grasping the eagle firmly by its wings, and began to declaim the readings again in English. 'A reading from the First Epistle of Saint Paul to the Thessalonians. We will not have you ignorant, brethren, concerning them that fall asleep, that you be not sorrowful, even as others that have no hope.'

Miles away to the northwest, in her room at Ravenhurst, Marie was preparing for the reception at which she was to make her *début*. She had looked over the clothing available to her in the wardrobe with some distaste; not so much that it was ugly or unfashionable, but that she was loth to give Augustus the satisfaction of dressing her, in however remote a sense. She had chosen to keep to her own black gown, partly as a private act of spite, and much more because she felt it only appropriate in her grief for her father. If she could not attend his funeral or mourn with her brothers, she could at least be shrouded for his sake. She had tried to pray for his soul once; the words had scalded her tongue and lips like molten metal, and the attempt had not been repeated.

But it was, after all, a visit to the ducal palace. She ought to be finely, if gravely, attired. She added a white choker with a brooch in the middle, and then, realizing that she would not be able to dress her hair on her own, grudgingly rang for Hyacinth.

A sickening idea crossed William's mind, for the first time. No, that was impossible. Not to be considered. Marie would never have gotten mixed up in that world for any price. It was quite impossible.

'… the Lord himself shall come down from heaven with commandment, and with the voice of an archangel, and with the trumpet of God: and the dead who are in Christ, shall rise first.'

Admittedly, she did know Lord Ravenhurst. She attended the occasional literary salons at his manor; she had mentioned them to him, a little shamefacedly, but that was only because Lord Ravenhurst had such a dubious reputation. She had had a chaperone, everything was surely fine. He would never have touched her under those circumstances.

'… Gospel according to Saint John.' William started, and hastily made the sign of the cross on his forehead, lips, and heart. 'At that time, Jesus came and found that Lazarus had been four days already in the grave. Now Bethania was near Jerusalem, about fifteen furlongs off. And many of the Jews were come to Martha and Mary, to comfort them concerning their brother.'

Tears welled up suddenly in William's eyes. Where *was* she? They had been all but inseparable for the last year, reading together, praying together, going to the theater together; they had received her father's blessing and been engaged six months ago. Those memories were bitter ones now, blended with her inexplicable vanishing.

'Damnation,' he whispered thoughtlessly, and then raised his hand to his mouth, hoping the blasphemy would be mistaken for a cough. The scowling personage in the pew in front of him turned his head slightly for a moment, and then turned back towards the lectern. William, feeling guilty for his persistent inability to attend, did the same. The Gospel had concluded.

'In the name of the Father, and of the Son, and of the Holy Ghost,' began the priest, crossing himself; the congregants imitated him, and then seated themselves again. He straightened the papers containing his homily, and looked out over the flock for a moment in silence.

'Death,' he said clearly, 'comes for us all, my sons and daughters. We lay our brother, James Redglass II, to rest here this night; as we laid his wife to rest years ago, and as we laid their parents to rest, years before. Grief is a bitter burden, but there is at least a unity and a universality in it, expressed with such magnificence by John Donne: *All mankinde is of one Author, and is one volume; when one Man dies, one Chapter is not torne out of the booke, but translated into a better language; and every Chapter must be so translated; some peeces are translated by age, some by sicknesse, some by warre, some by justice; but Gods hand is in every translation; and his hand shall binde up all our scattered leaves againe, for that Librarie where every book shall lie open to one another: As therefore the Bell that rings to a Sermon, calls not upon the Preacher onely, but upon the Congregation to come; so this Bell calls us all.*

'Yet every time it comes into our lives, death is as new as birth. For Catholic Christians, of course, it *is* a birth: a birth into the wonders of the invisible world. Being invisible, that everlasting world is largely unknown to us, but we know that it is defined by four things, what we call the Four Last Things: Death. Judgment. Heaven. Hell.

'Death is the door whereby we enter into this world. It is easy to accept the idea, so popular in our apostate age, that death is simply the end of everything. And none, save those that have themselves passed this door of death, can prove otherwise. We may offer this or that piece of evidence or line of argument about the immortality of the soul, whether derived from human reason or from our holy tradition; but we cannot prove it in such a way that any sane man must believe it—it is an act of faith. Saint Martha, so much maligned for her foolish rebuke of her sister's choice of contemplation before our blessed Lord, nevertheless had this faith abundantly. She, like Saint Peter, when Christ Jesus confronted her with the question of His identity, replied out of faith: first, that her brother would be resurrected; and secondly, that: *I have believed that thou art Christ the Son of the living God.*'

At a quarter to seven, Augustus and Marie departed for the ducal palace.

'Why are we bundling ourselves up, exactly?' she asked, as she wound a muffler round her throat. 'It isn't as though we need to protect ourselves against catching a chill.'

Augustus tutted. 'Use your head. On a night like this, anyone not warmly dressed would appear to be a lunatic, or worse, poor. Drawing attention to ourselves, other than that required to attract prey or establish our position, is bad; as you advance in your mental powers, you will learn that it is more important to suppress things in the human mind than to call them out. Come along, the landau is already waiting.'

They were bowed out of the house by Godalming, and strode into the darkness.

'Breathe.'

'What?' said Marie.

'Breathe when you aren't talking. There is no mist rising from your breath, it looks odd.'

Marie concentrated. What had once been mostly unconscious now felt like working a set of pipe-organ bellows, especially with a corset to struggle against. But she did manage to begin exhaling a faint fog of breath. Her sire, his exhalations pluming like the smoke of a dragon, extended his hand to help her into the ornate black carriage, gave an address to their driver, and climbed in himself. The driver snapped the reins, and they were carried off into the night.

'This same Christ,' Fr Weld went on, 'personally descended into Limbo, to His own beloved dead, who were at once His creatures and His ancestors, thus fulfilling spiritually the text: *I am the most mighty God of thy father: fear not, go down into Egypt, for I will make a great nation of thee there. I will go down with thee thither, and will bring thee back again from thence.* For He Himself said, when the Sadducees challenged Him, that God is not the God of the dead, but of the living.

'Yet Our Lord elected to descend into death and make His presence known there, as if to declare: *Yes, I am the God even of the dead, as well as the living, and shall restore the dead to life, so that you may know that I will fulfill My promise to judge both the quick and the dead, and so that My kingdom and the kingdom of My Father shall have no end, in heaven or on earth or under the earth.* And this brings us to the second of the Four Last Things, which is judgment.'

At last Augustus and Marie reached a great wrought-iron gate, in the center of which was a silvern representation of a manticore rampant. Behind the gate, in the distance, lay the palace. Between them and the edifice itself, as the gate slowly opened, Marie could obscurely distinguish expansive grounds, housing carefully maintained hedges and rows of cypress and flowerbeds—all dormant now—and, before the broad steps leading up to the main doors, a fountain: still active even in the late autumnal cold (presumably it was heated somehow), flashing in the brightness from the many tall windows and the outdoor lamps.

The palace itself was a baroque fantasy, spreading out left and right till its face spanned a full half-mile. Squared towers and a gigantic, octagonal dome reared into the skies, and pillared balconies, onto which immense, jewel-clear French windows opened, jutted out over the dim lawns. Over the great portico in the front was a broken pediment, in the center of which was a sculpture of a manticore, the same shape as that on the front gate, though vaster in size; its handsome face was disturbed by an unnaturally wide grin, and below, its true monstrosity was manifest: a leonine mane and brutal claws extended, with a serpentine tail ending in a stinging finial of spikes. Other heraldic and mythical animals were clustered around it, creeping at the manticore's feet—a crouching dragon with outstretched wings, a centaur with a barbed arrow in his hand, a three-headed ettin, the Calydonian boar, a sphinx, a brooding roc. In either direction, the fair stone walls were pierced by magnificent oriels, interspersed with colonnaded porches. The whole palace was scarcely less exquisite than Versailles.

Augustus spoke, softly but distinctly. '*Here thou must all distrust behind thee leave, Here be vile fear extinguish'd.* I am the Mercury to your Proserpina here, my dear. Follow my lead.'

'And eat the pomegranate seeds like I'm told so that I shall stay here,' she answered poisonously, before she could stop herself. Even as she spoke, she realized how shockingly insolent she was being, and put her gloved fingers in front of her mouth in horrified fear.

Her sire looked at her for a moment, expressionless; then his face split in a smile. 'A Danielle come to judgment,' Augustus jested, and exited the carriage, extending his arm for her as she descended.

The towering doors that stood at the top of the broad, deep marble steps were opened by a silent pair of Negro footmen. A haze of light flowed out over them from the chandelier in the vast entrance hall. 'You can stop breathing now,' he said carelessly.

The entrance hall was magnificent, far finer even than Ravenhurst Manor's splendid foyer. It was octagonal, floored and pillared in black Chinese marble, with two gigantic arches to the right and left leading to passageways to the rest of the palace, and opposite the entrance itself, a sweeping staircase fashioned of the same stone.

Overhead was a domed ceiling, divided into three unequal panels—a large central one and two lesser panels on either side—within which were copies of the panes of Bosch's triptych, *The Last Judgment*. Huge swaths of black, brown, green, and red dominated the viewer's eye, relieved here and there by smaller patches of celestial blue and white; but the total message of the painted ceiling was one of disaster. In the left-side panel was the Garden of Eden, lush and peaceful, with God hovering over it in a pale aureole; but even there, between earth and heaven were placed warring angels, and the temptation and ultimate expulsion from the Garden of Eden were depicted below. In the center there was the Judgment itself: at its height was Christ, clothed in red, surrounded by a sapphirine circle of angels and the blessed elect, but the mass of the painting that lay beneath was filth and chaos. Contorted bodies, weird machines of unknown function, gutted and burning buildings, beetle-like devils, and great clouds of black smog predominated. And to the right, in the final panel, lay only hell, and only more of the same: fires, demons, tortured sinners, monsters.

Marie shuddered a little, to release some of the *angst* brought on by contemplating the ceiling, and looked down to see a lithe, golden-haired male accosting her sire. He looked vaguely familiar to her.

'*Bonsoir, mon ami,*' he said smoothly to Augustus, '*et votre petit demoiselle, que ç'est tres belle! Votre penchant en la féminité, pour toujours excellent.*'

'*Oui, ç'est. Et bonsoir,*' replied Augustus, with a leonine smile. '*Comme vous et le Président de la Haute Cour de Justice, Monsieur Carroll?*'

'*Nous sommes bien,*' said Chastelard.

'*Ma nouveau fille, Marie,*' he said politely.

The other vampire took Marie's hand and kissed it. '*Enchanté, bien sûr, Mademoiselle de le Manoir de le Nid de Corbeaux. Parlez-vous Français, ma, si je peux me permettre, mignardise?*'

'*Non bien, Monsieur Chastelard,*' replied Marie.

'Then we shall converse in English with one another,' he said mellifluously, his English almost as liquid as his French. 'Ravenhurst, that is, our father Augustus, informed me of your recent elevation, and I must compliment his ever impeccable taste in companionship.'

Unsure whether she or Augustus were being complimented, Marie could not tell whether she should express thanks, but was rescued from making any decision by the flow of Chastelard's talk. They had turned to the right and begun to walk along one of the high corridors, the chandeliers shining in the polished black floors as if in mirrors.

Before long they came to a great ballroom—at a glance, more than an acre in extent, and something like a hundred feet high. Along one wall, the structure was pierced by gigantic windows, whose sills were low enough to sit in, but whose pointed peaks reached nearly to the moulded ceiling. Their massive drapes were drawn back, revealing a midnight sky pocked with planets and stars. Opposite each window was a mirror of equal proportions, silver-framed and adorned with sculpted wyverns, undines, sea-serpents, and Japanese dragons. Between the mirrors were small doors—at least, they looked small, in the context of the ballroom—with semicircular pediments and false columns surrounding them. The ceiling was raised in a barrel vault like a Romanesque cathedral, with painted panels featuring Bacchus, Proserpina, Venus, and other classical figures. Chandeliers and wall-mounted lamps illuminated the immense space. At the far end of the room was a low daïs, with an ornate black chair toward the left and a cadre of musicians to the right: five violins, two cellos, a French horn, an oboe, a flute, and a harpsichord. They were playing an ornamented, *legato* oboe melody supported by the strings, and accompanied by a delicately picked harpsichord line; Marie recognized it as a Marcello *concerto*. Its steady, strong rhythm was slightly hypnotic.

' *Voici*,' said Chastelard with an elegant gesture, 'the *massa damnata*.'

'Nor,' came Fr Weld's voice over the congregants at St John the Divine, 'shall the Lord abandon any soul, if it does not abandon Him. My children, judgment is not an arbitrary system of accounting on God's part: such-and-such a punishment for such-and-such a sin, weighed to a nicety in heartless fastidium; it is the simple spiritual effects of our actions, whose freedom God created, and ratifies. His judgment of us is more the revelation of the truth of our freedom, than the imposition of artificial consequences from without. As the Scripture says, *God made not death, neither hath He pleasure in the destruction of the living. For He created all things that they might be: and He made the nations of the earth for health: and there is no poison of destruction in them, nor kingdom of hell upon the earth.'*

The hall was filled with vampires. Dressed in unimpeachably tailored suits and stunning, voluptuous gowns—jet, violet, emerald, sapphire, champagne, and crimson flashed at Marie from every side—they were exchanging quiet talk or sedate, superior laughter that rippled through the mass of them. It could not quite be called a crowd, for there was no press, and indeed sufficient room in the hall that anywhere one stood seemed like an open space; yet in any direction one looked, one's view was interrupted by a vampire, or a knot of them, further away or nearer oneself. Here was one, a noblewoman in a steel-grey dress, a lacquered Oriental fan in her hand; here was another, a tall, imperious-looking female, with pale blonde hair and a copper-colored gown with black piping, setting an empty champagne flute on a tray being borne about the room by a footman; there was a third, a man, dressed in a cassock, which she was slightly unnerved to notice was surmounted at the throat not by the white clerical collar she would have expected, but a red one.

Chastelard espied someone, and passed from Augustus and Marie over to another guest, his teeth flashing brightly under the chandeliers. At almost the same moment, the blonde-and-copper vampire saw them and went over to them.

Marie's first thought was that she did not look like a woman to cross. She was as lovely as a classical goddess, but there was a sheen in the smile, a glint in the eye, a flexing of nails when she gestured, that created a more venomous impression than most goddesses exhibit. Augustus took her hand and said warmly, 'Lady Bath, how pleasant to see you here.'

'Lord Ravenhurst, a pleasure. And—'

'Ah, let me present my daughter, Mademoiselle Marie Redglass. Marie, meet the Marchioness of Bath and Wells, Lady Livilla Thackeray.' Marie curtseyed, bowing her head slightly.

'Charmed; I feel sure we shall be great friends,' said Lady Thackeray, in a voice that deceived no one. 'Lord Ravenhurst, have you heard about Secretary Mountjoy?'

'Not since the Michælmas Ball. Why do you ask?'

'Oh, it's too scandalous,' said Lady Thackeray, stopping a footman and selecting another glass of blood. 'He was caught carrying on with some young creature in the Duke's private hunting territory.'

'You cannot be serious,' Augustus replied, taking a glass for himself and passing a second to Marie, with a sidelong glance that told her she had better drink it. 'Violating the Duke's hunting rights is far too elaborate a method of suicide to bother with; the rumormongers have jumbled things, it's as simple as that.'

'Not this time,' insisted Livilla. 'Mountjoy wasn't hunting, you understand—he was fornicating, with some slip of a girl.'

'That I will believe.'

'Well, *I* hardly can, however many times I say it. It is disgusting. And *that* creature is Secretary to the Lord Chief Justice,' she spat.

'All the same,' Augustus said evenly, 'though it may be something of a *solécisme* officially, live flesh and blood make for a rather pleasing change of fuck. Now and again.'

'And again and again,' said Chastelard, who had reappeared, champagne flute in hand. He bowed, a little carelessly. 'Lady Bath.'

'Monsieur Chastelard,' she replied, not opening her mouth very widely. She turned back to Augustus: 'Speaking of Carroll, by the way, I feel he is going a bit too far in the statements he makes over his adjudications. He is beginning to sound like a Chartist.'

'Hell forbid,' sneered Chastelard into his glass.

'And Doctor Tinsmith's homilies these nights—really—'

At this Augustus laughed derisively. 'Forgive me, my lady, but if you listen to Tinsmith's homilies, you have no one but yourself to thank. A vampire's vampire, that one: at any rate he makes *my* skin crawl.'

'That is not the point,' said Livilla sharply. 'The point is, between them, they are fomenting a sensibility of—'

'Oh, stuff and nonsense. The Duke is our suzerain, we all acknowledge that—isn't that so? Marie, have a sip, this fellow's delectable. And in any case—ah, do excuse me. Good evening, Lady Ely.'

A smallish, olive-skinned female had joined the cluster. She was dressed in grey, her gown correctly but not attractively composed, and seemed to aim her eyes a little below the general level. She held a reticule in one hand, and grasped something black and elongated in the other.

'How do you do?'

'How do you do,' answered Lady Ely. The other vampires uttered nondescript civilities.

'My lady, permit me to present my daughter, Mademoiselle Marie Redglass. Marie, meet the Duchess of Ely, Carmilla Borgia.'

Marie curtseyed again, stealing a surreptitious glance at the new vampire's face. She looked nearly as nervous as Marie felt. As the latter rose, Lady Ely made a brave if not quite successful attempt at a smile, which was returned with a little more grace on Marie's part. She had to admit to herself, it was a small consolation that she was not the only one who was not at her ease in this place.

The musicians finished their piece; all the vampires stopped whatever they were doing and turned to applaud them. They bowed, and then began another movement. Conversation resumed. Lady Thackeray began talking to Lady Borgia, whose replies seemed to consist chiefly of monosyllabic agreements; they drifted in the direction of the musicians. Chastelard went over to a stately, dark-haired vampire, standing alone by one of the bays and looking at the night sky.

'That is Nigel Carroll, the Lord Chief Justice,' Augustus explained to Marie quietly. 'Since Livilla mentioned it, I have not noticed Mountjoy, who is usually in attendance on him; that is strange; it may be that His Grace the Duke has dealt with him after all ...'

'Is it a crime to—er—fornicate with humans?'

'Oh, goodness no. If it were there would be practically no courtesans at all, since many of them discover us first through acting as our mistresses and *cicisbei*, or through governesses' brothels. Hunting in the Duke's territory is a crime; fornicating without hunting could be read either way, and is manifestly criminal only in its *gaucherie*. But that is not the real reason the Duke would have for dealing with Mountjoy.' Augustus lowered his voice the way some people do to discuss medical matters. 'The fellow is a fool.'

'And that is a crime?'

'It might as well be; it certainly carries its own punishment. But stop interrupting me. He has expressed democratic sentiments on more than one occasion, openly, which amounts to fomenting sedition. In this instance, both Duke von Orlok and Lord Richmond want the same thing: for Mountjoy to be sacrificed. The Duke wishes to make an example of him, while Richmond needs to distance himself from the appearance of sympathy with the Chartists by approving of it.'

Marie looked around. 'Is it safe to speak so frankly here?'

He gave her a pitying look. 'Do you honestly suppose that I would so much as open my mouth in this hall if I were uncertain what would come out of it?'

She nodded and looked at the floor, chastised.

'Ordinarily, you would be right—or rather, you would have nothing to be right about, because I would have kept silence. But Mountjoy's fall is inevitable. The only uncertainty is exactly when it will be effected. The only person who does not know that is Mountjoy; unless it has already happened, in which case he knows something better than anyone for a change.'

'Are there any other crimes I ought to be aware of?' Marie asked.

He looked at her sidelong. 'Annoying one's sire with an endless stream of silly questions springs to mind.'

As Augustus finished speaking, a dissonant flourish issued from the musicians, and the vampires rapidly fell silent and turned to face the daïs. There was a loud bang, and smoke began pouring out of the floor, obscuring the great black chair. Marie gasped, but her sire laughed quietly at her ('His Grace likes to make an entrance,' he sneered), and the smoke cleared, revealing a tall vampire standing in front of the chair.

'Is he some sort of sorcerer?' she whispered.

'Of course not. That bang you heard was the trap-door in front of the chair being opened; he's then raised by a lever on a hidden platform. The smoke is to impress onlookers and hide the unsightly mechanism. *Câlice*, you're gullible.'

'His Grace, the Duke of London, master of all English vampires: Julius Otto von Orlok,' cried a voice from an unseen place. 'My lords, ladies, and gentlemen, hail your liege.'

Hail rose in a dull roar from a hundred throats. Bows of masculine and curtsies of feminine obeisance radiated outward from the daïs. Von Orlok seated himself; Marie took the opportunity to study him. He possessed a repellent physiognomy: his skin seemed to cling to his skull, as did his close-cropped, iron-colored hair, and his eyes were large and livid. He was excessively pale of skin, a feature accented by his evening dress. Nearly as bad as the eyes were the hands, long-fingered and slender, and periodically animated by a spider-like twitch. She shuddered.

A handful of polite formalities followed: greetings of this prominent vampire and that by the Duke, and a proclamation of a newly opened hunting ground in the East End (which had previously been the preserve of Livilla, it seemed, who now generously opened it to public use). Marie imitated her sire's deportment throughout, like a dinner guest surreptitiously eyeing her hostess because she is unsure which fork to use. After these matters had been disposed of, the Duke called out, '*Burggraf* Ravenhurst, come forward.'

Signalling by a small gesture that she was to follow, Augustus passed from the middle of the room to a spot directly in front of the black chair and its illustrious occupant. He bowed again, and stepped a little to the left, laying one hand on his breast and opening the other to the Duke. 'If it please Your Grace, meet my daughter, Mademoiselle Marie Redglass.' She curtsied deeply. Augustus had forewarned her to remain in that posture unless the Duke invited her to do otherwise, so she did, grateful that it would not be a strain on her undead limbs.

A heavy voice, soft and yet carrying—the Duke's—spoke. 'You are presenting a daughter to me, Ravenhurst.'

'Yes, Your Grace.'

'I had given you no leave to sire any children.'

'No, Your Grace. I have come to present her, and to solicit your pardon for my impetuosity.'

Marie risked a half-glance upwards without moving her head. Duke von Orlok was studying her in turn, teeth bared in what might be a crooked smile, his right hand raised. 'Had you any cause?'

'Your Grace can see better than anyone her exceeding beauty,' Augustus replied composedly. 'I confess that I was overcome, Your Grace. It was a crime of passion, not of malice.'

'Indeed,' said the Duke. 'But let her speak. You may stand, *fräulein*. Your name.'

'Marie Catherine Aurora Redglass, Your Grace,' she said distinctly, trying to keep calm, all of Augustus' instructions chasing one another through her brain. *Speak clearly and to the point. Back straight, do not slouch. Hands where he can see them. Do not look him in the eye, he doesn't like that—look at his chin. For Hell's sake stop fidgeting.*

'Are your parents living?'

She suppressed a wince. 'No, Your Grace, they are both dead.'

'Have you any surviving relatives?'

'Two brothers, one elder, one younger. The rest of my family live in Cornwall.'

'Do you intend to kill them?' he asked, without any great interest.

Marie gaped for a moment, and then managed to say, 'No, Your Grace.'

'Do you intend to resume residence with them?'

'Er, no, Your Grace.'

'You would refuse to do so.'

'I didn't mean that,' she said hastily. 'I—I only meant, if you ordered me to, Your Grace, I would—'

Augustus muttered, '*Whist, you fool*,' in a voice so quiet that even she could scarcely hear him. Von Orlok was grinning mirthlessly, his eyes untouched but his mouth pulled open like a sore. He leaned forward and quietly spoke.

'Come up here, *fräulein*.'

Marie stepped up onto the daïs. The Duke rose and began to walk slowly round her, inspecting her.

'Were there such a thing,' said the Duke aloud, 'it would have been a worthy defiance, Ravenhurst. I shall expect equally impressive excuses from all my subjects in future, if I am to show leniency.' He was standing behind her now, far too close; his strong, strange hand was on her waist; she felt her ringlets lifted gently from her neck and placed behind her shoulder. His other hand was suddenly on Marie, with cold pressure, just beneath her breasts. She was revolted, but held quite still. His breath wafted against her ear as he murmured, 'She is, as you say, beautiful.'

He struck. There was a blinding pain in her throat, and then, spreading from there through every vein, a horrible, stabbing sensation. Marie could not move, could not see—she struggled weakly, out of instinct rather than hope, but von Orlok's grip was heavier than lead—and then he abruptly let go. Her enervated limbs would not support her, leaving her to collapse onto the daïs. A confused picture of the hall swam back into view, its colors and angles bewildering. High above, a repulsive noise suggested that the Duke was licking up any of her blood that had escaped his mouth.

'*Fräulein* Redglass, you are hereby granted the freedom of the city,' he said idly. 'You may go.'

The room swam again. Everything went black.

William departed from St John the Divine immediately after the close of the Mass; he could make his excuses for not lingering to greet the other principal mourners by letter—the Redglass brothers would understand. He saluted a hansom.

'Where off to, my lord?' asked the cabman. William gave him the address, and the man gave him a disturbed look. 'Folk don't go that way, my lord, if you'll forgive me—'tisn't a right place, if you take my meaning.'

William scowled and produced ten shillings. The cabman's eyebrows flew into his hat. 'Three for speed,' said William, 'and the rest for silence.'

'Quick as you please, my lord,' the cabman answered. William climbed into the cab, and the fellow snapped the reins smartly. The festivities would not be over for some time yet, and afterward, Duke von Orlok would be expecting him.

CHAPTER V

THE DOCTRINE OF DOMINATION

A pleasant warmth filled the air, and an indistinct noise that seemed unplaceable but familiar. The noise was mildly discomfiting. But the warmth, and this soft whatever-it-was that she was lounging in, were the chief things. Anyway, the sound would go away presently.

That savage aching in her joints and muscles would go away too, she decided. Pleased with this attractive decision, she shifted slightly to get more comfortable.

At this point, Marie could not help but notice that the noise was still happening. The ache was also still there. It annoyed her. If they did not both go away this moment, she would open her eyes and sit up, she thought sternly at them. The sensations thus admonished remained unmoved. Marie frowned, and made good on her threat.

She was seated in a large armchair. The place was unknown to her: smallish and rectilinear, with mahogany panelling and a black, square mantelpiece that surmounted a—

'Fire,' she breathed aloud. Her voice rose hysterically. 'Put it out. Put it out, I say!'

'Marie, stop being a fool!' said a brutal hiss. Augustus. 'The hearth is grated and screened, it cannot hurt you.'

Gasping a little, if only out of habit, she looked around the room. To her left, in another of the armchairs, sat a tall, stately figure, whom she momentarily mistook for Lady Thackeray due to her fair hair; but she quickly saw that this was a different woman entirely. Another shape was in the corner of the room, indistinct in the wavering shadows, except that it seemed to be a male.

Augustus spoke, in a more normal voice. 'It is also worth saying that one should not form the habit of giving orders at the palace. His Grace the Duke does not like it.'

'We're still at the palace?' asked Marie miserably.

'Of course. Hell's hosts, child, did you really imagine I had carried your lifeless form out to the landau and whisked you back to Ravenhurst?'

'Lord Fairfax, be easy with her,' said the strange woman to her left in a serene contralto. 'She doesn't understand.'

'I am so glad that has been established,' Augustus snarled.

'My name is Vivien Glastenning,' said the woman parenthetically, turning to Marie. 'I am a friend of your sire's.'

Augustus turned to the shadowy figure. 'You—feed her. It's why you were sent, isn't it?'

'Yes,' said the fellow. Marie recognized his voice; it lacked the metallic ring that vampiric voices like Augustus' or Chastelard's had; it carried with it the human suggestion of moisture and warmth. But she was, for the moment, too distracted to identify the owner of the voice. 'His Grace asked me to attend to Miss Redglass specially. But—'

'Whatever you are about to say, whore, I do not care. I need to speak with the Chief Justice: excuse me, ladies.' He stalked out: as the door opened, the brilliant light of the ballroom shone in like a thunderbolt, and was then shut out as the door closed again.

'What did happen to me?' asked Marie in a small voice.

'The Duke drank from you, and then knocked you out.'

'But—Lord Ravenhurst said before that—that most vampires wouldn't be able—'

'His Grace the Duke,' said Miss Glastenning, pronouncing the words as though they tasted unpleasant, 'is not most vampires. He is centuries old, and strong in proportion; there are not many who have survived longer than he. Augustus is one of the few.'

There was a pause. The man in the corner (judging from Augustus' insult, she thought he must be a courtesan) had moved in front of the fire, where his silhouette was coming into focus, although he had his back to the women.

'I know you,' she said to him. 'But—who are you?'

For an answer, he turned around, stepped forward, and met her eyes. Marie was turned to stone.

William Vavasour. The Duke of Norfolk's chivalric nephew, whose wit and charm were the envy of dinner parties around London; he, the young Oxford scholar whose knowledge of the poetic and dramatic traditions of Western Europe was already second to none; he, the devoted and scrupulously observant Catholic, who had once challenged the Earl of Shaftesbury to an *au premier sang* duel for speaking scornfully of the Assumption of the Virgin. William Vavasour, to whom she was—or had been—engaged to be married. *He* was a courtesan.

She breathed his name aloud.

He looked downwards, like a man caught entering a bordello. 'In the flesh,' he said weakly.

Marie shut her eyes, unwilling to look at his face. To be tricked and ensnared by Augustus had been one thing. This was betrayal. Then, a wave of shame mixed with shock traveled through her, as she realized, too, that she was now exposed before him: sickly, cannibal, a thing more polluted than any chancred whore. She felt like Eve beholding, sudden and corrupt and irrevocable, her own nakedness and the nakedness of Adam.

'Get out,' she said through gritted teeth, not opening her eyes.

'Mademoiselle,' began Miss Glastenning gently.

'Get out,' she repeated. 'Please, I don't want you here.'

He drew a deep breath. 'Marie—'

'Don't. Don't you dare. Don't look at me!'

William swallowed and accepted their coinherent humiliations. He began again. 'Miss Redglass, please. Duke von Orlok has ordered that I restore you. He will be exceedingly angry if his wishes are ignored.'

'He is angry with me in any case.'

'He isn't,' said Miss Glastenning. 'His Grace's abuse of you was a tool, to punish Lord Ravenhurst for siring you without leave and for being too popular. He cares nothing about you at all. But if you ignore the Duke's express wishes now, then he will become angry with you. To say nothing of Mister Vavasour's possible fate.'

Then Marie did look at him. His eyes were on the floor and his hands limp at his sides. There was a faint smell coming from his clothes, aromatic and sweet, like incense.

'Why you?' she asked.

'It's another insult,' he said miserably, looking toward the door. 'Meant to suggest which vampire has the power to give life and to take it away. I'm his ... *client*.'

'And you didn't ask for this?' she demanded.

'No,' he replied, his eyes wide, pleading to be believed. 'No. Ma—Miss Redglass, I swear to you, I did not know you had been ... until I arrived for the— festivities tonight, and the Duke directed me to go to Lord Ravenhurst instead, and I remembered that you two knew each other; and I guessed it might mean ... And then he told me—'

'Don't,' Marie said. He shut his mouth. There was silence for a few moments.

'How long has this been going on?'

William shut his eyes and replied, 'A year and a half.'

'A year and a half?' she gasped. For a whole year before their engagement, he had been *steeped* in this world of physical and metaphysical disease. 'Did you know Lord Ravenhurst was a vampire when I was attending his salons?'

'Yes,' he admitted. 'But I thought he would never dare to hurt you; Lady fitzUrse was chaperoning you, after all, and the rules of secrecy so restrict predation that I ... But clearly I was wrong.'

'You fool,' said Miss Glastenning unexpectedly. 'Do you not know that Lady fitzUrse is a vampire?'

William choked, and his eyes began to stream in earnest. He sank to his knees in front of Marie, hands outstretched.

'Miss Redglass—I am sorry. I am utterly ashamed of … I … there are no words. Merciful God—I can make no defense for all I have done and not done, but I beg you to forgive me.'

She looked away and raised her hand to quiet him. Anger, sadness, love, and horror warred with one another inside her. Marie felt herself poised on a knife-point: the duty of forgiveness, laid upon every Christian, as against the relish and the strength of wrath. There seemed to be little point in forgiving him. There could be no absolution for *her* sins as she now was: scorched by every sacrament; her soul lost to an anonymous void. Whether she forgave or not, she would remain a child of Hell. And her wounds of both body and mind, from William, and von Orlok, and Augustus, and many more obscure figures, all cried out to her for vindication. Nor was she a stranger to the black pleasures of hatred. To hit back— not perhaps physically, but spiritually; not perhaps at the party chiefly responsible (whoever that was), yet at somebody—was crawlingly enticing.

Yet to extend peace and pardon would be, in its way, not only mercy but even justice, racked as she was by remorse for her father's death. William's deception of her, however contemptible, was nothing beside that; for could he have warned her in any way which she would have heeded? And compassion seemed one of her few links to her former life, and a kind of token rejection of the walking damnation into which she had been dragged. She raised her hand, as if in benediction, and opened her mouth, but at first, no words would come.

At last she spoke. 'I can't, Mister Vavasour. I simply can't. I am sorry.'

He shivered and nodded.

They seemed frozen there for a little while. Then, William stood up and, wiping his face with his handkerchief, began to unlink his left cuff.

'Mister Vavasour—no,' Marie said.

'If you do not feed, you may be too weak even to leave the palace, and you would be under His Grace's wrath,' he told her. 'Let me do this for you at least.'

'I will not,' she said, her temper rising again. 'Tell the Duke whatever you like. I am perfectly capable of making my way home.' To prove it, she rose from her armchair, whereupon she was seized with a fit of dizziness so severe that she collapsed back into it. The fresh wounds on her throat throbbed for a moment, and she became aware—or rather, was no longer able to ignore—the blind, gnawing hunger in the pit of her stomach.

He spoke, gently. 'Miss Redglass. Please, let me give you this.' He extended his wrist to her; the gesture reminded Marie irrationally of the arms of her parish's statue of the Virgin, outstretched in hieratic maternity. She took his naked hand in her glove, looking at the warm skin that concealed the veins and tendons within, and pressed her lips together firmly, shaking her head, less in refusal now than in uncertainty.

'What you do, do quickly,' said Miss Glastenning.

Her resistance snapped. Gripping his wrist firmly in both her hands, she thrust her head forward and bit into it: the hot, savory blood was flowing freely into her mouth, reviving her, exalting her, it was the nectar of the gods, more, and still more, the room was swimming about her—

'Enough. Enough, Marie!' came a voice from miles away to her left. She looked, but saw only a pale, swirling shape in the darkness. A strong hand was laid on her shoulder, and it pulled her back too firmly for her to remain immersed in the delectable feast. 'Take any more and you will hurt him badly.'

Her heart was beating, she had drunk so much. A vague yet vivid shape— William's—fell backward to the floor with a groan. Her surroundings began to solidify again. Miss Glastenning was on her feet, crossing to a cabinet; she removed a long strip of linen, which she wrapped tightly around his wrist in a rapid, well-practiced motion. In a weirdly homey gesture, she then produced a steel safety pin and used it to secure the bandage.

Revulsion swept over Marie, followed by hot, clinging shame. *Omne animal triste post cenam*, she thought wryly. Her eyes lit on a patch of the Persian rug that had been stained with the blood. William let loose an odd, drunken laugh. The blood-blackened patch was found by some moonlight that had spilt unwholesomely into the room, picking out each fiber in exquisite detail.

The ride home in the landau was grim. At first, Marie dabbed compulsively at her lips with her handkerchief, but she desisted after a wordless glare from Augustus. He spent the bulk of the journey staring out into the night sky and saying nothing.

She did not dare raise the subject of Duke von Orlok and his actions directly. But, when she opened her mouth to formulate some question about Miss Glastenning that would provide her with an avenue to inquire, she found that she had no need to, for her sire raised the matter first.

'Do not ever speak to His Grace that way again,' he growled.

'But what did I say?' she asked desperately.

'You spoke of his ordering you to do something! Time and time again, I told you not to offend his carefully maintained *façade* of impartial justice, and what do you do? You answer him like some sniveling peasant would talk to a tyrant!'

'He *is* a tyrant,' she said, with a sudden burst of spirit.

'In the name of every devil in Hell, girl, what has that got to do with anything? Save as another reason not to provoke him! Show a little intelligence—you've shown it well enough when talking about novels, it is high time you showed it in the here and now.'

'All right, Lord Ravenhurst, I am sorry. It won't happen again.'

'No it certainly will not. What a mercy *that* is understood,' he spat.

She twisted her fingers miserably in her lap for a few moments, trying to think of something to say that would diffuse the tension a little. The lace of the gloves pulled uncomfortably at her skin.

'Mr Vavasour—'

'Has known you for years, and in fact you were engaged to be married.'

'How did you know that?'

Augustus made a noise like an angry cat. 'Have you forgotten literally everything I ever told you about telepathy? Your brain is as secretive as thin air. We will begin lessons tomorrow evening at five o'clock sharp, merely to put *my* mind at rest.'

The remainder of the drive was conducted in silence.

A curt '*Au revoir*' from Augustus and a mounting of the stairs later, Marie was curled up in her bay window once more, watching the first faint intimations of sunrise, and thinking. The sky had gone from black to a rich blue-grey; since her window faced the west, the east was now probably blossoming slowly into rose and gold. The stars still shone brightly against the velveted roof of the world.

Her mind passed wanderingly over the chaos of the last several nights. A week already since her disastrous final visit to Ramshead Place. She thought of the *séance* by which Augustus had lured her in, the dreadful and sacrilegious longing to speak to her mother again, rather than waiting until she too had passed into Purgatory. Now, she was probably cut off from her mother forever; Marie could not quite see a vampire being admitted into the celestial court, even as the least of the least. What had her father's requiem been like? Abruptly it came to her that

William must have been there: James Redglass II would have been William's father-in-law, and he was an old friend of the family in any case. That was why he had smelled of incense. She thought of the feeling of his skin against her lips, and her mind flashed to the hideous feeling of the Duke's lips upon her skin.

An access of despair seized her. She flung herself to the vanity and pulled a fresh handkerchief out of it, forcing herself to weep, to expel some part of the horror. A few drops of blood seeped from her exhausted eyes.

After Marie had fled up the stairs, Augustus remained below, pacing the library for more than an hour. He hesitated over this volume or that at times, unable to drum up real interest in any. When some time had gone by, he murmured aloud, though no living soul could hear him:

'Quand la pierre, opprimant ta poitrine peureuse
Et tes flancs qu'assouplit un charmant nonchaloir,
Empêchera ton coeur de battre et de vouloir,
Et tes pieds de courir leur course aventureuse,
Le tombeau, confident de mon rêve infini.'

He rubbed his fingers together, as if to warm them. At last, he turned his steps out of the library and went to a door beneath the servants' stair, upon which hung a Mediæval portrait of St Clare. He reached into the collar of his shirt, and pulled a cord up over his head, from which there hung a heavy key; he opened the door with it and went inside, shutting the door behind him, and from the outside the noise of the lock being re-secured could be heard.

Marie passed the day in a trance-like languor. Except for her brief outburst of tears, she sat still on her bed, staring out of curtains she had never bothered to shut properly, and making no reply to Hyacinth's knocks. Slowly, the column of sunlight let in by the window, which she could see would never cross the bed itself, crept over the floor, the inverse of the shadow on a sundial.

At a quarter past four, there was a soft knock on her door. *'Bonsoir,'* came Augustus' voice through the wood. 'May I come in?'

'Yes,' she answered indifferently.

He did, and gave a sharp cry of alarm. 'Hell, child! Are you mad, leaving the drapes open like that? You could have been burned alive!'

'Not really,' she said.

Throwing Marie an invidious look, her sire went to the window, cautiously skirting the deadly light of the fading sunset, and pulled the cord that drew the curtains shut. He then went over to the wall lamp and turned it up, filling the room with pink-tinged light.

'How are you this evening?' he asked.

She said nothing. All of her emotions and reactions seemed to have been drained from her by the strains and shocks of the previous night. Everything, even looking from one object to another, seemed to require a Sisyphean effort.

'Come and have something for breakfast.'

'Have some*one* for breakfast, you mean,' she corrected him sullenly.

'Don't quibble.'

'I am not hungry.'

'Go on,' he coaxed, 'it'll make you feel better. Something from a glass again.'

'I am not hungry.'

Marie looked up at Augustus. He appeared—well, no, he appeared as unassailably suave as ever to the eye. But something about him *felt* different: anxious, or something.

She turned to face the *Holy Communion of Saint Teresa* on her wall. 'Did you paint that?'

He walked over to it, touching the frame lightly. 'Yes. I spent a whole summer on it, back in 1745—the days get so long, and there is little enough to do. I copied a number of paintings in the eighteenth century; most of the pictures you see about the house are my own work. Quite flawless, if I do say so, though I owe that more to my undead eyes and hands than to my native talent. There is a *Bacchus* in the library—Caravaggio's—and Fuseli's *Lady MacBeth* is in my private study. And of course you have seen Titian's *Venus With a Mirror* in the tower, among others.'

'How did you do it?'

'Paint?'

'Copy a sacred subject,' she asked. 'We are vulnerable to sacred things—aren't we?'

'Yes, *ma fleurette*, but this is only a picture.'

'I don't understand.'

'The sanctity does not come from the subject matter, but from the essential function of the artwork,' Augustus explained. 'In order for this to injure me or you, it would need to have been painted in order to serve as an icon, in a church or a chapel, and blessed accordingly. Without that, there is no sacramental power in the mere painted shapes, and it is simply' (he laid his hand over the saint's face) 'a picture. You'll find in the same way that you can, for instance, quote from the Bible or the texts of the Mass when your intention is purely literary, but that you are quite unable to pray.'

'Why is it that we are vulnerable to these things?'

'My dear, if I knew that I should have blown up Saint George's Cathedral. The traditional explanation is that we have no souls; though personally, I do not feel that I have seen any great evidence of souls in humans, either, so that the explanation does not explain. Be that as it may, a fact is a fact, and for practical purposes that is enough.'

Marie smiled, a little incredulous. 'You are a deathless creature who subsists on the life of others, can read thoughts, and must fear the words and gestures of a priest, and yet you are skeptical about the existence of the soul?'

He smiled back, not nicely, and replied, 'And do *you* feel any differently than you did before?'

Her stomach twisted around itself. She stared back at him, mute. Smug as a cat, Lord Ravenhurst put out his arm for her, and she angrily took it and went down with him to the dining room.

Half a bottle of Austrian later, Augustus began to explain telepathy. Marie, who had drunk as little as she could despite her hunger, sat stone-faced at his right and listened.

'The human mind is a subtle instrument. Ours are subtler still, and are subject to neither death nor sleep; but do not underestimate your prey's mind. It consists in a number of levels—so to call them; in fact the reality is rather more complicated than that, but I am giving you a basic sketch, upon which you may expand later. If it helps you, think of the human mind as being like those tiny boxes from the Orient, one nested inside another, each of which you must open in order to reach the next.

'Of those boxes that we have the power to open, there are four. We refer to the outermost as the mask. This is the consciously projected or social self; when you thank someone insincerely for inviting you to a dull party, for example, it is your mask which is thanking them. As you know from your own experience, the mask is stronger in some people than in others, and most people have multiple masks, shaped by upbringing and selected by circumstance.

'Unfortunately, the mask usually cannot be broken or dominated by force alone. It is possible to bypass the mask only by securing, in some degree, the consent of the person whose mask it is. That consent may be obtained through deceit, intimidation, or persuasion, but without it, penetration into the deeper levels of the personality is impossible. Even achieving dominance over the mind of a sleeping victim demands that you have established access through the mask at some prior point, although, under those circumstances, one can also simply bite them and have done with it. But it is more elegant and amusing to render the victim amenable to your predation.'

'How does one get beyond the mask?' asked Marie, beginning to be interested in spite of herself.

'That is the more pleasing part. It requires only enough manipulation of the interaction, by whatever means, to get the individual in question to express themselves directly instead of through a mask. In other words, they must allow you entry into the next layer, which we typically call the psyche proper.'

A thought occurred to her. 'Is this why we cannot enter houses without an invitation? Are houses connected to the mask of the owner?'

Ravenhurst gave her a faintly admiring look. 'That is the general opinion, yes. In any case. The psyche is a subtler organism: it consists in the conscious intelligence and will—the thoughts and emotions that the human thinks of as its active self. It is this which projects the mask and controls it. This level is invulnerable to direct influence, but can be influenced indirectly, and with considerable power, once you reach into the deeper levels of the personality.

'Beneath the psyche lies the memory. This level is directly accessible to the victim's psyche, but is not immediately under its attention, unless the person chooses to use it. It is the person's sense of self and of recollections—their basis of identity, if you will. At least, that is what they know about it. It sometimes contains things that the person has forgotten or prefers to ignore, but they have not eliminated these things from their awareness. Via the memory, one may indirectly influence the psyche.'

'How?' asked Marie.

'By discerning its contents and then strengthening or weakening them. One finds a given impulse, memory, *et cetera*, that is useful, and then concentrates upon it and thinks along with it; or one finds a disadvantageous thought, and either concentrates upon it and thinks its opposite, or else shifts focus to a different, contrasting impulse and strengthens that. Which method of suppression one uses is partly a matter of individual style, but also depends upon how strong-willed the victim is—the more obstinate or rigidly truthful the human, as a rule, the harder it is to neutralize a thought by mere concentrated mental contradiction, and the more one must try instead to strengthen opposing thoughts of their own.

'Learning to recognize the contents of memory is rather difficult, since they are not arranged systematically, nor expressed in the way in which one would express a sentence. Indeed, they are not, strictly speaking, expressed at all: that is why they reside in the memory and not the upper levels. There is an art to sifting this level and its contents, which can be acquired only by practice, although naturally some vampires show a greater autochthonous talent for it than others do.'

Augustus took a sip of blood and hummed with pleasure, and then went on. 'Beneath all these lies the unconscious layer of the mind. This contains the most repressed, most secret feelings and desires the human experiences, some of which reside only there and are not acknowledged by the upper levels of the mind. It is difficult, delicate work to get past the memory, which is a confusing layer since it is itself confused; but when you succeed in doing so, you will find that the unconscious affords you remarkable avenues for manipulation of the whole person.

'Mind you, you cannot quite master them entirely. As there is often an innermost box that is simply a cube of lacquered wood, with neither hinge nor lid, so the innermost will of the human prey remains impregnable; our power over them can be pushed to within one step of the inexorable, but that final step ever eludes us. That is, you cannot force their consent to anything; it is possible to dominate the body of a victim, for those with adequate mental strength and finesse, acquired through centuries of practice; yet it is always possible, in principle, for them to free themselves. Fortunately, most people are so unthinking that that does not matter.'

Suddenly, Marie demanded, 'And all this is how you murdered me?'

The air turned to ice between them. Augustus' mouth was fixed shut, his eyes unmoving, one brow slightly raised. The seconds lengthened.

'I am sorry,' she said, anxious. 'Please forgive me, Lord Ravenhurst.'

He said nothing in reply, but stood up sharply, knocking his chair aside a few inches. He went out of the dining room. As he passed through the veiled archway into the hall, he reached out without looking and, quick as thought, raked his hand across a painting on the dining room wall, ripping the canvas into four jagged stripes.

Miles away, Lady Livilla was being entertained by a fellow vampire. Her hostess held a champagne flute of blood in her left hand, and a jet-black, lacquered Japanese war fan in her right. Livilla was speaking.

'Fairfax is in disgrace! Why should we have to confer him at this juncture?'

'Are you a complete fool, or do you only pretend to be one?' asked the Lady with the Black Fan in an idle voice. 'His star will not remain at the nadir for long, *figlia*, if it was ever really there. In attacking him, the Duke made a blunder of the first order. Ravenhurst is too popular for a direct assault to work: if he had not been so angry, von Orlok would have done the clever thing and given him some impossible responsibility a few months from now, so that his blood would be on his own head when he failed. As things stand, His Grace's vindictive tantrum has only increased sympathy for Ravenhurst and hostility to the establishment. And anyway, that is no way to talk about your brother, my *dear*.'

'But surely von Orlok can rely upon the support of the cult …' said Livilla.

The other vampire laughed. She had a soft, melodious voice, but its laughter was somehow unsettling, as if it echoed more than it ought to. 'The Reverend Doctor has no more to gain from their alliance. The Chartists have been courting him, and they will succeed.'

'Disgusting creatures.'

'Admittedly; but it makes my plan far less work. Dispensing with von Orlok, backed by the full power and terror of *his holiness*, would have been tedious and difficult, even with you playing the distracting temptress. Without Tinsmith, the Duke will be both amusing and simple to eliminate.' The Lady with the Black Fan sipped her blood. 'And then, with me and Ravenhurst to back you up, you become the Duchess of London.'

Livilla frowned. 'What has all this got to do with the Redglass girl?'

'*Porco Iddio!* were you quite awake when you met her? I concede that she is as yet untrained, but I have not sensed that much raw power in a dragonet since Eyre disappeared. Give her a few months under Augustus Fairfax's tutelage, and she will be able to hold her own even against von Orlok. I want her on our side— or, at the very least, out of the way.'

The marchioness raised her eyebrows. 'You mean the Second Death?'

'Goodness, no. That kind of vigor is too delicious to destroy. She'll be as useful as Chastelard in the long run—he always *does* choose well. Neutrality, or some tantrum that causes her to run off for a while.'

'And you don't believe that Lord Ravenhurst would follow her.'

'No.'

Livilla drained her glass. The Black Fan frowned dispassionately at the figure prostrate between them on the floor, gasping and shuddering. It was a young manservant, dressed in sable livery with embroidery of human face and a skull side by side on the pectoral. Obscene gashes latticed his wrists and throat.

'It is rather a pity that he should have been the one to answer the bell,' she said. 'He had a genuine talent on the harpsichord. I shall miss that.'

'Why not change him, *Madre?*' asked Livilla. 'He must surely have lost enough by now.'

'No. Slaves who are suddenly clothed in immortality tend to wax insolent thereafter. Far better simply to exsanguinate him.' She leaned forward and used the razor-sharpened edge of her fan to open another wound below the servant's jaw, drawing a faint, choking gurgle from him. 'Besides, it will give me a little time to have the harpsichord tuned before it is played again—the strings on the two-foot choir have all gone flat. I simply *know* that if I kept him, alive or undead, I should be hearing an insufferably discordant rendition of the German Suites in a matter of minutes.'

Marie did not see Augustus again for the rest of the night. She went to the library, trying once again to revive her enthusiasm for novels and poetry. Around four in the morning, Godalming appeared, bearing a miniature bottle of Provençal that he said her sire had instructed be served her for dinner, mentioning that it happened to be some of the finest stuff in the manor. The grandfather clock tick-tocked a few rooms away as she finished it off in the empty dining room.

After that, she returned to her own room, carrying with her a copy of *The Duchess of Malfi*. She leafed through it listlessly until sunup, at which point she surrendered her pretended interest. She wandered vaguely about the room, stopping at times before the enchanting painting till she had memorized every brushstroke, or listlessly examining the dresses in the wardrobe, silk and taffeta and crushed velvet. The hours passed.

CHAPTER VI

THE WHITE DEVIL

But now, in this valley of Humiliacion, poore Christian was hard put to it; for he had gone but a little way before he espied a foul fiend coming ouer the field to meete him: his name is Apollyon … By this I perceiue thou art one of my subiects; for all that country is mine, and I am the prince and god of it.

—JOHN BUNYAN, *THE PILGRIM'S PROGRESS*

When evening finally came, Marie went back downstairs, pausing at the landing to gaze for a few minutes at the *Apollo and Daphne*. The shape of Apollo's face in Bernini's masterful sculpture reminded her of her sixteen-year-old brother, Henry. She wondered whether this sculpture too were Augustus' own work. It occurred to her that, given vampires' acute senses and exquisite control of their bodies, it was probably easy to sculpt even something of this magnitude and detail. After a little time, she resumed her walk downstairs—the house was very silent, save for the incessant ticking of the clock—and went into the library, where she found Hyacinth dusting.

'Good evening, Hyacinth.'

The maid screamed and dropped the feather duster, laying a hand on her heaving breast as she gasped for air. 'I'm frightfully sorry, me lady, I didn't know as anybody was abaout.'

'Not at all—I didn't mean to startle you,' said Marie, half amused and half bewildered. 'Isn't Lord Ravenhurst in?'

'No, me lady. He's gone off to see the Earl o' Richmond, I believe.'

'I see.' She went over to the bookshelf that carried most of Augustus' collection of modern poets—mostly Romantics, Pre-Raphaëlites, and Decadents—and began searching for something to read. Hyacinth picked up the duster and fidgeted a little.

'Was you wanting anyfing, me lady?' she asked.

Of course; Marie had forgotten: being fed upon by her master must have her and all the servants charged with more or less perpetual fear. Aside from the butler, who had some eerie calm out of his own resources. For a moment, Marie felt sorry for the poor, confused girl before her, and wondered what had led her to take, and keep, employment from a vampire.

'No, thank you, Hyacinth.'

'Very good, me lady. I'll give you your privacy, then.' She scuttled out, her task of dusting less than half completed. Marie shook her head, and glanced over the books before her, eventually selecting a volume of Baudelaire, to keep her French practiced. She supposed that the antiquity of the vampire population probably had something to do with how much French they used.

Almost immediately, there was a knock at the door, followed by voices in the hall. One, she could distinguish as Godalming's; the other was unknown to her, but made her skin crawl. She rose and went to the door of the library, at almost the same moment that the butler came to it.

'The Reverend Doctor Lazarus Tinsmith to see you, ma'm'selle,' he said. 'Are you at home to visitors this evening?'

'I suppose,' she replied, a little nonplussed. She remembered from Augustus' lectures that he was the head of what he called the vampires' cult: some sort of heretical Christian sect, or so she gathered. What could he want with her? 'Show him in.'

'I apologize for troubling you, but I shall need your assistance. I do not have the authority to invite him over the threshold.'

She considered this. 'Do you think Lord Ravenhurst would mind?'

'I cannot say, ma'm'selle. He and Reverend Tinsmith are not on intimate terms by any means, but his lordship instructed me particularly that you had the privilege of inviting guests into the house. In any case, he has come to see you personally.'

'I see. All right, I will invite him in.'

'Very good, ma'm'selle.'

They went to the foyer as the clock struck a quarter to eight. Reverend Tinsmith stood on the step, the night behind him dark as a cellar. Icy air flowed into Ravenhurst around his form. Tall, slender, and long-faced, he was unusually white of skin, even for a vampire, with a slightly Nordic physiognomy. He had spidery, tapering fingers that hung straight down at his sides, and was dressed in a black cassock, with a Roman collar—though it was in red rather than white, like Canon Glover whom Augustus had pointed out to her at the Manticore Palace; perhaps it was a sort of uniform. But it was his eyes that really arrested Marie's attention. The shadow from the doorway, combined with her own and that of Godalming, cast irregular patches of darkness upon the vampire's face; but his eyes caught the light like a cat's. A chilly shade of blue, they appeared capable of meeting any gaze, even the Duke's, without the smallest alteration or lapse of certitude. Yet they were not in the least passionate. They were the eyes of a corpse: not merely in the sense that the Reverend was, after all, undead, but in the sense that the affects and impulses that governed the life-in-death of most vampires—the jaded superiority of Lord Fairfax, the debauchery of Monsieur Chastelard, the cattiness of Lady Bath, the dominating sadism of Duke von Orlok—were all absent from this thing. She had a sickening sense, as she looked into his eyes, of staring into a bottomless pit.

Aloud, Marie told him, 'Please, come in.'

'I thank thee,' replied Doctor Tinsmith, stepping inside. He enunciated strangely, with the vowels of a bygone century, and a precision so absolute as to suggest that he was separately conscious of every letter and determined to wring the correct sound from each. He was not impossible to understand, but his words demanded a fixed attention. 'Thou art Lord Ravenhurst's daughter, Miss Redglass.'

'No,' she replied, keeping her temper with difficulty—'the late Baron Redglass was my father, and—'

'Thou mistakest me. I mean it was he which gave thee death, and not life.'

'Oh. Yes.'

'I have been wishing to visit thee.'

Marie shifted uncomfortably. 'Would you care to breakfast, Reverend?'

'I have broken fast. If thou wouldst, we shall retire into the dining room that thou mayst also, and I shall instruct thee there.'

'Instruct me?' she asked.

'Yea,' he said simply.

Unsure what to say in answer, she turned to Godalming and asked him to conduct them both to the dining room. He inquired whether he ought to bring her refreshment, and she grudgingly assented.

Doctor Tinsmith spoke in a low, continuous voice, pontificating on the theological role of vampires in human society. Or rather, not in society, for that was simply another name for the World, one of the seductions that persecuted the elect in life and in death. It was nothing more than an attempt to evade the utter sovereignty of God, which sovereignty willed vampires also as a part of the whole.

'I was taught my catechism,' she said, restraining the vexation from her voice as she privately added, *And was already discussing the finer points of Bossuet and Saint Alphonsus Liguori when I was fifteen.* 'I am a Catholic.'

The minister pulled his lips into a thin line. 'Thine erstwhile connection to the Great Harlot is of no moment. Having become a vampire, thy mortal ties are cancelled. Forget the lies and priestcraft of thy youth. As it is written, *Hearken, O daughter, and consider, and incline thine ear; forget also thine own people, and thy father's house.* Thy catechesis in the truth hath been reserved unto this night; it is written also, *This day this Scripture is fulfilled in your hearing.*'

Marie bristled. 'And what are you—sir?'

'I am a member of the true Church.'

'A dissenter, you mean?' she asked rudely.

'We have been called by many names—Dissenters, Precisians, Calvinists, Puritans. All this is whitewash, to obscure our fidelity unto the gospel.'

'I don't care. I am a Catholic.'

'Oh?' he said. 'And when shalt thou next hear Mass?'

Marie bit her lip and lowered her eyes to the table. A few moments later, she took a sip from her glass of blood.

Tinsmith resumed his homily. 'The Lord hath willed vampires, even unto His everlasting glory. Likewise willeth He pestilences, famines, wars, and all manner of death, for the mortification of our pride and the manifest punishment of our depravities after their kinds. And we ourselves are abominations: as it is written in the law, *Whatsoever man there be of the house of Israel, or of the strangers that sojourn among you, that eateth any manner of blood; I will even set My face against that soul that eateth blood.* Yet as the Lord by Sennacherib judged Hamath, and Arpad, and many other of the Gentiles, before He did judge

Sennacherib also; even so our judgment is reserved unto the Last Day, that by us He may judge many.'

She set down her glass and faced him, getting more exasperated by the minute. 'And how could we possibly know that the judgment of God has fallen on anyone?'

'That the Lord suffereth us to lay violent hands upon any man is adequate proof that he be under the Divine wrath,' Doctor Tinsmith replied. 'Otherwise He would assuredly preserve him. Such is the ineluctable fixity of the Divine purpose,' he continued, more to himself than to Marie, 'the several events in the lives of men and of vampires and of angels, and every manner of thing, being caused solely by His predilection: which cannot be said to be just, since to say thus would be to assert that there is any other thing by which God's acts may be measured. That cannot be. Say rather, justice is that only thing that conformeth unto His sovereign design.'

A step sounded outside the door, and Augustus appeared. His eyes settled on the figure of the clergyman with controlled distaste.

'Lord Ravenhurst, good evening,' said Marie quickly, with exaggerated brightness. She hoped at some point to redeem her *faux pas* of the previous night. But he did not seem to be listening.

'Reverend Doctor, what are you doing here? I was under the impression that you had despaired of me.'

'Scoff as ye will, my lord,' replied Doctor Tinsmith coldly, 'yet see I no cause that this maiden should be deprived of instruction.'

'So you came to bestow it without the approval or knowledge of her sire. I see. Have you any other business here?'

'I have. The Lord Chief Justice sendeth his compliments, and inviteth you both to a banquet at his own house, to be held on the thirteenth of December.'

'How kind. No.'

'He was most insistent,' urged the other.

'I am sure he was,' Augustus said in a honeyed voice. 'But if Carroll wants my company that badly, he can invite me in person, and not send along one of his catamites.'

'Ye confuse me with Chastelard.'

'Oh, goodness no. Chastelard is *welcome* company.'

Doctor Tinsmith stood. 'So be it. I shall convey your regrets to the Lord Chief Justice.'

'Shall you.'

The clergyman inclined his head to Augustus and Marie in turn, and then departed. Augustus sat down heavily at the head of the table.

'Be glad you weren't here for the catechism,' said Marie, sitting also. 'He is terribly …'

'Quite,' said her sire. 'I do understand your letting *it* inside the house, *ma chérie*; but next time, don't.'

'Oh. I thought you said he merely bored you.'

'I loathe people who bore me.'

'Oh.'

'Don't go on saying *Oh* like a guppy,' he told her irritably. 'Have you had any breakfast?'

'Yes.'

'Oh. Well, I haven't.' He summoned Godalming and requested a large glass of blood.

Marie pressed her hands together under the table, wondering how to apologize. 'My lord, I—'

But he waved his hand dismissively. 'Do not,' the other vampire said, 'even think of it.'

'How did you know what I was going to say?'

'Think about that question for a moment, please. If you would like to go to the library and wait there, I will resume your instruction after my breakfast.'

William emerged from the confessional, his head bowed, and went to do his penance. The November air had seeped in through the stone walls of St John's, so that it would have been more comfortable to say his prayers at home; but he felt that a little cold was a less stern a discipline than he deserved. He genuflected and crossed himself, and positioned himself on a kneeler in a pew near the front of the nave, where he could see the Tabernacle through the gaps in the rood screen, recumbent beneath the sanctuary lamp. The line of saints ranged upon the rood screen, each beneath their own window into the holy of holies, gazed with grave blessing over him: St George, bearing his white standard with its scarlet cross flying on his lance; the Magdalene, with curls of golden hair cascading over her bosom and shoulders, her alabaster jar in her hand; St Edward the Confessor, proffering his sword and crown to God; St Helena, mother of Constantine, with the True Cross in her hands; and amidmost, on either side of the central door, the Mother of God and St John the Divine. William removed a rosary from an inner pocket of his great-coat. Immemorial prayers flowed over his lips: '… to judge the quick and the dead. I believe in the Holy Ghost, the holy Catholic Church, the communion of saints, the forgiveness of sins, the resurrection of …'

As he prayed, the Redglass brothers entered the church. James motioned to the confessional, but Henry shook his head, seating himself in a pew about two-thirds back from the rood-screen and examining his fingers. James, looking nonplussed, went forward to avail himself of the sacrament.

William did not notice them. They did not notice him. All three were thinking of the same person: James, with a continual and often failing effort to govern the general ill-temper that, he knew, came from his despair of seeing his sister again; Henry, with a conscious confidence in her eventual return that, combined with a latent uncertainty about it, fed an ill-temper directed very specifically toward his brother; William, with a terribly divided heart, rejoicing that she was not (exactly) dead, aghast that she lived as she did, ashamed that she knew him now as he was, at a loss regarding what he might do to redeem himself to her. Their trinity of sorrows coinhered, without their will and without their knowledge.

James knelt inside the confessional; the dimly-lit face of Fr Weld showed through the grille. 'Bless me, Father, for I have sinned. It has been one week since my last Confession. I accuse myself of the following sins …'

Marie sat in the library, reading aloud to herself, relishing the precision of sound that she was now able to effect.

'In Xanadu did Kubla Khan
A stately pleasure-dome decree,
Where Alph, the sacred river, ran
Through caverns measureless to man
Down to a sunless sea.
So twice five miles of fertile ground
With walls and towers were girdled round;
And there were gardens bright with sinuous rills,
Where blossomed many an incense-bearing tree …'

'Do you know,' came Augustus' voice, 'I had actually forgotten I owned any Coleridge. I have hardly indulged myself in any of the Romantics of late, except for Keats and Byron.'

She turned in her chair to see him in the doorway looking at her, his nearly-emptied glass of blood in one hand. 'What have you been reading?'

'Oh, the Decadents and Symbolists, mostly—Baudelaire, Rimbaud, Mallarmé, Flaubert. Two years ago, when Verlaine and Rimbaud were in London together, I had the pleasure of having them here as guests—among other things,' he added with a wicked smile. Marie pursed her lips, but said nothing. 'And I dip into the Pre-Raphaëlites from time to time. Dreadfully underappreciated poets. Swinburne's *Laus Veneris* is truly hypnotic, to say nothing of *Dolores*.'

Augustus crossed the room and set his glass on the table by the vacant armchair. Then he clapped his hands and sat, saying, 'Speaking of hypnotism. Let us proceed with your instruction.' She laid the Coleridge on the table and composed herself to listen.

'You will recall the layers or spheres of the mind of which I spoke last time: mask—psyche—memory—unconscious. The innermost, as we discussed, is the will proper, which so far as we know is inaccessible; one cannot *quite* force a human to do something, though most of them are so subject to their passions (including the ones that think themselves strong-willed) that it makes short odds.

'Now, operating at these varying levels, there are a number of basic urges that underlie the motive forces of the human soul. Existence itself, liberty, pleasure, knowledge, and love: these are the things that all humans desire, and their deepest fears are of those things which negate or jeopardize them. Hence the fear of death, the fear of being trapped, the fear of boredom and pain, the fear of the dark, and the fear of loneliness.

'The first step in the practice of telepathy is simply to learn to recognize these things in a human mind. Not surface thoughts, you understand,' he said, rising and crossing to the black cord that rang the servants' bell, 'which are extremely easy to perceive. I am speaking of sifting through these and finding the shapes these fundamental desires and fears take, and the mode in which they animate these surface thoughts. When Godalming comes in, I want you to read his mind, and to identify at least two strands of desire or fear—so, for instance, to identify at least one thought expressing the fear of being trapped and at least one thought expressing the desire for knowledge. Or, what you will.'

'But—I—*how?*'

'Just concentrate and try. I assure you, foreign though it seems in the abstract, it comes very naturally.'

Just as he finished speaking, Godalming entered the library. 'Yes, my lord?'

'I have lost some of my correspondence with Lady Carmilla,' Augustus began, 'and it contained important information about the dispositions of six of …'

Marie concentrated on Godalming. Her sire cast her an occasional glance as he went on speaking about the letters, with ma'm'selle to one side. Godalming replied periodically, though for some reason he wasn't really speaking, only making a vague buzzing noise. Ma'm'selle seemed to be adapting to Ravenhurst Manor rather well, though admittedly her temperament was somewhat mercurial. The Norman and Flemish bloods of which his lordship is so fond are running rather low, although there is still that bottle of Slovak from the trip to the Continent in 1848 to which he was so partial it would serve as a good *aperitif* for this midnight's meal Godalming had forgotten to tell Hyacinth to sweep up the earth on the floor of the cellar and put it back in the *HOW DARE HE.*

Marie's concentration broke, and Godalming clapped a hand to his temple and gave a little gasp of pain. Her skull throbbed heavily for a moment, and she grimaced. Augustus rolled his eyes with annoyance, and picked up his glass and held it in front of himself. In an instant, in threes and fours, all of the books in the large case immediately behind him began shooting out of their shelves, striking Marie and Godalming like missiles. The gas lamps guttered. There was a faint, angry chittering in her head, which seemed to possess some pattern, but she could distinguish no words, and in any case she was trying to shield herself from the storm of books.

Lord Ravenhurst closed his eyes and raised his unoccupied hand in a gesture of command, and in a moment the books all fell to the floor, inert; the raging noise also ceased. 'Are you all right, child?' he asked; then, to Godalming, 'You may go. But get Hyacinth to come and pick up these books.' The butler bowed and exited, with a small gash on his forehead from the corner of one book and a button gone from his waistcoat due to the sideswipe of another.

'Yes, I am all right,' she answered in a small voice. 'Was that I? Did I lose control?'

'Oh, goodness no. Vampires do not possess psychokinetic powers to lose control of. I might have told you before, there is a poltergeist in the manor.'

'A poltergeist?' repeated Marie.

'Yes. It has been dormant for twenty years or so; I had begun to suppose it had reconciled itself to its death or joined the House of Commons or something. That psychic scream you heard was its voice; the nonsense noises belonged to it as well. The psychic structure of a poltergeist, such as it is, has little integrity to begin with, and they tend to break down over time.'

Marie shivered. The notion of something starting out as a raving specter, and then somehow decaying from *there*, was ghastly to entertain. 'What reawakened it, do you think?'

'Do you suppose I know everything?' he scoffed. 'I have better things to do than to keep track of the ravings of a dead madwoman.' A book wobbled at this remark, but Augustus raised his hand again and it was stilled.

'Wait a moment,' said Marie. 'A poltergeist, you said. Yet you told me that your Spiritualism was a *façade*.'

'So it is.'

'But—well, ghosts are real then, aren't they? Does that not prove the existence of the soul?'

'Poltergeists are not ghosts; at least, not necessarily. I suppose ghosts—that is, departed souls—may also exist, but I have no idea about that. The question doesn't interest me.'

She sputtered. 'But—but how can you not know? or at least care? There's a spirit living in your house! You are dead yourself!'

'And death has clearly given you great insight into the subject,' he answered nastily. 'In any event, *ma fleurette*, you are a vampire; what do you propose to find incredible?'

'You are impossible!' she shouted, making a black storm of her skirts as she abandoned the room. She knocked Hyacinth against the wall as she left, but did not look back, running up the stairs and bolting herself inside her room.

Hours later, she was still within. She was seated in front of the vanity, gazing into the mirror at her own empty dress. Though sickening, something about the sight fascinated her in its eeriness. Her gown was beautifully constructed: its black bodice and skirts being relieved by violet piping at the cuffs and the throat-high tatted collar, and intricate Celtic-knot embroidery over the bodice, with a rosette of baroque Tahitian pearls sewn into it over the point where the throat met the collarbone. She had not forgotten her fury with Augustus—that business about the poltergeist had seemed momentarily to tantalize her with the possibility of speaking to her mother again after all, and, as quickly, snatched it away once more—but her anger would not stay in focus; it distended its energies and dissolved when she tried to think of it. But the loveliness of her gown, which had not much held her attention before, was completely arresting. She found herself counting the number of stitches in the embroidery on the bodice and the number of holes in the tatted lace, and, when she had done that, peering more closely—it was not too difficult with her improved eyes—and counting the individual threads in each strand of the bombazine silk. *Six hundred and eighty-eight, six hundred and eighty-nine, six hundred and ninety, six hundred and ninety-one ...*

A timid knock interrupted her, and she lost count. She closed her eyes, barely suppressing a howl of rage; a moment later, the rage actually did dissipate, in her uncomfortable surprise that the disruption of such an unimportant occupation should have the power to make her so furious. But then the knock was repeated, and she asked who was there.

'Hyacinth, me lady. Only me lord said you migh' want a glass of blood, me lady, i' being the usual time.'

The idea of spiting him by refusing the blood passed momentarily through her mind, and was gone. Thirst overwhelmed her. She rose, crossed the room, opened the door sharply to see the diffident maid holding a tray with a Bordeaux glass full of scarlet liquid, snatched it from the tray, downed it in a single draught, and put it smartly back down.

'Thank you, Hyacinth,' said Marie colorlessly, as the room began to swim around her. 'That will do.' She shut the door again and managed to reach the bed before her senses became too inflamed for her to walk.

'Two letters for you, my lord,' said Godalming, lowering the service within arm's reach.

He picked them up. One of them said *Lady Livilla Thackeray* on the return, and Augustus tutted and tossed it, unopened, back onto the silvern tray. 'You can burn that,' he said.

'Yes, my lord. And the other?'

There was no return address on this one. He slid his finger under the flap and flicked it open, but then stopped, looking back at the seal. That it was in black wax was not unusual—using mourning wax instead of the proper crimson stuff was a traditional jest among vampires. But the imprint on the seal itself was not a common one. Augustus had seen it before, though not in many decades: it was a minutely articulated picture of a fan, with a picture of a blooming foxglove emblazoned on it. He smiled mirthlessly.

'Leave me, Godalming.'

The butler departed. The lord of Ravenhurst Manor took out the letter and started to read.

Miles away, the Reverend Doctor Lazarus Tinsmith knocked on the door of a finely kept townhouse on Cavendish Square. A servant came and opened it. The clergyman announced his name.

'Have you an invitation from the Lord Chief Justice, Reverend Doctor?' asked the servant.

'I have a standing invitation from Lord Carroll,' replied the vampire coolly. 'Now, if thou mind not.'

'Of course.' The servant stepped back, holding the door open and then shutting it behind Tinsmith, and taking his cloak and hat. They passed into the house, and another servant, carrying a tray with three champagne flutes and a bottle on it, collided with the vampire and stumbled to the ground. The glasses and bottle together fell, with a sound like a breaking piano, and blood seeped out over the floor.

'Titus, you fool!' snapped the first servant. 'My profuse apologies, Reverend.'

The man called Titus had managed to get onto his hands and knees in time to look up and see Tinsmith reach out with both hands, take the other servant firmly by the head, and move it suddenly at a strange angle. There was an ugly snapping noise; the servant's dead body fell into the blood and broken glass, spattering Titus' already dirtied face.

'What was that for?' came a different voice in mild tones. The terrorized servant looked over to see a lithe, golden-haired vampire dressed in flamboyant black and green silks.

'*Whosoever shall say, Thou fool, shall be in danger of hell fire*, Mister Chastelard,' quoted Reverend Tinsmith placidly.

'*Bien sûr*,' the other vampire answered with mock solemnity. 'Well, since you've killed him, you might as well eat him.'

'I do not pollute my blood with that of blasphemers.'

'*Zut alors*, I do. They have a sort of pungency to them.' Chastelard went up to the corpse and took it by the wrist, tugging it away from the foyer. '*Êtes-vous bien, garçon?*' he said to the remaining young man, not unkindly.

Titus spoke in strangled tones. 'Are you going to kill me?'

'Don't be silly, you look quite anæmic and would probably taste foul. And our friend the priest' (here Tinsmith protested angrily that he was not a thrall of the Romish Antichrist, but Chastelard talked over him) 'probably won't kill any more of his host's servants for the time being; admittedly he sets little store by tactfulness, but everyone has limits.' He sank his fangs into the warm corpse and began to suck; then, detaching for a moment, blood rimming his mouth, he said, 'By the way, *garçon*, since Frederick here has just been killed, you will have to announce the Reverend Doctor's arrival to Lord Richmond. So go on.'

He did not need telling twice. As he ran from the room, Titus could hear the obscene slurping noise getting louder.

CHAPTER VII

THE SICILIAN DRAGON

By day she wooes me, soft, exceeding fair:
  But all night as the moon so changeth she;
  Loathsome and foul with hideous leprosy
And subtle serpents gliding in her hair.
By day she wooes me to the outer air,
  Ripe fruits, sweet flowers, and full satiety;
  But through the night, a beast she grins at me,
A very monster void of love and prayer.

— CHRISTINA ROSSETTI, *THE WORLD*

Hours later, another knock disturbed Marie's solitude. The stream of interruptions was driving her frantic. 'What?' she called angrily through the door.

'Begging your pardon, ma'm'selle,' said Godalming's voice, 'but dinner is served, and Lord Ravenhurst –'

'Ravenhurst can hang for all I care,' she snarled. 'I am not thirsty.'

'He was most solicitous that you join him for dinner,' finished the butler patiently. 'He received a letter tonight that I believe he wishes to discuss with you.'

'What? From whom?' She wondered silently whether James and Henry might be on her trail: after all, even if they were on the opposite side of London, she was still here in the city; was it impossible to suppose that she had been seen and recognized? Then, more disquietingly, she wondered whether it was better for her brothers to find her or to be unable to. But Godalming was answering, and she suddenly realized she had not been attending.

'… lordship asked for his privacy. He said only, afterward, that I was to inform you of dinner and press upon you his desire that you should come down and speak with him.'

'I see. Yes—yes, very well, I'll come. Please inform Lord Ravenhurst I shall be down in a few minutes.'

'Certainly, ma'm'selle.'

He left, and Marie sat down to sort out her thoughts and straighten her clothes a little. Then she went downstairs and found Augustus in the pavilioned dining room. He was seated, a glass of blood in one hand and a page of a letter in the other; a slender bottle stood near the center of the table; another few pages lay before him, with the black border that signified mourning. She wondered whom he could possibly know who had a deceased relative nowadays (although the flippant reply entered her mind that surely everyone Augustus knew had an awful lot of dead relatives by now), and tried to espy the initials of the monogram at the top; but he suddenly set his glass down on top of the upper part of the letter, obscuring them, and spoke to her.

'Ah, Mademoiselle Redglass, thank you for consenting to join me.' He stood and pulled out a chair for her, and picked up another glass from the sideboard to set before her. The curiosity of Augustus Fairfax himself performing such menial tasks prompted her to look around the room; she noticed that the door had been shut behind her, with all the servants on the other side of it. 'Have some of this chap, he's quite delicious and I have not taken much yet. Yorkshire peasant stock, a refreshingly hearty flavor, perfectly tempered with a slight bitterness. Due to being still angry over the Pilgrimage of Grace, perhaps.'

He chuckled at the ugly look Marie cast him. 'By the way, I'm thinking of expanding the library. Is there anything particular that you want?'

She filled her glass. 'Godalming said you had a letter you wanted to discuss with me.'

'I have, but that can wait. The books, *ma chérie?*'

She thought. 'I don't know. I have not yet spent much time browsing in it; I have only looked at a few dozen volumes with much attention.'

'Well, what about Tennyson's latest—what is it called—*Gareth and Lynette*? I haven't yet read that one myself, which is why I was thinking of it, and I seem to recall your saying that you have a taste for Tennyson.'

'Oh, yes, the *Gareth* is more than lovely. I cannot recollect whether he drew more on the Italians or Malory for that one. I understand Matthew Arnold did not think much of it.'

'The man's a snob and a bore.'

'Very much so,' she agreed, taking a swallow from her glass. 'I suppose he thought its subject matter insufficiently serious ...'

The conversation continued along literary lines for a little time. The bottle of Yorkshireman grew lighter. The clock struck six.

'Ah,' Lord Ravenhurst said. 'The sun will be rising before long, and I have diverted myself with our pleasing chatter. Now, this letter. It seems that Lady Bath would like to express her condolences for your poor reception at the Duke's claws, and to give a *soirée* in your honor at her town-house in Mayfair. What do you think?'

'It does seem kind of her.'

Augustus smiled his most satirical smile and replied, 'No, this is not kindness. Nor an invitation. It is orders. As I have told you, Livilla is firmly in the favor of the Duke; yet she wants me on her side too. This *soirée* is meant to afford an opportunity to align myself with her, while also having it seen that it is I who come to *her*; given her standing with His Grace, she thinks, she will be able to ruin me if I oppose her. But she would sooner canvas my support. It makes her more secure.'

Marie was puzzled. 'What do you mean by her *side*? Secure from what?'

'Oh, postal mix-ups, backgammon matches, you know the sort of thing.'

'How could you discern all of that from the letter? I mean, it isn't what she said.'

'Of course not. Even Livilla has better taste than that. But you see, if she had really wished to console my feelings or yours, she would not have mentioned our bitter business with His Grace in so many words. She did; therefore she wishes us both to have it in mind, and therefore frightened, while at the same time impressed with her generosity—not to mention her confidence, in openly associating with us before this has quite blown over. Putting the, ahem, *invitation* into the same context makes it plain: the solution is to be in her own hands.' He took a sip of blood. 'You see how the game is played? Say, White: queen's knight threatens king's pawn; Black: king's pawn to K4; White: king's bishop to Q6; and Black to move. That, *mon petit chou*, is us.'

She nodded vaguely. She had never wholly mastered chess, even under her father's excellent tutelage, and could not easily picture the board he had described.

'As to sides ... ' Augustus made an indescribable face. *'Ce que l'enfant out au foyer, est bientôt connu jusqu'au Moustier.'*

'But there is nobody here except ourselves.'

'Don't be ingenuous, mademoiselle. Not all servants are above listening at doors. And not all servants are always, how shall I put it, quite themselves.'

'What on earth does that mean?'

'You will learn with time,' he told her. 'Now then, this *soirée* ... I believe the course indicated is graciously to accept our orders and attend. It is to be, let me see—the twenty-ninth of November. The wardrobe in your room is fully stocked, by the way: practically every color and style. If you want something but do not see it, inform Godalming, and he will see that it is obtained for you as quickly as possible. Hyacinth will attend to your hair, naturally.'

'I don't like Hyacinth.'

'Oh? Why is that?'

'She is completely foolish. She constantly forgets things, misunderstands me, drops things.'

'Well, that is partly my fault.'

'How so?'

Augustus finished his blood and poured himself another half-glass. 'She tried to run away, a few weeks before I sired you. I was obliged to employ my mental powers to force her to stay. I suppose the shock the nature of her employment caught her up at last.'

'You didn't dig out the motive telepathically?'

'Why bother? In any case, the experience seems to have addled her slightly. Or at least disordered her nerves. Probably there is no permanent damage, and if there is, there are always more maids to be had.'

Marie frowned. 'Why not—let her go? You've spoken of doing so with servants who give notice; why would running off be any different? After all, it hardly seems likely that anyone would believe her. And if she did say anything about it, she would probably simply be shut up as a deranged hysteric.' Although she had meant to hint at releasing Hyacinth as an act of private mercy, nonetheless, listening to herself talk, Marie was unsettled by an unwontedly chilly, practical note in her voice.

'Servants who give notice can hardly be stopped except by complete mental domination, which I don't care to waste my energy on; or else by killing them, which risks drawing attention, to say nothing of the mess. Besides, if they are coherent enough to give notice, they generally have more sense than to talk. But if a servant runs off, in most cases he or she is scared witless, and apt to babble anything to anyone (which mental disarray is also why a comparatively simple, if forceful, exercise of telepathy will do to stop it). Most people would respond to tales of vampires by placing her in a lunatic asylum, yes. But there is always the chance, however remote, that her tale could come to the ears of a vampire hunter.'

She gripped the table. 'Vampire hunter? They exist?'

'We exist,' replied Augustus drily; 'why wouldn't they? They *are* rare, and have grown rarer. Commoner in eastern Europe, among the Catholic and especially the Orthodox peasantry; you know the sort of thing: country priests, cunning folk, wandering exorcists, witch-finders, sin-eaters. Modern England has not seen a vampire hunter since the expulsion of the Stuarts. But there is always the chance. We know better than anybody that old things return. Hunters can be dealt with, but it is tedious and, on occasion, dangerous to do so. Better simply to avoid the whole business.'

'I see.'

'Don't be frightened,' he said, with a grin that exposed his fangs to the candlelight. 'As I said, they are rare, and often they are afflicted by zeal without knowledge. I met one in Paris in 1790 who attempted to destroy me with a large onion and a pewter fish knife.'

Marie laughed. 'Are you serious?'

'Perfectly,' he answered, chuckling with her. 'Though, in justice to him, he is wiser now.'

'He would have to be. What happened to him?'

'I sired him. He is Paul Chastelard.'

'Really? I had not taken him for a superstitious sort.'

'Oh, he was frightfully religious once upon a time,' Augustus replied. 'Lived in perpetual terror of the Four Last Things. But with death out of the way, and judgment rendered moot, he was liberated from hell and heaven. He would never have adopted Tinsmith's type of religious mania. Whether Tinsmith regards himself as an apostle of heaven or of hell, I never could answer for ... But unlike the sentimental English, whose religion is like their childhood nurse—thought of with fondness, but never attended to for any reason—Frenchmen come in two kinds: the devoutly religious, and the devoutly irreligious. Chastelard, on being clothed with immortality, converted.

'Well, I dare say you are beginning to sense the approach of sunrise, *ma chérie*. Don't let me keep you from your sedate seclusion; I shall be retiring to my own before long.'

Marie rose, and a thought crossed her mind. 'Where is it that you spend your days, Lord Ravenhurst?'

'There is a master bedroom.'

She stood there for a long moment, waiting for him to elaborate; he sat quite still, smiling his leonine smile and saying nothing. Then she bade him good day and went upstairs.

When she had gone, he got up and rang the bell. The butler entered.

'My lord?'

'I want to write a letter. Bring me the necessities, quickly, please.'

'Will your lordship be writing in the study?'

'No, bring them here.'

'Yes, my lord.'

The butler returned with the appropriate supplies and left again. Augustus spent several minutes in the composition of the letter. He read through it, frowned, tore it up, wrote another draft, read that, and smiled dispassionately and placed it inside the envelope. Taking the stick of black wax, he melted the end in one of the candles, and dripped a vaguely circular patch onto the back joint of the envelope. Then he picked up one of the linen napkins from the table and used it to pick up the signet ring, so as not to burn his fingers by touching the gold of which it was made. He impressed the wax firmly and set the ring aside. The seal glistened: a lion rampant regardant. Picking up the pen again, he wrote an address on the front of the envelope; the address was not that of the Marchioness of Bath and Wells.

At the same time that Augustus and Marie were having their last meal of the night, miles to the south in an opulent town-house in Belgravia, Tinsmith was conversing with Chastelard and Lord Richmond over the dregs of a prostitute from Whitechapel. The splendor of the town-house in which the cabal met was of a more restrained, Neoclassical style than that of Ravenhurst Manor—partly due to the intrinsic inhibitions of a town-house as opposed to a suburban estate, but also to a divergent taste. The floors and walls in the expansive dining room were ebony, and the columns were of veined black marble, with acanthus-adorned capitals picked out in silver. The undead men were arguing.

'I do not approve,' said Doctor Tinsmith.

'On moral grounds?' asked Richmond, with an ironical inflection.

'Yea. Your lax mores –'

Chastelard's eyebrows flew upward. '*Your?* The courteous plural?' he demanded sarcastically. '*Saintes putaines*, Reverend Doctor, you are being a positive *thuriféraire*.'

Tinsmith's mouth tightened. 'Accuse me of flattery or what else *thou* wishest, Mister Chastelard. But as I was saying, Lord Chief Justice, your lax mores scandalize the entire movement—my side, even as yours. I ask of you that ye take thought, and somewhat restrain your appetites.'

'I think you privately enjoy being scandalized,' Lord Richmond answered, smiling. He inhaled the bouquet from his glass, and spoke before taking another sip. 'And if we are, as you preach with such constancy, the walking damned, I fail to see how a little tasteful indulgence can mar matters more.'

'Do not sidestep this. If ye wish to retain the support of the church, ye must needs make certain cessions.'

'Surely you understand my reluctance to do so, Your Holiness.'

The clergyman bristled. 'Do not associate me with that rank human impostor. The Lord willeth that the damned too shall serve Him, and Him alone, nor consort with Antichrist.'

'For a damned soul, Reverend, I must say, you know the mind of God awfully well.'

Chastelard tittered. The brimstony face of the Reverend Doctor remained unmoved.

'Ye have yet given me no answer.'

The Lord Chief Justice considered this; then he took Chastelard by the nape of the neck, and kissed him with ostentation and brutality. At first the other responded enthusiastically, but suddenly he stopped, and then broke off, holding his lip. 'Ah! *Câlice, mon amour!*

'I am sorry,' said Lord Carroll, not sounding particularly sorrowful, 'I do get carried away. You taste so delicious, Paul.' A little trickle of scarlet was visible on his lip.

Tinsmith's face contorted with revulsion. 'Feeding off a fellow vampire,' he muttered. 'You are no better than von Orlok.'

'I am not the one who claims to be better. But speaking of His Grace, that is a pertinent point: the Chartists do not need to worry about our own credibility any more, because he has done us the favor of destroying his. Even—' he glanced at the dining room door, and lowered his voice—'even the Black Fan cannot buoy him up now, supposing she still wants to, which I doubt. The assault on Ravenhurst's daughter was a disastrous miscalculation. If the Duke will attack even the *arbiter elegantiæ*, who can be safe? And when the people see that, they will see that our message of egalitarian unity and revolt is the only possible response to the maniac who has ruled us these one hundred and eighty-six years.'

'*Put not thy trust in princes, nor in any child of man,*' quoted Tinsmith.

'I have never understood how you can drop Biblical phrases without scalding your mouth,' Chastelard said with mild interest.

'I accept the scalding,' he answered. 'Do not all things come from the Father of lights?'

'Especially hell,' Lord Richmond mocked. 'I shall have to sacrifice Mountjoy— not that I mind; the fellow is an incompetent—to keep the Duke's suspicions lulled a few weeks longer. But we need only those few weeks. You must see it, Reverend: the time is ripe.'

'I see it,' said Tinsmith slowly. 'But how are we to command the loyalties of the many vampires at stake? Some will never forsake the notion of monarchical government. And of those who will, how, if we are seen to be steeped in depravity, shall we commend ourselves to them as the worthy orderers of a new epoch?'

'You might just as well ask how we can commend ourselves to them if we are *not* seen to be steeped in depravity. Depravity is always fashionable.'

'I shall not be party to it.'

'Oh yes? Shall it then be Reverend Lazarus Tinsmith *contra mundum*?'

'I am always *contra mundum*,' said the clergyman drily. 'But I do not think it will be necessary to accent the fact. The elect are always few, but the light never wholly goes out.'

Richmond sighed. 'Reverend Doctor. I have given you my solemn guarantee' (here the clergyman snorted, but the other vampire ignored it) 'that with your support for the Chartists' *coup d'état*, the cult –'

'Church,' Tinsmith interjected brusquely.

'I apologize. With your support for our *coup*, the church will be granted an unprecedented degree of liberty in the new regime—such liberty as it has not seen since you yourself were a dragonet, and I no more than a twinkle on my sire's fang. It is to our mutual advantage.'

Tinsmith nodded. 'I know it. I know also, though ye would endeavor to disguise it, that it is more to your advantage than mine; and likewise more costly for you than for me, should I withdraw my aid. The church hath continued under Duke von Orlok, and shall continue, irrespective of his doom. I do not believe that the Chartists can persevere so easily.' He took a sip of blood from his glass and waited.

The Chief Justice sat silent for a moment, and then said, bitterly, 'I can make certain concessions.'

'Good.'

Chastelard smiled languorously and quoted:

'Du mécréant saisit à plein, poing les cheveux,
Et dit, le secouant: "Tu connaîtras la règle!"'

'Concentrate, Marie,' murmured her sire. 'You have to move gently. The way you're doing it is too obvious.'

'How can anything telepathic be obvious?' she protested.

'It is once you are experienced, *ma petite ingénue*. And that means it will be obvious to everybody; every vampire more than a year or two old has been thoroughly trained in these things. Now listen to me. You're simply barging into my mind. Use the less attentive chinks, as I told you. I'm directing my mind as hospitably as possible, and I can only do so much at once.'

'How can there *be* less attentive chinks if you yourself know about them?'

'Because *I* have mental discipline and am focusing on something else,' said Augustus patiently. 'And speaking of discipline, for hell's sake, *concentrate*.'

Marie sighed and recollected herself. At least the poltergeist had been firmly excluded this time; Augustus had set up what he called a ward, a telepathic barrier that prevented other minds from entering its confines. She felt around the surface of his thoughts, felt at his attention to the copy of *Les Fleurs du Mal* in his hands. A fascinating poet, Baudelaire, if perverse—but Augustus' attention was there, he would notice any ingress at once. Slow movement, slow movement. It was so tempting to rush things, he had said. Hmm … here were some thoughts about dinner. Modify the tone of her own thoughts, adapt them to his to be inconspicuous. Bring the æsthetic qualities in her own mind to the fore, then; pronounce her egotism … Dinner was to be a Danish bourgeois gentleman, not really to his taste, though Marie would probably like it. She was adjusting rather quickly, was she not? It was quite astonishing that she had read as much as she had from Godalming, on her first attempt and without eye contact, no less. She displayed a remarkable talent.

'Really?' she said aloud. Then her head gave a heavy throb, and she and Augustus both flinched. 'I'm sorry.'

'Do not break the link so abruptly,' he said, rubbing his temple. 'That is what causes the headaches. One more exercise, and then we shall have our dinner.'

'Yes, Lord Ravenhurst.'

'We have not yet practiced warding. I have given you the theory; repeat it to me nicely.'

'One imagines one's mind as a—'

'Ah ah,' he interrupted, 'what comes first?'

Marie winced. 'Concentration.'

'Just so. Now.' He gestured for her to resume.

'First one concentrates. One imagines one's mind as a hard shell, like the shell of a nut. To begin with, it should be pictured corresponding roughly to the skull itself. When one has this firmly in mind, one imagines the ward expanding to its desired size, slowly, maintaining concentration; if one is imagining correctly, some mild resistance is to be expected, which can be overcome through adequate focus. At the desired size, picture this shell being fixed in place, and this will render it active. Finally, when one wishes to dispel the ward, one simply pictures it dissolving.'

Augustus smiled. 'Flawless. Now do it.'

She nodded, a little nervously, and set her mind to concentrate again. A hard shell, the size of her skull, more or less spherical. She pushed it out a little; it held. A bit further out. There was indeed a slight resistance: a sensation somewhere between that of moving a sturdy piece of furniture and that of working out a difficult piece of arithmetic. The ward persisted. Feeling moderately pleased with herself, she carefully extended the sphere until it stood about two feet out from her body, and then attempted to fix it in place; but when she withdrew her attention from the ward, she could feel it start to shrink. She pushed it out again, but it shrank inward a second time.

Her sire spoke quietly; her concentration lurched at this, but she just managed to maintain her grip. 'Find an object—something stationary, it doesn't matter what—and picture your ward being fastened to that.'

Looking around for something in the appropriate range, Marie's eyes fell on the statuette of Diana and Actæon on the table beside her armchair. It was just a few inches further than she had made her ward at first. She focused, pushing the ward out again; the resistance increased, and she took a deliberate breath, to steady her mind by familiar behavior. The ward edged outwards slowly. It reached the statuette. She pictured the ward being affixed to it, imagined little tendrils growing out of the sphere and tying themselves in a knot around it. Then she turned her attention to Augustus; and the ward held. She beamed with triumph.

He smiled back at her. 'Magnificent.' He reached out telepathically—she noticed that, within the ward, her sense of his mental activity seemed sharper— and touched the ward, and it vanished like a soap bubble.

Her face fell. 'Not so magnificent, then.'

'On the contrary. Most dragonets your age would hardly have been able to craft a ward at all, and certainly not one of that size.' He rose and offered her his arm. 'Come and have dinner.'

The nights wore on, and a semblance of pattern was established in the manor: the lessons in telepathy and the use of her fangs and claws and other vampire qualities (occasionally interwoven with pæans on the superiority of vampires to man); the weird, sanguine, overtly decadent meals; the servants' routines, comforting in their prosaicism; the shortening hours of daylight that lengthened the night, and gave Marie a delicious sense of freedom. Since the cold did not matter, she sometimes went out into the grounds, gazing at the dry gardens and the empty fountains, or up into the sky at the stars. Here on the northwestern outskirts of London, away from the haze of the streetlamps, they shone more brightly and distinctly than they had in Lambeth.

Now and again, Marie would be overcome by the death of her father and her separation from her brothers, and would take refuge in the sacrosanctity of her own room, forcing a few bloody tears out into a handkerchief. Even the comfort of attending Mass was denied her; she did not know whether her undead constitution could endure an entire liturgy, but regardless, she felt sure Augustus would never permit such a thing—not to mention the fact that most Masses were said during hours of daylight.

Still, Ravenhurst had grown familiar enough to act as a cushion. Its sumptuousness and luxury was oppressive sometimes, like an over-rich cake, but it was after all familiar, and that was what counted. She often found herself frozen, for an hour or more, before one of the many pictures or sculptures that graced the castle, half-involuntarily analyzing its every detail. The library was also consoling, containing hundreds of volumes, especially of poetry. She lost many hours absorbed in the glittering conceits of Marvell, Donne, and Crashaw, the mysterious and private mythology of Blake, the fantasias of Keats and Shelley, or the experimental depravities of Baudelaire and Rimbaud.

One event did interrupt the mostly improved temper of her relations with her sire. Two days after the letter from Livilla, Marie had come down the stairs and smelled an unfamiliar scent, like cold earth. She had looked around, more and more curious on account of its persistence, and at last traced the smell to a door in a small side-passage, the same where she had met Godalming and Peter the night when she was trying to get a newspaper, with the archaic painting of St Clare hung upon it. The door stood slightly ajar. Marie drew close, and was reaching out to open it, when a hand shot out from behind her and slammed it shut, almost catching her fingers. She let out a sharp cry and spun around, finding herself nose to nose with Augustus, who was glaring at her with white-hot anger. She stepped back, and he advanced, until she could feel the cold of the wall against her, and her sire's arms were against it to either side of her. Trapped. She did not know how long he stood there, pinning her to the wall with his eye.

'That is not your concern,' he breathed at last, and lowered his arms.

She nodded, shaking with terror, and walked quickly around him and out of the corridor, daring to glance back only once. The rage on her sire's face had not subsided. Marie went back to her room and locked herself in. A few minutes later, though she was unable even with her sharpened hearing to make out most of the words—something about *irresponsible* and *never*—Augustus' shouting voice came up the stairs from the deeper recesses of the house, accompanied by human screams.

As the date of the *soirée* drew nearer, Augustus seemed to be getting generally cross. Marie did not often go to his second-floor study, as this tended to precipitate flare-ups, but on the rare occasions she did happen by it, she noticed a remarkable volume of correspondence. Given his reclusive, sybaritic life, it seemed a little out of character; but she hardly knew what to say or ask. Some of the envelopes he addressed bore the names of living men and women, whom Marie for the most part did not know personally but did by reputation: influential members of the aristocracy and the capitalist class, in whose affairs (and profits) Augustus had a hand. There were also a few undead names she recognized—Lady Thackeray, Lord Carroll, Lady fitzUrse, Chastelard—but more that were unknown to her, and a handful without any name at all.

CHAPTER VIII

A BURLESQUE OF WISDOM

There is one end for all of them; they sit
Naked and sad, they drink the dregs of it,
  Trodden as grapes in the wine-press of lust,
Trampled and trodden by the fiery feet.

I see the marvellous mouth whereby there fell
Cities and peoples whom the gods loved well,
  Yet for her sake on them the fire gat hold,
And for their sakes on her the fire of hell.

— ALGERNON CHARLES SWINBURNE, *LAUS VENERIS*

On the evening of the twenty-eighth, Lord Ravenhurst came upon Marie in the library at about ten. She was curled up in one of the armchairs, catlike, reading Keats' *Lamia*. She looked up and greeted him politely.

'Well, your *début* at Lady Thackeray's town house tomorrow night has been fully arranged. We will go over in the landau at a quarter to eight, and the reception will last until half past one: light refreshment, conversation, the usual sort of thing. Her ladyship has a taste for German … well, I suppose one has to call them *thinkers*. If you have not read much Kant or Hegel hitherto, I advise you to find my volumes of their works and glance through them.'

Marie's heart sank at this. 'I'll hardly understand a word with so little time to think,' she remarked. 'James was the clever one with that.'

'Oh, you needn't understand it, *ma mignardise*. Livilla doesn't. Only acquire enough familiarity with them to nod meaningfully at the appropriate times. All she wants is to be allowed to play the queen bee; fall in with that and she will find you perfectly charming.'

'I see. Well, as I am still fairly tongue-tied around everybody, that shouldn't be too difficult.'

'I wish,' he said, a little tartly, 'that you would not be so diffident, child. Toward me it is fitting enough as your sire. But generally speaking, it is poor strategy: quiet vampires are not left in peace as you suppose; they are used, by stronger, smarter, quicker ones. It would be better if you learned to show your fangs with cunning and elegance. And besides, it's better *style*.' He turned to go, then looked over his shoulder and added, 'There is a letter for you, by the way.'

'There is? From whom?'

'I don't know; the envelope is sealed, you see,' Augustus answered drily. 'Probably the Reverend Doctor Tinsmith wants to take you as a lover.'

She grimaced involuntarily with disgust. 'You don't really think so?'

'Obviously not. The fellow was as cold as a corpse even before he died. I doubt that the intervening two hundred and twenty-five years have done anything to excite his animal spirits. Anyway, whenever you want it, you have only to ring for it.'

'Thank you, Lord Ravenhurst.'

'And talking of letters,' he muttered. Marie waited for him to go, and then rang for Godalming, who brought her the letter. There was no return address; she looked closely at the seal, which was impressed on traditional scarlet wax, not the black she had learnt to associate with the morbid humor of vampires. It consisted of a Jerusalem cross above a lion rampant—William's personal seal. She retreated with it to her room.

Her hands trembling slightly, she broke open the seal and pulled out the letter. It said the following.

My dear Miss Redglass,
I hope you will pardon my writing to you without your permission; under the circumstances, I have little right to request your attention. Nonetheless, desire to regain some morsel of your favor emboldens me.
First, permit me to express my deep grief for your bereavement of your father. I admired him profoundly, as a man of character, intelligence, and piety,

and he will be much missed even by his merest acquaintances; so that I can scarcely imagine the wound that afflicts your heart. I was able to attend his funeral Mass, and can assure you that it was said with great dignity.

Secondly, I must apologize for my conduct over the last six months. I had no right to ask you to marry me, caught in a net of impossible perversion as I am. I had been hoping, in marriage, to escape from this underworld, and allowed the passion of that hope to dominate my reason. I refused to see that my intemperance was in the long run a danger to yourself, and one of which I could not even warn you, for fear of being dismissed for a madman. I regret it bitterly: it was unjust and selfish of me, and I can only implore you to believe that my error was born rather of thoughtlessness than of malice. I have asked your forgiveness once before, and you justly refused it. I cannot wish to gainsay you, nor to impose on your kindly nature; but to be thus beholden to your deserved ill-will leaves me utterly without rest. I dare to hope that, now or at some later time, you can find it in your heart to pardon my unpardonable conduct.

With or without your forgiveness, I place myself at your disposal, out of love and justice alike; and I beg to remain
Your obedient servant,
William St George Vavasour

Marie read the letter four times with rapt attention. Same old William, she thought: the same debonair affection, the same exacting sense of honor, the same funny curve to his *f*'s. And it was the only condolence letter she had received, or would. It certainly made a sharp contrast to Augustus' brutality the morning of her return to Ravenhurst Manor, or the night she found the obituary in the *Times*.

She thought. The letter must be answered. With forgiveness? She had tried before, and failed. Could she try again? Angry as she was still over the whole affair, she could never believe that, had he known the danger she was in, he would have stopped at anything in trying to protect her. And what did forgiveness mean, if she extended it? It was hardly to be thought that they could still marry. Yet even so, he would be a friend, among these monsters. It would be pleasant, consoling, even just to sit with him and talk to him. A human companion.

Marie discovered suddenly that she could forgive him and had, in a single, self-luminous act. Why and how, she could not explain even to herself. The forgiveness was simply and joyously *there*, feeling less like a decision than like a function of her being. She had only to tell him. She rummaged in the vanity and found some writing paper, then rang for Hyacinth and asked for a pen and inkpot, an envelope, and some sealing wax. The necessaries before her, she sent the maid away and sat down to write.

Dear Mr Vavasour, Marie wrote, and stopped. Her brain was blank. She tried to marshal her thoughts into sentences; they flitted around in disobedient happiness. She looked down at the paper and found that she had been absent-mindedly drawing, in minute detail, a picture of the *Diana and Actæon* statuette in the library. Pursing her lips, she crumpled up the page and threw it in the waste paper basket, then began again with the same words. Her mind was stubbornly uncooperative. She laid down the pen as a precaution, and put her head between her hands, trying desperately to think clearly.

This expedient actually succeeded, as her brain deposited a single word in her consciousness: *Augustus.*

Augustus, the master telepath, whom no waxen seal would keep out. Obviously he could not read her mail without opening it, because letters did not have minds to read, but once read, its contents were inside her memory. As would be anything she wrote. Was there any way of keeping her correspondence private? Warding her memories, maybe; but she was still a beginner, and in any case, he had literally centuries of experience to toy with, as against her fortnight or so.

Scowling, Marie rose and made a pace of the room. There must be a way to be private from him. There had to be.

Lord Richmond straightened his collar as he paged idly through the sheaf of papers in front of him. The other members of the judicial council—Br Horace Dane of the Oratory of the Divine Sovereignty, pale and bony; the Viscount of Chelmsford, Gabriel Culpeper, outwardly a stripling of sixteen, yet sired before the death of Louis XIV; the Baroness of St Sepulchre, Francesca fitzUrse, her glance scornful beneath her iron-grey hair; the Baron of Pontefract, John Finch, once a member of the Star Chamber under Charles I; Mr Malcolm Whitgift, a dark, small, twitchy fellow—were seated with him in the judgment chamber of the Pantheon, in the towering hemicycle of grey-veined Chinese marble that composed the bench. Below them stood Mr Petroc Mountjoy. Ordinarily he would be seated immediately below Lord Carroll as the court's Secretary; but Mountjoy was, in this case, the accused. Whitgift smiled nastily at him as he passed another leaf up to the Lord Chief Justice, who studied it side by side with his other notes, and then looked down at his erstwhile Secretary. He spoke in a clipped voice.

'Mister Mountjoy, you have been convicted of illicit hunting in the private territory of His Grace the Duke on the following occasions—'

'But I wasn't!' cried Mountjoy desperately. 'I've—'

'Silence. The ninth of December 1873, the ninth of January 1874, the fourteenth of March 1874, the third of April 1874 …'

'It's a lie! I've told you, I was there, but I never hunted, not once!'

'Order, Mountjoy!'

'This is Whitgift's doing, isn't it!'

'Keep your tongue behind your teeth,' shouted Lord Richmond over the prisoner's continuing protestations, 'unless you want to be summarily sentenced for contempt of court as well!'

But Mountjoy, it seemed, was past caring. 'How can you, of all people, uphold these convictions? Even if they were true, what do they concern you?'

'I am the Lord Chief Justice of His Grace, Julius von Orlok,' replied Richmond in a terrible voice. 'Every trespass against his rights and privileges concerns me.' To his left, the Baroness allowed herself a twisted smile.

'Liar!' Mountjoy screamed. 'We all know *you're* the one who wrote the Chartist Letters!'

Carroll transfixed him with a glare. 'I think, Mister Mountjoy, that you must be beside yourself. It is well known that Lord Arden's sad treachery to His Grace was a matter of public confession and has been dealt with equitably. And if you repeat this raving nonsense, I will have you charged with slander on my own initiative.'

'You said you would protect me, Nigel! How can you perform this— this farce!'

Chelmsford rose. 'My lady, my lords, Mister Whitgift, I think we have heard more than enough from the convicted. If my Lord the Chief Justice cannot prevail upon him to conduct himself orderly, perhaps he should be consigned to the Solarium, and informed of his sentence later.'

The other members of the judiciary council agreed, over the irrelevant screams of the criminal, and he was led away.

'Such preposterous accusations,' remarked Lady fitzUrse as the council members rose to recess. 'Anybody would suppose he wanted to disgrace himself.'

'Faithful Secretary though he once was, Mountjoy was never a vampire of sterling intellect,' said Lord Richmond sadly. 'Perhaps the strain of being found out has disordered his wits.'

She nodded. 'And the idea that you were the author of the Chartist Letters! Quite impossibly insolent.'

'Whether it was insolent is hardly relevant. The point is that it's false,' snapped Richmond.

'Oh, yes, entirely false,' agreed the Baroness.

The next evening found Marie standing in front of the wardrobe at seven, frowning at the forest of lace, taffeta, and brocade, of grey and ivory and yellow and crimson. She was hoping that the maid's assistance would be superfluous for this at least. She wished, for her father's sake, that she could simply retain her current black gown, but Augustus had warned her that after the damaging episode with His Grace, other vampires would be apt to sneer if she turned up in the exact same dress. At any rate she would go decently sub-fusc. Fine, but not ostentatious.

At last she settled on a dark, shimmering thing in the emerald green of Augustus' house, with a cuirass bodice drawing to a sharp point below the navel, where the skirt was rouched over the bustle. The rich color was accented by contrasting copper-colored piping and a pair of copper-colored satin evening gloves that went with it. The fabric felt beautiful against her skin, like cool water. Then she realized that, as the mirror was useless to her, she would have to call for Hyacinth to find out whether the dress flattered or insulted. She sighed deliberately and rang for her.

'Yes, me lady?'

'Tell me truthfully, Hyacinth. How does this gown look? On me, I mean.'

'Very smart, me lady,' the girl said, with a hesitating smile. 'I expeck you'll be wan'ing your hair put up wivvat one.'

'Yes, please,' Marie said, seating herself at the vanity. She tried not to look at the gown's vacant reflection. Hyacinth applied herself to her mistress' hair. Marie could not help but notice that the maid lost something of her perpetual nervousness as she did so: her hands moved deftly, arranging lock over lock, placing hairpins just so in order to conceal their operation while accenting their effect. It was only a few minutes before the maid announced that she was finished.

'Oh, and 'ere did used to be a ligh' shawl wha' went wivvis one,' Hyacinth said brightly. 'Muslin, you know, me lady. I' did ough' to be in the wardrobe, I'll fetch i' for you.'

This she did, and arranged it over Marie's shoulders in smooth, artful folds. The girl beamed. 'Cor, you do look a picture, me lady!'

'Thank you, Hyacinth.' She ran her fingers over her hair, feeling an elegant knot high in the back, with a fan-shaped set of ringlets descending from it. Dismissing the maid, she went to find Augustus.

He was in the entrance hall, looking like a relic of the French Empire in tails and a green cravat. As she floated down the stairs, she could feel his eyes fixed upon her.

'*Mon doux plaisir*,' he said. 'You do look a picture.'

'That's just what Hyacinth said,' she replied, smiling.

'Shall we?' He proffered his arm.

They arrived at Lady Bath's house just off Sloane Street a tasteful five minutes late. A footman took their coats, and the butler led them into the parlor, announcing, 'Augustus Fairfax, Lord Ravenhurst, and Mademoiselle Marie Redglass.'

A small knot of guests was there already: Chastelard, Lady Ely, a male vampire whom Marie did not know, and Miss Glastenning. Chastelard detached himself from the group and advanced to greet the new arrivals. He kissed Marie's hand with zest, saying, '*Bonsoir, ma béatifique beauté, et ça va?*'

'Very well, thank you,' she replied. 'How do you do?'

The unknown was introduced to her as David Tudor, the Earl of Monmouth. He was a friend of Lady Bath's, with a great interest in political theory. Monmouth made the necessary courtesies to Marie and she to him, and then he posed a question about the judiciary to Augustus. The latter had begun to answer when two more vampires entered the room: Lady Livilla Thackeray herself and Lady St Sepulchre.

Marie bit her lip. Livilla was wearing a gown practically identical to her own, down to the copper piping; it was like a coincidence out of some cruel novel of manners. Livilla's eyes widened momentarily at the sight of her, the silk-gloved fingers clenching slightly as she advanced to greet her guest.

'Mademoiselle Redglass! How lovely to be able to welcome you more properly into our society,' she proclaimed in a bright, toxic voice. 'We have all been hoping that Viscount Fairfax would take himself another child. The change shall do us good.'

'Thank you very much, Lady Bath. How do you do?'

The marchioness smiled patronizingly, without separating her lips. 'As a *junior* member of our community, I feel sure you will not take a word of advice amiss, my dear. That shade of green does nothing for your complexion. Sable, I think, is your proper color.'

Marie set her jaw firmly. 'Thank you, my lady.'

A dinner gong was rung, and Lady Bath clapped her hands together. 'Now! If you would all follow Phillips, please.'

The butler led them into a lavish and suffocating dining room. Their hostess took her place at the head of the table. To her right was Augustus' place, and Marie to his right; Lord Monmouth was to Livilla's left, and Lady St Sepulchre to his left, across from Marie. Chastelard was on Marie's other side, and then the Duchess of Ely. The foot of the table was empty. To its right sat Miss Glastenning, and then came another space between her and Lady St Sepulchre.

'The Chief Justice and Canon Glover, I fear, shall be late,' announced Livilla, as a footman filled their glasses. '(This is a Burgundian blood, by the way, taken from a courtesan of noble ancestry.) Lord Carroll's duties at the Judiciary have him in arrears, and Glover, being his chaplain, is in attendance on him.'

'I hope Lord Carroll can keep talk of his curious political ideas to a gentlemanly minimum tonight,' said Monmouth. 'Not that they aren't amusing in their way. But one cannot help imagining the consequences if they were taken with the gravity *apropos* to an official of the state.'

'I agree with you absolutely, Lord Monmouth,' said Chastelard cordially. 'Why, if Richmond's ideas were taken seriously, certain of the rights of His Grace the Duke could even be called into question.'

'That is not terribly funny,' said Lady Thackeray coldly.

'No indeed,' interjected Augustus mildly as he set his glass down. 'But, if you will all forgive my changing the subject: my lady, I have been reading the *Phänomenologie des Geistes* lately, and there is a passage that I would be grateful for your opinion on.'

'Certainly.'

Augustus began to declaim something in German; Marie, though her Latin was good and her French middling, had no German at all. Livilla listened for a few moments, and then interrupted her guest.

'Ah, yes—please forgive me, Ravenhurst—that passage is a favorite of mine. It is a detail of the question of the master-slave dialectic, itself a subcategory of Hegel's general treatment of the phenomenon of consciousness. His language is rather obscure here, but I have devoted extensive study to the matter.' (Chastelard gave a tiny false cough.) 'Beginning from an attenuatedly Hobbesian notion of the state of nature, Hegel posits an encounter between two ideal or mythic individuals, who by means of this encounter experience themselves for the first time as the object of another's consciousness, rather than purely as the subject of their own— monarchs of reality, now confronted with a pretender to the throne, as it were. Thus, they find a contradiction between their own subjectivity and the subjectivity of the other.

'In order to resolve this contradiction, the two fight, as to the death, so as to leave a single claimant to that monarchy. However, inevitably, one of the two will fear death more than the other, while that other would prefer to die rather than to lose. The one who fears death the more will, therefore, consent to a truce: he who is less afraid of death shall be the master, and the other his slave, and a single relation of subjectivity and objectivity shall prevail for both once again.'

'I see,' answered Augustus.

'It is truly fascinating,' Livilla went on, warming to her subject, 'to consider the implications of Hegel's philosophy as applied to the dialectic between ourselves and the human race.' (Marie gripped her gown momentarily under the table.) 'In his thought, which, owing to his ignorance, he applied only to man, master and slave are eventually brought to equality, once the slave realizes that the master depends upon him for the production of goods. This allows the slave to reassert the original duel to the death. Yet the existence of the duel depends upon the fact that both fear death. To ourselves, this fear is inapplicable; we can win any duel to the death, merely by waiting long enough, to say nothing of our physical and psychical mastery of their race. The wheel of fortune imagined by Boëthius, the pattern of rise and fall, has no relevance to us. The vampire is above the accidents of history.'

'A hypothesis borne out by our unseen domination of human culture,' put in Augustus cheerfully.

'Quite. We have filled their cities, their fortresses, their exchanges, their colleges, their councils, their palaces, their parliaments, their squares …'

'*Sola vobis relinquimus Templa*,' said Miss Glastenning—quietly, but everyone heard her.

'And it is equally borne out by contemplating the Darwinian hierarchy,' Lady Thackeray continued, a little too loudly. Marie surreptitiously glanced at Miss Glastenning, who was calmly studying her in return. Marie took a swallow of blood uncertainly and attended again. 'The lowest creatures subsist upon slime, and are slime themselves, shapeless and ugly. The next order, plants, have constant form, and subsist upon the lowest; the lesser beasts have both form and movement, and subsist upon plants, but the greater beasts live off the inferior kinds of animal. Humans are higher still, possessing shape, motion, and reason, and subsist on the lower orders, with the exception of the very lowest, the aforementioned slimes: men reach down, yet do not stoop to eat. This is the same principle which we discern throughout. The deduction follows: vampires, who have shape, movement, reason, and immortality, and feast only upon the highest of these kinds, are above every other order. Devourers, ourselves undevoured, we are the noblest creatures of all.'

'And here we sit discussing nothing but human ideas,' said Marie suddenly. 'If we are so splendid, have we come up with nothing of our own?'

The effect was electric. Lady Thackeray turned as scarlet as a tiger. Lord Tudor and Lady Borgia looked shocked almost to the point of fright; Lady fitzUrse looked at once angry and scornful; Augustus and Chastelard seemed to be trying not to laugh. Miss Glastenning alone seemed unsurprised, a small smile playing at her lips.

Livilla opened her mouth, and Marie braced herself to be eaten alive—but at that moment, Phillips announced, 'The Lord Chief Justice, the Earl of Richmond and Kingston-upon-Thames, Lord Nigel Carroll; and Chaplain to the same, the Reverend Canon Dominic Glover.' A tall vampire with dark hair entered first, followed by a young, fair, slender specimen in a cassock, whom Marie recognized from the palace. Footmen came in after the two vampires and collected the half-finished glasses of blood.

'Pray forgive our lateness, your ladyship,' said Lord Carroll as he and his companion were seated, he at the foot of the table and the Canon between Miss Glastenning and Lady fitzUrse. 'Duke von Orlok has brought to my attention certain irregularities on the part of my Secretary, Mountjoy—former Secretary, rather. I have been obliged to dismiss and chasten him.'

'Oh, what a sad loss to you,' said Lady Thackeray happily. 'My lords, it is a great pity that you were not able to be here for the opening course, but I know you will appreciate this one. A sweet, full-bodied Spaniard, a southerner.' The said blood was put before them in sherry glasses.

Augustus spoke. 'While I have your ears, my lord, and Reverend Glover, I hope that you will forgive my immense rudeness to Doctor Tinsmith the other night. I never speak that way, unless I dislike somebody. Please do not suppose that my loathing for your associate, though profound, inhibits my equally profound respect for yourselves.'

'I quite understand the delicacy of your position,' Carroll replied. The canon simply nodded with closed lips. 'But I would hate for our untimeliness to disrupt what I am sure was a lively conversation. May I ask its subject?'

Chastelard smiled wickedly. 'Mademoiselle Redglass and Lady Thackeray were giving us an invaluable lesson in mastery and slavery, my lord.'

The bloods that followed were a Provençal man of letters, a country girl from Lombardy, a Bordeaux industrialist, a Breton of a cadet branch of the illustrious Penthièvres, and finally, as they retired to the drawing room, a young Polish girl—'Just twelve years old,' Livilla bragged. Marie recoiled at this, but said nothing under a warning glare from Augustus. Unable to bring herself to drink it, she pretended to take a sip once or twice and set her brandy glass down, trying not to let her hand shake.

She glanced longingly in the direction of the door; but this was (in theory) her own *début*. She would have to wait it out. Conversations drifted and multiplied. Augustus and Livilla resumed their dissection of Hegel; Chastelard was pontificating to Carroll and the other noble females about Sir Henry Irving's characterization of Hamlet; Monmouth and Reverend Glover were discussing the divergent merits of French and Austrian opera. Miss Glastenning approached her.

'You lost your father recently,' she said.

Marie stared at her, taken at unawares by the reminder; then, recollecting herself, confirmed that she had.

'Please let me offer you my condolences.' She had an air of—not friendliness exactly, but—courtesy. Not the cynical charm of Chastelard or Ravenhurst, but sincere, grave respectfulness. 'He was a noble man.'

'Thank you,' Marie answered, controlling her voice. 'You are very kind, Miss Glastenning.'

The woman inclined her head and withdrew, drifting toward Augustus and Lady Thackeray. Marie looked around at the slate blue walls of the drawing room, and her eyes fell on a painting of the death of Julius Cæsar, all jet and white and scarlet. It struck her that she knew almost nothing of the histories of these vampires, either individually or as a society. She knew that Augustus had become a vampire in the middle of the fourteenth century, he had told her that much; and that he had sired Chastelard only eighty-five years ago. (Did that make him a sort of sibling to her, she wondered?) But the rest—how old were they? What had they been like in life? Did any of them, like her, have living relatives, many generations removed from themselves, maybe? How much history they must have witnessed in the making!

'… the next thing to impossible without monarchical and aristocratic patronage,' someone was saying. Livilla.

'I cannot agree with you there, my lady,' said Lord Richmond. 'Consider the seminal accomplishments in sculpture, architecture, oratory, and drama bequeathed to us by classical Athens, one of the few pure democracies the world has yet seen.'

Lady fitzUrse said, 'Yes; and it lasted just over a mere hundred years, before being overthrown by Sparta.'

'Admittedly. But the artistic accomplishments remain.'

'Well of course they remain,' replied Livilla in a peevish tone. 'They weren't going to get up of their own accord and take a holiday in Majorca, were they.'

'But they were never surpassed, and scarcely rivalled, for a thousand years of European monarchic civilization among the Mediævals,' Chastelard argued. 'And even when the Renaissance arrived, it copied its classical forebears in everything. Brunelleschi, Donatello, Botticelli, Bramante, Ghirlandajo—*quid autem habetis quod non accepistis?*'

Richmond pointed at him. 'Precisely. If we propose to speak highly of monarchies on the grounds of their true and worthy contributions to beauty, it is equally possible to speak highly of democracies for the same reason.'

'You sound like a Chartist,' said Lady St Sepulchre with a hint of spite.

'I don't know that the Chartists are altogether wrong,' said Augustus; a spasm of disgust passed over Livilla's face. 'The Duke has not said so much.'

'That may be, but their ideas would undermine our entire society as it has stood since the Duke's accession,' St Sepulchre replied.

'That is more than I know,' Augustus said, taking a sip of blood. 'I can claim little acquaintance with Chartist ideas, after all.' The suggestion that she perhaps could was allowed to hang strangling in the air for a moment. 'But consider: the marchioness and I have been discussing the Hegelian *Weltanschauung* and its implications, and it seems to me that, among vampires, it prevents a purely pragmatic justification for monarchy—since, as everyone knows, we are immortal, destroying the ground on which Hegelian dialectic exists. How, then, are we to understand the nature of vampire monarchy?'

Reverend Glover spoke. 'It seems to me that the only possible justification, in that case, lies in the thesis of Divine Right. That monarchy is a traditional form of rule is mere sentimentality, and pragmatic reasons have already been dispensed with. What remains is simple submission to the will of God, expressed in acceptance of whatever in fact is.'

'Always supposing there is any God,' Chastelard sneered into his glass for all to hear.

'But surely, Reverend,' said Marie, and then stopped, suddenly shy as all eyes turned upon her.

'Yes, my dear, what is it?' said Lady Thackeray poisonously; 'you know how much we love your philosophical reflections. And it is after all *your* party.'

Emboldened by a fresh wave of dislike for her hostess, Marie continued. 'If the will of God is expressed equally in everything that happens, how can any one thing be justified rather than another? In that case, a revolt that succeeded in instituting democratic government would have quite as much claim to Divine Right as any monarch whom it dethroned. Acceptance of every fact simply as fact would leave every course of action acceptable.'

Silence followed these words. The Chief Justice and Chastelard both seemed to be hiding smiles with their hands; the Canon was impassive; most of the others looked appalled and furious. Lord Ravenhurst was openly smiling a bright, false smile, and said at last, 'We are the *enfant terrible* this evening, aren't we, *mon petit chou?*'

CHAPTER IX

THE DOCTRINE OF BEAUTY

She dwells with Beauty—Beauty that must die;
And Joy, whose hand is ever at his lips
Bidding adieu; and aching Pleasure nigh,
Turning to poison while the bee-mouth sips:
Ay, in the very temple of Delight
Veil'd Melancholy has her sovran shrine,
Though seen of none save him whose strenuous tongue
Can burst Joy's grape against his palate fine:
His soul shall taste the sadness of her might,
And be among her cloudy trophies hung.

—JOHN KEATS, *ODE TO MELANCHOLY*

The rest of the *soirée* was steered quietly away from political theory by Ravenhurst, Carroll, and Monmouth. At a quarter past one, the guests began to make their excuses and thank Lady Thackeray for a lovely night; twenty minutes later, Marie and Augustus were in their carriage, on their way back to Ravenhurst Manor. He wore a mute, catlike smile as they rode, bumped now and then by a loose cobblestone.

'I'm sorry if I was rude to Lady Thackeray,' Marie said.

Her sire, to her great surprise, laughed. 'On the contrary, you humiliated her with a correctness worthy of great envy, and that has endeared you to me. Livilla is a parasite. Her self-conceit is of no moment to me. Your sole miscalculation tonight was to imply that the theology of the Oratory, from which Canon Glover hails, could be used to support a Chartist insurrection.'

'Couldn't it?'

'Obviously. But one doesn't *say* so.'

Marie nodded. 'Who are these Chartists, anyhow? I keep hearing the name and nobody has explained it to me. Are they the disciples of Lord Carroll that you spoke of once before?'

'In good time, *ma fleurette*, all in good time. At the moment I am conjuring the expression on Livilla's face when you outraged her pride at the dinner table.' He closed his eyes lazily.

Vivien Glastenning sat in her house, alone. She did not need a house for her own use; but some of those who came to visit her needed her to have a house, and so she had one. Others, such as the visitors she was receiving that night, had no such need.

Had anyone else been present, they might have seen her crowned and bearing a wand-like scepter. She had been seen that way more than a thousand years before among the worn limestone hills of the south-west, by a few stray Romanized Britons who carried strange tales to their refuge from the Saxon warriors in Armorica. Humans might, too, have seen her visitor in a stranger shape: a vast, pinioned, whitish-yellow thing. But these attributes, his and hers, were—so to call them—tricks of the light: a kind of ceremonial vestments, courtesies to the dignity of matter and of man, not men or matter themselves. They themselves had a different nativity.

For the operation Miss Glastenning was conducting, most human beings would close their eyes. It made no difference for her, any more than the recitation of a set pattern of words made any difference. What requires deliberate mental effort for a human was, for her, simply another facet of her existence, ever present to her mind, to which she could direct her particular attention, as simply as one looks from one face to another in a room. She was neither all-knowing nor all-powerful; yet her modes of knowledge and of power lay rather in the immediate contact of her mind with the inner structure of reality, within her own sphere and capacity, than in the sensation of shapes and movements. The visitor whom she received—

or rather, of whom she was more specifically aware than usual—knew and acted similarly, though his sphere and powers differed from hers.

The two minds met. Put into human terms, she smiled.

The morning of the thirtieth of November, the First Sunday of Advent that year, dawned cruelly cold, with a raw, blotchy light. William walked quickly, his scarf pulled up and his hat pushed down, his hands stuffed deep into the pockets of his great-coat. There was a smell of woodsmoke and snow in the air. He crossed Stanhope Street, which still lay quiet under the winter sunrise, and went inside St John the Divine.

The earliest Mass had already been said at six that morning, and another was due to begin at half past seven, but Fr Weld always sat in the confessional for about twenty minutes between liturgies. Blessing himself with holy water from the stoup, William walked quickly up the aisle, his boots making an uncomfortably loud *tock-tock-tock* on the flagstones, and ducked into the ornate box. The priest's profile could just be made out through the veil and the grille.

'I attended on Duke von Orlok again,' William said in a rush.

'*Bless me, father,*' Fr Weld said gently.

He swallowed and looked down. 'Bless me, father, for I have sinned. It has been one week since my last Confession.'

That night, when Marie (having resumed her black gown) came down for breakfast, it was to discover Chastelard, Miss Glastenning, and a tousle-headed stranger whom Marie sensed immediately to be a mortal, all sitting with Augustus in the library. At the sight of her, Augustus and Miss Glastenning smiled, and Chastelard began to applaud. '*Brava, brava!*'

Augustus rose and went over to her, giving her a kiss on the cheek. 'Come. I've arranged for something pleasanter than last night—a salon, a proper one. And by a great stroke of good fortune, Monsieur Arthur Rimbaud himself is in town to share it with us.' He extended a hand towards the young man, who gave Marie a slight nod.

'It is a great pleasure to meet you, Monsieur,' said Marie, curtseying. 'I have long admired your poetry.'

'Mmm,' Rimbaud explained.

'Now,' Augustus said, as he and Marie seated themselves. 'This evening, our symposium will discuss the nature of beauty: what is it, if anything? And what is its place in our existence—or, what is ours in its?'

Chastelard leaned forward with an elegant, effeminate gesture. 'I say that there is nothing at all in life or death, except beauty. *La vertu* is but the cowardice of the passions; *la vérité*, the senility of the intellect; *la volupté*, a passing childishness. But beauty, this is Venus herself. Faithfully I dwell with her in the Hörselberg, and worship no other goddess.'

'But does not beauty give pleasure?' asked Miss Glastenning.

'Pleasure! it is a nothing. Pleasure soothes the heart; beauty breaks it. Pleasure is the Law to which beauty is the Gospel: the hedonists are mere Jewish usurers, exacting the payment from what is soon used up. Beauty is perpetual, self-renewing, *quod Moses exaltavit serpens in deserto*, the worm Ouroboros.'

'But what, in your view, *is* beauty?' insisted Augustus. 'Like Meno you give us parts and not the thing in itself.'

With a concessive nod, Chastelard answered, '*Alors*, but to philosophize about Venus—*c'est impossible*. She belongs to mythology, that is, to the spirit, not the mind.'

'I cannot agree with you there,' said Miss Glastenning sedately. 'Why fissiparate the spirit and the mind so?'

'*C'est dans l'ordre de choses*. As the sage Apollonius destroyed the beautiful Lamia in the poem of Keats, so the mind naturally destroys all things of the spirit. To know a thing is to kill it.'

'I haven't found that to be the case,' said Marie. 'I generally find things more beautiful when I can understand them.'

Chastelard smiled at her, as one who smiles at a child whose remarks reveal their innocence.

'And what of love?' said Augustus.

He shrugged attractively. 'It makes the time pass.'

'Nothing more?'

'Nothing more,' Chastelard confirmed.

'I cannot believe that,' said Marie. 'Love is among the noblest qualities of human nature; it makes men kind and brave and self-sacrificial. How could it be a mere pastime?'

Rimbaud's face became ugly, and he unbuttoned his left cuff and extended his wrist; a purple scar was spattered upon it. Yet when he spoke, his voice had a terrible calm. 'Verlaine and I were lovers once. This is where he shot me.'

Marie could only stare.

'And you, you fool, say, *a pastime*,' he continued, rounding on Chastelard. 'Men do not do this for that. Love is no pastime. It is a devourer.'

'All the more reason to make no oblation on its altar,' the vampire replied coolly.

Augustus smiled and said, 'Yet you are amorous enough with Nigel Carroll, and were with me, once upon a time.'

'That is the pattern by which one loves. One must play the game according to its own proper rules. Otherwise, where is the fun?'

'I thought fun was childish.'

'*Oui*. But childishness may have its own kind of beauty.'

At that moment, Howard entered, bearing a tray with five wine glasses full of dark red liquid on it, and held it out for each of the conversants, beginning with Chastelard. Marie cast a bewildered glance at her sire as Rimbaud took the next glass; Ravenhurst smiled and shook his head slightly, which she took to mean that she ought to keep silence. Rimbaud took a sip, his face showing no sign that anything was wrong. She looked to Chastelard as he too sampled his glass; and it could not be wine, for he did not wince. Then Miss Glastenning, then Marie herself, and finally Augustus. Marie took a sip. It was indeed blood. And the living poet was drinking it.

'What vintage is this, Lord Ravenhurst?' Rimbaud asked, holding the glass up to the light. 'I have never tasted its equal.'

'Barbaresco, from Piedmont. I have something of a weakness for Italians.'

Marie's stomach turned, and she set down her glass with a grimace. She carefully looked anywhere but at Rimbaud as the conversation resumed, and said little. After about ten minutes, the discussion had become an earnest debate between Rimbaud and Augustus, and diverted itself into specifically literary channels, particularly the overlapping yet incompatible trends to be found in the Romantics and William Blake. Chastelard yawned ostentatiously.

'*Ma belle soeur*,' he said to Marie, 'they have gone and begun to philosophize. Tedium awaits. Would you care to join me for a walk in the grounds?'

She assented, and they went out into the icy night. Lindens and willows were scattered about the grounds, and a semicircular line of cypresses stood around a silent fountain that lay a little way north of the house, looming over it like attendant spirits. The flower-beds were all in their winter hibernation, but with her sharpened eyes, she was able to distinguish the shapes of the few dried leaves that were still caught among the branches or against the stones, and could identify moonflowers, poppies, and asphodel.

'Do you really agree with Rimbaud? About love being a devourer?'

'*Oui.* But that is not what makes the difference. As though beauty were not a devourer!'

The pair stopped on their walk beneath a tall Glastonbury hawthorn, sprinkled with the small white blossoms of its winter flowering. Chastelard studied them for a few moments, and then turned back to Marie.

'*Alors, comme regardez-vous nôtre père, Auguste?*'

'He is … very clever.'

'Marie, there is no need with me for the best behavior,' he told her in amused tones. 'I have known him these eighty-seven years: I have been his son, his pupil, his lover, and his friend, and nothing that you say will surprise me.'

She nodded, and thought. 'I do not quite know what to make of him,' she admitted at last. 'At times we seem to get along well enough. But then I lose my temper over something or other, or he loses his, and—I do not understand it.'

'Do you not?' Chastelard smiled again.

Marie smoothed her dress against the crinoline beneath it, and asked, 'Why did he sire me?'

He gave her a sidelong look. 'Do you suppose that he was being untruthful at the Palace?'

'When he said he was overcome by my beauty?' she scoffed. 'I dare say I have as much reason to be vain as many women, but not so vain as that!'

'You have not been a vampire long. It was all true, what I said in there, you know. For us, beauty is everything. In entering this, *le demimonde de l'Enfer*, all other chains are struck loose. For religion and statecraft and family, all these things presume the generation and corruption, birth and death. Yes, even religion— especially Catholic religion. Your Redglass family were *Catholiques occultes*, what is it you English say, the recusants, yes?'

'Yes,' she said proudly, 'in both branches. My father's mother was a descendant of Thomas Darcy.'

'And the holy Church, does she not teach that all this life is a preparation for death? But that is of no moment to me and to you, *ma soeur*. Only the contemplation of beauty remains.

'*A thing of beauty is a joy for ever:*
Its loveliness increases; it will never
Pass into nothingness; but still will keep
A bower quiet for us, and a sleep
Full of sweet dreams.'

'Keats again. *Endymion*,' said Marie. 'Though I suppose the line about *health and quiet breathing* isn't very apt."

'No. And yet—
'*Of the gloomy days,*
Of all the unhealthy and o'er-darkened ways
Made for our searching: yes, in spite of all
Some shape of beauty moves away the pall
From our dark spirits.

'To sire a beautiful vampire—this is the ultimate *beau geste*.'

They drew up beside a cluster of rosebushes. Chastelard disengaged his arm from hers and said, '*Attendéz.*' She folded her hands and watched. He crouched, studying the dry plant as if it were a piece of Greek statuary. Suddenly, he thrust his hand into the middle of a rosebush and drew it rapidly out again, tearing open his skin on the thickly massed thorns.

'Paul!' she cried, startled out of formality—but he laid a finger on his lips, smiled knowingly, and whispered, '*Attendéz.*'

He shook his savaged hand over the bush, and great pearls of blood fell onto it. Marie gasped: as they landed, the rosebush sprang to life. Leaves as green as malachite unfurled themselves in a matter of seconds, and buds formed, no bigger than peas at first, but then swelled and burst into saffron-yellow blossoms under the starlight. The wounds on Chastelard's hand vanished, and he straightened up again and said, '*Il vous plait?*'

'It's miraculous,' she said. She bent to inhale the fragrance of the flowers. 'How did you do it?'

'Any vampire can. It is one of the properties of the blood. Do you not remember? *Anima enim omnis carnis in sanguine est.*' He winced, swallowed, and went on. 'That, how shall I say it, that *élan vital* is what we take from mortals: in them it is animal and crude, but in ourselves, it is pure and pulsing and unadulterated life. It would be far stranger, *ma belle*, if the rose did not bloom—ah, but see, already it wilts; even in the cold the blood dries quickly.'

He was quite right. Even as they watched, the leaves turned brown and brittle and fell to the ground in the mild breeze, and the flowers withered into wraiths of themselves and fell apart, bearing no fruit.

'And yet you hate our father Augustus,' Chastelard sighed.

'What? No, I don't hate him.'

'This gift of deathlessness and eternal beauty he has given you, and you hate him for it. *Ça ne fait rien; c'est dans l'ordre de choses aussi.*' He took her arm again and began to walk around the garden, gazing up into the constellated blackness. 'And Lady Bath, what do you think of her?'

'Nothing that would look better unveiled,' she replied acidly.

He laughed; it was a metallic sound, like jangling copper. 'And of her opinions the same! I hope that you like Lord Carroll. He also is Venus; I left his room this evening in only my shirtsleeves and a smile. Do you like him?'

'I don't know what you mean,' she said cautiously, somehow perceiving a subtlety in the inquiry that she was not prepared to plumb. 'He seems a noble gentleman.'

'Ha! It is the truth you speak, but do not say it to him; nobility, in his philosophy of government—ah, stop my mouth lest I say inconvenient things!'

Marie frowned for a moment, calculating her response. A direct question about what he was driving at felt wrong, so she said, affecting carelessness, 'I had the impression from our sire that the Lord Chief Justice does not greatly care for the society of His Grace's court.'

'*Non*, he finds its elegances snobbish and its ritual tedious. Yet often must he be there, on account of his duties to the Duke.'

'Why does he not seek to simplify the elegance and ritual?'

'So he has suggested,' said Chastelard, 'on more than one occasion. But our good lord is rather set in his ways. Sired before the inauguration of modernity, he retains the forms and the habits of mind of the Renaissance: all absolutism and power politics. Von Orlok has no notion of what a truly *égalitariste* society among us could mean …'

The vampire trailed off wistfully, waiting for the question—but Marie's curiosity had been aroused in a different direction.

'Monsieur, when was Lord Carroll sired?'

'*Zut alors*—perhaps two centuries ago. A little before the War of the Spanish Succession.'

'And Lady Thackeray?'

'Oh, she is quite young; only 1813.'

'What about Lady Borgia?'

'Why?' asked Chastelard, as if the conversation were taking a turn he didn't like.

'There must be so much history preserved among us,' she said eagerly. 'Eyewitnesses, continuing for hundreds of years –'

'Sometimes.'

'What do you mean, sometimes?'

'Has our father told you nothing?' he said spikily. 'If we lasted so long always, the world would be crowded with vampires, from the elders of the world to the dragonet of yesterday, like seven children trying to suckle at a single breast. But between *les chasseurs* and those who are executed and those who go mad with their own ancientry and kill themselves or vanish, it is exceedingly rare to find a vampire more than five hundred years of age.'

'But—but you said—and Livilla too, I mean, Lady Thackeray—that we have nothing to fear from death.'

'Death, *oui*, as men mean the word. The Second Death may yet claim us. But after all, what is that? Our souls are departed already, so that if the body should die, there will be no suffering; only oblivion. And that is not so bad.' He didn't sound as though he quite believed it.

Marie shivered. A gust of wind, high above them in the dark, tore a small cloud across the sign of Leo like a ragged ribbon.

On the other side of London, her brothers were also out in the cold.

'Get inside, Henry.'

'I only—'

'Now, please.'

Scowling, Henry did so, and James followed him in from the balcony. The inhospitable flow of icy air into the house was stopped as James shut and locked the French windows.

'What in God's name were you doing?'

'I was looking at the stars.'

'At three in the morning? In your night things? *Again*?'

'What concern is it of yours?' Henry snapped. 'I cannot sleep. I've been trying to for hours.'

'You'll get ill, going out in the cold like that and staying up all night. I'll have Harker send for more laudanum in the morning. Now please, go back to bed.'

'And why are *you* up and about, James? Unless you prefer to be addressed as *Baron Redglass*.'

The elder brother sighed and pinched the bridge of his nose. 'I was going over a letter sent us by the metropolitan police.'

Henry's demeanor changed instantly. 'The police? Did they find Marie?'

'No. A woman was seen in Gravesend who matched her description, but when found and interviewed her it turned out to be somebody else,' said James dismally. 'I didn't tell you about the letter because I didn't want you to get your hopes up, and clearly I was right.'

He scowled again and folded his arms, his eyes glittering. 'We should be looking for her ourselves,' he said firmly.

'Not this again,' James sighed, but his brother began to speak over him.

'Yes, *this* again! Marie is our sister, we have a right and a duty—'

'The police were created for a reason, Henry, and given this job for a reason—there is a way these things are done—'

'A way they fail to be done, more like—'

'Do you really imagine that we would be better at finding her than—'

'Yes! And I can't understand why you won't even—'

'I won't risk you as well! Especially not for a sister who might be *dead* for all we know!'

An ugly cracking sound and a roar in James' ears, like the sound of a train, were rapidly followed by horrible pain. Henry had broken his nose.

Suddenly the brothers were boxing each other, bellowing like wounded bulls. Bone, blood, and skin met with every movement; both men were fighting, not to win, but to hurt. The air was filled with glittering shards of something like ice, refracting the light of the stars and the gas-lamps of the drawing room. Freezing wind restored their choler-ridden senses to an agony of precision, and they fell apart, panting and gasping.

Slowly they realized that they were outside, and that they had gotten there by breaking the French windows. James was bent over, massaging his knee, blood running freely from his nose; Henry was erect, his left eye blooming into midnight purple, feeling the edge of his jaw gingerly. At that moment, an indignant voice split the darkness like a gunshot: 'What the devil do you think you're doing?'

James groaned. 'I'm coming in,' the voice called to them. It seemed to be a few yards away, at the gate. A few seconds later, there was a heavy clunk, and the voice had evidently picked the lock, for the gate opened and then shut again.

'My lords?' came another voice—Harker's, from inside. 'I heard a frightful noise, and—oh, my lords.' The old butler clucked his tongue.

The first voice came into view, rapidly ascending the exterior staircase on the balcony. It was William Vavasour. He looked at the Redglass brothers and asked sternly, 'What is the meaning of this?'

Both Redglass men were silent, the elder with chagrin, the younger defiant. 'Are you injured?' asked Harker.

William had moved forward to study them, and was met by resentful looks but no actual resistance. 'They'll be all right in the long term,' he said grimly. 'Come inside, gentlemen. We can sort the particulars of your quarrel once you've both been cleaned up a bit.'

They suffered themselves to be conducted to the study by their friend and the butler. The latter went to the kitchen and came back a few minutes later with hot water and a few cloths, handing one to James to stanch the flow of blood from his nose. Harker and William mopped up the various wounds, picking a few pieces of broken glass out of the brothers' skin. Harker also brought a cold compress for Henry's eye, and then set about sweeping up; William poured three brandies, handing two to his unlooked-for hosts and sitting down with one himself. The men drank in silence for a few moments. At last, he prompted, 'Well?'

'What were you hanging about for, anyway?' said Henry.

'I had an errand to make in the service of a lady.'

'A lady? That was quick,' Henry answered sourly. 'Marie's only been gone for a month.'

'It's nothing of that kind,' William replied, coloring slightly. 'An eccentric time for it, I concede, but no other would serve. And why were the two of you performing the mystery play of Cain and Abel?'

'Mind your own business,' James grumbled.

'Your answer to every question,' Henry said spitefully, 'and it's wearing rather thin.'

James glowered and opened his mouth to respond, but William broke in sharply. 'Gentlemen. Your father, *requiescat in pace*' (here all three made the sign of the cross), 'is dead, and your sister, my sometime *fiancée*, has disappeared. This is no time to disgrace yourselves with a feud—if there ever is a time for any such thing. Above all, you must be at one now.'

They sat in silence for another moment. Then, William clapped his hands against his thighs and stood up, clapping his stovepipe hat back onto his head.

'But perhaps, as you say, Lord Redglass, it's no affair of mine. I ought to be on my way in any case; the hour is late.' He drained his glass and pulled his gloves back on. 'A pleasure to see you both, gentlemen. Goodnight.'

James and Henry sat quietly for some time after he left. The clock struck half past three, and Henry stood up, still clutching the compress to his eye. 'I'm going to bed,' he muttered.

'Goodnight, Henry,' said his brother. There was no reply; the younger man shut the door with a click.

When Marie and Chastelard reëntered the manor, they found Augustus and Rimbaud deeply involved in a game of chess. At first glance, Rimbaud's position was a strong one, developed from the Dragon form of the Sicilian defense, with his queenside mounting an aggressive assault on one half of the board and Augustus' attack with white on the kingside; but as she studied the position with her quickened wits, she recognized the delicate trap that her sire had crafted. Chastelard went over to watch them, lazily sipping from a fresh glass of blood. Marie sensed someone behind her, and turned to see Miss Glastenning. Rimbaud moved his queen, and picked up his own glass.

'How can he drink that stuff?' Marie said under her breath.

'You mean wine?' asked Miss Glastenning.

Marie looked at it again, and sniffed the air. Sure enough, the hue was ever so slightly different—nothing a human would pick up on without close attention— and, from yards away, she could pick out the smell of wine amidst the blood. She opened her mouth to ask why Augustus hadn't told her at the time that the poet was receiving wine, realized what a terribly silly question it was, and shut it again.

Augustus took the black queen with his king's bishop. 'Check.'

Rimbaud studied the board, and a brief light went through his eyes as the real situation broke upon him. He sighed. 'And mate in … five.'

CHAPTER X

THE WARS OF THE MANTICORE THRONE

Let's skip a few short years of hollow peace,
Which peopled earth no better, Hell as wont,
And Heaven none—they form the tyrant's lease,
With nothing but new names inscribed upon't;
'Twill one day finish; meantime they increase;
'With seven heads and ten horns,' and all in front,
Like Saint John's foretold beast …

— GEORGE GORDON, LORD BYRON, *THE VISION OF JUDGMENT*

It transpired that the guests of the salon would be staying for a few days, so that continuous attendance on them as a semi-hostess did not bind Marie. She chose to withdraw early that night, and sat in her room, trying to think of ways to get a letter to William that Augustus could not perceive. The hopelessness of circumventing a telepath seemed insurmountable no matter which way she looked at it, but at last, she decided that she would rather risk discovery than risk losing William altogether.

She crossed to the window and shut the drapes, keeping out the pearlescent light of the approaching dawn. Then she went over to the vanity to write a reply.

She struggled with this for a surprisingly long time. Formality and informality, affection and distance, all seemed equally out of place. *Mr Vavasour* seemed safe enough to start: all right, then, start with that. *I am exceedingly grateful for your kind letter. Thank you for assuring me of my father's decent funeral.* Yes, good. He would be worried about her, so *Everyone here is*—well, they certainly weren't *most kind,* as she had been about to write, and he would see through that at once. Below her, faintly, the grandfather clock chimed eight in the morning. The thought of Lady Thackeray popped into her head, and she was tempted to add sarcastically *most well-dressed,* but it seemed incongruous to include a sneer in a reply to a condolence letter. Hmm ... *doing their best to make me feel at home,* which was not a lie, even if the idea of the relevant *everyone* as to what it meant to feel at home was a morbid one.

Now for the truly difficult bit. *Please be assured of my forgiveness. I understand the*—invidious? no, too arch; delicate? that minimized the problem; impossible? hyperbolic, and therefore paradoxically weak; hideous? true, but that word might inhibit her message of pardon ... well—*the desperate circumstances you found yourself in, not least because I am in a rather desperate state myself nowadays. I thank you for your chivalrous offer of your services; I shall certainly apply to you if*—if what?—*I find myself in need of anything. For the present, would you oblige me simply with news of my brothers? With warm regards, Miss Marie C. A. Redglass*

It was a clumsy reply, but it would do, and she was wary of writing many drafts; each one was an opportunity to slip up and let it fall accidentally into the hands of Augustus. She put the letter in an envelope and addressed it, and then realized that she had no sealing wax and no signet ring—she had been wearing her own ring when she was changed, but it was made of rose gold and had begun to scorch her finger, so she had pulled it off and dropped it somewhere, she couldn't remember where. Very well, she could do without a crest for the present. But sealing wax could hardly be dispensed with. And the only place she knew to find it was Augustus' own study.

Perhaps he would not notice.

Marie took a deep breath, if only out of habit, and went out into the passageway, to find its leftward course, down toward the staircase, flooded with deadly sunlight. Apparently Hyacinth, with her usual lack of attention, had forgotten to let down the curtains before sunrise. And the cords to let them down were on the far side of the tall, diamond-clear windows. Naturally.

She was fired with an irrational determination to get the thing done, sunlight be damned. The first step for that was wax, which meant the study, and that at least was in the opposite direction. Hopefully her sire had gone to his own room, wherever exactly that was.

She crept up the hallway like a cat, almost inaudible even to herself. One door, two, three, four, five. Here it was. She looked cautiously around the doorjamb, seeing and hearing no one within. Good. With infinite patience, she edged into the room, re-scanning it for every inch she moved forward. It was empty.

A smile of joy and relief passed over her face. Now, sealing wax. She went over to the capacious mahogany desk in which Augustus kept his writing things. As silently as possible, yet trying to work quickly lest someone come in and find her, she went through the drawers. Paper, no. Pens, nibs, and inkpots, no. Postage stamps and envelopes, no. Drawing pins, pencils, here we are! Half a dozen blocks of wax. Only one of them was scarlet; all the others were coal-black mourning wax. She decided that he was likelier to notice use on the scarlet stick, so she selected one of the black ones, rummaged further for matches, and gingerly lit a candle that stood on the desk.

At that moment, a loud rattle made her heart leap into her mouth. She froze. The sound was not repeated, so she slowly turned around, expecting to see Augustus there with a sardonic look on his face, awaiting an explanation.

There was no one there. It had probably been the wind.

Marie returned to her task. She heated the wax, dripped some onto the fold of the envelope, and blew on it slightly to cool it. That was done.

The rattle came again. She looked up quickly this time. Without visible agency, the drapes that covered the small window of the study pulled apart, and the window rattled a third time. A mad chittering, yet faint, as if coming from a great distance, seemed to sound in her brain. The poltergeist—it must be trying to open the window. She extinguished the candle, slipped the wax back into its accustomed drawer, and darted from the study.

Now then, the passageway and its windows. Might the gown she was wearing protect her? It could be seen in mirrors, so obviously vampires' clothing was unaffected by the change. But she would need gloves and a thick veil if she were to chance it.

She went back to the wardrobe in her room and rummaged, finally coming up with a muff—all the gloves were thin, decorative things, except the assorted pairs of evening gloves, which would not fit over her sleeves—and a long *crêpe* veil designed for mourning. She arrayed herself in these, re-entered the corridor, and edged up to the light.

Marie experimented, putting an elbow in awkwardly. In seconds, it was as hot as a brick oven. She jerked it back out again, nursing the burn resentfully. She wondered for an idle moment whether (even as a mortal) she could have walked an equal distance over hot coals, as *fakirs* were said to do in India. If she ran through the passage … it would hurt, but she could probably make it … Squaring her shoulders, she moved back a few paces, and took the brightly illuminated passageway at a run.

It was ferociously painful, like being stung by wasps all over, but she clenched her teeth and persevered. A moment later, she was at the top of the stairs, grimacing and gasping, her flesh as raw and tender as a skinned peach. She smiled proudly and began to descend the stairs, wincing with every movement.

'And there's no need to tell his lordship about it, all right?' she said kindly to Peter. She tried to sound pleasantly conspiratorial, but was unable to keep a note of pleading out of her voice. 'Just take it to the address here.'

The errand boy blinked up at her owlishly. 'Was there anything else you wanted, me lady?'

She frowned. 'No. Thank you.'

'Yes, me lady.' He left.

Pensive, Marie walked back toward the staircase, unconsciously keeping step with the pendulum of the grandfather clock. A deep, feminine voice interrupted her thoughts.

'Whom?'

She looked over, to see Miss Glastenning standing in the library, close to the doorway, looking out at her.

'What?' Marie said.

'Whom? The letter?' the other said serenely.

She shifted uncomfortably. 'That is my own affair.'

Miss Glastenning said nothing; she simply looked at Marie. She felt increasingly anxious (though she could not articulate why to herself), and advanced toward Miss Glastenning.

'All right, it was to Mister Vavasour. We knew each other before—well, *before*. What of it?'

'I know. I would counsel you to be careful of knowing him much more henceforth. One is apt to regret ongoing acquaintanceship with those one knew in life, later on.'

'Why?'

Silence. Miss Glastenning withdrew to the other end of the library and seated herself at a table, on which a large book lay open. Evidently she had been reading it for some time, since it was open to a page a little more than halfway through.

'The letter is sent now in any case,' said Marie, with a mixture of unease and defiance, advancing to the table herself. Then she added, 'Will you—'

'I will not tell Augustus.'

'Oh. Thank you.'

Marie ran her hands over her skirt and licked her lips. The clock struck a quarter past. She curtseyed politely and turned to go.

'That will not be enough.'

She turned around again. 'I look after myself. I can hide things from him adequately.'

'No, you don't, and no, you can't,' said Miss Glastenning placidly.

'He has taught me how to ward my thoughts.'

'Which means that he knows better than anyone how to penetrate your defenses. As you realize perfectly clearly. You need something at once stronger and more subtle.'

Marie sat down at the table. 'What do you want?'

'To help you.'

'Why? Why should I trust you?'

Unexpectedly, she smiled, and asked, '*Do* you trust me?'

A score of denials died on Marie's lips. 'Yes,' she admitted at last. She had no idea why she did, but she did.

Miss Glastenning reached into a sash around her gown. Out of it she took a little metal box, roughly the size and shape of a pyx. Holding in in her right hand, she extended it to Marie and said, 'This is, let us say, a kind of talisman. It will make telepathic defenses almost entirely unnecessary, and Augustus will not notice its effects for some time. However, in giving it to you, I am making you the protectress of a powerful object, and one that is precious to me. There are, accordingly, certain conditions for its use. I want you to repeat them back to me as I tell them to you.'

Mystified, Marie nodded her assent.

'First of all: you must never, ever open the box. Not even when you are absolutely alone.'

'Never open the box.'

'Second, you must keep it on your person at all times. It can never be allowed out of your sight.'

'I must keep it with me at all times.'

'Lastly, you must speak of it to no one.'

'I must speak of it to no one.'

Miss Glastenning nodded, as if satisfied, and placed the pyx in Marie's hand. It was curiously hot to the touch, though not painfully so. She stared at it for a moment, utterly bewildered. She looked up at her companion and asked, 'Why do you trust *me?*'

The other woman smiled again. 'A sensible question. But I have known you and your family for some time: I know what to expect of you.'

'What? How have you known us? I had never met you until the night at the palace.'

This query was ignored. 'With that in your possession, only the most talented telepath will be able to detect any of your thoughts, unless you actively broadcast them. That will hold for some time, until Augustus begins to search your mind for it.'

'Don't you mean if he begins to do so?'

'I said what I mean,' Miss Glastenning said simply. Apparently she had entirely finished with this remark, because she returned her attention to her book and was silent again. A little taken aback by the abrupt end of the interview, Marie rose, curtseyed again, and headed back up the stairs.

She examined the pyx as she walked. It was made of some plain, pewter-like substance, rather than the gold of a true pyx (since of course the Blessed Sacrament would be placed on no lesser metal). It bore a curiously solid lock as well—Miss Glastenning, presumably, had kept the key. She gave it a cautious shake, but it made no sound. Frowning, she concealed it in a pocket of her dress as she reached the top of the staircase.

The sun-splashed corridor lay before her, but this time, she was on the advantageous side. As she walked, she reached up to each cord and let down the curtains over each tall window, drowning the passage in hospitable darkness.

A few evenings later, the guests took their leave. Augustus and Marie bade them farewell together, and then went to the dining room for a late breakfast. As they drank, she recounted the conversation she had had with Chastelard in the garden to her sire.

'What was he actually talking about?'

'Surely you can work that out for yourself, *ma fleurette*,' he told her evenly. 'Consider: he was sired during the French Revolution; he is the lover of the Earl of Richmond, who happens to be the Lord Chief Justice; he speaks of Duke von Orlok only in ironies and circumlocutions; he discourses freely on the implications of a democratic and even an egalitarian society; does all that suggest nothing to you?'

'But I thought you said that Chastelard was indifferent to politics.'

'As much as myself. But he dotes on Lord Carroll, who is not; it could be argued that he, Chastelard, would canvass anyone on Carroll's behalf.'

'So—he was trying to enlist my support? For the democratic faction?'

Augustus raised his eyebrows. 'Who said anything about there being a democratic faction?'

'You did.'

'I said nothing of the kind. What I did say is that his words and actions could be taken in that way, which everybody knows.'

'So is there a democratic faction or isn't there? Is that what the Chartists are?'

'What makes you think I know anything about it?'

She scowled. 'Heaven's sake, Lord Ravenhurst, when did you become so taciturn?'

'This is not taciturnity, *mon amour*, this is evasiveness. The two are quite divergent arts.'

'It comes to the same thing,' she insisted.

'It doesn't. The one is practically an admission of guilt; the other is merely the common sense of the underworld.'

'But you seem to know practically everything about the world of vampires. Won't you tell me about this?'

'I don't know *quite* everything," he said with a twinkle in his voice. "But I do know the greatest thing.'

'What is that?'

He tented his fingers and looked at her. 'When to keep my mouth shut.'

Disconcerted, and feeling that they were at an impasse—his sophistical cleverness could run rings around her younger intellect for hours on end—Marie said, in a more subdued voice, 'Have I done something to forfeit your confidence?'

'Many things,' he replied cheerfully, 'but those were mistakes, and I expected that. You are only a dragonet as yet, after all: under my tutelage, you will become a mistress of all our arts in a very few years. I am teaching you something of those arts now. Think it out.'

She thought. Chastelard had been trying to canvass her, whatever Augustus said, or more precisely declined to say. Lady Thackeray was a favorite of the Duke and hated Lord Richmond, that was obvious. That suggested two sides at least. Doctor Tinsmith had tried to convert her to his weird, deathly church; whose side was he on? Wait—Canon Glover, he had appeared at her *début* in his capacity as Richmond's personal chaplain; that was suggestive. But her sire plainly would not answer a direct question: it seemed to be either bad tactics or bad manners to pose them among vampires. He had said before that the walls had ears. Perhaps the servants couldn't be trusted, or perhaps their minds would simply be read: a vampire could ward himself, a human servant could not. So she had to find a way to ask without asking.

'Augustus—who ruled London when you were sired?'

He smiled broadly and began to talk.

At the time he was sired, in 1347, London was ruled by a coalition government: a limited monarch, Saturninus de Ville, shared power with an ancient collection of nobles and priests. He was the first to use the title *Duke*, as he professed to be a descendant of Charlemagne himself, and therefore to be restoring the mantle of the Holy Roman Empire into England—lost since the days of Arthur, when Rome had withdrawn behind her shrinking borders on the Continent. So he claimed the title of Duke, that is, *dux*, a military commander of the Empire. The story might even be true—by all accounts, de Ville was at least three hundred years old when Augustus was sired. Miss Glastenning went back to that time, too; there was a persistent tradition that she had been a part of the household of St Edward the Confessor, but that was all before Augustus' time, and he knew little about it.

The aforementioned priests were an amalgamation of changed clerics, of whom there was no shortage in Mediæval England, with assorted cunning men and even witches. The religion they practiced was vaguely Christian in theory, though of course no sacraments could be celebrated; mostly it consisted in superstitious observances in honor of saints' days, mixed with folk customs, sorcery, and a few survivals from Druidic ritual of mostly forgotten significance. Not many vampires who had known the pagan Britain of Cæsar, Boadicea, Vortigern, and Hengist were still in existence even then.

The coalition was relatively stable, allowing for the usual machinations for hunting rights and prestige, for some decades after Augustus was changed. But in the mid-fifteenth century, paralleling or, who knew, adumbrating developments in human society, the power of Saturninus de Ville had waxed out of all proportion to that of his parliamentary cohorts. An illustrious priest, one Stephen à Tintagel, grew paranoid. In 1453, he attempted to consolidate and expand the power of the cult by siring a wealthy and devout German margrave, while the latter was on a pilgrimage at the tomb of the sainted Becket. The notion was that the wealth and Imperial connections of this noble would be employed in pressure on the blood trade, which, with improvements in transportation, was now going like a house on fire; but the margrave was so horrified by what he had become (once he had been made to understand it) that he went quite mad, and rampaged around the home counties for a year, before stowing away on a ship back to the Empire, where he began siring depraved duplicates of himself all through Silesia and Hungary and into Ruthenia; no one knew what had become of the 'Mad Margrave' after that. His luckless get had for the most part inherited his madness along with his vampirism, or so it was said, and there was a rumor that the Orthodox Patriarch of Kiev had begun training hunters about this time to deal with the crisis. In any event, this disaster robbed the priesthood of most of its prestige and influence, and tipped the scales still further in de Ville's favor.

So then Tintagel himself went a bit mad, and became convinced de Ville was scheming to destroy the priesthood altogether. He therefore began to counter-intrigue with a number of nobles and priests; and in 1499, he launched what he believed to be a preëmptive strike against de Ville, attacking the Duke's seat—which at that time lay in the South Downs, the palace that von Orlok inhabited being of later date—and, with his co-conspirators, burning the place to the ground. A score of vampires were killed, de Ville among them. The remainder of the Duke's party, enraged, seized control of the parliamentary offices, then in a secret location under the streets of Westminster, and managed to capture Tintagel and about thirty of his followers. They were put to the Second Death.

'I saw them die,' Augustus mused, his eyes glassy. 'It was at a manor outside Saint Ives; I was staying there with a noblewoman of my acquaintance. They chained them to trees on the grounds, within screaming range of the house, and left them to the sun. One of Tintagel's personal attendants, in his habit and chaplet, was chained to an immense yew not a hundred yards from my bedroom window. He was begging to be let go, saying that he had no part in the conspiracy, that he had known nothing about it. That was probably a lie. Even so … As the dawn touched his flesh, he began to scream like a frightened infant. The sunlight was searing his whole body within minutes, and finally he caught fire.'

'Caught fire?' Marie blurted out.

'Yes. That is what happens when we are exposed to the sun too long. I was perfectly safe, I was inside the house looking out at them as they burned: looking out at sunlight is safe, you simply mustn't let it actually touch you … He did not die quickly. A human suffocates in the smoke before long, if he is burned to death. For us who do not need to breathe … It was four hours before the fellow died. The yew was scorched on that side, but it survived.'

Marie shuddered. 'And was that the end of the conflict?'

The conflict, he explained, had scarcely begun. After the St Ives Massacre, as it became known, the city erupted into a full-blown civil war. A clutch of heirs presumptive had arisen—de Ville had chosen carefully in siring, and his children were tough and cunning specimens. The parliament was deadlocked, unable to obtain a majority in support of any candidate: fruitless negotiations went on for a few weeks, and then broke down, each of the eleven heirs of de Ville fighting all the others. At first there were fears that this would draw the notice of the humans, and thus inspire the increasing numbers of exorcists and witch-finders to turn their attention to vampire hunting; but as the era of the Tudors wore on and became more rent by strife of various kinds—Henry and his many wars and wives, the regencies for irrelevant Edward, the vacillations of Mary, the brilliant and carefully ambiguous Elizabeth—it provided ample cover for the civil war of London's vampires. It dragged on over sixty years, picking off claimants one by one.

In 1563, when the Black Death returned to London and prey was rendered uncomfortably scarce, a truce was reached among the five surviving offspring of de Ville. Each took a segment of London—one in the center, the other four arranged on the points of the compass—and a new coalition was, formally, established. But the prosperity of Elizabethan England led to continued instability, for every time the populace recovered and expanded, there was more to intrigue for. None of the five succeeded in eliminating any of the others while Elizabeth lived; but in 1611, the rulers of eastern and northern London were both assassinated (one by an ambitious subordinate, the other by a wandering witch-finder), and vampire society reverted to a state of open warfare.

It was during this time that Julius von Orlok—reputed to be a grandchild of the 'Mad Margrave' whose siring had precipitated the crisis more than a century before—came to England. He was frustrated by the populous fields of the Holy Roman Empire, where there were many ancient vampires with whom he could hardly compete; England, where he at first believed his great-grandsire Tintagel still dwelt, might be more hospitable to his lust for power. Undeterred by his disappointment in finding Tintagel long dead, he began to gather followers and, once he had a coterie large enough, entered the conflict with vigor. He had considerable native powers, being uncommonly strong and fast even for a vampire, and was able to frighten where alliance or bribery would not do. He it was who, in the year that Cromwell took power, sired a Cambridge divine of Anglo-Saxon blood and Puritan opinions, a certain Lazarus Tinsmith.

Von Orlok's design had been that Tinsmith, who despite his Calvinism had been known to fanatically support King Charles I, would consolidate the fragmentary remains of the priesthood and use it to bolster his, von Orlok's, political designs. He was thinking of the formidable position of ecclesiastical lords in the Empire and in France, and thought to find in Tinsmith a Cardinal Mazarin to his own would-be Louis XIV. But Tinsmith had his own ideas. Consolidate the cult he did, and took the opportunity to refashion it completely, in accord with his own severe ideas of Protestant orthodoxy. He showed no propensity to unthinkingly support all, or indeed any, of von Orlok's claims. He commenced a hunt for heretics, to whom he offered the choices of conversion or execution; none took the latter.

But in the long run, von Orlok got what he wanted anyway. Tinsmith did not hinder his sire any more than he helped him, and his power over the now disciplined, militant cult was frightening to many, who wanted to see him checked. And so, exhausted by two hundred years of intermittent war, fearful of the witch-finders' depredations, and reduced in numbers by the Great Fire in 1666, a treaty was finally reached by the vampires in the year following, and Julius von Orlok was proclaimed the Duke. To satisfy Tinsmith, and, if possible, reëstablish some measure of control over him, Duke von Orlok declared his cult the binding religion of London vampires.

Marie's head swam as she tried to disentangle the maze of plots and counter-plots, false starts and reversals. 'Who was your sire?' she asked.

Augustus gave her a twisted smile. 'In a way, no one of any consequence.'

'Do you mean—well, so far, all the vampires I have met through you have been from old families, mostly of the aristocracy. Are there vampires among the lower classes as well?'

He stared and said harshly, 'Do you suppose that I am professing descent from a line of undead serfs?'

She bit her lip. 'I didn't mean that.'

'Good.' He took a large swallow of blood. 'There are such creatures, but they've nothing to do with me.'

'So what did you mean about your sire being of no consequence?'

'Ask me no questions and I'll tell you no lies,' he said with a leer.

Marie asked him what happened after the Duke's accession. He answered that in 1696, Nigel Carroll, the son of an unknown sire, crossed over from Ireland, and was inducted into undead society in London. A little less than a century later, when the Lord Chief Justice Jonathan Eyre disappeared, Carroll (who had already been made the Earl of Richmond, when its previous lord went mad and killed himself) was chosen to replace him. Thereafter, official society had more or less the shape that it retained in 1874—save that the siring of Lady Bath took place in 1813, and her subsequent ascendancy as a favorite of the Duke began not long thereafter. She had little official position, but she did have influence with him, silly though she was, on account of her beauty.

The only other events of any consequence in the nineteenth century, he told her, stemmed from the publication of a series of anonymous pamphlets, starting in 1848 and continuing for about ten years, at intervals of a few months. They proposed the abolition of the dukedom and the institution of parliamentary government. They were nicknamed the Chartist Letters for their close resemblance to the human Chartist movement, with which of course Marie would be familiar from its periodic riots throughout the country. Von Orlok had been furious over the Letters, as well he might be, and had ordered Lord Richmond to seek out the author with all the power at his disposal; Richmond, it was said, had devoted considerably less energy and intelligence to the search than he might have done, and it was speculated by some that he was himself the author of the Letters, though there was no proof of that—naturally. Augustus knew nothing of their provenance. A minor vampire called Arden, a grandchild of the Duke in fact, was eventually charged with the crime and subjected to a chastening—a type of punishment which could be as mild as forcibly losing a finger to sunlight, or as harsh as having a fang removed; in this case it was the latter, and he had left the court in shame and (rumor reported) gone to live in Scotland. But everyone knew that Lord Arden had not written the Chartist Letters. Still, after his chastening, they had stopped.

'So,' Marie said, 'Duke von Orlok has ruled London since, er, 1667. Without successor, and with little check.'

'That is correct.'

'And—while certain of his decisions could be criticized by—unthinking persons, who might even advocate for, er, a change of government—no one could accuse you, Lord Ravenhurst, nor myself, of voicing seditious sentiments.'

Augustus' wet fangs glittered. 'How perspicacious of you, *ma fleurette.*'

Miles away, William was awake. His habitual attendance on von Orlok as a courtesan had begun to take a toll; he was often listless and fatigued, yet he almost never slept properly any more, owing to the strange hours he kept.

He sat in his shirtsleeves, smoking a pipe and reading an anonymous volume of Arthurian epic, titled (by a modern redactor) *King Arthur the Holy.* It had been lent him by a clever, flashy fellow called Wilde up at Oxford. It was an unusual, strikingly archaic telling of the story: Galahad and Lancelot were missing, and Bedivere, Kay, and above all Gawain were to the fore. It might well predate Chrétien himself, or be taken from sources that did. Even the verse form belonged to the long-neglected Alliterative Revival of the fourteenth and fifteenth centuries:

Wynd out of þe westelond wouen aboute him
As he had ryden riȝt harde vpon rouþeless Badon.
Caliburn clouen hem, crested heddes fellen
In swych scarlet as swete wyne
Flouyng in þe far feldes of fayre Camalot.

It was a wonderfully, consolingly *English* thing to read: though he enjoyed the classical poets and mythographers, and the Romantics as well, there was a rough, windswept quality to British verse to which no Greek, Latin, or French could compare. Homer came the closest; but his myth was too distant from the native fancies of a Briton to achieve the same sense of familiarity, the same feeling of digging one's fingers into the old, white earth.

The bard went on to describe the Saxon army at Badon Hill, howling to their gods and rattling their spears against their shields. The charge of Arthur's Romano-British infantry was surprisingly realistic to William, who was reading History at Magdalen, and the strategy of the Saxons was convincing, too. Whatever their other merits, Mediæval poets did not often rise to such an exact standard of realism.

The poem passed from the battle itself to the aftermath: pools of blood freezing in the moonlight; ravens, buzzards, and owls troubling the sleep of the living; King Arthur seated in his tent and having a wound in his thigh dressed by Lady Morgan. One could almost feel the frost on the polluted earth, and hear the calling of the birds.

And then came something odd. William re-read it twice to be sure he had not misprised the antiquated English; but it seemed strangely, shockingly, familiar.

Loobly wher he leyde Lytch himself awaken
For to prollen þe pasture of Mars peple.
Euer he eketh lyf endyng anoþeres,
Baryng for þe blood þe bones so whyte.
Swych schall he be swelt, sweuenes troubel,
Lyuen not, and lust, nor may he leue
Til Domes Day and deþes dien,
Except a meke mayde schall amenden his synnes.
Wedded as a widwe to þat whyte deuel
Sche schall grace get him, the graue to undoen.

His heart was beating rapidly. Had he discovered a reference to a vampire in this old epic poem—and to a traditional *cure?*

He mustn't get his hopes up. It was probably a superstition, like the convention that a unicorn could be captured by setting a young virgin in a forest and allowing the beast to find her, whereat it would be perfectly docile. For that matter, perhaps it was not even about vampires. Yet: a *lytch*, a corpse, getting up of its own accord and prowling around a battlefield? *He eketh lyf endyng anoþeres*—he increased his own life by killing other people? and did so, moreover, by extracting their blood? And if he had *sweltan*, died, why bother to add that he *live not*, unless the question were not capable of a simple answer? And what corpse would linger till Doomsday anyway? It all pointed to the creatures that he knew as vampires.

The last two lines clutched at William's chest. *Wedded as a widow to that white devil, Grace she will get for him, the grave to undo*, he rendered in his head. It sounded like the indicated remedy was for a virgin to marry the vampire and thus, supernaturally, render him mortal again. William could not help but release a gasp of fierce yearning for it to be true. What Marie would say!

But he could not tell her of a mere suspicion. What would he do, suggest that they keep their original engagement, on the strength of an Arthurian poem of uncertain provenance? A matter of this gravity demanded investigation, of the sort that justified not mere longing, but conviction. And when one came to think of it, who said it was impossible? The placid scorn of Matthew Arnold for the historical veracity of ancient poetry had only recently been countermanded by the miraculous findings of Heinrich Schliemann in the Troad, suggesting that the very hexameters of the *Iliad* might themselves be historical.

Where to start? Where could he find useful evidence of the history of vampires, and, more to the point, any tradition of vampires being turned back into humans? The easiest solution would simply be to ask von Orlok or one of the undead to whom the Duke occasionally 'lent' him; but William intuited that they would not greatly appreciate the question. The oldest vampire he knew of was Lord Ravenhurst, but William had no claim on him to justify an approach, and anyhow, that brought the whole inquiry very close to Marie.

Could Fr Weld help? He had taken it with amazing calm when William had, for the first time, made a clean breast of what he had been doing at the Manticore Palace, some months ago in the confessional. Was it possible that he knew about vampires independently? It could not hurt to ask, the next time he made his confession.

Thrilling with anticipatory joy, he continued to devour the epic, line by delicious line.

CHAPTER XI

DANSE MACABRE

While loud thunders roll, troubling the dead, Kings are sick throughout all the
earth,
The voice ceas'd: the Nation sat: And the triple-forg'd fetters of times were
unloos'd.
The voice ceas'd: the Nation sat: but ancient darkness and trembling wander
thro' the palace.
As in day of havock and routed battle, among thick shades of discontent,
On the soul-skirting mountains of sorrow cold waving: the Nobles fold round the
King,
Each stern visage lock'd up as with strong bands of iron, each strong limb bound
down as with marble,
In flames of red wrath burning, bound in astonishment a quarter of an hour.

— WILLIAM BLAKE, *THE FRENCH REVOLUTION*

The next night, Marie received a few curiously elated lines from William full of effusive thanks for her reply, and also reassuring her that her brothers were well enough under the circumstances, and in fact he had paid them a visit recently. He also asked whether she would be at the Yule Masque, and if he might speak with her there.

The Yule Masque?—this was the first she had heard of it. She decided to ask Augustus about it, and concealed the letter with its predecessor, under a false bottom she had discovered in one of the drawers of the vanity. Then she went downstairs to look for Augustus.

'What's this I've heard about a masquerade ball?' she asked as she found him in the orchidaceous conservatory, working on a copy of Titian's *Assumption of the Virgin*.

'The Yule Masque?' he asked, not looking up from his palette. 'A farcical bore. Everybody running about in costumes and saying to one another *Did you see me cut Lord So-and-so viciously just then by pretending I didn't know it was he?* I haven't attended it in forty-nine years.' He made a deliberate stroke on the Virgin's pale red inner tunic. 'Why, who told you about it?'

'Chastelard.'

'Hm. That is quite typical, he loves it. Of course, one must strut like a peacock now and again; it's in the nature of things. But I strongly prefer anything else, including nothing at all, to that particular peafowls' pen.'

'Well I think we ought to go,' Marie said boldly. 'I would rather like to attend a public event where, even if I do humiliate myself, I have a mask to hide it behind. And surely I ought to acquaint myself with the manners of … our kind more thoroughly. This seems an ideal event at which to do so, doesn't it?'

Lord Ravenhurst looked over at her, and seemed a little impressed. 'Well spoken. All right. We shall go. But I have got a condition.'

'What's that?'

'Don't enjoy it. If you did, after that it would be like living with Livilla.'

She smiled charmingly. 'I promise never to resemble Livilla unnecessarily.'

Duke von Orlok and the Marchioness of Bath and Wells were reclining together on a *chaise longue* in one of the more private rooms of the palace. One of his maidservants was dancing for them, in the grandiose Russian style. Her eyes were utterly blank as she leapt gracefully between *arabesques* and *fouettés*. She had been dancing for three and a half hours before she finally came to a standstill, shuddered slightly, and then abruptly fell unconscious to the floor. The Duke blinked and raised a hand to his forehead.

'Are you in pain, Your Grace?' asked Lady Bath tenderly.

'No, Livilla, thank you. There is always a slight tingling in the brain when one releases a dominated slave, that is all.' Two other servants appeared, and bore the stunned body of the dancer out of the room. Von Orlok reached to the table beside them and took a sip from his intricately etched glass.

'Your talents as a dancer are quite taking, Your Grace. Thank you for the display—I feel truly privileged to have seen it.'

'Flattering woman,' said the Duke fondly. 'But it was a pleasure to celebrate. To be rid of Mountjoy is a delicious prelude …'

'Are you speaking of your designs for the insolent Carroll?'

'*Jawohl.* With him chastened, my grip will be complete at last. Tinsmith will come to heel; even Fairfax will have to pay me sincere honor, unless he wants to go the same way.'

Livilla laughed. 'Delicious indeed, Your Grace, that is *just* the word.'

The Duke fixed his dour eyes on her. She kept hers downcast, a demure smile dressing her features. He leaned over and grazed her chin with desiccated fingers. 'Give me your mouth.'

She raised her face, and he kissed her. Cold lips and dead tongues crawled over one another like creatures of slime.

It was three interminable weeks before the Yule Masque came, and Marie went almost frantic with waiting. But come it finally did.

As she was getting ready, just after sunset, she realized abruptly that it was Christmas Eve. At this time back at Ramshead Place, the cook would be sending up trifle and *petits fours* and pudding with brandy butter; a great fir tree would be standing near the drawing room hearth, precariously decorated with candles and colored globes of glass; they would go to Mass in the morning, as the sun rose pale over the rooftops of London, the altar half-concealed behind the black cassocks and white cottas of acolytes, and above them, flashes of gold from the priest's chasuble and the sacred vessels, a crown of Christmas roses resting upon the statue of the Mother of God.

There was no help for it. Her family and her God were lost to her, and she to them. Perhaps, on the Day of Judgment, some mercy could be found; though she felt small hope of that. But to go to church, or even back home, now, was a further journey than to go to Doomsday.

She shook herself. Morbidity. It was probably more sensible to ignore it, if she could do nothing about it. So she told herself. She didn't feel as though she quite believed it. Nonetheless, she returned her attention to her costume.

Half an hour later, she and Augustus were on their way to the Palace. He was aloof, almost surly (though too proud to display his temper visibly). His attire for the Masque, however, was impeccable: he was dressed as the lion that symbolized his lineage, in the rich and acidic shade of green that it wore on his crest, with a great false mane like an ugly halo around his head, and gigantic teeth stretching below his exposed chin. Marie—with Miss Glastenning's amulet hidden away inside her corset—was dressed as a raven, partly in homage to the house of which she was now a member, and partly because it gave her a pretext to remain in black, for her father. The headdress itself was mostly black, with lines of blue and violet forming cryptic sigils near the eyes and a large beak extending from the center, though the bottom of the mask was open to allow speaking and drinking; with it was a pair of wings, bound by a sort of harness to her shoulders, and coming up and over them as if in flight, fashioned out of ravens' feathers (relieved with a handful of blue and purple plumes from birds-of-paradise) affixed to a black frame. She could not help but think of Icarus when she saw them.

'I shall be avenged on you, my dear,' Augustus was saying carelessly. 'I do not lightly forgive others for subjecting me to boredom. I shall do some dreadful thing and force you to participate, and you shall regret that you ever bullied me.'

'Oh, as you please, my lord,' she answered mockingly.

He continued, 'By the way, telepathy is forbidden at the Masque. You may guess at who is who, three times, and if you fail then you have to tell them who you are. But that is the only recognized way of picking one person out from another. Of course, it is never exactly good form to use telepathic powers on a fellow vampire, but at the Masque it quite ruins the game of guessing, so it is formally banned.'

'You mean, everybody will be doing it.'

'Quite.'

The landau rumbled to a halt. A footman opened the door for them, and they exited into the frigid night air, hardly taking in the expansive grounds in the dark, and walked up the steps of the palace.

The opulent interior now housed a charade of stylized and mythical beasts, trading philosophical observations.

'Oh my. Don't drink this chap, he tastes of onions.'

'I suppose that, with a certain generosity of spirit, that could be described as a sculpture.'

'Isn't she a shame?'

'Isn't that a fright?'

'Who'd have thought she'd wear *that* dress tonight?'

Some people had hardly bothered to disguise themselves: His Grace the Duke, to nobody's surprise, had clad himself as a manticore, his grinning and many-toothed face modeled after the monster on his gates; the spiny false tail and sleek folds of blood-red shantung silk that formed most of the costume seemed more natural to him than a human body. Lady Bath was likewise transparent: her owl-of-Athena costume was admittedly stunning, the bodice decorated with the plumes of peahens and strixes, its mask studded with mother-of-pearl and brown agate about the eyes ('Although the owl's reputation for wisdom is less suited to her than the fact of its blindness,' Augustus had whispered in Marie's ear when they caught sight of her); nonetheless, the great chignon in which her white-blonde hair was arranged and her imperious manner gave her away instantly. By contrast, Chastelard had so outdone himself, eerie and strange in a grey wolf mask and gauntlet-like gloves, that even Augustus did not realize who he was until he allowed Lord Richmond, whose Father Time was among the less convincing costumes, to kiss his hand.

The courtesans who had been summoned for the festival would in any case have been recognizable by their auras, but they were also distinct by dress. They had apparently not been permitted to wear full masquerade attire; they had only small masks, large enough to cover the eyes, in a small range of colors: black, silvern-white, yellow, and scarlet. These, her sire explained, signified the different strains of blood they had to offer; four main savors were identifiable, with regional and ethnic variations: earthy, saline, sweet, and savory. Ordinarily a courtesan would stick to his or her patron vampire, unless the patron consented to lend them, but tonight, anyone could dine or be dined upon as they pleased—the masks were pretended to hide identities and make anything licit. Marie did occasionally see a vampire engage a courtesan with a commanding gesture, and the latter would respond in the court's fashion, head slightly bowed, palms upward and crossed over each other, exposing the wrists. The vampire would lead the courtesan into one of the rooms set aside for the purpose, and they would emerge a little time later, the living person pallid and out of breath. They generally left the ballroom at this point and went down to the kitchens, where the palace alchemists would give them a restorative, and they would return and service two or even three more vampires before they could stand no more. Marie looked carefully, but did not see William.

The curtains of the ballroom's towering windows were thrown open to the night. At one end there sat a group of musicians; as Augustus and Marie entered, they were just concluding an *allemande*, and followed it promptly with a *courante*, in which he led her. She was rather proud of her skill as a dancer, which was improved by the greater strength she could exert now, but Augustus outstripped her even so, moving with a grace and control more complete than almost anyone else on the floor.

After they finished the *courante*, he spotted a courtesan to his liking and excused himself, and Chastelard took his place at Marie's side.

'*S'il vous plait*,' he said, extending his gauntlet as the musicians started a *sarabande*. She accepted, and they began to dance.

'The first dances are set according to the baroque suite, you see,' he explained. 'This allows the puritanical vampires to pretend that they are tired when the immodesty of the *sarabande* arrives.'

'Like Reverend Tinsmith, you mean?' she asked.

'Ha! *non, ma belle*, he never shows his face here if he may avoid. The frivolity, the license, these things he cannot abide. Yet still he sends other Precisians here to be his eyes and ears, lest he fail to have knowledge of all the things that happen everywhere …' As they performed a turn, he cast a significant glance at a pair of vampires across the room. One, a very tall fellow clad as some creature she did not immediately recognize in silver with sulphurous yellow accents, was facing away, speaking to someone. The other, who looked the right height to be Canon Glover, was standing sedately beside him, his hands folded, in the costume of a white cat.

'White seems an odd color for a vampire to wear,' she remarked.

'That will be Glover, *sûrement*. Still he thinks of himself as a Christian—*bon sang toujours ment*. But he is not completely tasteless; the cat at least might be a witch's familiar.'

Marie laughed, but turned it into a cry of surprise halfway through as Chastelard dipped her almost to the floor. His willowy figure belief his vampiric robustness, and he pulled her back up effortlessly, as the flute trembled over the harpsichord and the *sarabande* came to its climax and closed. Chastelard released her and bowed, and she curtseyed to him.

'And now, *ma douce rebelle*, I must leave you. I have promised the *gavotte* to the Baroness of St Sepulchre, and her temper—*zut alors*, I would not offend her.'

'Am I likely to?' she asked impishly.

He smiled through his wolf-mask and wagged a gloved finger at her. 'Never anger the woman who has the Italian mother; the Furies inherit through the female line.' He turned and went, leaving Marie close to the edge of the room.

'Good evening, miss,' said a hoarse voice close at hand. She started and turned: beside her loomed the Precisian cultist whom Chastelard had pointed out, dressed (as she could now see) in a silver and yellow wyvern costume. He was a massive specimen, and something about him unsettled her—perhaps his smell, which was more rankly necrotic than she was accustomed to.

'Good evening,' she replied warily.

He studied her silently for a moment. 'Lady Carmilla Borgia,' he said.

'No.'

'Miss Vivien Glastenning.'

'No,' she repeated. His large hands in their glittering, metallic gloves twitched slightly; he was standing much too close to her. She wanted to leave, but she felt rooted to the floor.

'No, of course—your hair is the wrong color. Lady Francesca fitzUrse.'

'No,' said Marie. She dropped a hasty curtsey and turned to go.

'Wait,' the stranger said, 'I have to tell you who I am. Those are the rules.'

With extreme reluctance, she turned around and waited. The wyvern bowed and pulled a card out of a concealed pocket. 'My name is Horace Dane. I am a student at the Oratory. The Reverend Doctor is deeply solicitous of his whole flock, miss,' he said ominously. 'We look forward to your formal induction into the church; and if ever you need to consult him on any matter, he resides here with his disciples.' He handed her the card, which said *The Oratory of the Divine Sovereignty*, and bore a Whitechapel address and a short series of names.

'Thank you,' she said, in a voice not intended to deceive, 'er—Brother Dane.' She curtseyed again and positively fled across the room and into a side chamber, merely to put a door between herself and the skin-crawling monstrosity.

There was a crowd of variously costumed vampires within, about six. All were huddled around a table with their heads bowed. Something large and long and black, difficult to make out in the dimness of the gas-lamps, was lying on it, and making a strange sound that she did not at first comprehend. None of the vampires took any notice of her; she peered at them, and at the thing on the table, and stepped forward for a better view.

One of the vampires raised her head. It was Lady Bath. She stared unseeingly at Marie; her mouth dripped blood. At the same moment, the thing on the table became distinguishable as a girl, about Marie's own age, being fed upon simultaneously in different places by the whole coven. She was talking, pleading, and at first Marie thought the poor girl wanted them to let her go, but when she was able to make out the words, the girl was moaning, 'Harder … harder …'

As Livilla lowered her maw back to the girl, Marie recoiled. She bolted out of the room, past the mass of dancers, through a wide passage, and out onto one of the balconies in the icy night air. She was shaking and crying.

'What the devil?' said a familiar voice. 'What is the meaning of this performance?'

She looked over to see a small clutch of figures already occupying the balcony: Augustus and two unidentifiable others. One, a male, was dressed as a peacock in iridescent blue and turquoise, with bronze and indigo accents; the other, a female, was in unrelieved black from head to toe, and held a black-lacquered fan.

'I'm sorry, my lady, my lords,' Marie stammered, 'I—I didn't know there was anyone out here, and—I'm sorry.'

'Quite,' the peacock man said sourly. 'Ravenhurst, do excuse me a moment. I find I am rather thirsty.' He stalked inside the palace.

The woman stepped forward, opening and shutting her fan with a regular *clack-clack-clack.* Marie noticed that it bore the design of a male nude and a skeleton dancing together. The woman said nothing. Her eyes could not be made out behind the mask, which was in the shape of a skull; and in her distress, a horrible fancy took hold of Marie that there was no one actually inside the costume—that it simply walked about of its own accord, endlessly and emptily watching, and snapping its fan open and shut like a pendulum.

'Lord Ravenhurst,' Marie rasped, 'may I inquire …'

She had meant to ask for an introduction, since none seemed forthcoming, but she was unable to get the words out. Something about this woman in black seemed to be draining her of the power to think. The air was pressing in on Marie, squeezing her, and suddenly she could feel scorching heat emanating from the concealed pyx at her breastbone.

'Leave us,' the woman whispered. Marie did not need telling twice.

Shivering, and dabbing the forced tears out of her eyes with her handkerchief, she wandered listlessly through the lesser rooms of the Palace, careful to avoid the ballroom and the smaller chambers lest she stumble upon another blood-orgy. Occasionally when another vampire would pass her, she would smell blood on his or her breath and draw back instinctively, wondering whether it had been taken from that wretched, perverted girl. Trying to clear her head, she found another balcony, a smaller one that she made certain was empty, and sat on the railing to look at the stars for a while.

After a few minutes, there was a faint whine of hinges. She braced herself for another scene of some kind.

'Good evening, Miss Redglass,' said William Vavasour's voice.

She looked up to see him standing in front of the French windows that formed the entrance to the balcony, smiling. His hands were folded at his waist, and he wore a small black mask around his eyes. The blaze of the chandeliers behind him would have left him a silhouette, but the starlight and moonlight silvered him. He looked like Titian's handsome portrait of Actæon.

She tried to answer, but no words would come. His brow clouded. 'What is it? What's wrong?'

'Too many things,' she said, shaking her head. 'I—oh, God, William—they're a pack of complete monsters!'

'I know,' he said quietly, sitting down beside her. He gingerly put his arm around her shoulder, seeming unsure at first whether he had the right to comfort her so intimately; but she clasped his hand in her glove, and he held her more tightly. Warmth flowed into her body from his. There was nothing adequate to say about what was happening inside, so they were silent for a while, looking up into the sky.

After a little time, William said, 'I see you persuaded Lord Ravenhurst to attend. That was quite a feat.'

She let forth a single 'Hah' of unhappy laughter.

'Marie,' he said suddenly, taking one of her hands in his—'if you will allow me to be so bold. I am deeply, truly sorry that you have to be in this underworld. I cannot express my bitter regret at not having done something to protect you, to, to ...' He began to choke on his words.

'Shh, Will, it's all right,' she said, laying her other hand atop his. 'There was nothing you could have said that I would have believed. And I've forgiven you, remember?'

'I would do anything for you,' he insisted, his eyes glistening. 'I am yours to command, heart's lady ... I ...'

Only half-aware of herself, Marie was leaning in quite close to him. She could smell the lamb and burgundy he had had for supper, could see an eyelash that had fallen on his cheek. Their fingers moved gently over one another.

Miles away, in the rectory at St John the Divine, Fr Weld lay awake. He was thinking about Mr Vavasour's confessions. The sin, simply as sin, was of course no business of his: in the confessional he was simply the mouthpiece of Christ, who alone forgave sins, blotting them out of the memory of the very Godhead; and so far as he was able to forget, Fr Weld retained no recollection of what his penitents told him, for that was between them and God—hence the seal on the sacrament. But he could not help but reflect on the broader significance of what Mr Vavasour had told him. It implied a commerce between realms that he had thought impossible, and multiplied the number of creatures that ... there was no use beating about the bush in the privacy of his own mind, was there? Vampires.

He shifted in his bed. Every day, he saw bread transformed into the Body of a Man, and wine into the Blood of his God. He did not lightly consider things to be impossible. But, until a few months ago, he would have considered stories of vampires to be imaginative fiction, superstitious hysteria, or lunacy. The obvious lucidity and sound temperament of Mr Vavasour (apart from this particular besetting sin), however, seemed to forbid that interpretation.

And it did have an eerie accord with certain unsettling observations of his own, in the rookeries of the city. He had seen things at times, as he rose in the small hours of the morning to recite Matins and Lauds before opening St John's for Mass: a vagrant grabbing a bat out of the air with inhuman precision, and then licking his lips and stealing into an alleyway with it; a pale young boy reciting a blasphemous litany outside his window in the dark; a woman in black, darting through the streets alone, and clapping her hands over her ears at the sound of church bells. Nothing conclusive, and yet nothing that he felt able simply to dismiss.

The priest wondered whether he might consult Archbishop Manning about it. He was the bishop of Westminster, after all, and an erudite, holy man. He ran mentally over what he knew from outside the confessional; too little, much too little. Would the Archbishop dismiss him as a madman, perhaps even deprive him of his faculties as a priest? That would do nobody any good, Mr Vavasour least of all. There *must* be some way of finding hard evidence.

He sighed and turned onto his side, murmuring a few phrases from the Litany of the Sacred Heart, and tried to sleep.

'Fascinating,' remarked the Lady with the Black Fan. 'She seemed so ordinary at first.'

'She was,' Augustus said. 'Aside from her beauty, and her voice.'

'She sings?'

'Excellently. She is a bit shy about it, but she possesses a sweet, gossamer timbre, without too much *coloratura*.'

'In other words, just the sort of soprano that rarely survives the transformation,' said the other vampire with satisfaction. She picked up a champagne flute half full of blood from the balcony railing. 'I want her support.'

'I don't understand. Marie is so young.'

'And my designs are not,' she said. '*Augusto*, be sensible. When was the last time you encountered an infant telepath, any telepath, with the raw power to withstand *me*? You train your *dragotte* well, but not *that* well, and certainly not that quickly.'

'She is quite gifted. But I—'

'*Quite gifted*,' the Black Fan scoffed. 'And Dante Alighieri was *quite gifted* at finding clever sets of rhymes. I repeat, I want her on my side, *figlio*. And what I want I'll have.'

Augustus lowered his head. 'Must this be done?'

'Surely you have not developed a perverse affection for His Grace.'

He made a dismissive noise. 'I fear the consequences of the struggle, *Madre*. How can we be sure Livilla will both get power and retain it? Everyone will know she is a puppet.'

'She will get power, and retain it, with you and me making it happen. All the more reason to enlist your new daughter's support as an enforcer; if it comes to open violence, as I think it probably will, *she* could tip the scales.'

Augustus said nothing, looking out gloomily over the grounds.

'Look,' said the woman. 'I have kept von Orlok in power for over two hundred years, even despite the major blunder of his siring Tinsmith. That move, combined with von Orlok's own hypocrisy about religion, doomed the incipient alliance between the monarchy and the cult the moment it was made—and yet, thanks to me, here they stand, still looking like fast friends.'

'While Tinsmith makes backstairs deals with the Chartists,' he muttered.

'Which is what Chastelard is *for*, as you very well know,' she answered firmly. 'It was a great piece of luck that he fell in love with Lord Richmond when he did, so we could keep all the powers that be in the family. In any case. It has required all of my cunning to keep the current regime afloat, and as I have told you several times, I have come to find it a tedious exercise. I want a new power. Also I want the chance to melt the flesh from von Orlok's bones; really *new* sensations are too rare, my dearest, far too rare.'

'Do you really believe it will be easier to keep Livilla afloat than him?'

'Of course. Livilla is compliant. It takes wits to deal with him, to keep him from ruining himself with a proud tantrum. You can see that. And as for everyone knowing she is a puppet, why should that matter? They will assume that you, or Richmond, or one of the other noble ladies, hold the strings; not I.'

The Black Fan set down her glass again. 'Get your daughter's support. Do not tell her much; nothing, if you can help it. Just see to it that her thoughts and sentiments are all on the side of monarchy, and when the time comes she will do what is needed.' She snapped open her fan, holding it by her left ear.

Augustus bowed as one dismissed from a royal audience. '*Si, Madre.*'

Marie and William pulled gently apart from their kiss, her hand resting on his chest, his on the nape of her neck.

'Oh, Will,' she said softly. 'What are we to do?'

'I don't know.'

'I wish we could just, just run away, and hide from all of this.'

A sudden light came in William's eyes. 'Well—why can't we?'

'What?'

He repeated, 'Why can't we? We can hide. Take ship to the Continent, or to America. People do, all the time. I have the money we would need—my great-grandfather settled a good sum on me in his will, and I had set it aside anyway to start a family with. I would be honored to use it for your benefit.'

She looked into his eyes, bright and grey as the sea. 'What exactly are you saying?' she whispered. 'Do you mean …?'

He slid from the railing into a kneeling posture before her. 'Marie—my lady—I asked you, once before, if you would consent to marry me. I dishonored the trust that you placed in me then. But if you have found it in your heart to forgive me, and if, by doing so, I may be of greater service to you, I beg you leave to ask again for the honor of—'

'Good evening,' said a bass voice. The pair started and rose. Before them was the blood-red manticore that was Duke von Orlok. He moved with such quiet that it was impossible to tell how long he had been watching them.

'Good evening, Your Grace,' Marie managed in a strangled voice. 'What a pleasure.'

'My reputation precedes me, I see,' he said with false ruefulness. 'My masques never seem to come off. But let me see … You are *Fräulein* Redglass, *Burggraf* Ravenhurst's daughter, I believe.'

'Indeed I am, Your Grace.' She dropped a deep curtsey.

The Duke stepped quite close to her, till she could smell a tinge of blood on his tongue. She was petrified. William, at whom the Duke had not yet even looked, was standing with head bowed, his wrists crossed and upward-facing, court-fashion. Von Orlok leaned forward until his face was almost touching Marie's, and spoke softly.

'Filth. On your lips. You need a napkin.'

She was utterly still. Were there laws about how vampires and humans were permitted to interact? Would she be punished? Would William?

Without taking his ghastly eyes off her, the vampire spoke again. '*Mein hure.*'

'Your Grace,' William replied promptly, flushing visibly in the dark.

'I am rather thirsty. Come.'

'Yes, Your Grace.'

The Duke went back inside. William clasped Marie's hand for a fleeting moment, eyes shimmering with humiliation, and was gone. She turned away from the palace, looking at the dim, chill expanse of the grounds without seeing it. For the first time she could recall since her change, the night felt freezing cold.

At half past four, with the dancing and drinking still going strong in the greater halls of the Manticore Palace, the green lion came to find the black raven and take her back to their own manor.

She was sitting in the palace chapel, into which she had wandered about half an hour before. It was a large, whitewashed room, spacious enough to seat as many as five hundred worshippers. It was full of simple wooden pews, from the back all the way to the chancel rail, broken in the middle by the nave. Beyond the rail was a long wooden table, covered by a white cloth, and a lectern to the side. A second and shorter lectern was on the hither side of the chancel rail. A large book lay open on it—printed, without illuminations; Marie assumed it was a Bible. The rest of the room was bare: there were no windows, paintings, or statues anywhere, no finial carvings on the pews, no choir loft.

It was the shape of the place that had arrested her attention. When she first looked in from the outside, it appeared to be cubical. As it did not seem specially interesting from this cursory glance, she turned to go, but as she did so, the proportions of the room seemed to slide and twist, and all the angles went acute or obtuse. She looked again. Again it seemed a perfect cube, but as she stared longer, her confidence wavered. Its semblance of Euclidean exactitude, she became convinced, was a mirage. The geometry of the place was *wrong*: it was hard to say exactly where and how, but it was; that corner looked like a ninety degree angle, if you looked at it directly, and the lines that came out of it looked like perfectly straight lines, but if that were true the rear wall could hardly meet *that* wall the way they did; the table was clearly flat, but the cloth on it behaved as though the surface were somehow concave; this wall and that wall were the same height, as not only æsthetics but even physics predicted, and yet the ceiling told the eye that it was slanted. Augustus found Marie seated in one of the pews close to the entrance, examining the eerie space.

'If you've finished not praying, mademoiselle, I should like to go home.'

She nodded and stood up. 'No choir?'

'Does the Reverend Doctor seem to you like the sort of fellow who would approve of anything so ornamental as music?'

They walked out. 'I don't like that place,' she said. 'I don't know why it had me so fixated.'

'It has an arcane structure. The student of architecture or of geometry can scarcely help but be fascinated by its quiet defiance of mathematics.'

'I thought you said,' she remarked quietly as they reached the door of the palace, 'that His Grace was an atheist.'

'Not an avowed one,' Augustus said impatiently. 'Almost none of us are *avowed* atheists. The cult is too powerful, and as I told you, the Duke gave it a decidedly privileged position. Since the subject has come up, I may as well tell you that I have postponed your own induction into it rather too long; that will have to be seen to, soon.'

'I won't join any cult,' she told him stubbornly as he helped her into the landau. 'Not for anything. I'd sooner die.'

'I don't doubt it, but that won't do you much good now,' he quipped. 'Anyway, you don't have to *mean* the words, you only have to say them.'

'That's even worse!' she cried.

'Oh, shut up,' he said testily.

They rode in silence for a few minutes; then, to make peace, Marie asked who had designed the palace chapel.

'His name would mean nothing to you. A talented fellow, but when he had finished building the chapel the Duke ate him. He has a touch of Ivan the Terrible that way.'

She nodded, and then asked, a little more hesitantly, 'Who was that woman in black? The one with the fan.'

'Oh, her. An old friend.' He said no more.

'Do you know,' she said after a little time, 'I believe I've come round to your way of thinking.'

'How's that?' he asked.

'I hate parties.'

Her sire smiled.

'*Hier raus*,' the Duke said. '*Schnell.*'

William bowed and re-buttoned his shirt, adjusting his waistcoat as he left the drowsily half-lit chamber. Hot, prickling shame ran up and down his neck. It was always like this, and he always came back for more—being fed upon gave a rush more powerful than a fencing match or a hunt. During the act, he felt drugged and ecstatic. Afterward, self-disgust set in; but the memory of that self-disgust always weakened eventually.

At least he had also had another, better reason to come to the palace tonight. His pallid face reddened a little as he walked down the stairs to the kitchen, gripping the banister tightly to avoid stumbling. The kiss he and Marie had shared had been more than he had dared to hope to receive from her, ever again.

Could he rescue her, and himself, from this nightmare kingdom and its horrible pleasures and dangers? His mind went back to the haunting lines of *King Arthur the Holy*, and he was inflamed with resolve to see them proven right. If they were, the two of them could marry before they left—there were a few priests in London who could be relied upon to perform, ah, *discreet* marriages—and that would allow them to obtain new traveling papers for Marie, which would make them harder to track if anybody tried to do so. Lord Ravenhurst had been known to travel on occasion, and of course there were the Redglass brothers … He could never separate her from her brothers permanently, but he could not risk having them try to keep her in England, either, where it was so unsafe for her. Better to summon them to the Continent. Switzerland, perhaps. Or better, Austria-Hungary, which was tucked still further away from the British Isles, and was besides overwhelmingly Catholic, which would make it a hospitable environment for them as recusants. Probably with plenty of vampiric apotropaics, given Vienna's character as the gateway to Eastern Europe; likely some solid, earthy, soundly superstitious peasantry, too. How much money would they need for travel? Let's see. There would be a fee for the marriage license, and they would need private cars on the trains, and if—as seemed probable—they would be obliged to live abroad, he ought to see about getting Marie a proper German tutor …

He needed his wits about him, to think all this out properly. He gripped the banister more tightly and increased his pace.

CHAPTER XII

THE TOWER OF SLAUGHTER

The worlds whole sap is sunke:
The generall balm th'hydroptique earth hath drunk,
Whither, as to the beds-feet, life is shrunke,
Dead and enterr'd; yet all these seem to laugh,
Compar'd with mee, who am their Epitaph.

Study mee then, you who shall lovers bee
At the next world, that is, at the next Spring:
  For I am every dead thing
  In whom love wrought new Alchimie.

—JOHN DONNE, *A NOCTURNALL UPON S. LUCIES DAY*

Augustus and Marie alighted from the carriage, and he sent Howard to stable the horses. As Godalming let them into the house, the grandfather clock chimed a quarter past five.

'I think I shall retire early tonight,' Augustus said. '*Bonjour.*' He kissed Marie's hand.

A thundering noise came out of the library. The door, close at hand, was shut, but it began to rumble and shake, as though someone were beating on it with angry fists. Augustus sighed deliberately and rolled his eyes.

'The poltergeist. I shall have to put it to sleep. Don't let me keep you, please.'

Marie opened her mouth to ask how he dealt with the spirit, but he was paying her no attention. Rather than going upstairs, she lingered, watching from the foyer. He opened the door: one of the smaller tables was hovering in the middle of the room, closer to the ceiling than the floor. Around it was a revolving circlet of books, like a parody of the rings of Saturn. This ring was expanding every second, as more and more volumes were flung violently from the walls and into its rattling course. The door shuddered on its hinges in a rough rhythm, and the drapes on the library windows opened and closed together with each shudder. The jingling of metal against metal, as the curtain hooks scraped along the bars that supported them, reminded Marie irrationally of a music box.

Striding confidently into the bedlam, Augustus stood directly beneath the levitating table and raised his hand. Though she was not yet skilled enough to see how it was done, she could feel him exerting prodigious telepathic force, and the spectacle slowed to a standstill, holding itself tremblingly in place for a few seconds; then, all at once, everything fell to the ground or stood limp and inert. Augustus caught the table above his head with one hand, and nimbly set it down again in its proper place. With a vexed air, he began to shut the curtains and pick up the books.

Marie advanced to help him, but as she reached the threshold he said, without looking up, 'I will gather them. *Bonjour.*' Mystified and a little chastised, she went up to her room.

She rose from her daylight lethargy a little earlier than usual, and went down to the library. It was wholly still: not so much as a rap came from the poltergeist. She traversed the floor like a ghost herself, her feet silent in their slippers and invisible beneath the hem of her skirt. Finding the copy of Donne's *Songs and Sonnets*, she decided on a whim to let it fall open where it would, and it found *The Expiration*. She read it aloud to herself:

'*So, so, breake off this last lamenting kisse,*
  Which sucks two souls, and vapors Both away,
Turne thou ghost that way, and let mee turne this,
  And let ourselves benight our happiest day,
We ask'd none leave to love; nor will we owe
  Any, so cheape a death, as saying, Goe;
Goe; and if that word have not quite kil'd thee,
  Ease mee with death, by bidding mee goe too.

Oh, if it have, let my word worke on mee,
  And a just office on a murderer doe.
Except it bee too late, to kill mee so,
  Being double dead, going, and bidding goe.'

A palpable hit, she thought. The wrenching memory of her father welcoming her home for the last time, and the bewildering roar of images that followed, in which she could distinguish almost nothing— *Whether I suffered, or I did*, she added wryly to herself, quoting Coleridge … Yet the truth was that she did not have the energy to live in perpetual grief. What then?

She turned back firmly to the beginning of the volume and began to read from there. When she finished, she passed on to William Blake's *Jerusalem: The Emanation of the Giant Albion*, which she had attempted before but been defeated by. Its imagery was too confusing and secretive. Now, with more time at her disposal, she hoped to be able to make something out of it.

Around seven, Augustus came and found her. '*Ah, ma mignardise, bonsoir.* I hope you had a pleasant rest after the Masque.'

'I did, thank you.'

'Would you care to breakfast?'

They went to the dining room and were brought glasses of blood. 'By the way, *ma fleurette*,' he remarked as they began to drink, 'I have arranged my revenge upon you.'

'Oh? When is it?'

'The night after next.'

'And am I to know what it is?' she inquired.

'Certainly not.'

'Very good.'

'Do you still sing much?' he asked her. 'You sang for your supper, of course, but I don't recall hearing your dulcet tones often since then.'

She replied that it rarely occurred to her, especially since breathing was no longer normal.

'Oh, that doesn't make any odds. You can breathe exactly as you choose, and in fact being dead can make you a better singer, since you need not worry about straining your lungs and throat. One or two operatic *virtuosi* have been vampires.'

'I see. I wouldn't mind taking it up again, if it please you.'

'If it please you, *mon petit chou.* I should like you to be happy, whenever it does not conflict with my own amusement.'

'Naturally. Are there any instruments in the house?'

'Alas, nothing but an ill-tuned pianoforte. I have not indulged much in music since Chastelard left; I turned more to sculpting and painting. Lady Borgia has quite an array of instruments, some of them venerable and all punctiliously maintained. You could practice with her. And it would ingratiate you with the palace clique, who are great music lovers.'

Marie grimaced. 'Is that necessary?'

'For the moment, yes,' he said heavily. 'Everyone is being frightfully boring and pretending that they care what the Duke thinks, and one must always do what everybody else does. Of course, it is better to have him as the locus of power than nothing at all, don't you agree? But it is dull nevertheless to have to involve oneself. Still, all the more reason to do so through something that is pleasing in its own right. *A thing of beauty is a joy forever.*'

Marie smiled. 'Chastelard quoted that too. Do you sing? Or did you? You seem to have a fine voice.'

'On occasion. I was once offered the part of Don Giovanni by the Paris Opera.'

'Really? And did you take it?'

He shook his head. 'It was when I had just sired Chastelard, in 1790. I wanted time at my disposal to educate him. Besides, Paris was becoming dangerous as the Revolution took hold; such gentlemanly gentlemen as ourselves would have been regarded as prime targets before long, even if we were taken for mortals. Still, I seduced and nearly exsanguinated the fellow who offered me the part, so in a way I did play Don Giovanni.'

Marie half-smiled, unsure whether to laugh.

'Oh, he lived,' Lord Ravenhurst said dismissively. 'Though, the city being what it was at the time, I cannot guarantee how long. You have not touched your glass, my dear, is everything quite all right?'

She picked it up and took a sip, the familiar heady sensation flowing through her. 'Mere absent-mindedness, Augustus.'

At Ramshead Place, James was kneeling on a prie-dieu before the altar of the family chapel. It bore white flowers, candles, a wooden crucifix, and two icons: one depicted the Assumption of the Virgin, the other St Edward the Confessor, from whose line the Redglasses claimed a distant descent. A book was open on the slanted shelf before him, and he was drumming it with his fingers.

The chapel door opened and shut, and Henry knelt beside his brother. 'I'm sorry I'm late.'

James did not reply, but moved the book so they could both read it. He made the sign of the cross over his heart with his thumb and pronounced, '*Converte nos, Deus, salutaris noster.*'

'*Et averte iram tuam a nobis,*' Henry replied.

'*Deus, in adjutorium meum intende.*'

'*Domine, ad adjuvandum meum festina.*'

'*Gloria Patri et Filio et Spiritui Sancto.*'

'*Sicut erat in principio et nunc et semper …*'

The well-worn Compline prayers flowed fluently over their lips. Outside, a few snowflakes were falling, and an ornamentation of hoarfrost had begun to form on the window panes.

The evening of the promised revenge, after a light breakfast, Augustus departed, saying that he had business to attend to, but that he would see Marie later that night, and that some guests would begin to arrive about ten o'clock. She went to the library and nestled into her favorite chair to continue her laborious but pleasant reading of Blake. Seven wore into eight, and eight into nine, and her mind wandered a little. She was thinking of music. Carmilla Borgia was rather a boring specimen, but she was at least considerably less terrifying than most other vampires; it might be nice to spend time with someone like that.

Her mind suddenly returned to William, and she glowed. *He still wanted to marry her.* Was it possible for them to escape, as he was planning? Would she have the nerve, if it was? She felt sure she would; nothing was holding her in England in any case, except that it was the land of her birth, and she could give that up for the sake of—in a sense—coming back from the dead.

Until William died, she realized. There he would be, getting older and weaker, and there she would be, still fresh-faced and cold as snow. No children. It would not be so embarrassing, perhaps, as *him* remaining forever young while *she* became a crone; but all the same, she could see in her mind's eye the conversations where they would decide that it was time to start pretending he was her father instead of her husband, and then her grandfather instead of her father … Marie could give up England, but could she do it only to do that to him? She laid a hand to her mouth, wondering.

A loud knocking startled her from her reverie. At first she thought it was the poltergeist, but then she could hear Godalming opening the door and receiving a visitor, who turned out to be Paul Chastelard.

'You are eagerly awaited,' the butler was telling him. 'His lordship is in the usual place.' (Odd, she thought, that she had not noticed his return.) 'Mademoiselle Redglass is in the library, if you would care to greet her first.'

'*Charmante*,' he replied, and came into the library, dressed in sleek black silks that made him look luxuriant as a cat. Marie rose, and he took her hand and planted a light kiss upon it. '*Ça va, ma soeur?*'

'I am well, thank you,' she said. 'And you, Monsieur?'

'*Je suis bien, ma belle diablette, je suis bien.* Our father Augustus has instructed you about the evening, no doubt.'

'He hasn't, actually. He only said he would revenge himself upon me for persuading him to attend the Yule Ball, and that it was to be a surprise.'

Chastelard's face opened in a mischief-making smile. 'Ah, then it is not mine to say what comes. So does he amuse himself. Only do not be afraid, and let things develop as they will, and it shall be an excellent night, *mon ami.*' He laid his hand lightly on her arm, and then turned and went. A little puzzled, Marie returned to her book.

It was not long before another guest had arrived: the Baroness of St Sepulchre, Lady fitzUrse. Marie gave her a curtsey as she entered the library. She too was dressed in black, with a *crêpe* veil. Marie had known the Baroness slightly before her transformation; it was on the strength of her presence that poor William had supposed Augustus would not harm her, not realizing that the Baroness too was a vampire. Her mannerisms had nothing of the lingering, sensuous quality that characterized Chastelard: she gave rather the impression of a woman accustomed to being listened to, and disinclined to waste energy in unnecessary talk. She exchanged courtesies with Marie, a touch brusquely, and then asked her where Lord Ravenhurst was.

'I don't rightly know, my lady. Monsieur Chastelard arrived a few minutes ago, and Godalming showed him in—he said something about *the usual place.*'

'I see. Have the Dees arrived yet?'

'Er, no, my lady. I believe not. I have not met them.'

'Very well.' She left, snapping open a broad black fan as she did so.

A few minutes after ten, the mysterious Dees still absent, Godalming came to the library and said that Augustus had sent for Marie. He led her to the spiral staircase that ran from the ground floor to the tower that sat in the middle of the western wall of the manor; hitherto she had only seen the tower room used for *séances*, but surely that would be too cruel a revenge, even for him. It was a claustrophobic and chilly space, with dozens upon dozens of steps, insulated only by tapestries that appeared to date to the fifteenth century. After minutes of climbing, she came to the top, where there was no door—only a thick, heavy curtain. She pulled it aside and entered.

The exquisiteness of the topmost, circular room formed a stark contrast to the rude staircase that led to it. The floor was of grey-veined marble, as were the engaged columns that marked the walls at intervals, alternating with mahogany boiseries. There was no chandelier, but nine wrought iron candlesticks formed a circle at the edge of the room, providing enough light to read by. The exposed flames panicked her for a second, but she controlled herself with an effort. Marie knew, having seen the room before, that there were windows in it, but these were each blocked by a painting hung carefully in front of it, hiding it completely. One was a copy of Titian's *Orpheus and Eurydice*; the next was of John Everett Millais' drowning *Ophelia*, splashed with greens and greys and small, colorless flowers; one was a reproduction of Pieter Huys' chaotic, Bosch-like *The Harrowing of Hell*; and the fourth was a treatment of Pluto's abduction of Proserpina, which she recognized but could not place. The round table was draped with a dark cloth, and surrounded by six chairs, in three of which sat the other vampires, all in black. Even Augustus had not a speck of the color he usually displayed so proudly.

Several curious objects were placed about the room. To Marie's right as she entered was a lectern, on which lay an immense Latin Bible opened to II Maccabees 12, with a quartz crystal sitting on its pages. On the opposite side of the chamber was a little pillar, bearing a vase holding a single lily in bloom; she rightly guessed that the water had been mixed with vampire blood to keep the flower fresh. On the far side of the table, behind Augustus, were three more pillars. One bore a small dish with a fine, whitish substance in it, the next a handbell, and the third a steel knife. In the center of the table was a glass bowl, full of a cloudy, greenish substance that she judged from its aroma to be olive oil.

'Ah, Marie. Please, sit.' Augustus indicated the chair to his left.

She didn't move. 'A *séance*,' she said bluntly. 'You're holding a *séance*.'

'I am. You are to assist me.'

'I won't.' Her submerged wrath with her sire rose like Leviathan out of the sea. She ought to have known, once she had heard that his revenge was to take place in the tower—but she could scarcely believe even he would sink to this. After he had deceived her with this exact device, to require her to assist in the corruption of another innocent? How dare he even ask her?

Augustus said sweetly, 'I was not asking, my dear. I did warn you that I would avenge myself upon you. Sit; our two seekers after the eternal wisdom will be arriving shortly.' A soft rustle of laughter passed through the vampires.

'I won't,' she repeated more loudly.

His smile never faltered. *Like the Cheshire cat*, she thought giddily. He rose, went about the table, gripped her by the arm, and marched her to the chair beside his, forcing her down into it.

'You will.'

She sensed a telepathic pressure mounting upon her. Cursing herself for having left the pyx on the vanity (she had taken it out the previous night, having been so disconcerted by its burst of heat the night of the Masque), she tried to ward herself, but she could feel the tendrils of Augustus' mind already sliding into hers, and she wasn't strong or dextrous enough yet to pry him out. Afraid he would find her thoughts about herself and William, she said hastily, 'All right. I'll do it.'

The pressure ceased at once, and he withdrew. 'Now then.'

He began explaining the means he used to fake his *séances*: unlike the notorious Fox sisters, they could not rely on cracking knuckles, so a small metal box with pliable sides was fastened under the table, where it could easily be reached without drawing notice in the semi-darkness. Manipulation of the size and stiffness of his vocal cords, attained through practice, sufficed to produce the hoarse, eerie voice of the medium's control. Faking ectoplasm was more of a challenge, and required an expenditure of blood to stimulate the mucous glands, but it could be done; he saved it for the more skeptical guests.

The pair who were visiting tonight, a Mr and Mrs Edward Dee, were definitely not skeptical. Nor were they trying to communicate with a lost loved one, as Marie had been guiltily doing. Like the self-styled necromancers of old, they were simply thirsty for hidden knowledge, and for the harrowing glamor of cryptic rites, and were willing to credit almost anything that Augustus tossed their way. Any control would do, provided that it was the spirit of someone possessed of adequate mystique; Cleopatra was a great favorite, and he had also made use of Nostradamus, and of the seventeenth-century French poisoner and witch, La Voisin. Marie's role, working in tandem with Lady fitzUrse, would be to telepathically move Mr Dee into a state of extreme susceptibility to all suggestions, while Augustus and Chastelard did the same to Mrs Dee. In this semi-hypnotized state, practically anything would seem plausible—even being fed upon.

A minute or so after he had finished speaking and summoned them all to silence, the heavy curtain was pulled aside again by a man. He was perhaps in his late twenties, tall, fair, and square-jawed; presumably this was Mr Edward Dee. His wife came in behind him, slender, with black locks of hair hanging loose. Both were dressed as if in mourning. Marie set her mouth firmly. Augustus had said that they rarely killed. They would feed, and then it would be over—probably he would confuse their memories somehow to protect the secret. *Just get through it,* she thought.

But she could not help remembering the room as it had been on Hallowe'en night a mere two months ago.

Marie pushed the curtain aside, and there were Viscount Ravenhurst and Baroness fitzUrse. 'Mademoiselle,' Augustus said warmly, rising. 'We shall make another effort tonight. I feel certain that your mother's spirit will not be barred from us this time; she has a great love for you. It shall triumph.'

She thanked him and seated herself, trembling a little. She knew it was wrong to be here; the Inquisition itself had pronounced Spiritualism to be a mixture of fraud and commerce with evil spirits, and she burned with shame at the violation of her conscience. Yet the messages that Lord Ravenhurst had shared with her had given her such hope, just when her belief in the next life was wavering— surely that could not be the work of a demon. If she could only hear her mother's voice, once more, from Heaven or even from Purgatory, she would be comforted enough to return to obedience.

Now Augustus was introducing her to the Dees, saying that she was his niece. Marie and Mrs Dee exchanged courtesies, and Mr Dee took her hand and said 'How do you do,' in a deeper voice than he had been using. Augustus indicated the chairs that they should take: Mr Dee to Marie's left, with the Bible at his back, and Mrs Dee on the opposite side, so that the table alternated between males and females.

'If I may have a volunteer for the drawing of the blood,' Augustus said, 'and then we can begin.' Mr Dee put out his hand, and Augustus made a nick in his proffered forefinger with the steel knife, and flicked a few drops of blood into the bowl of olive oil. He smiled reassuringly at Mr Dee and continued:

'Lay your hands flat on the table, everyone, so that your smallest fingers are touching those of each person next to you.' Marie did so, trying to keep her breathing steady. The other women and the medium himself seemed much more relaxed. 'Concentrate upon the bowl, and keep as quiet and still as possible ...'

The edge of Mr Dee's finger brushed Marie's, and she came back to the present with a start. Her sire gave her a surreptitious glare—the Dees both had their eyes closed, so it hardly mattered. She mouthed an abbreviated apology at him. He looked at the faces of his guests and said in a solemn, soft voice, 'Is there a spirit here who wishes to speak to us?'

Mr Dee stifled a cough. His wife's eyes flickered, but she kept them shut. Their eagerness was palpable, flowing out of them in involuntary psychic waves; and something else was detectable in the husband, something even less savory than a curiosity so ravenous it would turn to necromancy to satisfy itself. Something with a hot, jagged, twisted feel to it, clinging to him, like a parasitic fungus: a perverse and passionate appetite, secretly cherished, inflaming his brain and body with lust. She nearly gagged with revulsion.

'I sense something,' said Augustus in a hoarse whisper. 'There is a spirit here.'

'Who is it?' Marie asked faintly. 'Is it my mother?'

'Hush, mademoiselle. Let it make itself known in its own time.'

She restrained herself and waited. The pause lengthened, and she was losing patience, but then a strange calm stole over her. It seemed to settle on her from without, lulling her mind and pacifying her nerves. She need not be afraid. Lord Ravenhurst was an experienced medium; he knew what he was doing.

Mr and Mrs Dee seemed noisy and fidgety to Marie, until she realized that in fact they were being extremely rigid for mortals. What was making them seem so loud was the absolute stillness of the dead that surrounded them. The aroma of blood, discernible over the olive oil, was making her fearfully thirsty.

'We welcome thee, O spirit departed into the blissome realm. Wilt thou commune with us?'

Acting as one, Augustus and Chastelard began telepathically radiating their wills into the young woman. Lady fitzUrse began to do the same to her husband, and Marie, suppressing her disgust, moved to assist her. She found that she could not help but despise this young man, so foolish as to be almost beneath pity: even apart from the operations of the vampires, she could clearly feel him making every effort to be complaisant and credulous, pushing back every skeptical instinct.

A single, loud rap startled the table.

They waited for another rap, or for a voice, but none came. Ravenhurst groaned, as if in pain, and said, 'Something is restraining the spirit's power of speech. There is another presence here—another spirit, I think. Or a force.'

'What is it?' Marie breathed.

The nobleman's eyes drifted dreamily halfway open. 'Mademoiselle Redglass, am I right in thinking that you wear a scapular?'

'Yes," she said. 'I've worn the Brown Scapular of Our Lady of Mount Carmel ever since I was a little girl.'

'I am afraid you must lay it aside for the course of the séance.*'*

'But—my lord, I couldn't do that.'

'I do not make this request lightly,' he said, his face and voice serious, like one who asks another to make a sacrifice that neither one of them desire. 'But the sacramental power that inhabits that sacred object is too strong for this spirit to speak to us within its orbit. Take it and lay it on the lectern, beside the Bible; that is no disrespect, and will give the spirit adequate space to operate.'

'But I can't,' she protested. 'The scapular must be worn continuously. That is one of its conditions.'

'No matter what?'

Marie wavered. She did take the scapular off to bathe and to sleep—she never could sleep with something lying across her throat. And Lord Ravenhurst, though not a Catholic, clearly understood its importance, both in itself and to her personally. He would hardly ask her to do it if it were really unnecessary. And this spirit could be her mother. The only way to find out was to take off the scapular. Take off the scapular.

'Your Majesty? Cleopatra the Queen?' said Augustus. 'Is that you?'

'Is something wrong?' whispered Mr Dee. 'She has never had trouble speaking with us before now.'

'I don't think there's enough blood in the bowl,' Chastelard whispered back, but the medium gently told them to be quiet.

'La Voisin, is that you?' he asked; and then, with a great false gasp, 'Oh my—Catherine of Alexandria? The great martyr herself?'

Marie glared at him, outraged; he wordlessly gloated back at her. The table shivered, but did not lift into the air. Augustus said, 'I think it is Saint Catherine.

More blood may make the communication smoother. Dee, shall I ask another this time, or are you up to the task?'

Marie reached up to her collar and undid the uppermost buttons. Then she reached in carefully under the hem of her shift and grasped the cords of the scapular, pulling it over her head gingerly. She crossed to the lectern and set it down, keeping the little pads of brown wool together, the embroidered crosses facing outward. Then she returned to her chair and sat.

Lord Ravenhurst, his eyes closed again, smiled sweetly. 'The spirit is speaking now …' He shuddered and gasped, and then began to talk in a different voice, guttural and cracked.

Dee twitched—not, as Marie could feel, from reluctance, not even from the weird thrill of the necromantic operation, but with lecherous arousal. She grimaced. He uttered a faint 'Yes' and extended his hand again.

'We will need a larger quantity this time, I'm afraid. But do not be alarmed. It won't hurt,' said Augustus, looking around at his fellow monsters with a vicious leer. His fangs elongated; so did Lady fitzUrse's; so did Chastelard's. Marie cast him a mute, pleading look, but he thrust a finger of brutal command at her, and she extended her own, and followed the Baroness' lead in positioning them just beside, not quite touching, the dupe's throat.

'I am Ahriman, guardian of the threshold of the spirits. Why dost thou trouble me?' said the medium in his alien voice.

'I want to speak to my mother, please,' Marie replied. Her forehead was glistening with sweat, but her voice was steady.

'Who art thou? Why dost thou seek the counsels of the dead?'

'My name is Marie Catherine Aurora Redglass. I want to speak with my mother. Only her.'

This time the table did levitate, and a growl was emitted from the medium's throat. 'Who art thou so to dare?'

'At any rate I do dare,' she insisted, trying to keep her tone steady. 'Please let me speak with my mother.'

The growling grew deeper and quieter. 'Very well. But there shall be a price.'
'What price?'

'To speak with the dead,' proclaimed Lord Ravenhurst as Ahriman, 'thou must come among the dead.'

Marie shrank, and her burst of spirit failed. 'Will I come back?' she managed to ask.

'Thou shalt.'

Again she hesitated.

Augustus held out a hand with three fingers up, to signal when they should, in unison, strike. Three—

'All right,' she said.

Ravenhurst abruptly returned to himself. Marie leaned forward to explain what had happened and to ask what to do next. He replied comfortingly, 'Don't worry, Mademoiselle Redglass. This is actually quite common; I am surprised we have not met Ahriman before now, in fact. An invitation to come among the dead is a good sign: he would not let you pass unless you were a woman of worth.'

—two—

'But how do I do it?'

'Simply close your eyes, and I will guide you.' He moved his chair close to hers, putting one arm around her shoulder and taking her hand with his other hand. She closed her eyes.

—one—

He struck.

Mrs Dee's eyes flew open in shock as Augustus and Chastelard sank their fangs into her flesh and began to drink. Mr Dee's hands gripped the table, hard: the bowl of oil and blood quivered. Lady fitzUrse was biting him. Still Marie sat inert, torn between horror and desire, present and past defiling one another. Hardly a trickle of blood escaped the greedy lips of the monsters, closed over obscene wounds. Chastelard slurped noisily from Mrs Dee; a bolt of fierce hunger shot through Marie at the sound, and her resistance failed.

She tried, at first, to take only a little from Mr Dee. But despite herself, the intoxicating flavor of fresh, hot blood, pumping into her mouth direct from a living heart, combined with her victim's badly suppressed cries of pleasure, drove her frantic. Time and place receded. There were no other vampires, there was no *séance* or tower-chamber, there was no victim and no predator; there was only the taste of this divine nectar …

'Marie. Marie, stop!' Augustus' voice broke in on her, and she withdrew a few inches, licking her lips, dizzied and giggling. Her eyes refocused—and she saw Mr Dee with his head hanging backward over his chair, his arms splayed out, only the whites of his eyes showing as he convulsed. His breath was coming in fitful gasps.

His wife had darted to her feet and set her back against the wall and begun to scream, over and over. The little pillar with the lily had been knocked over, and the vase had broken in pieces; Marie didn't know when it had happened. Chastelard and Augustus had leapt to their feet, and each grabbed Mrs Dee by one of her wrists. Augustus was staring behind her for several long seconds, controlling her struggling without effort, mouthing silently, and then suddenly he looked back up.

'Oh, look, you've gone and killed him,' he said in an annoyed voice. 'Well, under the circumstances you might as well finish.'

'No! No, I can't have done! He could still live!'

'Not after losing this much in one go,' Baroness St Sepulchre answered.

'What about this?' asked Chastelard, lifting Mrs Dee's wrist. She stopped screaming and burst into terrified, slobbering tears.

'Oh, for hell's sake, shut up, girl,' said Augustus.

'Whatever for?' Chastelard said merrily; 'her voice is lovely—*c'est le ton qui fait le chanson*, you know.'

'Let me go!' Mrs Dee screamed. 'Let me go, I beg you, my lords! I'll tell no one!'

'Better kill her too,' Lord Ravenhurst said briefly. 'We don't want any witnesses of this, it would ruin my reputation.'

Marie recoiled, as the young woman redoubled her shrieks. 'You said we did not kill!' Marie shouted.

'I said nothing of the kind. I said we *rarely* kill, and that is for practical reasons, not moral ones. I've begun to think you would lecture the Devil himself for behaving diabolically.'

'Let me go!' Mrs Dee sobbed. 'I won't tell a soul, I swear it—don't kill me!'

Chastelard said sweetly, 'But *ma chérie*, do you not remember where it is written that *the wages of sin are death*? Everyone else in the room has been paid their wages in full; it were mere churlishness for you not to accept your own. Or do you not confess that you are a sinner? How extreme in wickedness you are,' he finished with a laugh.

'Are you going to have any more, or aren't you?' Lady fitzUrse asked Marie, waving a careless hand at the twitching man dying in front of them. 'If you just let him sit, the blood will grow tepid, you know.'

'Miss!' cried Mrs Dee, appealing desperately to Marie. 'Miss, I beg you, save me—'

'I told you,' Augustus said testily, 'to shut up'—and he ripped her glove clean off her hand and punctured her wrist with his fangs, directly in the great vein that runs back to the heart. The wretch screamed again, but her voice was growing ragged; Chastelard returned to his erstwhile suckling place on her white throat. Within a few moments, she too was shaking violently, her eyes dim; she was being held up only by the vampires that were killing her. A few moments more, and they detached. Her corpse fell to the floor.

'You're mad!' Marie shrieked. 'You're all damned madmen!'

'Mad?' said Augustus mildly, as though he had been accused of picking up the wrong fork at a dinner party. '*Mon petit chou*, surely you see that if we had left either of them alive, they would have tattled sooner or later. Besides, it is better manners to—'

What precisely was better manners she never found out, for she howled, clapped her hands over her ears, and tried to run from the room. In her confusion, she ran straight into the lectern,

knocking her scapular onto herself. It scorched her. She stumbled, feeling faint. Then she noticed the ugly, sticky sensation around her mouth. She licked her lips: a weird, coppery taste clung to them. Looking over to Ravenhurst for an explanation, she saw him stanching a great gash in his arm with a length of linen— and then the last few minutes, which had seemed at the time like a laudanum-riddled dream, came shockingly back to her.

His teeth, strangely elongated, had somehow sunk into her throat, and yet the feeling was not like a wound, but one of exquisite, fiery pleasure. He had drunk from her for minutes on end, and she did not want him to stop. Then, as the world around her became cloudy and dark, his voice had come to her, saying something about dying, and that she had to drink from him also. An arm with a great wound in the wrist had been placed before her. She had been too bewildered to question or resist the command, and had leaned forward and placed her mouth on the deep, bleeding gash, and had begun to suck ...

This time the scapular was not there, but a tiny patch of exposed skin, between her glove and her cuff, brushed against the pages of the Bible, reminding her of its presence. Without thinking, she picked it up, ignoring the scalding pain, and hurled it at Augustus. His open-mouthed shock, visible for a split second, gave her a delicious sense of revenge; then the Bible hit him in the face. He howled. It fell onto the table, catching the edge of the bowl of oil and blood and flipping that into her sire's face as well. She could see a magnificent rectangular burn, raw and glistering under the oil.

'You little bitch!' he bellowed. 'How dare you!' He began to move toward Marie, but she roughly shoved the Baroness into Chastelard, and gained the doorway before anyone could catch her.

'What have you done to me?' she demanded, her voice quaking.

'You are a vampire now,' Lord Ravenhurst said.

'That's impossible. There are no such things.'

He smiled. A rosy tint gleamed on his curiously elongated canines.

Marie, knowing at that moment that she was in the presence of a deranged killer, picked up her skirts and fled from Ravenhurst. She did not even stop for a carriage or a horse; her sole thought was to get back home.

As she hurled herself down the spiral staircase, her wits began to return to her. She could hear Augustus and the others in hot pursuit—he was shouting at her— but she had the advantage of two dozen steps, and had drunk more blood than any one of them, so that her energy was at its peak. Within a few seconds, she had found the door that led to the second floor landing, and dashed out onto it, where she was surprised to find Godalming. She slammed the door shut and held it, and within a second, it was being pounded against by raging fists.

'Give me the key,' she told the butler fiercely.

He merely raised an eyebrow at her. Snarling at his insubordination, Marie picked up her skirts again and darted forward around him, so that the three vampires tumbled out of the door unprepared; for good measure, she gave Godalming a savage kick from behind, so that he would stumble into their path. Not pausing to look back, she raced furiously for the stairs that led down to the door—

An iron pincer of a hand closed around her elbow, and she stumbled at the top of the staircase. She looked up, and was shocked to see that the hand was the butler's. His face was utterly empty.

She tried to shake free of his grasp, but he was as strong as she; and then Augustus caught up to them both. His face was dripping with oil, burnt by the holy book, and contorted with uncontrollable anger. He snatched Marie's wrists, shouldering the butler aside. The Baroness and Chastelard were standing by the doorway: she looked haughty and amused; his face wore a strange mixture of contempt and pity.

'Look at me,' growled Augustus.

The burn was healing as she watched, as he exerted his blood. She shut her eyes tightly and tried to pry her wrists free of his grip, but he was too strong for her. Suddenly she seemed to be flying. She opened her eyes, and screamed. He had swung her bodily over the balustrade, and was now suspending her, by her wrists, over a drop of two floors. The drop in itself was not disastrous, or so she tried to remember; but she was hanging directly over the grandfather clock in the entrance hall, whose gold ornamentation on its crown would puncture and sear her body as surely as the Bible had seared his.

'No! Augustus, don't, please!'

He let go with his right hand; she swung about, and let loose a shriek of fear, at which he laughed. She reached upwards, kicking with her legs, trying to reach the balustrade and get some purchase against it, but he kept jerking her from one place to another and twisting her around, preventing her from having any constant frame of reference.

'*Monsieur Chastelard, la Bible, s'il vous plait,*' he called out gaily. '*Mes gants son en—*'

'No! Lord Ravenhurst, I beg you, I'm sorry, *please* don't do this—'

'*You shut your mouth!*' he screamed, jerking his face back to her; he looked completely insane. 'You disgraceful creature, how *dare* you! I am your *sire!*'

'*Augusto,*' said a powerful, unmoved voice. '*Basta.*'

He looked to his right, where it had come from. Marie looked that way as well, but, suspended as she was under the balustrade, she could not pick out who had spoken. Augustus' mouth compressed into a grim line.

'*Come si desidera, Madre,*' he replied. He lifted Marie back up onto the landing. She staggered into the wall, and slumped against it, crying and shaking. Godalming, who had withdrawn behind the vampires, nodded.

'Go to your room,' Augustus said.

Chastelard came forward and helped her up. As soon as she was on her feet, Marie pulled her hands out of his, flinching at every suggestion of touch. She clung to the wall, away from the balustrade, all the way down to the floor below, and left him behind at the door of her room.

CHAPTER XIII

THE CHANTRY OF SAINT CLARE

Dans tes jupons remplis de ton parfum
Ensevelir ma tête endolorie,
Et respirer, comme un fleur flétrie,
Le doux relent de mon amour défunt.[3]

– CHARLES BAUDELAIRE, *LE LÉTHÉ*

Following the aftermath of the *séance*, Augustus, Chastelard, and a third figure were shut in his study. It was unlit. The two vampires were standing in the traditional posture of submission, with their wrists crossed over one another and facing upwards, their heads slightly bowed.

The third person, who was seated, spoke. 'I see my increased watchfulness was fully justified, you idiot.' Its gloved fingers tapped the arm of its chair.

Augustus tried to conciliate. 'Please, *Madre*, it was an error of judgment on my part, I quite admit that—'

This was met with a mirthless 'Hah' and a glare so fierce that he desisted.

'You,' the figure continued, with perilous restraint, 'have made our task incomparably more difficult. All for the sake of a silly joke and the compensation of your wounded egotism. Obviously the Redglass girl is being a fool, but what

---

[3] 'And in your garments that exhale your perfume

I would bury my aching head,

And breathe, like a withered flower,

The sweet, stale reek of my love who is dead.'

did you expect? Did you not take a moment to calculate the effect of your prank upon her? *Porco Iddio!*—I expect a great deal more foresight from you, *Augusto*. If you continue in this fashion I will take charge of the girl myself, and as you know, I loathe being bored quite as much as you do. And when I have cause to revenge myself, I do not do it with jokes.'

Augustus nodded, the whites of his eyes wide. 'I shall repair the situation, *Madre*. I swear to it. Only give me a little time.'

The figure extended an imperious hand at Chastelard. '*Paolo*. Do what you can with her in the evening.'

'I will.'

The person nodded. 'I shall leave now; and I shall drop back in whenever I please—no amount of revoking invitations will do to keep me out, as you know very well. *A domani sera, figlio.*'

'*A domani sera, Madre*,' replied Augustus.

Godalming rose and left the study, and shut the door behind him. He walked a few paces down the corridor outside, slowed, and then collapsed.

'And Henry's eye is better as well, I trust?' asked William, setting down the clotted cream and taking a mouthful of his tea.

'Yes, much,' said James. 'Thank you again for intervening; I know we were both beastly to you at the time, but—'

'Never mind that,' William said. 'Anyway, I didn't come by only to play the amateur physician. Tell me more about your study of Arthur.'

James smiled broadly. 'I have come across a truly exciting copy of *Le Morte D'Arthur*, since you mention it. I happened to be visiting Winchester College a few months ago, around Michaelmas, and I came upon a manuscript which—well, I cannot be sure yet, but it *appears* to predate Caxton.'

'I thought Caxton's printing was the first.'

'It was, if you're speaking of prints. This is a manuscript proper, you see; it's older still. Written in an elegant fifteenth-century minuscule, without illuminations, aside from a few decorated capitals. It might even be …'

William leaned forward. 'What?'

'It could be the autograph,' the other replied. He licked his lips. 'I don't want to rush to judgment, you know. But it *just* could be.'

'But James, this is fantastic. Can it be proven? Can I help you at all?'

'I don't know. Possibly.' He finished his tea and poured himself another cup, adding an embarrassment of sugar and stirring it briskly. 'I'll tell you, if I ever find out a way—I am eager to *be* helped, you know, I just haven't yet worked out how to proceed … But what about your own researches? I trust Magdalen is treating you well?'

'Yes, very,' William said. 'Though I do wish I had the time to dig more deeply. One of the frustrating things about literature and history both is the sheer difficulty of tracking down a reference to verify it, however minor. Poets especially should be made to give bibliographies in their work.'

'Thinking of becoming a professional academic? Oxford is certainly the place for it.'

'Quite true. Bodley's stacks are more expansive than I had dared to hope before I came up. All the same I should like to see more in the way of commentary on the Alliterative Revival in the fourteenth and fifteenth centuries; there is a particular saga I'm studying at the moment that displays a genuine—'

The clock struck half-past four. 'Oh, high heaven, is that really the time?' said William suddenly. 'Talking of stacks, I had meant to be at the London Library a quarter of an hour ago.' He turned to his host to ask pardon for his abrupt departure, but James waved his hand.

'Believe me, I understand. It is the scholar's lot; go in peace. *In omnibus requiem quæsivi, et nusquam inveni nisi sed in angulo cum libro.*'

William grinned at him and took his leave, hailing a hansom cab and rattling off towards Westminster.

Caxton and the autograph of such an important epic were valid inquiries, of course, and under other circumstances he would have been intensely interested. But he had been hoping for some reference, any reference, that might touch on his own recent investigations. He had not, and would not have, shared his full zeal over *King Arthur the Holy* (still less his reasons for it) with James at that time; but he was increasingly hopeful. He had spoken with Baron Houghton, the Library's current President, and had some promising first-hand accounts of vampire superstitions in Eastern Europe to look forward to for the night.

Hours had passed; a full day, perhaps. Marie did little. She lay on her bed and stared at the ceiling, paying no attention to the little line of sunlight that graced it for a few minutes; or she sat up on her bed and stared at *The Holy Communion of St Teresa*, its delicate baroque lines fading in and out of focus. Now and then she wondered idly what Augustus would do to her.

At last she got up, and went over to the window and sat in the bay with the curtains opened, after determining that night had fallen again. Orion, Taurus, and Aries were visible in the sky, brooding like rocs over a distant copse. She wondered what it would be like to be positioned in some strange planet, in one of the constellations of the zodiac, and watch the sun rising as a distant star.

There was a soft knock on her door. 'Go away,' she said.

'*Je suis, ma belle*,' came a musical voice. 'May we speak together?'

'Please go away, Monsieur.'

'Let me in.'

Marie sighed a defeated sigh. Chastelard would not remonstrate, it was not his way; but she could scarcely handle any conversation at all. Yet she felt that she could handle a conversation conducted through a locked door even less than one held face to face, so she reluctantly rose and let him inside.

'*Merci*,' he said. 'Such an hospitable dragonet you are.' He sat down before the vanity, looking into the mirror with an amused expression. Marie curled up in the bay again and waited.

'I never cease to be fascinated by this.' He gestured to the empty reflection of his clothes in the mirror. '*Ô beauté si ancienne et toujours nouvelle.*'

'What do you have to say to me?'

He gave no sign he had heard her. 'Unique is the lot of the vampire. *Homo natus de muliere brevi vivens tempore*, we alone remain after death itself. The rest, they are resolved into the ash and the earth. Is it not strange to you, *petite fleur*? To contemplate these vessels, brimful of life and vigor, tenaciously bound together with ropes of muscle and sinew and reinforced with bones, withering into dust? Is it not strange? Indeed, they are like *the grass of the field, which to-day is, and to-morrow is cast into the oven*. But you and I, Marie, and our father Augustus, we are like gemstones—lovelier even than hothouse lilies, and we wither not. Drop a gemstone on a blossom or a blade of grass, and it is crushed; *c'est dans l'ordre des choses.*'

Chastelard finally turned to face her. 'Let this settle into your bones, and allow you the freedom to sing, to dance, to praise, to love.'

'Monsieur,' she said bitterly, 'we did not fall on those two like gemstones on flowers. We were like—like strixes preying on mice.'

'*Et puis après?*'he responded placidly. 'Do you lecture these owls on the error of their ways, and send them to the confessional for penance or to the court for punishment?'

'But we are not beasts, we are—'

The word caught in her throat. Chastelard waited, and at last finished the sentence for her stingingly: 'Human?'

She tugged out her handkerchief and crushed it against her eyes, not to absorb tears, but simply to shut out the waking nightmare. The silence lengthened. She thought she could hear the clock tolling ten.

Chastelard stood up. '*Remords a noyé plus de gens que Neptune.*'

'Please go away.'

He did. The door clicked shut. She raised her head and looked back out into the black heavens.

The next several nights at Ravenhurst were almost unendurable. Augustus did not dine with Marie, speak to her, or even look at her. The servants were more skittish than ever. She did not dare try to initiate any conversation. Her only company was the books (when Augustus was not in the library), the occasional rattle from the resident spirit, and the incessant sound of the clock, which seemed to infect every room in the manor.

She began to think that the isolation would drive her mad.

She thought often about Chastelard's little speech. *Remorse has drowned more than the sea*, he had said. It might be a fair point. Nevertheless, the four of them had murdered that young couple. That they were both fools, and he a sexual pervert to boot, might make it a morality tale from one perspective, but it did not justify *them*. Every time she thought of Mr and Mrs Dee having their lives drained out in that little room, nausea all but blinded her.

When six nights had gone by, Godalming brought Marie a note from her sire. It informed her curtly that he had arranged for her to go to Lady Ely's townhouse and start to practice music with her. The duchess' carriage would arrive for her at eight in the evening, and bring her back to the manor at four. Grateful for an escape (and suspecting that Augustus was grateful for a pretext to have her out of the house), she wrapped herself in furs, put the pyx into a little pocket inside her corset, and, at eight, went down and was met by the carriage.

Curiously for a vampire, Lady Ely's house was not in the privacy of the city's outskirts or one of the fashionable boroughs, but in, of all places, Whitechapel—overcrowded, dirty, and dangerous. Commercial Road, on which her dwelling stood near the intersection with York Street, was fine enough, but it fronted some of the most squalorous and reeking warrens in London. Angry shouts, snatches of drunken song, and the foul smells of tanneries, foundries, and charnel-houses drummed against the senses. Marie did not linger on the doorstep, but knocked quickly and was as quickly let into the house.

Servants took her furs and showed her into the music room: an open, pleasant place with cream-colored walls, dominated by a three-choired harpsichord in its center. Its lid was lifted, and the interior bore a familiar *danse macabre* motif. A black-robed skeleton stood to the left, showing his disciples their way into an open grave: a pope in funereal regalia, a queen in snowy samite, a yellow-clad huntsman with an arrow on the string, a young girl in a crimson dress carrying a lute, and last of all a nude man (perhaps the traditional image of the beggar was implied). Other instruments were set in stands or on low tables here and there, many of them dating apparently to the Renaissance. She could see a shawm, a large viol, three lutes, a trumpet, an hautbois, two recorders, and a harp. The only other piece of decoration was a statue, about ten inches high, of a mænad brandishing the savaged head of a victim of Dionysian frenzy, presumably Pentheus'. Carmilla was also there, waiting. She sprang up with a sincere if quavering smile at the sight of Marie, and greeted her with pathetic affection.

'Mademoiselle Redg-g-glass, it is so w-wonderful of you to c-come by. I understand you sing b-b-beautifully.'

She demurred, which Lady Ely evidently took as confirmation. The latter produced some sheets of music from a mass setting of Palestrina's, and offered to play for Marie if she would simply sing the soprano part as best she could, so that the two could familiarize themselves with one another's musical styles. She sat down at the harpsichord and began to play immediately; Marie, caught slightly by surprise and unfamiliar with that particular piece, followed as best she could.

It turned out to be a good deal more straightforward than she had expected. She was familiar with Palestrina in a general way, and she found that the caution and occasional strains that would have been necessary before for her to sing this soprano part were quite unneeded now. Before the mass setting had ended, she had begun to enjoy herself a little; and she had to admit, too, that her companion was a talented harpsichordist.

They brought the *Agnus Dei* to a close, and Carmilla clapped her hands and said, 'Oh, lovely, lovely! You have a splendid voice, mademoiselle. Now, I have a few p-pieces prepared—here, see if there's one you would like to start with ...'

They went through all of Victoria's *Officium Defunctorum*, Carmilla singing the alto part and Marie the first soprano; des Prez's *Nymphes des Bois*; the *Te Lucis ante Terminum* of Thomas Tallis; and Carmilla accompanied her as she sang the aria *Smanie Implacabili* from *Così fan Tutte*, which Marie had never even heard before. Occasionally they would pause for Carmilla to give her instruction in how to take best advantage of her undead lungs, losing her stammer almost entirely as she did so. Marie thought privately that she could have been—perhaps once was—a genuinely charming gentlewoman, without the terrorizing effects of dwelling among vampires. She felt a rush of pity, and resolved to return periodically, and to make a point of being kind to the duchess.

At half past midnight, they paused for refreshment. A servant brought them glasses of blood (exceptionally fine stuff, as Marie could now tell, though her hostess did not brag of it) and they sat and talked over them for a little time.

'You were so d-diverting at Lady B-B-Bath's,' Carmilla said, with a timid laugh, as though afraid the marchioness might hear her. 'I c-could not say so at the time, as m-my st-stammer keeps me from saying m-much in company. And I am always intimid-dated by her. But it was hard n-not to laugh w-w-when you said that about mortal phil—phil—' she smacked the table she was sitting by impatiently, and blurted out, 'philosophy. How ever do you think of such things?'

Marie smiled. 'Thank you, my lady. Actually, at the time I wasn't even thinking clearly—it simply popped into my head and I said it. If I had stopped to consider it, I likely would have said nothing! I certainly did not earn Lady Bath's good will, though Lord Ravenhurst—' She bit back the remainder of the sentence.

'Y-yes?'

'Oh,' she went on, with an awkward attempt at carelessness, 'Lord Ravenhurst said it would be all right and that he would smooth things out with her, that's all.'

Carmilla smiled brightly. 'He is such a c-cl-clever, capable fellow. You must be g-glad to have him as your sire. I was so f-f-frightened when I first b-began to navigate v-vampire society. It was all t-t-terribly confusing.'

'Lord Ravenhurst is a very competent guide,' Marie said shortly. She did not want to talk about Augustus.

'Quite. Do you know—' she looked around, as if afraid of being overheard, then leaned in close to her guest and whispered, 'I sometimes think that *he* would make a better D-D-D-Duke than von Orlok d-does!' She concluded with a sort of terrified giggle.

'I suppose. He doesn't seem greatly interested in governance, though.'

'No, that's t-true. Content to leave things as they are. And th-that isn't so bad, r-really. Anyway it's better than the ch-ch-chaos a d-democratic system would probably bring.' She set down her glass, and picked up a sheaf of music. 'Would you like to do the aria *Una Donna a Q-Quindici Anni* next?'

Marie assented, and they resumed their work. Sooner than she realized, four o'clock had come. Carmilla clasped her hand and thanked her profusely for coming by, and said that she looked forward to seeing her again. Marie warmly returned her farewell, and went out into the reeking streets of Whitechapel to take the carriage home.

Across the Thames, that same night, in the cozy townhouse that belonged to the Vavasour family, William was shut in his study poring over several thick, aged volumes he had borrowed from the London Library. He had already spent most of the day reading at the British Museum, except for taking tea with the new Baron Redglass. Scholarly works on Slavic and Levantine folklore; legends and poetry and a precious few annals from the misty origins of Wessex, Wales, Iceland, and Brittany; crabbed religious texts from the decay of the Byzantine Empire; even a few volumes of studies in the occult, which he was by no means sure were permitted to a Catholic to read without a formal indult. He felt, and prayed, that his desperate need to confirm those hope-giving lines in *King Arthur the Holy* justified him.

He closed the book he had been working with, and shut his eyes and rubbed them gently. It was a difficult read: a compendium of Gypsy, Hungarian, Romanian, and Slavonic traditions about *strigoi* and *upirs*, regional equivalents of vampires, and it was a challenge to sort out what might be genuine local differences among vampires from mere alternate superstitions. Few, and none outside of Gypsy sources, contained any suggestion of a possible cure. Some sources did suggest—with a consistency that encouraged him by being there at all, but frustrated him with its vagueness about details—that those who had died married were immune or resistant to being turned into *strigoi*, but did not explain why.

Deciding to take a break from the labyrinth of Balkan mystagogy, he pulled a different book towards him, opened it, and began to read.

There was a rapid-fire knock on the door, and a slightly scruffy, ginger-haired footman came in, his tie and jacket missing, with a steaming cup and a saucer. 'I've wet you a tea, sir.'

'Thank you, Desmond. If you'd just set it here.' William sighed. 'High heaven, this cold just eats into your bones, doesn't it? You can go to bed if you like—if I want another cup I can go down and fix it, I don't mind a bit.'

'I'm happy to, sir, truly,' replied Desmond with a broad smile. 'What is it ye're up over, anyhow?'

'Research,' William answered. 'There's a curious passage in an old epic poem I'm reading through, and I want to be sure that I understand it.'

'Oh ah. I wish I had your sort o' wits at times, sir. My second sister, the one what became a nun, she had brains herself as ye would hardly credit—could speak Latin and Greek and all, and such a head for figures! And all that was before she went off and got herself wedded to God.'

'Not all of God's brides are as clever as that,' he replied mischievously. 'I am glad He took an intelligent one this time.'

Desmond laughed. 'Well, I'll leave you to it, sir.'

'Oh, actually, now that I think of it. Help me remember tomorrow to cancel the re-glazing order for the kitchen windows—if we put it through just now we won't have enough money to pay your wages at the end of the month.'

The servant's friendly face grew serious. 'Has something gone quite wrong now, sir? Ye never do have this sort o' trouble. I should have thought the Duke o' Norfolk would keep you nice and proper.'

'He does; there have been a few unexpected bills, that's all. Don't worry, it's nothing drastic. We will get that wall repaired, it will just have to wait a bit.'

'Would it help if me and the boys pitched in a bit?' he asked, scratching his head. 'I know some chaps what's handy with that sort o' work.'

'Desmond,' said William with affectionate disbelief, 'the last time you and your bold boys *pitched in a bit*, it cost forty guineas to put things back to being *only* as wrong as they were before you started.'

The valet laughed again and said, 'That it did, sir, and 'tis a damn fine story if I may say, pardon me tongue. All right now. I think I shall go to bed. Only do ring the bell if ye find ye want anything.'

'All right. Good night, Desmond.'

'Good night, sir.'

William sipped his tea and bent his brain to the cryptic book on the table in front of him again. It was a little-known piece, purportedly commissioned by King Cynegils of Wessex shortly after his accession, professing to record the history of the area between the withdrawal of Roman forces from the island and Cynegils' own reign in the seventh century (though the manuscript was imperfect, and came only to the coronation of Cerdic as King of Wessex in 519). William thought it might be authentic. The important thing about it was that it corresponded closely to *King Arthur the Holy* in certain passages, to the point that some sections of the poem seemed simply to be dextrous versifications of the chronicle. That could be corroboration. It did also contain some long digressions about the history of Spain, which seemed quite confusing and out of place—though one such digression did throw out a tantalizing, although unexplained, hint about *þe lytches cell hard by Sanctiagou vpon þe montaines of Galæcia*—but perhaps it was only a reflection of the persistent Celtic tradition that their people had come to the British Isles from Iberia. The pages were old and friable as dried bread, and he had to be cautious as he turned them.

Marie continued to visit Lady Borgia and rehearse with her, and even managed to make a small remark to Augustus about it one night, about a week along. He had begun to see her at mealtimes again, though the expression on his face still warned to her say nothing at first. He responded to her gambit with an indifferent nod; the next evening he made a small remark on the subject himself, and the evening after that they succeeded in a shallow, short conversation.

The next night Augustus was away, visiting Livilla. He did not explain why, considering his great dislike of the marchioness; but perhaps paying court to her was needed in order to keep on the right side of the Duke. Marie did not mind having the manor to herself in fact, as she so often did in practice, and decided to explore it more thoroughly than she yet had.

She began in the conservatory. Lord Ravenhurst had finished his copy of Titian's *Assumption of the Virgin*: it was standing on its easel in front of an exotic fern, waiting to be framed and put in whatever place it was he wanted it. There were no other paintings there at present, though there was a copy, not yet complete, of Bernini's early sculpture *The Rape of Proserpina*. She stared at this for some time, captivated by the perfect detail of each whorled lock of hair of Pluto's head and beard, and by the formation of his finished hand, so flawless as to leave one half-surprised that it was cold to the touch. His bones and musculature were almost complete, brutal in their grip upon the goddess. Though naturally the shapelier of the two, Proserpina was by far less complete. Her smooth, tapering legs were done, and most of the body, with its breathtaking simulation of tender and yielding flesh, and the left arm was completed, laid modestly before the breasts; but, aside from the lowest third of the braided curls of her hair, most of the goddess' head and face were sketched in only the roughest degree. Marie moved closer and a little to one side, trying for a better look—and then started when she heard the clock chime, and realized she had been mesmerized by the piece for nearly a full hour. She shook herself and moved on.

Library; dining room; smoking room; drawing room. Another library, which she had not seen before. This one seemed to be filled mostly with mathematical and scientific works, and a few specimens, all out of date. If Augustus had been interested in science hitherto, he must have lost his enthusiasm sometime in the eighteenth century. Beyond that, a solarium, though of course it was not used as such: the wide, sun-catching windows were firmly shrouded by ponderous drapes, and Japanese silk screens were placed in front of them, depicting pines, bamboo, and herons in mountain landscapes half-concealed by swirling mist.

She went upstairs, where most of the rooms were bedrooms, with the exception of Augustus' study. She was a little surprised that she was unable to find one that seemed to be his own bedroom. There was a master bedroom, certainly; but it contained none of his effects, and indeed no sign of being inhabited or even used in the last twelvemonth at least. Yet one of the bedrooms, a fan-vaulted, blue and grey fantasy, was clearly set aside for Chastelard's use on his regular visits. She could make nothing of the puzzle.

Marie ascended another stair to the uppermost floor (barring the tower, which she did not revisit that night), where she found a small door that led out onto the lower battlements. She undid the latch and walked out into the night. It had snowed, and a thin white coverlet lay on the stone; but now it was clear, and the snowflakes caught the starlight and moonlight, and sparkled like gems.

She walked to the edge of the roof and leaned against the parapet, resting her elbows on the crenellation. London lay before her, dim and distant, huddled in a vaguely glowing smog. She had not greatly liked the city in life: she always knew in the back of her mind that, for most of its people, it was a dirty, overcrowded, unhappy place; and her privileged position as a member of the gentry, however minor, was not lost on her. She had preferred the romantic loneliness of the country, with its glens and hillocks and ponds, untouched by human griefs and cares. But now, standing at the edge of the countryside and looking inward, she could see that London did have a certain beauty. Its overcrowding was simply another word for its being teeming with life; the dirt was the old soil of England, creeping up over the restrictive cobblestones to remind the inhabitants that there was life under them and around them—even, for all their anguish, inside them.

A wind sprang up from the east, disarranging her hair. She closed her eyes and savored the faint bite against her skin, which reminded her of past winters, when it would have been pain unendurable to stand here without so much as a muff. Little whirlwinds of snow danced on the rooftop, and the bare trees creaked in the gardens far beneath her.

Finally, after making a circuit of the roof and peering out as far as she could in every direction, Marie went back inside. She brushed the stray snowflakes off her sleeves and out of her hair, smiling. Then she descended the stairs, getting warmer with each step down.

As she came to the ground floor, she remembered the door under the stairs, the one Augustus had warned her off of more than a month prior. What could he have been so determined to hide?

He was not here now. The servants would not come unless they were called for.

She looked about. Then, suddenly making up her mind, she walked quickly in the direction of the mysterious door.

Fortuitously, it had been left unlocked. Marie checked the corridor again, to be sure that Godalming was not watching; as she did so, her hand brushed against the painting of St Clare and was scorched. She just managed to stifle a cry, more of surprise than of pain, and nursed the burn for a few seconds as she healed it, giving the nun a mutinous look. Then she slipped inside and pulled the door to behind her, being careful to make sure that it did not latch.

She was at the top of a lightless, damp, coffin-narrow stairway. It was cold. Putting out her hands to steady herself, Marie advanced, one cautious step at a time. The stairs were deep, about eight inches, and though the first few dozen were made of wood, the lower ones seemed to have been cut out of the living rock. There was a thick smell of earth in the passage; it was hard to dismiss the fancy that she was being buried alive. She counted the steps at first, but lost track somewhere after sixty, and still they went on.

Finally she put out her foot and was startled to meet only more floor. This seemed to be the very fundament of the house. The wall had ended to her right a little time ago, so she stretched out her arms and slowly advanced into the cellar.

'Hello?' she said, more to test the size of the room than to see if anyone else was there. It proved to be a cavernous space. A faint, ugly dripping sound echoed from somewhere. The air was close, cool, and moist. The chamber was unlit. Or no—there was a dismal, unsteady light far to the left. She went to find it.

Almost immediately she cracked her nose painfully against an unseen structure. She gave a sharp cry and stopped, nursing what felt like a break, until she remembered that she could simply heal it at will and did so. Then, with more care, she reached forward and found the thing she had accidentally drawn up against.

It was a solid, square column, made of stone, with metal brackets bolted into it on all four sides for holding torches. She felt inside the brackets. The first two were empty, the third did contain a torch, the fourth a mess of rubbish and aha! a matchbox. She opened it, finding several matches inside, thankfully free of the damp that pervaded the cellar. Striking it against the box, she lit the torch with little difficulty and shook the match out. She had to fight down a sensation of panic when the torch caught and sputtered alight, but steeled herself.

Extracting the torch from its bracket with extreme delicacy, so as not to risk contact with the flame, Marie took it and looked around. The place was immense: it was about thirty feet high, and lay under perhaps the whole of the house. It was obviously much older than the rest of the manor—that is, whereas the upper floors had been periodically updated, this place had remained unretouched since its construction. Its ceiling, curiously, was lierne vaulted, and thus vaguely reminiscent of Trinity Cathedral in Ely. The column she had struck was one of many, forming a long, rectangular area in the middle of the space, with the entrance in one of the aisle-like sides. The will-o'-wisp illumination appeared to be inside the rectangle, away at the far end. The floor was swept quite clean. It bore eldritch patterns, not painted, but carved into the stone direct; she decided to examine these later. There were a number of defaced bas reliefs on the walls, but these were so water-worn that she could make out little of their original character.

Around the edges of the room was a litter of objects, lying as if they had been pushed there to keep them out of the way. Some, rotten with time and moisture, were past identifying, but the ones she could make out were strange. There were gem-studded goblets lined with gold; a heap of bead-sized fragments of jade-colored glass; a great copper ewer encrusted with verdigris; icons in gold leaf and costly enamels from Byzantium and Russia; a delicate rose-gold thurible; empty candlesticks of irrecoverably corroded brass; a reliquary of fine Venetian glazing and wrought iron, decorated with silver filigree.

There was a tearing screech and a rattle, and Marie spun around. A spark from the torch fell and nearly lodged itself in her dress, and she let loose a hysterical curse and stamped it out. No one was there. Perhaps the poltergeist had followed her down, and was amusing itself. Or maybe it had only been a subterranean bat. She moved back toward the center of the room. The torchlight made the columns and their shadows shift and sway like giant dancers. She made for the dim glow, now ahead of her.

At the head of the chamber was an alcove, deeply recessed into the rear wall, somewhat in the style of a Lady chapel. In it were three indistinct objects; large, boxlike things, black, or at least they looked black in the obscurity of the cellar. A three-pronged candlestick stood on a table behind them. She approached.

As she did so, the rattling resumed. An offensive, metallic squeal and some mental noise illuminated Marie: it was the poltergeist, playing with the torch brackets. She decided it would be best to ignore it, and moved forward, almost stumbling at a wide, shallow step that ran across the chamber at about a quarter of its length, measuring from the alcove. She lifted her skirts and kept moving. The boxes were clearer now, even in the guttering torchlight: elongated, with a curious bulge in the middle, and brass plaques on the ends; two were rather dingy, but the one furthest to the right was well polished.

As Marie drew nearer to these, the poltergeist began to babble and scream into her brain. *Impudent filth strumpet I shall have thine head whoreling how dare he HOW DARE HE bitch murderess FAITHLESS TRAITOR liars the both of ye.* She tried to ward herself, but the wraith's resistance was surprisingly strong—she had left Miss Glastenning's phylactery upstairs, and apparently despite its madness the creature was a psychic force to be reckoned with—

The torch went out.

The poltergeist began to giggle and babble about revenge. Frightened, Marie stupidly threw the torch in the direction that seemed to be the focus of the poltergeist's mind, only to have it seized by the spirit and hurled back at her with terrible force. She hardly parried the missile that would have taken out her left eye. The candlestick behind her flared ferociously, spitting out sparks. From the other direction, a second projectile struck her, tearing open a small gash in her forehead. It was one of the bolts—the metallic screeching had been the poltergeist pulling the torch brackets to bits.

All at once, the air was full of jagged, ripped-up pieces of metal, whirling round her and hurling themselves at her like a murder of crows. She screamed for help and ran, trying to find the staircase, but the poltergeist snuffed out the three-pronged candlestick, chittering hideously, and she could not find her way in the absolute black. She banged into a column and reeled, tried to run again, hit another column and almost fell over. Shards of iron were slicing her skin. The cellar-wide step was suddenly under her feet, and she lost her balance and was struck by the floor, hard. There was a strange pounding in her ears, and Marie wondered whether the poltergeist had the strength to dismember her, and whether that was one of the ways a vampire could die.

The pounding grew louder, and a ghostly light appeared. She looked up. Augustus was coming down the last few steps of the staircase with a lantern in his hand. He caught sight of her, and his mouth fell open with shock. For a split second they merely stared at one another, he standing, she prostrate. Then, expressionless, he closed his mouth, lifted an imperious hand, and looked toward the alcove. Marie felt a wave of telepathic force pass over her, not directed at her but at the poltergeist; the insane chatter ceased, and the broken pieces of the metal torch bracket clanged to the cellar floor.

Augustus came over to her, hoisted her up by the arm, and marched her to the stairs. He pushed her up with his left hand and trailed the lantern behind them with his right, casting irregular shadows on the moisture-beaded walls.

'Lord Ravenhurst, what—'

'Shut your mouth.'

They emerged from the stair into the gleam and warmth of the ground floor. Augustus hurled her from him down the passage, and she ran involuntarily a few yards and tottered, catching herself against the wall. He came after her. Eyes wide, lips compressed, Marie began backing away rapidly, her feet eventually finding the main stair and ascending it unsteadily.

Augustus paused for a moment at the foot of the staircase. His glare slid into her, as if with eyes alone he could tear away every veil of privacy and defense. He began to speak, in a voice gorged with horrible calm.

'Did I not tell you, in words of one syllable, that that cellar is not your concern? Didn't I?' He took a step onto the staircase, and Marie backed away again. 'Well?' he barked.

'Yes, you did—'

'*I did.* And what do you do, when my back is turned? Why did you go down there, when I had expressly forbidden it? I ask so little of you, Marie, so *very* little!' He suddenly flung the lantern down onto the stairs, smashing it, and glittering fragments of glass skipped over the varnished wood. 'Why? Tell me!'

She was crying with terror. 'I, I didn't mean to—'

'*Liar!*'

He was advancing, and Marie was giving way before him, stair by stair. 'I gave you immortal beauty! Without me, you'd be an old, ugly woman before the century was out! Is this how you repay me? Embarrassing me before the Duke, disrupting my *séance*, and now trespassing upon my chantry! You dithering mess of afterbirth! Do you have eyes for anything but your own *idiot* curiosity?'

'Lord Ravenhurst, please, I'm sorry—'

Marie tripped backwards at the top of the staircase, and Augustus let forth a nightmarish laugh. She scrambled away, crab-like and clumsy, but he was too quick. He swept down on her like Pluto in an access of wrath, grabbing her by the waist and the thigh; she struggled and pushed back against him, but it was no use. He half-carried, half-dragged her to a bedroom—not her own—and then, dropping her legs, seized her by the arms and shook her violently.

'Stay out of my chantry, do you hear? *Out!* Set foot in there again, and you'll *wish* you could still die, Marie! Do you understand me?'

'Yes!'

'*Say it again!*'

'I understand you! I won't, I won't, ever again!'

He threw her against the wall. The impact cracked the plaster; she could feel blood trickle sluggishly over her scalp. Augustus slammed the door shut, making the room tremble. A heavy clack proclaimed that he had locked it. A ghastly heat swept through her groin. Marie opened her eyes in naked terror, expecting to see blows beginning to fall on her, or worse—but he had left her alone. She lay on the floor, blood leaking from her scratches and out of her eyes, sobbing and screaming.

Up late again, William took a swallow of tea, took his flask out of his pocket, and added a little whiskey to it. A new book was open before him: the diary of an eighteenth-century hunter, a peregrine fellow based near Lublin, written around 1760. He ran down the page with his finger, murmuring his translation aloud to himself—his Polish was poor, and the text was terse and archaic, but he was determined to get through it all, and he had a Polish-English etymological dictionary open on his lap for good measure.

'*The* wampir *outpaced me for forty-seven nights … but I persevered by—by God's grace, and at last I trapped him in the*—oh, what is that word—' He flipped a few pages, peering at the dictionary. '*In the sacristy.* That's odd. *I said that I would kill him in the name of God, to avenge his crimes … and he said to me that he willed to—wished to repent. I told him that only a creature with a duchy was capable of penitence*—what?—ah, no, *with a soul was capable of penitence, and the* wampir *pleaded with me that I help him get a soul.*'

William had another mouthful of his fortified tea, and glanced out the window. Snow was falling.

'*I asked him how he could acquire a soul. He said that … there was a tradition among the* wampiry *that true love, sealed by the*' (flip flip flip) '*the mystery of matrimony, would restore their lost souls to their bodies. I said that I did not believe him, but he said he would swear upon the relics of Saint Hyacinth … that he was speaking me—telling me the truth.*'

He reached out for his teacup, but his hand was shaking so much that he began to spill on the book, and he set it down again. Independent corroboration, from a source removed by hundreds of miles and centuries of time, of the belief—and one not merely reported among men, but professed by the creatures themselves—that vampirism could be cured.

Tears of joy gathered at the corners of his eyes, and his breath came in gasps. His eyes went to the crucifix on his wall, and he began to pray. 'Thank You. Oh, blessed Lord Jesus, thank You. Glory be to the Father and to the Son and to the Holy Ghost, as it was in the beginning, is now, and ever shall be, world without end. Amen.'

CHAPTER XIV

THE LADY WITH THE BLACK FAN

But should I love, get, tell till I were old,
I should not find that hidden mysterie;
    Oh, 'tis imposture all:
And as no chymique yet th'Elixar got,
    But glorifies his pregnant pot,
    If by the way to him befall
Some odoriferous thing, or medicinall,
  So, lovers dreame a rich and long delight
  But get a winter-seeming summer's night.

— JOHN DONNE, *LOVES ALCHYMIE*

Augustus left Marie in the strange bedroom for two days and a night. It had been perhaps an hour shy of dawn when he had caught her in the cellar: the following day, the next night, and the next day were all spent in slow, dry fear. She felt her thirst little. She hardly even thought. She simply stared at the locked door, waiting for him to come and throw her out of the house to die.

As evening fell, there was a harsh clunk at the door—it was being unlocked. She hastened to her feet. If she was going to be put to the Second Death, she would meet it standing. It wasn't much; but it was what she had.

The door swung open. It was Godalming, with a champagne flute full of blood on a tray.

'His lordship's compliments, Mademoiselle Redglass, and if you should like to go riding you are welcome to accompany him. He will be leaving in about half an hour. He expected that you would be thirsty, and instructed me to bring you this.'

To work oneself into a state to withstand martyrdom, and then be met by an offer of food, is a disorientating experience. Marie considered spurning the drink out of pride, but this thought did not last more than a few seconds. She moved forward with what she hoped was great dignity in spite of a slight wobble, and took the blood. Draining the glass, she set it back on the tray and asked whether her sire was still angry with her.

'I am not aware that he has been angry with you at all, mademoiselle. He has made no remark suggesting it. But that is of course his lordship's business.'

She nodded. Would it be worse to sit in the manor and wait for him to return, or to go riding with him and endure his—whatever mood he was in—at once? That was easy; far better to get it over with as rapidly as possible. Waiting would be unendurable.

'Are there riding clothes in my wardrobe?'

'Yes, mademoiselle. Shall I send for Hyacinth to assist you?'

'No, I'll do them up myself. Thank you, Godalming.'

'Very good, mademoiselle.'

The butler left, and she went down the hallway to her own room. Having donned a midnight blue riding habit and a fine, masculine top hat, she proceeded cautiously down the stairs and went to the stables, steeling herself. Augustus was already there, dressed in a pale grey jacket and white jodhpurs. He was standing by a fine palomino stallion of about seventeen hands' height, patting its neck and cooing to it. He caught sight of Marie and, unexpectedly, smiled.

'*Mon doux plaisir*, there you are. I'm glad you chose to join me. This is Chlorus. Say hello, Chlorus.' The horse whickered as if in reply. 'Take any horse you please—I recommend Lancelot, the black one there. Or Regina, the chestnut over there.'

She stood dumbly for a few moments, half wondering whether Augustus actually remembered his recent savagery. Fumbling for language, she tugged at the fingers of her kidskin gloves. 'Lord Ravenhurst, why—'

'Again, child. Call me Augustus,' he said promptly, without quite meeting her eye. Something in his voice told her that he would sooner forsake his ride and walk right back into the house than entertain inquiries about their last, disastrous meeting. She walked along the row of horses and found a dappled grey cob. 'What's your name?'

Augustus walked over. 'That is Foamflower. An affectionate mare, and very spirited—she will tug at the reins now and again, but if you handle her properly you ought to have no trouble.'

Marie looked at him. 'I like her,' she said.

'I do too. Take her.' He undid the padlock and saddled and bridled the animal, which stood patiently as she stroked its neck and fed it a few lumps of sugar from a stray saddle-bag. Once he had finished preparing Foamflower, he hoisted himself lightly onto Chlorus in a single leap, without even the assistance of a mounting block.

'Goodness, you're strong,' said Marie.

'So are you, if you remember,' he answered with a chuckle. 'Go on, leap up onto her, just the way I did. You won't hurt her unless you mean to, or are too clumsy to be riding horses in the first place.'

She gave it a try, and was pleasantly surprised to succeed on her first attempt. She settled her feet into the stirrups, and followed Augustus and Chlorus out into the glimmering night.

'Have you ever been riding by starlight before?' he asked her.

'No, I haven't.'

'Trust Foamflower. She knows her way about the grounds. And keep your eyes open—don't forget that you can see a great deal more clearly now.'

She nodded. Without another word, Lord Ravenhurst set off at a brisk trot, rising rapidly to a canter. She urged her filly on behind them. The horses' hooves kicked up bright crescents of snow and ice, and the night air was turned to a wind that wove about them as they rode. The path they followed was far from level, but her sire was right: Foamflower was a clever beast, and kept her rider seated with ease, finding her footing with perfect surety even on the slippery winter lawns. They followed a roughly circular track around the edge of Ravenhurst's grounds, bridles jingling. The horses' breath came up in great plumes of steam, as if they were riding dragons.

They came to a pond on the grounds, its surface like frosted glass. A great ring of naked trees surrounded it. Augustus and Chlorus pulled up suddenly, and Marie followed suit. He pointed to a well-used track that ran about the pond, just discernible in the folds of the snow.

'Do you see that path?'

'Yes.'

He turned his head and gave her a puckish smile. 'The devil take the hindmost,' he said, and instantly he was off. She spurred Foamflower and followed, racing him.

Soon they were galloping at full tilt. He was laughing, and Marie began to laugh as well; anguish and tension flowed out of her like water. She urged her horse ahead. The liquid moonlight fell irregularly on their ride, interrupted by waves of cloud.

Fr Weld sat close to the stove with his cup of thin tea, frowning over the letter that William Vavasour had sent him. He knew the young man had been engaged to be married to Marie Redglass, the daughter of the late baron, but that she had disappeared three months ago. He had not known Marie well, but he had liked her, and her brother Henry. (Their elder brother James was a very decent fellow, although *likeable* was not the adjective that sprang immediately to one's mind to describe him.) Henry had been much affected by the tragedies that afflicted the family, it seemed: he had stopped his habit of coming to daily Mass, and one of his friends had remarked in passing that he was not answering his letters.

The priest shook his head; he was losing his train of thought. William, a mere three months after the disappearance of his *fiancée*, was now asking Fr Weld's consent to marry him—immediately!—to an unidentified young woman; and what was more, to do it without even publishing the banns. It was quite unlike William's open, chivalrous character to be so abrupt and secretive. The only explanation he could think of was that he had gotten this anonymous young woman with child and wanted to do the honorable thing, but, given the temperance and chastity of the young man's life, that seemed scarcely possible— barring, of course, his habits with respect to ... On the other hand, perhaps it *was* possible; a moment of weakness could overcome anybody. Or perhaps an acquaintance had fornicated with her and then jilted the poor girl, and William had determined that the child should not grow up fatherless, and said nothing about it out of concern for the cad's reputation, hoping he would repent if given a chance.

Fr Weld sighed. It was impossible to make any decision on the matter without knowing more. He rummaged for some paper to pen a reply.

'Father?'

He turned his head. A scrawny, wall-eyed adolescent with straw-colored hair was standing in the doorway, scratching behind his ear and yawning. With Archbishop Manning's approval, the priest ran an *ad hoc* orphanage at the rectory of St John the Divine: taking boys off the street, at times out of the very mouths of the pickpocket gangs or, worse, the workhouses, he would typically board three or four at a time. They would stay until they could be fostered out to parish families, go to sea, enter seminary at St Edmund's, or otherwise make their own way in the world. One way and another, few of them stayed longer than a couple of years. At that time there were two: John Hellriegel, a thirteen-year-old bantam, and Michael Stride, a seven-year-old.

'John, what are you doing up? It's late, you ought to be in bed.'

'I know, but I was thirsty, and the water in our jug has frozen.'

'Oh, yes, it would be. Well, I made myself a pot of tea a little time ago, it's here on the stove. Help yourself to a cup and then go back to bed.'

'Yes, Father.'

The boy did and stumped off, and Fr Weld returned his attention to the letter and picked up his fountain pen. *My dear Mr Vavasour,* he began, *I gather that you are in a somewhat delicate position over this, and I am loth to increase your difficulties. Nonetheless, not to mince words, it is quite impossible for me to fulfill your request, unless you can furnish me with more detailed information on the nature of …*

'And how is she?' Godalming's mouth asked of Augustus, as Marie stepped lightly up the stairs at the end of the night.

'Well enough, *Madre.*'

'*Well enough.* Will she coöperate if it proves necessary?'

'I believe so.'

'I am not interested in your beliefs, *figlio,* I am interested in what will happen. Now. What else needs to *happen* to turn your belief into a certainty?'

Augustus shifted uncomfortably. 'I suppose she would have to see the hopelessness of Chartism first-hand, somehow.'

Godalming frowned. 'That will not be easy to arrange. And once it is, it may be too late, and the false start may coincide with—and so strengthen—the attempt at a true start that Carroll wishes to launch. No. Give me something else.'

He thought. 'Binding her more closely to yourself, directly, would probably work,' he said slowly. 'If she spent more time with you, *Madre*, you could guide her thoughts into the appropriate channels ...'

'Also too slow,' said the other, 'unless I merely dominate her—a clumsy approach. Yet it may have to do. There is not enough time to do the thing properly, it seems. *Cazzo!* I do not like working face to face, it is why I sired you and Livilla in the first place.'

'Your plan for von Orlok is rather face to face,' Augustus said mildly.

'That is different. I have been looking forward to his downfall for decades, and I intend to drain that chalice of pleasure to its dregs: no hand but mine shall lift it. Anyway, there are many pieces on a chessboard besides the queen. That I shall perform the *scacco matto* proves nothing to anyone.'

He nodded.

'By the way,' she said, 'the armillary sphere has arrived. You ought to see it before it's put to use; it's some of the finest glasswork of Venezia. Rather a pity that it shall be smashed.'

The next night, Marie went back to Lady Ely's house, where she was surprised to meet not only her hostess but Lady fitzUrse. It was not an altogether welcome surprise: Marie had conceived an extreme dislike for the Baroness of St Sepulchre, partly for having deceived her about Augustus, partly because the other was inclined to be imperious and severe. But Lady Borgia wanted to do some scenes from *Don Giovanni*, and Lady fitzUrse had an exceptionally deep voice that would serve for the tenor and even baritone parts, so she had made her a third that night.

They ran through several arias and duets. Lady fitzUrse stopped them a few phrases into the first and corrected Marie's pronunciation of the Italian, which the latter begrudged but could not argue with. A little after midnight, they paused for refreshment.

'Has your r-reception into the church b-been arranged, Mademoiselle Redglass?' asked Carmilla brightly.

'Not yet,' she evaded. 'I believe Lord Ravenhurst is working out the details with Tin—excuse me, with the Reverend Doctor.'

'He ought to have had it done by now,' Lady St Sepulchre said shortly. 'Three months is far too much time.'

'He and Doctor Tinsmith don't get on,' Marie began.

'That's no excuse. It's what one does, by tradition and by the orders of His Grace the Duke.'

'Yes, but why is it a tradition? If there are religious vampires, why not simply leave them to their own devices?'

The Baroness sneered. 'You jest, child. That would foment incessant intrigue at the court, one faction lining up against another, all stability lost. It would be intolerable.'

'Oh, quite,' said Marie in a hard voice.

'And aside from that,' Lady St Sepulchre went on (speaking over Carmilla, who had ventured some weakly conciliatory remark), 'have you failed to observe that most other religious services take place during the day? It would be impossible to attend *them*, save perhaps in private chapels; or by sneaking into a church before daybreak and remaining there until after nightfall. And even if one were to do that, I could only wish her luck in dodging the panels of light coming through the stained glass windows. And there is the *little* problem of being scorched by everything in sight, from the most exalted sacrament to the smallest blessed medal. Unless one accepts the silly superstition about marriage, I suppose.'

'Perhaps we could return to—' the duchess began, but she was talked down again.

'Have you any religious feeling yourself, my lady?' asked Marie with false politeness.

'Little. Mostly I have common sense.'

'So—I ask merely for information—your participation in Tinsmith's cult is unqualified hypocrisy?'

Lady St Sepulchre stood up. 'Insolent child,' she hissed. 'I will not be spoken to in this fashion.'

Marie stood up too. 'And *I* will not say and do things I don't mean. I have more self-respect than that.'

The Baroness' face fell open in shock and anger. Carmilla turned round on the bench and began to play and sing much too loudly. '*Il passo è periglioso, può nascer qualche imbroglio.*'

'As Ravenhurst's dragonet,' cried Lady fitzUrse over the noise, 'I will do you no harm as yet. When you come of age, girl, we are enemies.'

'As your ladyship wishes,' Marie retorted with a deep curtsey.

Lady St Sepulchre swept furiously out of the house, shouting to the servants for her effects. Carmilla gradually petered out on the harpsichord with a crumpled expression, her head low. It suddenly came to Marie that she had ruined her hostess' evening, and possibly one or both friendships as well. She made a shamefaced apology.

'Th-that's all right,' Lady Ely answered meekly. 'I d-d-don't have c-company much in any c-c-case, it fl—it flusters me rather.'

They heard the front door open and shut. The next moment, a wave of fierce telepathic power washed over Marie—she recognized it, from her training with Augustus, as an attempt at domination—and the concealed amulet turned scorching hot for a moment. The attack could not break the protection afforded by the pyx, and was repulsed. She and Carmilla both let loose sharp cries of shock.

'What was that?' asked Marie.

'A p-p-parting shot from the B-Baroness, I expect,' replied Carmilla anxiously. 'Oh, dear.'

Marie left early that night, after sitting with the duchess a little while longer to make sure that her nerves were calmed. The poor creature was still trembling when Marie left, though she seemed able to cope. The landau ride back to Ravenhurst was charged potently with thought.

Lady fitzUrse had attacked her. Why? Merely to satisfy her outraged dignity? That seemed a bit impulsive—more like Livilla or von Orlok. And if that *had* been the motive, why try to dominate her? Why not try to knock her out, or confuse her nascent powers? Yet, what other motive could there be? Unless it were that, as a clear partisan of the monarchist party, the Baroness wanted to get ahold of Marie and make her an agent of that cause. It seemed far-fetched that she would try something so inept, and for such a small prize as herself—after all, Marie thought, she was only a few months old (as they measured things), and of little social significance; what she did have all came from her connection to her sire. It occurred to her that, depending on just how powerful the open-secretive Chartists were, things might have come to such a pass that any vampire was worth commanding. She would have to not-ask Augustus about it when she got back.

She had asked what Lady fitzUrse's curious passing remark regarding *the silly superstition about marriage* was meant to refer to, and Carmilla had explained distractedly that there was an old legend among vampires that they could get their souls back if they married a mortal. Obviously there was no truth to it; it was just one of those tales that people tell—indeed, it was probably derived from the identical tradition about fairies. Nevertheless, despite Carmilla's dismissal, Marie could not help but imagine herself and William … It was probably better not to think of that. Not to torment herself.

Before she knew it, the landau had reached the manor. She exited, trotted up the steps, and went in and asked Godalming where Lord Ravenhurst was.

'In his study, I believe, mademoiselle. By the way, you have received a letter.' He handed her an envelope with no return address.

'Thank you, Godalming.' This would be from William; her talk with Augustus about her night with Carmilla and Lady fitzUrse could wait a few minutes, and anyway he did so hate to be interrupted in his study. She retreated to her room, tore the envelope open with a letter knife, and read:

My dear Marie,
I hope this finds you well, my lady.
Please destroy this letter as soon as you have read it—I know that, vampires having the powers they have, that is an imperfect protection, but it is better than nothing, and I charge you urgently that what I have to say must on no account be allowed into the hands of Augustus Fairfax, or any other undead creature. Henceforward I will send all my letters in the astrological code.
I believe I have found a remedy for vampirism. I have been studying the matter assiduously since I encountered a passing reference to the matter in a Mediæval poem, and—having verified it as far as I can—there seems little question that this remedy is no mere folk tale, but a scientific fact.
I hope this does not seem incredible; but we live in a world of wonders, and one more is not perhaps so strange. The remedy these texts report is marriage to a mortal.
My lady, my beloved. I know well that I have no right to ask you to give me your hand—but may I give you mine? To restore you to the life that is yours by right would be an honor I never would have dreamt of aspiring to. I appeal to your generosity, to suffer me to render you this service: do not refuse me, I implore you.
Your obedient servant,
William St George Vavasour

The letter slipped gently out of her fingers and onto the vanity.

There was a way out. She could go home. *Alive.*

After several minutes of dazed bliss, Marie recollected herself, rolled up the letter, and slipped it inside her sleeve, to be thrown into the fire some time when Augustus wasn't looking. She could hardly think or move; she could not remember being so utterly happy since her childhood. She felt as though she would float up to the ceiling if she didn't keep a hold on her chair.

But she must think; she had to plan, if she wanted this to happen. To begin with, if all this was to come off, she could take no chance of Augustus' discovering her intentions and stopping her. She resolved to feign complete reconciliation to her condition, so as not to arouse any suspicion, and to keep the pyx with her every minute, as Miss Glastenning had told her before. She would write to William and tell him—a letter could be intercepted, but that would not much matter if it were coded. And William had already suggested the astrological code, which the two had amused themselves by creating for their letters to one another months ago. It was a pity, he had once said charmingly over dinner with the Redglass family, that the Baron her father was so amiable, as it prevented William from courting Marie in the style of Robert Browning with Elizabeth Barrett; but he and she had invented the code together in any case for fun, serendipitously as it now appeared.

Navigating the intrigues of the court might still be necessary; her mind returned to the startling assault that Lady St Sepulchre had made upon her earlier that night. Granted, Marie would not have to do so with an eye to perpetual consequences any more (and at this thought she could not help but laugh aloud with delight), but all the same, if she got caught in someone else's web somehow, it could have a disastrous impact on her elopement with William. Or if, God forbid, he were targeted for some reason—but no, he was courtesan to Duke von Orlok, surely nobody would dare touch him. The wisest course was probably to feign indecision, so that no one would have a reason to try and get rid of her, or to use her loyalty to one group as a tool for exerting pressure on another.

Her head felt as if she were trying to hold an entire game of chess inside it, keeping track of every piece and movement solely by memorization. This wouldn't do. She needed her mind clear. One thought at a time, then: the only action to be taken just now was to destroy William's letter, before anybody else could lay their hands on it.

Augustus was currently in his study. He might easily be there until dawn. Marie crept downstairs to the library. The hearth was burning lowly, but it was enough. Closing the door as softly as she could, she cautiously moved the screen aside and fished the letter out of her sleeve. She tossed it in, and patiently watched it burn, shoving straying pieces further in with the poker to make sure that no suggestive particle of paper remained. Then she replaced the screen, left the library, and went back to her room.

The next evening, at breakfast, Augustus talked about the cult.

'I have written Tinsmith, with as much politeness as I can stand, and made arrangements for your induction. It will be at the Oratory itself; ordinarily a function of this magnitude would take place at the palace, but Tinsmith has dispensed with that tradition this time. All told, the business will take perhaps an hour—nothing too formal.'

'I see. Where is the Oratory? I was given a card, but I threw it away.'

'As one does,' her sire said, and then pulled a face. 'It's in Whitechapel.'

'Hm, that is where Lady Ely lives.'

'In a manner of speaking; she is on the high street. The Oratory is back among the proletariat warrens.'

Marie pulled a face in return.

'Never mind, we shan't be there long.'

'Who will be there?'

'Well, Tinsmith and his acolytes, naturally,' Augustus said; 'Glover and Dane are the two chief ones. Stay away from Dane, by the way—the fellow's a brute and a fanatic. And a few of my own familiars: Chastelard, Monmouth, Chelmsford.'

'Do courtesans come to the Oratory at all?' she asked lightly.

'Oh, no. Doctor Tinsmith does not approve of courtesancy. He regards the appetite to be fed upon as perverse, and he prides himself on never feeding upon ritually corrupted blood. How he reconciles that to his teaching that vampires are suffered by God to lay hands upon their victims as punishment for their sins, I cannot answer for.'

'Really?' replied Marie with a laugh, inwardly cursing that William would not be there. 'It sounds as though the doctrine of this cult must be rather confused.'

'To say the least. But let's not talk about it; it is terribly complex, and the only people who actually believe it are Tinsmith and Glover.'

'I thought you just said that Dane was a fanatic.'

'He is, but his fanaticism is institutional rather than creedal. It is the cult, more than the cult's beliefs (such as they are), that animates him.'

'So if the cult officially disapproves of courtesans, why do so many vampires keep them? They seem to have a more or less official status.'

Augustus said with a withering sort of pity, 'You *are* darling, Mademoiselle Redglass. Have you known any Christian monarch to keep no mistresses as a matter of principle? Well, aside from Queen Victoria.'

'Charles the First didn't. Or Queen Elizabeth,' said Marie stubbornly.

'I will concede that Elizabeth's Masters of the Horse were *exactly* as chaste as she. And as for Charles the First, look what happened to him!'

She pointedly ignored this. 'Will I be expected to do anything at this ceremony?'

'Profess to believe in this and that and the other, when asked. Aside from that, there is a ritual drinking of blood and a—well, I suppose one has to call it a *benediction*, inapt though the word is. And after that, we shall be free to go.' He finished his glass.

She nodded. 'What is the date for this?'

'The night of the eighteenth.' Howard removed their glasses. 'Oh, by the way,' Augustus said to her, rising, 'we still need to—'

Augustus' shoulder jarred Howard's elbow as he stood up, and the tray in the servant's hands slanted, sending the two goblets to the floor with a racket of shattering glass. Howard flinched. Augustus stepped over to the debris, got cautiously down on his hands and knees, and began to stare at the particles of broken glass, his lips moving silently.

'Augustus?' said Marie. He held up a hand, indicating that she would have to wait.

'What is he doing?' she asked of Howard in an undertone.

'Counting, my lady,' the servant replied.

'Does he often do this?'

'He does, my lady. My lord has an obsession with it. Almost every time he comes across a spread of lots of tiny things—seeds, sand, what you please—he cannot rest until he's counted every bit of it, though now and again he's able to put the counting off till later, when he's in a passion, like. Only the other night he was counting out all the grains in a little dish of salt.'

She stared at her sire, hunched down, utterly still save for his lips and his eyes. 'How strange. Have you any idea why, Howard?'

'I haven't, my lady. Best just to leave him; he'll finish in a bit, and then Hyacinth can come along and sweep up the mess.'

'Yes, alright. Thank you. You can go on back to the kitchen with the tray.'

'Yes, my lady.'

Not knowing what else to do, Marie sat and waited awkwardly for her sire to finish with his compulsive need to count the glass shards.

Several seconds after Howard's departure, Augustus suddenly said aloud, 'Ninety-seven,' and stood up again. A look of mild confusion passed over his face, and then vanished. 'Oh, *ma fleurette*, I apologize. I got rather absorbed just then.'

'Why do you do that?'

'Do what?'

'Count groups of minuscule objects.'

'I have a passion for arithmetic. Is that so eccentric? But I was going to say, we still need to train you in hunting. You will rarely need to do so, but it is on occasion a necessity.'

'I've been hunting before,' said Marie. 'My brother Henry and I used to go when we stayed in the country.'

'I don't mean foxhunting or the like. I mean hunting for human prey.'

'My God—*no!* I will not do it!' she gasped.

He gave her an amused look. 'My dear, don't you think it's wearing rather thin?'

She let out a mirthless laugh, but could think of no retort, and he went on. 'Hunting is not difficult, but it is always best to be prepared. And you need not go mad and throw a tantrum—'

'Tantrum!'

'—as we practically never kill when we hunt. We'll do it after your reception at the Oratory, I think. Whitechapel is a good place for it; Shadwell, Shoreditch, Limehouse, anywhere that odd behavior is likely to be put down to drunkards and opium eaters, and disappearances, to be ignored.'

Marie glowered. 'I will not do it. I refuse.'

'It's funny, I have this unaccountable recollection of your saying much the same thing about being inducted into Tinsmith's cult,' he quipped.

'I'm going for a ride,' she snapped, and went to change, followed by Lord Ravenhurst's quiet and insufferable laughter.

CHAPTER XV

THE DOCTRINE OF PERDITION

By the ravenous teeth that have smitten
* Through the kisses that blossom and bud,*
By the lips intertwisted and bitten
* Till the foam has the savor of blood,*
By the pulse as it rises and falters,
* By the hands as they slacken and strain,*
I adjure thee, respond from thine altars,
* Our Lady of Pain.*

— ALGERNON CHARLES SWINBURNE, *DOLORES (NOTRE-DAME DES SEPT DOULEURS)*

The next night, Augustus produced a pair of opera tickets for *L'Orfeo*, which was playing at Covent Garden. They bundled themselves up for the look of the thing, and took the landau southeastwards into London: they passed through myriad rows of shops large and small, cramped houses, and sooty railway stations, and at last disembarked in the square outside the theater. The scents of smoke, horses, frost, and cider clouded the air. To her surprise, Marie spotted Lady Ely going inside, and began to go over to greet her; but Augustus suddenly laid a hand on Marie's shoulder and turned her around, looking her in the eye with a calculating, curious expression.

'What is it?' she asked.

He was mute for a few seconds. 'Nothing,' he said at last. 'Let's go in.'

A servant led them up the burgundy-carpeted stairs to the box Augustus had reserved. The fellow took his Imperial sable and her mink, offered to fetch them drinks, opera glasses, or anything else they wanted, and retired. The two vampires settled into their chairs as the orchestra tuned up.

'I,' proclaimed Augustus, 'have never liked the opera. It was not quite so bad when it played only before courtiers, as it did in its earliest days. But then they began catering to the lowest *hoi polloi*, provided only that they had enough money to get in. It is impossible not to smell them; it distracts me from the music; and it is so vexing to have to wade through them all to greet the musicians afterward, as I like to do—save that I often lose patience and leave immediately instead.'

She could not deny that there was a smell, faint but discernible to her, of mingled sweat and perfume and wool coming up from below. 'Then why did you make the reservation?'

He tutted. 'One can hardly *never* attend the opera, my dear. One must be seen to appreciate its fineries in order to maintain a *rapport* with humans of the right type. It is like knowing which fork to use: it would be humiliating to eat one's hostess and know all the while that she had seen you use the salad fork while pretending to consume the joint. Besides, I anticipate being consoled by Orpheus tonight. I do not follow opera closely, but I happen to know Giacomo Borgia personally.' Seeing her blank expression, he added, 'He is the lead performer tonight, and is an incomparable, delicious baritone. To hear him sing is like listening to amaretto find a voice.'

The orchestra began to play a toccata prelude. Augustus asked her, 'Have you considered singing for the opera yourself? You could not start for twenty years or so—too much risk of your being recognized till then, unless you went to the Continent of course—but that is not so long, and I am told it's a capital way to amuse oneself.'

'I have given it a little thought,' she admitted, 'and it does sound diverting.'

The mythical figure of La Musica strode onto the stage, declaiming in a captivating soprano on her celestial power to soothe troubled minds and hearts. The opera had begun.

When it concluded, Augustus, whatever disdainful remarks he had made, was in an expansive mood. Giacomo Borgia's Orpheus had plainly exalted his spirits, and Marie felt much the same: the fellow had a controlled, dark, penetrating voice, and carried off arcs and *arabesques* of sound without even the appearance of effort. She turned to her chaperone.

'Well, will we seek the *primo uomo*?' he asked.

She assented, and they gathered their furs and made their way downstairs. 'You have contacts, I suppose,' she remarked as they walked.

'Everybody thinks so. No one is ever quite certain who they are, but surely it would be impossible to simply walk back and be allowed in on the strength of the confident look on one's face.'

He led her backstage, the guard letting them past when he caught the confident look on Augustus' face. After a little investigation, he knocked on a door that said, on a little card tacked to it, *Giacomo Borgia*.

'*Avanti*,' called the room's inhabitant. They entered to find a smallish, black-haired, olive-skinned fellow, somewhat of Chastelard's type though less effeminate, writing a note.

'*Giacomo*,' said Augustus affectionately. '*Buona sera, e bravissimo*.'

The singer looked up at them with delight. '*Signore Chiarachioma! E una Signorina—vostra figlia, amico?*'

'*Sì sì. Signorina Vetrosso*.'

Giacomo rose, taking Marie's hand and planting a kiss on it lightly. '*Una molta bella donna, sì, bellissima. Come sta, Signorina?*'

'I'm afraid I don't speak Italian, *Signore* Borgia,' she replied.

'*Ahimè*, but it is the fairest of languages!' he cried. 'Pleasanter to the ear than English, if you will pardon me, and much more straightforward than French, with its continual rummaging in the nasal passages and the back of the throat. I never sing Rameau or Bizet if I can help it.' He turned to Augustus. 'I trust you found the performance tedious?'

'Oh, utterly. It made me wish I were dead. Well, more so.'

'Ever you do *but jest, poison in jest, no offense in the world*,' said Giacomo merrily. 'And yet, *Signore*, I believe you truly do dislike every moment you spend in places like this, away from all your beautiful books and sculptures and paintings. And all the rankest people clotting your nostrils, too—I can scarcely imagine what could drive you here.' His eyes went to Marie.

'Good God,' she gasped, 'you know.'

'Know what?'

'About us.'

Augustus intervened. '*Signore* Borgia was a courtesan for a short time. I took a fancy to him when we were both in Savoy in 1850.'

'Was? Did you … retire?'

Giacomo laughed. 'That is not done. *Cortigiani* are expected to remain such for the rest of their lives. No, I escaped to Florence when I changed my mind.'

'I arranged it,' Augustus said.

'Not without help,' retorted the baritone. 'And you, *Signorina* Redglass—did you enjoy the opera?'

She said, without thinking, that she had, and then stopped, wondering whether her saying frankly that she had liked what both her host and the performer had criticized made her look a fool. But Giacomo seemed quite pleased, and they talked a little about the techniques of singing opera. Then her sire spoke again.

'Would you care to stay at Ravenhurst a few days, *amico*? No need to offer your services, if you'd rather not—only for company.'

'I should have been most pleased, a month ago or more,' he answered, 'but I return to Florence soon. The vampires here …' He made a deprecating gesture.

'There are fewer here than on the Continent,' Augustus said reasonably.

Giacomo gave him a twisted smile. 'True; but the Florentine vampires are not in foment. I have spoken with one or two here already.'

The two men paused. Some understanding seemed to hover between them that Marie could not identify.

'Not—'

'*Il Ventaglia Nera*,' said Giacomo. '*Burattinaia tua*. She warned me.'

Augustus looked fairly affronted. 'Burattinaia *mia?*' he challenged.

'Deny it.'

The Englishman's countenance grew ugly. 'Mademoiselle Redglass, I believe we are trespassing upon *Signore* Borgia's valuable time. Let us be on our way. *Signore*, my compliments for a very fine performance.'

'*Quell'osservazione era fuori luogo*,' said Giacomo in a hurt voice.

'*Negarlo*,' said Augustus nastily, and exited. Marie was left standing uncertainly near the door, not knowing whom to be rude to.

Giacomo stepped over to her, clasped her hand, and spoke graciously. 'It was a pleasure to meet you, *Signorina*. Go and catch up your father. And permit me to apologize for that second and inartistic performance. In our differing ways, we two are both old men, and when the passions cool and indulgences are harder to find, resentments flow in to supply the defect.' He kissed her hand again and released it. 'Go on. *Buona notte.*'

'*Buona notte, Signore Borgia,*' she answered, noting happily that Italian rolled off her tongue as easily as French did despite her ignorance. She departed and caught up to Augustus, who was parting the crowd with a stormy face.

He continued to be taciturn and sour as they got into their carriage and rode back to the manor. As they drove past Primrose Hill, Marie gathered her courage and asked him what was happening.

'Why are you asking *me?*' he said sarcastically. 'If you trust me to tell you anything, you might consider discarding the ward that you keep up perpetually about yourself.'

'What are you talking about? I—'

'Oh, Hell's sake, Marie, don't play innocent with me, it's unbecoming on *you,*' he snarled.

They continued in an uncomfortable silence for a few minutes. 'Chastelard should have told me about this,' Augustus muttered as if to himself.

'About what?'

He gave her a hard look. 'Listen to me, *ma fille.* The next time we are at the palace, no matter what happens, you must obey me in every particular, do you understand? There is to be no adolescent willfulness and no clever evasion. You must obey me in *every* particular.'

'But why? I mean, why then so specifically?'

He did not answer.

Lord Richmond's townhouse, which he had bought on arriving in London and kept after his appointment as the Lord Chief Justice (even though office gave him the right to live in the Pantheon Manor, near the Manticore Palace), had no lights in its windows. The servants had been allowed to go to sleep, after what was for Carroll and Chastelard a rousing round of boxing, complete with such salacities as bloodied noses and dripping cuts. The two were now conferring in the dark, warded against possible psychic eavesdroppers.

'I for one do not believe that Tinsmith will break his word,' Richmond was saying. 'The demise of the Duke will benefit the cult, and though von Orlok is his sire, I believe Tinsmith is wholly prepared to betray him due to his irreligion. We can dispose of the cleric *after* that; doing so now would draw attention rather than diverting it, even though it would be a little easier to do it in the lull before the storm that we currently enjoy.'

'*Oui, oui,* I understand; but I wish even so there were some way we could deal with Tinsmith first—it is he that is the truer threat. Of course, at this point, is it even necessary to maintain strict secrecy?' Chastelard asked idly. 'Von Orlok can hardly do anything about our plan at this stage. Though admittedly surprise does make it more delicious.'

'I'm surprised at you, Paul, darling. You perhaps forget that I have been dealing with him for a hundred years longer than you have. Even without his lackeys, his own raw power makes him a force to be reckoned with. And the Black Fan, what of her? It is no light task to defeat the most powerful telepath in the court.'

'She will not at all oppose us. She is as amenable to the destruction of the Duke as we.'

'All the same, it would be easier for me to plan round her if you would consent to tell me who she is,' Lord Richmond remarked.

'*L'Enfer.* I have told you,' said Chastelard impatiently, 'that that I am unable to do. Augustus and Livilla are the only ones who know; she reveals herself to her own children only, and for them to pass on their knowledge is forbidden—a forbidding enforced, I suspect, by telepathic safeguards. I am but her grandchild, Nigel. I know of her only because Augustus has spoken to me of her at times; I have spoken *with* her only through a mouthpiece, the Metatron of her Ayn Soph. Do you know, I think Augustus is a little afraid of her.'

Lord Carroll's mouth tightened slightly at the mentions of Augustus. 'Regardless of all that, I want some insurance against her. Our plan is adequate to deal with the Duke and with Tinsmith, and I am convinced that we can also deal with her somehow.'

'*Dixit insipiens in corde suo,*' retorted Chastelard. 'Her you have dealt with never at all.'

A knock on the door of the rectory made Fr Weld start. He had just finished Compline, and left his breviary on the prie-dieu before the simple crucifix on his bedroom wall and went to the door. It was Mr Vavasour.

'William,' he said with interest. 'This is a surprise. I thought you would write.'

'I thought of it, but this would be communicated most safely in person.' He looked around. 'Is there anyone else here?'

'Young John and Michael—they are asleep by now; that's all.'

'All right,' he said, and stepped in and took off his coat. 'Forgive my boldness, but I think this will take some little time. And you'll probably think I am mad before I've finished, so I'd rather be warm when the men come here to take me to Hanwell.'

The priest smiled. 'If I was prepared to think you mad, I should have come to that conclusion a long while ago.' He led his guest into the kitchen, where he set the kettle on the stove and began trying to light the burner. 'I know it's late, but I generally have a cup of tea myself about half past ten, before I go to bed. Will you join me?' William nodded and seated himself at the table. 'Now. What is it?'

'The creatures that I've spoken about, in my confessions.'

'Vampires.'

The young man swallowed. 'Yes. Father, I believe I have found a way to cure them.'

Fr Weld paused and sat down. 'I suppose that is no more difficult to believe than their existence itself, in principle. Continue.'

'If I may ask, do you really believe ...that is, I mean—why are you so—so credulous of their existence, Father?' asked William anxiously.

'I have seen strange things, of which they seem the most coherent explanation. And I have your own personal testimony. Can you think of a more straightforward set of reasons for accepting the thesis that they exist? Why do you ask—are you worried for my sanity? Or your own, maybe?'

'No, I suppose not. It's only—I keep feeling as if your acceptance is too good to be true. I always thought that was a rather trite phrase, but nowadays—'

'If I thought you were a lunatic, I should have gently said so before now,' Fr Weld said again. 'Pray continue.'

William reached into his great-coat and pulled out a crumpled sheaf of papers, typed and heavily annotated thereafter with a slightly leaky fountain pen, and a pair of small books. 'I've been researching legendary evidence on vampires, and comparable revenants in various folklore traditions: litches, *draugar*, *lamiæ*, ghouls, *strigoi*. It is difficult to sift the merely superstitious from what may be factual or based on fact. It would be easier to do at Bodley, but I haven't the time to make a trip to Oxford.'

'Why the rush?'

'There's a revolt brewing among the vampires here,' William whispered. 'I want to get Marie out before it bubbles over.'

'Marie,' said the priest sharply. 'Marie Redglass?'

'Yes. She's—well, not *alive*, I suppose,' he said angrily, 'but up and about.'

'You mean she has been turned into a vampire?' Vavasour nodded, his face cloudy. The kettle began to sing, and Fr Weld rose and fetched cups and a pair of tea balls, and began spooning the dried leaves into them. 'Well. Well. Forgive me, but does she know who killed her father?'

'That I don't know for certain. I couldn't have brought myself to ask her, the first few times I saw her; she has barely been coping with her new state of existence. And after that, I was always thinking chiefly of how to protect her, as best I could. But personally, I think the murderer was the one who sired her, Lord Ravenhurst.'

'The Spiritualist medium?'

'The same. She had been visiting him in secret, trying to speak to her mother— Marie was terribly grieved when she died, and practically raised Henry after that. Ravenhurst played on that. I believe he took a fancy to her and decided to change her, and came down to Lambeth and took her right out of the house, and killed Baron Redglass when he tried to stop him. But of course you couldn't take *that* story into a court of law; and even if you could, Marie being as she is, she could give no evidence: the daylight, the Bible ...'

Fr Weld nodded grimly as he sat again, pushing a mug to William and setting the other before himself. 'Yes, I see. Well. What is your plan?'

'Marry Marie and get her out of London. Out of England, in fact. I mean to take her to Austria; it is far enough that I believe we will be safe from Ravenhurst's searching there, and I have enough money from my own family and from Cousin Henry—you know, the Duke of Norfolk—to keep us comfortably there for a long time.'

'Good. And what is this cure, William?'

'Marriage,' he replied, and smiled and flushed a little, 'hence that part of the plan. Considering my own failures, I had been too ashamed to press my suit after she found out about me. But when I came across the possibility of her, her *resurrection*—well, I could endure absolutely anything for that. I'd tell Her Majesty and both Houses of Parliament about my depravities to help Marie, though' (he smiled again briefly) 'I *am* glad I won't have to. But about marriage. It appears all over the different traditions. I first found it in this.' He lifted up the more battered of the two books. 'It's an obscure Arthurian epic; judging from internal evidence, I'd put it in the last or next-to-last decade of the fourteenth century.'

'Wherever did you find it?'

'My friend Wilde lent it me at Magdalen, this past Michaelmas term. You remember him, the one who's gotten rather interested in the Church, the one who's reading Greats? Anyhow, the bit about marriage curing *litches*, as it names them, is only mentioned in passing, so I went to other sources to verify it—particularly this.' He laid the other book on the table, a worn but solidly bound blue volume that said in bronze-colored letters on its cover, *Wampiry: Ich Natura i Maniery*. He leafed through the volume as he spoke. 'It's a practical manual on vampires, compiling information from original sources all over Eastern Europe, from the Baltic to the Ægean and from the Volga to the Elbe. This priest, more than a century ago now, was an autodidact, professional hunter. He describes several cases in Prussia, the Austro-Hungarian Empire, Romania, the European parts of the Ottoman domains, Russia—the borders were different then, of course, but that same area. He either killed or cured each one. Here is a cure, one Petar Blagojevic, in the village of Kisilova, which was part of Austria at the time.'

'I didn't know you read Polish,' said Fr Weld.

William nodded, and flipped through a few pages. 'Here is another one, whom he chased for over a month and finally cured, a Jan Vanik. And here is another—he had to kill this one, sadly: a Ruthene named Avgustyn Voloshyn. And another cure, Maria Mazur, outside Warsaw.'

'It is quite a list,' Fr Weld said, taking the journal and leafing through it, engrossed. He said, only half-attending, 'So this is what your letter was about, and why you were so circumspect about the young lady's identity.'

'Yes. I did not want to reveal too much in case the letter went astray.'

'Have you told her brothers?'

'Not yet. If the wedding does not come off for some reason,' William said, his voice dropping, 'I would not have them so cruelly disappointed. And publishing the banns would risk the attention of Ravenhurst or one of the other London vampires. The whole thing must be *entirely* secret. I am not telling even my own family; they know only that I am taking an extended holiday in France.'

The priest raised an eyebrow. 'You are lying to them?'

The young man shifted in his seat and muttered, 'Not exactly. I *will* be going to France, after all. I just won't be staying there, and it is not an *ordinary* holiday. Once it seems safe to tell them, I will write them.'

'Judging from what you've had to say, that could be many years from now, William.' He sipped his tea, pensive. 'Would you like me to speak to them, privately?'

'Do you think you can persuade them?'

'Hm! I see your point. Well. I can be as Jesuitical as the next man, I suppose; if Rahab could conceal the spies of Joshua among the stalks of flax, perhaps I may be suffered to conceal you and Miss Redglass among the leeks of France.' He rubbed his fingertips against the hot porcelain to warm them. 'Have you already arranged your passage to the Continent?'

'I have: we will take ship from here to Dover on the eighth of next month, and cross from there to Calais; after that, we go by train via Paris and Geneva to Innsbruck.'

'Wouldn't the train from London to Dover be quicker than sailing?'

'Yes; but the thing is, while vampires don't mind trains in the least, they don't like boats. Too easy to get caught in a vulnerable position without an escape route, you see. Not that there's anything to stop them from jumping into the water, but if they did, it would be hard to tell the difference between day and night, which for them can be disastrous. And the boat I have booked us passage on is only stopping at Dover, so that we needn't disembark until we reach France. I think it affords us more safety from pursuit.'

'Quite. Well, I will remember you both in my Mass for Saint Apollonia,' said Fr Weld, smiling. 'And—as you have been waiting with the patience of a second Job for my answer—yes, I will marry you and Miss Redglass. I'll do it here in Saint John's, at night, so that she can get here without difficulty. When will you be able to get her here?'

'I really cannot be certain, I'm afraid,' William admitted. 'How much notice do you need?'

'I prefer at least a few weeks, really; but under the circumstances you may regard yourself as having a standing invitation to rouse me from sleep. *Awake thou that sleepest, and arise from the dead, and Christ shall give thee light*,' he quoted.

They stayed up laying plans over their tea till a quarter past one. At last William rose, shaking Fr Weld's hand and showering him with thanksgivings and pleas for prayer, and set off for home.

Having seen him out, the priest went back into the kitchen and sat down over a second late cup of tea. Ordinarily he was never awake past eleven, but this business had his nerves too excited to sleep just yet. He looked meditatively over the books and papers that Mr Vavasour had left in his safekeeping, and the realization slowly coalesced in his mind that he now had hard evidence with which to approach Archbishop Manning. Textual backing, spanning six centuries and half of Europe, penned by eyewitnesses or by those who had spoken with them. And a living eyewitness whom the Archbishop could, with a little planning, interview in person—soon, if all went according to plan, *two* such living witnesses. The Church surely had to have some established way of dealing with this kind of thing, some customary procedure; after nineteen hundred years, she had seen practically everything humanity and inhumanity had to offer.

Fr Weld pulled a piece of paper and a stub of pencil toward himself, and sketched out a rough draft of a letter. He knew he was far too tired to write anything worth sending that night, and anyway the posts would not be open until tomorrow morning. But he could set out his chief thoughts, and be ready to write a coherent letter immediately after Mass the next day, and have it posted straightaway.

The night of the eighteenth of January fell clear and chill. The pearlescent light of the stars and the moon rested gracefully upon Augustus and Marie as they picked their way through the filthy streets of Whitechapel. When they had reached the intersection of Angel Alley with the High, Augustus had bidden the carriage not to wait ('I don't want my landau, or my coachman come to think of it, damaged by the local wildlife'), and the two vampires proceeded up the street, which was cramped between ill-kept blocks of buildings. It was noisome with rotting vegetable matter, fæces, and the occasional scrap of meat thrown out of a window as unfit for human consumption. The gutters were alive with rats, who squalled in chittering voices that reminded Marie of the poltergeist.

They came to Wentworth Street. It was unusually quiet and dark. Even at that time of night, and even in winter, it was not unknown to see illuminated windows showing the pale, underfed faces of men in the company of overpainted prostitutes, or the vacant stares of factory boys doing their level best to drown their memories of the day in gin, laudanum, and morphia. And it was nearly impossible to travel through this or any London rookery without being disturbed by shouted quarrels and drinking songs, day and night alike. But tonight, stillness.

'Has something happened here?' asked Marie in a whisper.

'Horace Dane has probably been making the rounds,' Augustus told her. 'When someone is to be received, Tinsmith likes there to be silence, or its nearest approximation. Dane's face purchases a great many near approximations of silence.'

Remembering his importuning of her at the Yule Masque, she privately sympathized with the people of Whitechapel. She would have taken ship for Timbuctoo, there and then, for the pure joy of putting a few extra inches of ground between herself and Dane.

They came to a rickety white door, on the left-hand side of the thoroughfare, a little before the junction with Commercial Street. The paint was peeling. It bore a crude sigil: a depiction of a chimæra in charcoal, below the unadorned knocker. Augustus struck this twice, and waited. After about thirty seconds, the door was opened, by Dane.

'Welcome, Lord Ravenhurst, Miss Redglass. You are expected. Come in.'

They did. He informed them that the reception was to be held in a private room on one of the upper floors, and that they might go ahead of him up the staircase. Augustus went, the steps whining sourly under him; Marie followed; Dane came to the rear. Marie could feel his horrible eyes on her skin like leeches, and set her jaw ferociously, determined not to give him the pleasure of knowing that he could make her uncomfortable.

The upper floor, to her surprise, contained a substantial chamber, rather larger than the drawing room at Ravenhurst Manor. It was lit with excessive brightness, full of gas-lamps and candles so arranged as to obliterate all shadows, and painted dead white from floor to ceiling. Despite being located in one of the most impoverished, filthy boroughs of London, it was unnaturally clean: Marie, already feeling a little hysterical, had to bite back a delirious giggle at the fancy that perhaps dirt and dust were afraid to enter the room. Marks on the ceiling, floorboards, and walls suggested that some interior partitions had been removed to make this into a single room.

Tinsmith was there already, as were a small number of congregants, whom her sire had mentioned. Tinsmith was dressed in his usual black cassock and carmine-red collar, but over these he had donned a more familiar plain surplice, and a standard black tippet draped over his neck. It depicted at its decorated end what Marie presumed to be the coat-of-arms of the heretical cult: a scarlet sword thrust through an argent chalice, and words embroidered beneath it: *The Greate Day of the Wrath of the Lamb That is to Come.*

The Reverend moved forward and gave her a slight bow, and shook Augustus' hand. Then he went back to a lectern, before the center of the rear wall, on which lay a volume with a few ribbons protruding from it, evidently some sort of sacramentary. There was a long table behind him; Canon Glover stood at one end of it. Dane went forward and took his place at the opposite end. A tall cup stood in the center of the table, carved apparently from ivory or bone, and a paten-like dish of similar make, containing some clotted, dark substance.

After a pregnant silence, the ancient clergyman spoke. 'Man that is born of woman hath but a short time to live, and is full of misery. He cometh up, and is cut down, like a flower; he flieth as it were a shadow, and never continueth in one stay. In the midst of life we be in death: of whom might we seek for succor, but of thee, O Lord, which for our sins justly art moved? Yea, O Lord God most holy, O Lord most mighty, thou hast delivered us of thy holiness into the bitter pains of everlasting death. Thou knowest, Lord, the secrets of our hearts; Lord most holy, O God most mighty, thou most worthy Judge eternal, suffer us not, having passed the hour to seek thy mercy, to fall from thy purpose, who sufferest us to be thy instruments by which thou exactest revengeance upon thy people.'

The foul parody of the Prayer-Book service for the dead, once she recognized the vaguely familiar words of the Protestant service, made her want to retch. A great, distracting vomit would be a relief, and a clean affair compared to the blasphemies now being recited; and the words themselves, at least the ones directly quoted from the Scriptures, gave her shooting pains in her skull. But she steeled herself, thinking of William and her hope of returning home—returning to humanity—and being cleansed again in Confession.

Bearing the book from which he was reading in one hand, and grasping a handful of the something from the dish in the other, Reverend Tinsmith advanced into the center of the room. Augustus nudged Marie out to meet him there. She reluctantly did so. He was holding a handful of earth mixed with ashes and sulphur, which he sprinkled over her head; its pungent smell met her nostrils as he continued. 'I commend thy body, forsaken by its impenitent soul, to God the Father Almighty; earth to earth, ashes to ashes, dust to dust; it is now raised, and hath no other hope but to meet the eternal and Second Death, through our Lord Jesus Christ; who shall destroy our vile body, to the fulfillment of his glorious will, according to the mighty working whereby he is able to subdue all things unto himself.'

'I heard a voice from heaven,' declaimed Glover, 'saying unto me: Thou art righteous, O Lord, which art, and wast, and shalt be, because thou hast judged thus. For we have shed the blood of saints and prophets, and thou hast given us blood to drink.'

He handed the bone cup to Tinsmith, who took a deep draught from it, and then held it out to Marie. Reminding herself that she could soon forsake this activity forever, she drank the remainder of the blood—it was horribly cold, like spring well-water—and handed the cup back to the Reverend Doctor.

He prayed again in a lower voice. 'Almighty God, we give thee hearty thanks for this thy slave, whom thou hast forsaken to the miseries of this wretched world, into the body of death, in recompense for her many temptations. Grant, we beseech thee, that at the day of Judgment her soul, and all the souls of the reprobate departed out of life, may with us, and we with them, fully receive damnation, to the perfection of thy glory in thy Son Jesus Christ our Lord.'

The three members of the Oratory began to say a psalm. Marie clenched her hands, wishing she could pray for some consolation. She shut her eyes (though the glare of the room passed through her eyelids like foxfire) and waited for the black, gory business to be finished.

'… and my life draweth nigh unto hell,' declaimed Dane and Glover.

Tinsmith recited: 'I am counted as one of them that go down into the pit: and I have been even as a man that hath no strength.'

'Free among the dead, like unto them that are wounded, and lie in the grave: who are out of remembrance, and are cut away from thy hand.'

'Thou hast laid me in the lowest pit: in a place of darkness, and in the deep.'

'Thine indignation lieth hard upon me: and thou hast vexed me with all thy storms.'

'Thou hast put away mine acquaintance far from me: and made me to be abhorred of them.'

'I am so fast in prison: that I cannot get forth.'

'My sight faileth for very trouble: Lord, I have called daily upon thee, I have stretched forth my hands unto thee.'

'Dost thou shew wonders among the dead: or shall the dead rise up again, and praise thee?'

Marie shut her ears and eyes to the remainder of the psalms, pretending to be nursing her headache. After several minutes, she found that it had lulled, and she opened her eyes again, wondering whether the necrotic rite was over. But Tinsmith was only turning a page.

'It is thought good that at this time (in the presence of you all) should be read the general sentences of God's cursing against impenitent sinners, gathered out of the seven and twentieth chapter of Deuteronomy, and other places of Scripture; and that ye should answer to every sentence, *Amen*: to the intent that, being admonished of the great indignation of God against sinners, ye may behold the justice of his wrath in handing yourselves, and specially this our sister' (he indicated her with a gesture,) 'over to the torments of hell upon the face of the earth; and may walk more warily in these dangerous days; and may select your prey from among those who practice such vices ...'

Until now she had hardly paid any attention to the doctrine of the cult, and she was shocked, and a little mesmerized, by the careful, line-by-line bowdlerization of every reference to the divine mercy. She could see what Augustus had meant about the nightmare perversion of Calvinism that Tinsmith had introduced. No John Knox or Cotton Mather could ever have sunk to such depths.

'Cursed is the man that maketh any carved or molten image, to worship it,' he said.

'Amen,' murmured the vampires all around her.

There was a pause. Marie looked at Tinsmith, who was staring expressionlessly back at her. Suddenly she realized that he was waiting for her response. Thinking firmly of William, she repeated, 'Amen.' Her tongue and throat burned for a moment.

The clergyman continued. 'Cursed is he that curseth his father or mother.'

'Amen.'

'Cursed is he that removeth his neighbor's landmark ...'

It seemed to take hours, but the ugly liturgy was completed. At its conclusion, Doctor Tinsmith caused her to kneel, solemnly placed his hand upon her head, and said:

'Take thou authority to execute the office of a vampire, to shew forth upon living sinners his displeasure, when they be committed unto thee and fall into thy power, even as thou suffer the same; in the name of the Father, and of the Son, and of the Holy Ghost. Amen.'

She rose to her feet, and the Reverend presented her to the assembly as a newly consecrated member of the cult. A murmur of greeting came from their throats. She was unsure at first whether some sort of reception was to follow; but the other vampires began to leave immediately, and when she thought about it, socializing with Tinsmith and his lackeys would not be, for most people, an obvious good time. She caught sight of Dane, staring at her with an unhealthy leer stretched over his face, and grimaced; then she crossed back to Augustus and asked if they might go home.

'Quite soon, my pet. Have you forgotten that I was going to teach you a bit about hunting before we went back?' he asked, as they left the room and walked down the stairs. 'Just a quick lesson and a quick practice, and then we'll catch up the landau on the High.'

They passed out into the icy night again. The stars winked at them, their silvern light combining with the dull gold of the streetlamps and producing a glitter on the dirty snow and frost-slicked cobblestones. Her heart went out to the grime and stench as things refreshingly natural and familiar.

'That was absolutely horrific,' Marie said, once they were around the corner from the door of the Oratory. 'Blasphemous, disgusting.'

'I know, my dear, I know,' he told her tenderly. 'If he were a werewolf one could understand it. But that Tinsmith should have absolutely no feel for *décor*—it's quite unforgivable in a vampire.'

She glared at him. 'I meant the so-called prayers.'

'Oh, those,' said Augustus, as though he had only just remembered the religious element of the evening. 'Yes, I can see why you might find them to be in poor taste.'

'*Poor ta*—Oh, go to the devil,' she snapped.

'I doubt that would solve anything; isn't the devil supposed to have the worst taste of all? But soft, what light through yonder window breaks,' he said, pointing to a pub whose door had just opened, permitting a drunken, fat man to stumble from the premises. 'It is the east, and Falstaff is the sun. Arise, Marie, and kill the envious sun, who is already sick and pale with drink.'

'I won't kill,' she said hotly.

'It's just an expression. Go on.'

'I thought you said you were going to teach me about hunting first.'

'Well obviously you aren't going to succeed on your first attempt,' he told her impatiently. 'Give it a try, and then I will know what to teach you. After that, the lesson.'

She rolled her eyes and turned toward the drunkard, who was meandering up the road away from them, slobbering out a wildly inventive and personal version of *Cam Ye O'er Frae France.* As she followed him, she tried to think what to do. The man reeked even as far back as she was, so she was little worried that she would get carried away while feeding. She would simply go up to him and … what? With the Dees, the chief telepathic work had been done by the others; and anyway they had been offering their blood deliberately, though for another purpose. She could hardly expect that of this fellow. Perhaps—repulsive though the notion was, for moral and æsthetic causes—a seduction? Well, a flirtation, not a full-fledged—anyway. She irrelevantly wondered for a moment whether the succubi and terrible nymphs of myth were, in some cases, really female vampires.

She drew up close behind the stranger, whose gin-and-sweat stench was almost tactile. He heard her footsteps and turned around, his mouth hanging open in a stupid smile. He was rather startlingly ugly: three of his teeth were broken, he had a weak chin, his hair was sparse, and his nose was bent to the left as if it had been broken and then healed out of place.

'Wossit, love?' he asked her.

Marie was slightly surprised to hear herself answer, quoting, '*Ah, Lycius bright! And will you leave me on the hills alone? Lycius, look back! and be some pity shown.*' She supposed that the *Lamia* must have been hovering in the back of her mind when she was thinking about succubi.

His face grew awed. 'And 'ow did you know as my name is Lucius?'

Her unintentional near-accuracy took her aback, but she maintained her composure enough to give a charming false laugh, and to say, 'Now don't be like that, my darling. I know we have quarreled a good deal, one way and another. I dare say I have been quite in the wrong. But please, my own Lucius, find a little pity for me in your heart, won't you? I shall do my level best to make it up to you.' She set to work on the telepathic techniques she had learnt from Augustus: little resistance here thanks to the alcohol, and an easily diverted mind; this would probably be extremely simple.

The fellow peered at her. He seemed sufficiently soused to mistrust his senses and memory (or perhaps it was only the eternal optimism of his sex), and began to tell her vaguely, 'Oh, dear, ye needn't go on so …'

'No; I must make it up to you,' she said, laying her lace-gloved hands on his lapels, and grateful for the first time that she didn't need to breathe, lest she inhale of his pungency, and ruin her performance by choking. 'Go on, let me,' she said, laying her head softly on his shoulder, to edge her mouth closer to his throat.

'Well … I … if ye do feel so strongly about it …' he replied happily.

Marie inched in, extending her fangs. Repulsive as this fellow was, this was the way to keep Ravenhurst from suspecting. Not that she was thirsty. No. But this way, she could protect their secret. Her fangs tickled the ugly man's skin, and she lifted caressing fingers to his cheek, to keep his head steady.

A strong hand seized her upper arm and pulled her abruptly away. Shock and indignance on the face of the man called Lucius, when it met hers unveiled, abruptly gave way to naked fear; he raised a shaking paw to point at her as Augustus half-dragged her away. After a few paces, the vampire pulled her up beside him, and marched her down the road toward the High.

'Use longer words next time, it sounds better,' he told her waspishly, and hurried her across the street toward the waiting landau.

CHAPTER XVI

THE GATHERING OF THE HOSTS

They rush in red and purple from the red clouds of the morn,
From temples where the yellow gods shut up their eyes in scorn;
They rise in green robes roaring from the green hells of the sea,
Where fallen skies and evil hues and eyeless creatures be;
On them the sea-valves cluster and the grey sea-forests curl,
Splashed with a splendid sickness, the sickness of the pearl;
They swell in sapphire smoke out of the blue cracks of the ground, —
They gather and they wonder and give worship to Mahound.

– G. K. CHESTERTON, *LEPANTO*

The next night a letter arrived from William. Conveniently, Augustus was still in a mood over her instantaneous success at hunting (Marie privately suspected he had not been talented at it when he was her age) and was sulking in his study, and she therefore had no need to circumvent him. She took the letter from Godalming with careless thanks, and retreated to her room to open it.

On it was a long series of hastily-drawn symbols:

It was the astrological code they had crafted together. Each symbol represented a letter; the correspondences were determined not by constant values, as that would be far too simple for an outsider to crack, but shifting according to the date on which the letter was posted, which of course was set on the postmark. She set to work with a pencil, faintly scribing each letter over its corresponding symbol.

The letter read:

My dear Marie,

I have spoken with Fr Weld: he has consented to marry us, God be praised! I have also booked passage to France. From there we can go to Austria, where, I believe, we will be safe from pursuit—though it would behove us to use false names. We will depart by ship from London on 9th February at nine in the evening.

His so-called Grace von Orlok will be announcing a reception at the palace on 7th February. It will be announced as a primarily social event, but this is a lie. It is an excuse to get rid of Lord Richmond, who has been intriguing against him for decades now, or so he believes. (One of the compensations of being a courtesan is that vampires say things in one's presence that they would never say openly before other vampires.) The Duke will proclaim a chastening against him, and Richmond will then commit suicide while imprisoned; Lady Bath is to be his successor as Chief Justice.

I do not think that you will be in any direct danger, as Lord Ravenhurst's child: he is universally respected. However, I do think we can expect disarray in the wake of the announcement, and I suggest that we take advantage of it to slip out and lie low at my family's house in Lambeth. Fr Weld can marry us at St John's on the night of 8th or 9th, and then we can depart immediately.

I love you so much, my darling, my lovely Marie. You have given me joy inexpressible, and do, daily. I can scarcely thank you enough for your illimitable generosity in giving me your hand; each morning I wake with a smile to think that it is a little closer to resting in mine. Keep yourself safe, beloved. God be with us both; and I beg to remain,

Your obedient servant, yours in every way
William St George Vavasour

She beamed. So soon! She rose and went over to *The Holy Communion of St Teresa of Ávila*, touching the depiction of the Host gently with the tips of her fingers. The painting almost seemed to glow in response. Ignoring the sting of the words, she whispered ardently: 'Lord Jesus, save us and help us.'

The rectory at St John the Divine was quiet. Fr Weld had recited Vespers with John and Michael and sent them to bed, and was enjoying a small glass of tawny port, which his niece had sent him for Christmas; he had been careful to make it last, less out of asceticism than out of a patient, disciplined epicureanism. A soft knock surprised him, and he rose to answer the door, wondering whether Mr Vavasour had come back for further advice, or had possibly even defied the odds and spirited Marie away from Viscount Ravenhurst already.

Standing in the doorway was a man in a cloak and hood—a fellow parochial priest, to judge from his cassock. 'Good evening, Father,' the stranger said. 'May I come in?'

Fr Weld had opened his mouth to say *Yes*, when the thought struck him that this person might—if William had been in any way found out by his *patrons*— not be what we generally mean by the word *person*. He gripped the latch and said, 'Would you please put back your hood, Father?'

The figure chuckled. Knuckley hands pulled back the cowl, revealing an angular face with bright, living eyes. Standing before Fr Weld was none other than the famous convert, one of the most prominent ecclesiastics in the British Isles, a well-known favorite of Pope Pius IX and rumored to be fated for a Cardinal's hat: the Archbishop of Westminster, Henry Manning.

'My sincerest apologies, Your Excellency!' said Fr Weld, opening the door wide and bowing him into the rectory. 'I—I hardly know what to say.'

'You acted rightly, Father,' answered the Archbishop. 'Please don't be embarrassed in the least.'

'Has a letter perhaps gone astray? Ought I to have expected Your Excellency tonight?'

'No, no. There was no reply to your letter that could safely be put to paper, so I preferred to come myself, as soon as I could spare the time to do so. I apologize if I have thus incommoded you.'

'Not at all, Excellency, not at all. I'm sorry Saint John's is so ill-equipped to entertain a cleric of your standing—'

Manning waved a hand. 'That is of no importance.'

'May I offer your a glass of port?'

'Perhaps later, thank you kindly. I wish to speak privately with you first. Is there anyone else here? Another priest, a charity case, anyone at all?'

'There are John Hellriegel and Michael Stride, my current foundlings. They are both asleep in bed.'

'In bed but not asleep, I'll wager,' said the Archbishop, smiling. 'Have you forgotten what boys are, Father? Come, we shall speak in the sacristy.'

They walked through passages over aged, creaking floorboards to the private door between the rectory and the church. Another pair of cunning feet, stepping with care and unheard by either of the priests, followed them.

'Foundlings?' asked the Archbishop conversationally as they walked. 'Do you mean that literally?'

'In young Michael's case, yes. He was found by one of my parishioners in '68, in a gutter near the Poplar Workhouse, swaddled in rags—we only know his name because whoever abandoned him there left a note pinned to him. No indication why the poor child couldn't be taken to the Foundling Hospital; but here we are. We looked for his mother, but there were no women with the surname *Stride* of child-bearing age in the records, and the only man of that name was at sea—no help there. As for John, his parents died of cholera about three years ago. They were German Jews, immigrant converts to the Catholic faith. He has no relatives in England: all his family still live in Bavaria. I tried to contact them for two years, but when at last I did succeed, they would have nothing to do with their apostate relations.'

'I see.'

They came into the sacristy, where the consecrated vessels were carefully locked away, and the vestments with their damask and embroidery hung side by side. Fr Weld shut and latched the door. Archbishop Manning coughed, and began.

'Now, Father. In your letter, you laid before me certain evidence, and inquired of me whether there was anything repugnant to the faith in the hypothesis that there were other rational animals than man. I noticed that your phrasing was very deliberate, and that you did not touch on how precisely you came by the aforesaid evidence.'

'That is true, Your Excellency.'

The cleric transfixed Fr Weld with a stern eye. 'Am I to understand,' he said, 'that you are using knowledge obtained *in* the confessional to acquire further and more certain knowledge *outside* of it?'

The priest stiffened and held up his head. 'It is *only* on the basis of things that I have been told of *outside* of Confession, or have seen myself, that I have been so bold as to seek Your Excellency's counsel.'

Manning's face softened, and he nodded and exhaled sharply. 'Now then. I can confirm that it is possible; and, in the case of the creatures you seem to have in mind—actual. I do not quite know whether to call them rational *animals*, since the relationship between mind and body that they exhibit does not seem entirely analogous to that displayed by men, but let that pass. I suppose there may be many such creatures, alien to the life of man, as the angels are; they might even dwell in other stars than this; but, as Saint Augustine wrote of the salvation of satyrs and centaurs, that question is of no final consequence to the Church until we meet any. The relevant matter for us is the inhabitants of our own star, which do include the species of vampires.'

It was odd to hear the word from the lips of someone else. Despite his researches and even the strange things he had seen with his own two eyes, Fr Weld realized now that all the time, his investigation had had something of the quality of a philosophical game he and Mr Vavasour were playing together. Now, it was irrevocably objective. Exterior. Something that other people might do things about, things altogether outside his control or knowledge. He thought of his childhood fantasies of exploring enchantment-woven woods, like Chrétien de Troyes' Sir Yvain questing in the forest of Broceliande. It looked as likely to come true now as ever. He put a hand against the wall to steady himself against a swooping sensation in his stomach. Forty-five, he thought silently, was not a good age at which to begin going on adventures.

'What are we to do?'

'I have no intention of allowing my sons and daughters to be preyed upon by such creatures. It is an unnatural and unholy mode of existence. What can be done for the vampires themselves, I confess I do not know; but the predation must stop.'

'Certainly,' said Fr Weld. 'One of my sources left some documents in my possession that have a bearing on the subject. Your Excellency is welcome to them, of course. One of them is in Polish, however—' he picked up *Wampiry: Ich Natura i Maniery* and handed it to the Archbishop—'and it seems to be the most important source, unluckily enough.'

'Thank you, Father. As to that particular document, one of my secretaries, a Mister Kowalczyk, happens to be a Pole, by God's grace. I shall reassign his other duties and set him to work translating this at once. I will also confer with Bishop Danell in Southwark, to see what we can do as far as protecting London itself; and I will write to the Holy See, and find out what can be done in the Church at large.'

'What about the Anglican clergy? Should we inform Bishop Jackson? Or perhaps contact Archbishop Tait?'

'I will think about that. I don't know how much we can expect; anti-Popish prejudice does not dictate the life of the Church of England as it once did, but we are not exactly popular, especially not since the defections of 1845.' The Archbishop smiled bitterly. 'Tait especially and the Oxford Movement were no great friends to one another; I dare say he has not forgotten my intransigence. More important, I believe, would be the mere difficulty of getting them to credit the *existence* of vampires. Probably they would dismiss it as another, characteristically Roman, superstition, or, if confronted with direct evidence, as imposture. Particularly when they found that their sacraments were ineffectual as apotropaics …' Manning passed a hand over his eyes. 'All the same, one can hardly leave the Protestant masses of London to be attacked by vampires for the sake of the obstinacy of their leaders. There must be *something* we can do for them. I will think, and pray.'

'Of course, Your Excellency. And—in the meantime?'

'In the meantime, Father Hellriegel, I authorize you to organize whatever defensive measures you can. Strictly defensive, you understand: bear in mind, until we receive word from the Holy See explaining exactly how vampires are to be regarded on theological grounds, we must proceed on the assumption that they have rights as men have by natural law. After all, they were once men, and perhaps they still are. It would be far too horrible to find out that that was true only *after* we had assumed the opposite and acted accordingly. But by the same token, if you find your own safety or that of others threatened, defense is entirely justified. I have not studied the matter closely; but I am given to understand that vampires generally do not operate during the day, and that sacraments, gold and silver, the scent of garlic, and fire in any form, are all effectual apotropaics. I also understand that they cast no reflections; though that hardly seems possible, and may be no more than a superstitious exaggeration. I will give you more detailed instructions once I am better informed by His Holiness.'

'Thank you,' said Fr Weld faintly. 'Your Excellency—how long is all of this process of investigation and verification likely to take?'

The Archbishop scoffed. 'Far too long, depend upon that. But no, I am wrong: our Lord's timing is the best timing. Let us bear that in mind, Father. If it is accomplished quickly, so it is; and if not, not, and so be it.'

'As God wills,' murmured Fr Weld in reply.

'As God wills,' whispered John Hellriegel to himself on the other side of the sacristy door, before sneaking back to bed.

'Lord Ravenhurst—'

'Hell's sake, child. Call me Augustus.'

'Augustus. What is a blood chastening?'

He looked at Marie with interest. 'Where did you hear about that?'

'Lady Carmilla mentioned it once. Just in passing.'

'It is the second-worst punishment that can befall a vampire,' he replied, taking a sip of blood. The green silks that pavilioned the dining room shimmered above them. 'The victim is locked in a cell with gilt bars and a small aperture in the ceiling, and left without blood to drink for a given amount of time (the old tradition is a year and a day, though most rulers are compassionate enough to cut the time short). The sunlight that gets through the window is not enough to set the inmate ablaze, but it does leave scars, for of course without a fresh supply of blood the vampire cannot heal himself.'

'What happens to a vampire deprived of blood?'

'He goes mad,' Augustus said coolly. 'Depending on his initial size and native vitality, it takes a month or more. The tougher and more stubborn the vampire, the longer it takes. He also weakens: within a fortnight he is no stronger than a human, and after another month or so he is generally too weak to move about.'

Marie grimaced involuntarily. 'Do they starve to death?'

He gave her a supercilious look and replied, 'You haven't altogether grasped the concept of being dead already, have you, *mon petit chou*?'

'So what happens when they are released?'

'They often aren't; many of them commit suicide in captivity, or are unofficially murdered. But, if they are released, they can be nursed back to health in a few weeks, given enough fresh blood. All the same, they will never be quite right in the head afterward.'

'I wonder if that ever happened to the duchess herself,' said Marie. 'It would explain why a vampire of her age is so anxious and diffident.'

'It is possible,' her sire conceded. 'Regardless—'

The door opened, and Godalming came in. 'My sincere apologies for interrupting, my lord, but you have a letter from the palace that the courier said was most urgent.'

'Oh? Who brought it?'

'One of the nigger slaves of the Duke's retinue. He came on horseback, and departed immediately upon delivering the message.'

'I see. Thank you, Godalming.'

The butler bowed and left as Augustus slit the envelope open with a talon. His expression became wary as he read it through.

'What does it say?' prompted Marie.

'There is to be a grand reception given by the Manticore Throne. It will be on the seventh of February, and all are earnestly solicited to attend by His Grace.'

'Meaning?'

'Meaning he thinks he has finally caught up to the Chartists, and intends to crush them in a single move.' He handed her the letter. 'What he has forgotten is that the king is the most vulnerable piece on the board—a knight and a pawn between them can deliver checkmate.'

'And what do we do?' asked Marie.

'Attend the reception; what else? There'll be no show like it for a hundred years.'

The Lady with the Black Fan sat alone, gazing at the blue orb of Venetian glass she had acquired. It was a hypnotizing piece of craftsmanship: an armillary sphere, silver-fretted on its surfaces with the appropriate lines and symbols, and rather bigger than a grapefruit. In the center was a tiny sphere of solid glass, with a perfect map of the earth's surface etched upon it, the seven continents and the seven seas; the other spheres, thinner than her little finger yet wonderfully strong, were arranged according to the Ptolemaic universe: the Moon, Mercury, Venus, the Sun, Mars, Jupiter, Saturn, and finally the *Stellatum*, the sphere of the fixed stars. The signs of the Zodiac were set in a slanted belt on its surface, and fifty-eight more constellations graced its upper and lower hemispheres. It was a pity to destroy it—but, all told, it was worth ruining even such an incomparable work of art in order to revenge herself upon von Orlok for being such a crashing bore, and nothing less would be worthy of the occasion.

She stood up, and went over to a wooden cask. She opened it and looked at the container of sacred chrism that lay inside, gloating over it. Most vampires who were bold or mad enough to concoct the scheme that she had laid would have used holy water for the purpose, which was easier to obtain. But the Black Fan liked the ostentation of chrism, and its cruelty: water would scald and then slide off the body or evaporate, but blessed oil would cling and crawl along the flesh like a parasite.

The nights marched on. Ravenhurst Manor sat aloof in the icy gloom; the house of the Lord Chief Justice was quietly alive with rebellious traffic; Carmilla and Marie played and sang at regular intervals; William worked and prayed in a passion of patience; Fr Weld and his wards and flock observed their Masses and recited the Office; Duke von Orlok meditated savagely on the prestige and power of the Manticore Throne; Tinsmith and the other members of the Oratory repeated their traditional blasphemies; the dispirited Redglass brothers waited and wondered and said their prayers and rarely spoke to one another.

Slowly, January wore through into February, and the night of the grand reception at the palace was at hand.

'Paul!' called Lord Richmond up the staircase. He was resplendent in black coattails and a copper-colored waistcoat, his arms folded against his chest. His eyes were tense behind his wire-rimmed spectacles. 'Paul, please hurry up. I do not want to be late.'

'*Une moment plus, s'il vous plait, mon coeur,*' called Chastelard's mellifluous voice from above. Carroll scowled and tapped the fingers of his right hand against his arm, turning away from the stairs. After a few seconds, he picked up a tiny bell and rang it vigorously. A valet appeared.

'Morris,' he said icily, 'if you would ensure that tonight is a peaceful one down in the servants' quarters, I would be exceedingly grateful. I might even see fit to forego Thursday evening's games.'

The valet paled. 'Yes, my lord.' He scuttled off.

Carroll paced at the foot of the stairs in the foyer, beneath a chandelier decorated with white-and-black sardonyxes and darkly tinted opals. He took out his pocket-watch and checked it, and tutted. After a few more minutes, Chastelard came down, dressed to the nines in a coat of deep plum, pearl-grey gloves and cravat, and a polished walking stick in one hand, which he was twirling puckishly. His saffron-blonde hair was thrown over his shoulders, Caroline-wise.

'*Une beau geste pour vous,*' he said sweetly.

'Charming of you, beloved,' said Richmond in a cross voice, 'but we are now late, and this *is* rather an important occasion, you know. Do you think we have Mademoiselle Redglass' support?'

'I have told you,' said Chastelard tartly, 'a dozen times at least, that she will most likely do nothing. My efforts to gain her allegiance were unsuccessful. We cannot secure Lord Ravenhurst that way; nor, probably, at all, until the revolution is a *fait accompli.*'

'And the Lady with the Black Fan?'

'I still believe we can manage her. She does not much care who wears the mask of power—'

'I don't want to wear the *mask* of power, my darling, I want the substance of it,' insisted Lord Richmond hotly. 'If all you can offer me is a pretense of my own in place of von Orlok's—'

'*Assez!*' Chastelard snapped. 'Have you no patience? Only for thirty years have you been laying out this scheme. If you will not work with her, you shall work against her, and she against you. And in that Augustus will surely not be neutral.'

Carroll controlled himself a bit more and remarked, 'I still don't understand why he *is* neutral, even in this conflict. Whichever faction he lent his support to would almost certainly triumph. I believe he only does it to annoy.'

Chastelard smiled. '*A tout pourquoi il y a un parce que.* You have nothing to offer him, and he has nothing to lose by preferring accidie to wrath, do you not see it? He has all the powers and pleasures he wants under the current government, and we do not propose to take anything away from him. Besides, he does not enjoy the intriguing. He always preferred lazily to watch others play than to set a board of his own.' He fiddled with a finger on his glove. 'I suppose the Reverend Doctor will do something tedious tonight.'

'It hardly matters. We have his word that he will honor the alliance, and the monster does honor his word—one must give him that credit. Anyway, I find it hard to believe that even he would be as gauche and fanatical as that.' Lord Richmond extended his arm, and Chastelard took it, and they walked out to their carriage.

Several neighborhoods to the southeast, in Whitechapel, the relative softness of midnight was ripped by a scream out of Angel Alley. It quickly came to a diminuendo under a hideous baritone laugh. A door opened in one of the grime-blackened walls, and from behind it there hissed a commanding voice.

'Come inside at once, Brother Dane.'

'What about this?' the vampire whined.

'Bring it within.'

Dane obeyed. The bleeding man choked and sputtered as he was dragged over the threshold onto a stone-paved floor in the harshly lit Oratory.

'If I have told thee once,' said Reverend Tinsmith, 'it is a myriad of myriads of times that I have told thee. Do not kill men in that alley. What if someone were to take notice, and contact the metropolitan police? A gaudy night that would make, mopping up after thy carelessness.'

'We should eat well for days off their men, surely,' replied Dane, biting another vein in the man's neck. Another yell frothed out of his mouth.

'Simpleton,' sneered the other vampire. 'Thou forgettest that even though we left none alive, they should put up a search for their missing men. And another, and a third, as need were. The Oratory itself could be discovered. Nor am I a skilled enough telepath to blast their memories or dominate their wills: still less thou, or Glover. Th'art a thoughtless fool.'

Dane bent himself slightly, assuming a look of remorse. 'I apologize.'

'Sin no more.'

'Would you like a mouthful, Brother Tinsmith? As fresh as it comes ...'

The victim coughed thickly as his lungs filled with ichor. 'Please, milords—I don't know who you are or what you've done. Let me go and I'll say nothing, nothing to anyone, by God. I, I have four children, and a wife—'

'And art a sinner,' said Tinsmith coldly. 'As are thy wife, and thy sons and daughter. It is the will of the Lord that they grow up fatherless, lest thy sins corrupt them further; else would He not have delivered thee into the hand of Dane. For He protecteth the widow and hath compassion upon the orphan, but His wrath abideth upon the sinner's head.'

The man burst into ragged sobs. 'Please don't kill me. Don't kill me.'

'Thou hast none to thank save thyself. Dane, finish thy supper, and that right soon. I do not want it to distract me from my work. Send Brother Glover to me when he returneth, and even ready thyself.'

Tinsmith stalked from the room. The wretch's shrieks became increasingly erratic, and the energy seeped out of them. Over the racket, the vampire called loudly, 'And forget not thy napkin this time, glutton.'

At Number Four, Ramshead Place, Harker was bearing the fruit to James and Henry. In the upheaval that had followed on their father's sad death and their sister's disappearance, several of the staff had given notice; James, now head of the household, did plan to hire more, but the departures had been abrupt and were followed by a heap of bills related to sorting out their late father's affairs, so that at the moment the household staff consisted solely in the butler and the cook.

The brothers were sitting in silence. James looked gloomy, as usual, and Henry was scowling. Harker set the plates before them: slices of sour apples dusted with brown sugar and nutmeg. He tried to think of something comfortingly commonplace and affectionate to say, to ease the tension that—as so often of late—plainly simmered between them, but nothing would come to mind; he ached badly after a long day's work. 'Would either of the gentlemen care for dessert?'

'No thank you,' said James dully. Henry shook his head. The butler sighed gently and retreated, and the two young men ate for a time in silence.

'You shouldn't be so short with Harker,' said Henry. 'It is not his fault that he has so little help.'

'I know. I don't mean to be short with him. I just don't find that I have much to say.'

There was a long pause, as Henry watched his brother eat. Suddenly Henry threw his fork onto his plate.

'I shall.'

'I said no,' said James.

'So stop me.'

James looked up, beginning to be concerned by his brother's demeanor. 'I have explained, time and time again—'

He never finished. Henry stood up, throwing his napkin onto the table, and stormed out of the dining room. James groaned and followed him upstairs. Henry was in his bedroom, already wearing his heaviest coat, and stuffing things into a mostly-filled knapsack.

'This is lunacy.'

Henry made no answer to this, but yanked the cord on the top of the knapsack, closing it. Then he crossed to his bedside table, pulling open the drawer and extracting a leather holster, a flintlock pistol, and a rattling box of bullets.

'What on earth!' James cried. 'When did you buy that?'

The other made no reply, silently strapping the holster to his thigh and shoving the gun into it, then stuffing the bullets in his pocket and marching up to the bedroom door.

'Get out of my way.'

'Please stop. Think about this—you mustn't—'

'Say what you like, Marie has been out there for over three months and you, *we*, haven't moved a finger to help her. I am going to find her, and I am going now. So stand down before I *knock* you down.'

The elder brother's face turned a blotchy puce. When he spoke, his voice shook with badly suppressed anger. 'Two losses are more than enough. I will not lose you as well.'

Henry's mouth split open in a mirthless smile. 'Coward.'

Twenty seconds of blind fury later, Henry was barreling down the stairs, blood running freely from his nose; James was in hot pursuit, a great bruise blossoming around his left eye. The younger, though ajangle with gold and weaponry, was the quicker, and gained the door before James could catch up. Henry flung himself out the door into howling darkness. James tried to follow, but he slipped on the icy steps at the front door, and sprawled in the road, weeping and shouting after his brother. The night wind cut his skin like a razor.

The horses' hooves clop-clopped against the cobbled streets. Within the landau sat Augustus and Marie: he was in a smart black coat, with a waistcoat and cravat in the emerald green satin that signified his house, and a stovepipe crowning his grey-flecked hair; Marie had chosen a gown of fine taffeta, midnight purple shot with pale silver, and silver ornaments. Hyacinth had put her hair up again, arranging a delicate headdress upon it that consisted in a thread-like chain from which were suspended more than forty minuscule teardrop pearls. Against her lustrous black ringlets they looked like falling comets. Tired of the crinoline, which scarcely fit under the skirt of the purple gown in any case—and having a private reason to desire greater mobility that night—she had traded it for a more modern cuirass corset, with the pyx secreted away in the bust and secured by a ribbon.

'I still fail to see why we need to hunt at all,' Marie remarked. 'After all, between courtesans and the cook and—'

Her sire chuckled. 'The cook. Tell me, *ma fleurette*, how old do you suppose the cook is?'

'I don't know. Nearer fifty than forty, I should say. Why?'

'That woman is not yet thirty years old.'

She gaped. 'How? I mean, why is she like that? Is she quite ill?'

'You would taste it in her blood if she were ill. Most sicknesses produce a sour or mildewy flavor, extremely unpleasant. (Though I admit, I have got a silly little weakness for consumptives; the way they cough up blood is so provocative.) No, her rapid aging is a byproduct of being fed upon so regularly, and, to a lesser extent, of the alchemical work she conducts to keep our older and more exotic bloods fit for consumption. Being fed upon regularly, as opposed to the periodic assignations one conducts with a courtesan, strains a mortal constitution considerably— allowing for variances in the *élan vital* of the individual. Psychically, it tends to stunt development, resulting in a certain juvenility and stupidity; physically, it saps vitality, and thus slows maturation in those not yet fully grown when they begin such a career, while accelerating aging in those who are. The current cook began when she was nineteen, and has been with me nearly a decade, which is longer than some of my cooks have lasted. They rarely see forty years of age—though I did have one, back during the reign of James the First, who reached fifty-two. Quite a hardy specimen.'

'Is the cook already dying?'

'I expect so. It should take another four years, maybe,' replied Augustus lightly. 'Why?'

'But it's ghastly,' she insisted. 'I—I mean, she is a human being.'

'*She* is; you are not. Hell's sake, child. Even as a mortal, you must have replaced a dog every few years; it is not so very noteworthy.'

Marie compressed her lips. Probably it was an illusion, but the landau felt colder than before.

Her sire resumed. 'But, in answer to your question. One cannot rely solely upon cooks and courtesans and the import of donated or stolen bloods. Foreign trade is easily disrupted, for obvious reasons: ships sink, trains crash, cargoes are discovered and cast out with uncomprehending horror. As for the willing humans, servants would scarcely last more than two or three years if we depended upon them exclusively, and besides, that would become both insipid and conspicuous; the last person to try it was Elizabeth Bathory, and you know what happened to *her*!'

'Er,' began Marie, who didn't.

'And when it comes to courtesans,' he went on, 'there are enough of them to furnish symbols of status, to supply additional blood for high occasions, and to vary one's diet; not more. One can extend the usefulness of all of these people through the cultivation and telepathic manipulation of the right house guests, of course. I do. But there is a point at which relying thus upon pastured humans, as opposed to the undomesticated types found via hunting, begins to be gauche. We are, after all, *predatory* creatures. Besides, if one feeds on nothing but these tamed people indefinitely, one's own energies tend to become sluggish and timorous; *der Blutsauger ist, was er ißt*. And the company of courtesans in particular can wax tedious after the first eight or nine seconds. One can only spend so much even of eternity being bored; why any vampires take courtesans as lovers, I cannot imagine.'

She shifted in her seat. 'Vampires can take human lovers?'

Augustus hummed his assent. 'It is the height of vulgarity, but, in a cosmos so large as this, more or less everything happens sooner or later. The vampires who do so are as a rule inexperienced, the type apt to cling to the past—though I believe that for some it is a kind of erotic deviancy, not unlike the obsessions of the Marquis de Sade. It is short-lived, by our standards: a mortal woman will lose her beauty and energy after twenty years or so, and the men don't last a great deal longer. And even that is supposing one maintains enough self-discipline not to drink them dry during a particularly stimulating *folie à deux*. Goodnight, sweet and savory prince.'

'But surely,' she said, keeping her voice placid with difficulty, 'if one were in love with a mortal—'

He let forth a derisive hoot. 'Oh, you charming idiot! Love!' he guffawed, and clapped his hands. 'Ah, me.'

'Why is your library stocked with so many volumes of Metaphysical and Romantic poets, then?' she challenged. 'To say nothing of the Pre-Raphaëlites and the Decadents.'

'Well, one must read something,' he said, adjusting his hat, which, in his mirth, had been knocked a little askew. 'Besides, the god Eros may be a delusion and a madness; but the right sort of madness, played against the right backdrop, can be quite elegant in its way. Oh, Marie! Why do you go on supposing that the standards you have learnt, which were meant to serve you for a terrestrial life of seventy years, will suffice for an unlife for seven hundred? and more, and yet more. Romance, religion, philosophy—can't you see it's all whistling in the dark? Humans are afraid of death, and tell themselves comforting tales on the road they take to it: some of the tales are about the road, and some are about the destination that they wish to lie beyond it, but all are only a kind of Decameron; the Black Death lies all around, and will greet them at the gate with a smile. To this we are immune. We are the haunters of the dark, in whom men tell themselves they do not believe. We have no need to whistle. And once romance and religion and philosophy and all the other forms of consoling claptrap are done away, my dear— the only thing left then is to amuse oneself.'

'What a hideous prospect for eternity,' Marie answered spitefully.

She expected him to flare angrily, or turn cold and silent. But Augustus' features were severed by a diabolical leer.

'That's it, child: show your teeth. Once they get long and sharp enough, you can sink them right into the hideousness, and savor its pungency. It is not as though you have anything else to do.'

Biting her lip, she folded her hands and looked at the floor. The rattle of the wheels and the clapping of the horses' shoes on the street punctuated the night.

Chapter XVII

RAGNAROK

And now was acknowledged the presence of the Red Death. He had come like a thief in the night. And one by one dropped the revellers in the blood-bedewed halls of their revel, and died each in the posture of his fall. And the life of the ebony clock went out with that of the last of the gay. And the flames of the tripods expired. And Darkness and Decay and the Red Death held illimitable dominion over all.

— Edgar Allan Poe, *The Masque of the Red Death*

Three carriages, their crests emblazoned on their doors—a sprig of foxglove in silhouette, a sable dragon segreant and nowed, a rising swan proper—arrived at the Manticore Palace almost simultaneously. The wrought man-eater at the summit of the gates glistered over them. Duchess Carmilla Borgia of Ely disembarked from one as Earl Nigel Carroll of Richmond and Monsieur Paul Chastelard got out of another.

'It's b-been ever so long since the last f-f-formal reception,' Carmilla stammered. Her slate-colored dress was unflattering as usual, almost a perverse masterpiece of insulting sartorial. About the only well-crafted thing she had about her was a messaline reticule in her left hand, though even that bulged awkwardly.

Another female, Livilla, was exiting the third carriage. She was clad in yellow ochre with a black, lace-edged shawl, and a matching black fan. She exchanged looks of polite hatred with Richmond, the one with a faint curtsey, the other with an infinitesimal bow. Lady Ely glanced awkwardly between them; Chastelard merely smirked.

A fourth coach pulled up to the gate, and the other vampires drew back a little. It was a plain, utilitarian thing, clearly not built to sate the lust of the eye, but possessing an air of resolve that suggested it would outlast the gaudier contraptions most vampires favored. It was from the Oratory; a milky chimæra was daubed upon its door. Out of it, almost as soon as it had stopped, climbed the gaunt, erect, white-and-black shape of the Reverend Doctor Lazarus Tinsmith. Horace Dane and Canon Dominic Glover followed. All three were in Sarum cassocks: as for Tinsmith himself, the only spot of color about him was the livid red clerical collar at his throat. All else was black wool, ivory skin, and weird, white eyes. He stalked toward the gates, his disciples behind him, all ignoring the aristocrats.

The Chief Justice shook himself slightly, and made as if to follow them, but Chastelard laid a gloved hand on his shoulder and said softly in his ear, '*Alors, mon amour, attendéz.*'

Yet another carriage was arriving, its fineries a perfect balance of robust craftsmanship and indisputable good taste. A green lion rampant reared haughtily upon its door. Its owner exited, and helped his companion down from her perch within: her coal-black curls were twisted into an elegant knot at the back of her head, and her gown was a purple aureole about her, glinting with rays of silver in the starlight. Livilla might have been the boldest beauty there till then; but the sickly goddess Envy, examining the newcomer as assiduously as she examined Arachne's web for Minerva, found no flaw in her. Marie dropped a curtsey to the ladies and gentlemen before her.

'Augustus, how charming,' said Livilla icily; and to Marie, 'Hello.'

'Good evening, Lady Bath,' replied Augustus, in that tone used exclusively to mock others by one's own excruciating correctness.

'Good evening,' repeated Marie around clenched teeth.

Once all the undead present had traded obligatory pleasantries, they went in through the gate of the palace. Ten yards ahead of them was the contingent from the Oratory.

'I see our divines are at their sacred stuffiest,' observed Augustus lightly.

'*Oui,*' Chastelard said. 'Understandable in the circumstance. It reminds me of the time …'

While his friend reminisced, Ravenhurst murmured to Marie, 'Livilla has dropped us. That's interesting.'

'The insult?' she asked, to clarify.

'Exactly. His Grace has offered her something. But what?'

Marie said nothing, partly because she could not guess, and partly because she did not care. Tonight, she was to make her escape with William. What were the intrigues of this lunatic asylum to her tonight?

All the same, her nerves fluttered as they passed through the baroque magnificence of the entrance hall, and turned with the remainder of the crowd toward the throne room proper—not the ballroom that Marie's original and disastrous *début* had taken place in, but a room she had never entered before, used only (her sire explained) for the loftiest events. Even the throne in the ballroom was only a smaller copy of its original, which they would see shortly. The maids and footmen gave them anxious obeisances as they walked through the corridors, passing by hangings of burgundy bordered with silver, neoclassical statues of figures from history and myth, the copied paintings of Renaissance masters, gilt and carven ceilings. Finally they arrived at a pair of looming bronze doors, guarded by footmen with nauseatingly empty eyes. They stared straight ahead, unmoving, as if blind. They kept their hands behind their backs, which for some reason struck her as the most *macabre* element of their pose.

'Slaves, under complete telepathic domination,' Augustus told her in an undertone. 'The technique is rarely used, since its subjects are so easily picked out, but Duke von Orlok delights in doing it. He likes to remind us of his own native powers before delivering his edicts.'

Operating evidently on some concealed mechanism (for the servants remained motionless), the gigantic bronze doors opened inwards, with a slow, shuddering groan of metal. Behind them lay a dim, monstrous room, floored and walled and roofed in black marble and porphyry. The distant ceiling was raised in a tunnel vault, with a baroque dome in the center—windowless, but with a huge lamp hanging from its zenith and slanted mirrors arranged octagonally around it, so that its light was magnified and reflected downwards. Bas reliefs on the walls between engaged columns, from the floor all the way up to the ceiling, suggested an Egyptian temple or of Spanish Rococo, though the colors were of the brooding, shaded cast more favored by the painters of the Romantic age. Yet even in the muted hues of Persian orange, russet, indigo, and carnelian, the knotted reliefs of fantasticated beasts and warriors, leaping from one Corinthian-entablatured pilaster to the next, dizzied the eye.

At the end of the room was an elevated platform, higher than the simple daïs that graced the ballroom; five steps led up to it in the center, and the rest of the platform was a precipice. On it, larger in scale, sat the original Manticore Throne, its fangs and claws and tail-spines bristling as if it were really about to strike—and yet, despite all that, with a face handsome enough to charm an Amazonian queen.

'When was it made?' she asked Augustus.

'1690 or thereabouts. Von Orlok wanted to buttress his authority, so he did something splendidly popular by commissioning a new work of art, that just so happened to exalt his position as well as his prestige.'

'Duke von Orlok did something splendidly popular?'

'This was a long time ago.'

Vampires were milling about the immense space, individually and in clusters. Marie had never seen so many together before, not even at her *début*; there seemed to be three hundred at least. There were some courtesans in evidence, though they were rather fewer than she had anticipated. Footmen carrying trays of champagne flutes full of blood were going about the room, and some of the vampires were helping themselves to the refreshment.

'*I had not thought death had undone so many*,' Marie murmured to herself.

'What's that, child?'

'Nothing.' She reached out for a glass of blood, but Augustus' glove closed around her wrist, and he shook his head. 'What?' she asked.

'Look at the footmen,' he said in a low voice.

She did. At first they looked unremarkable, if flushed; then she perceived that they were all as painted as prostitutes. It was skillfully done, so that a careless eye, accustomed to ignoring servants, would probably not notice. But an attentive look revealed powder, rouge, and even lipstick, reddening the anæmic faces of every servant in the room. Some of the courtesans, she saw, were thus reddened too. She looked quizzically at her sire.

'The Duke wants us to be thirsty,' he told her quietly.

Marie glanced surreptitiously about the room. Not many vampires seemed to have realized the possible danger—yet here was Tinsmith coldly refusing the offer of a glass, there was Chastelard declining with a sugared smile.

Augustus murmured in her ear. 'I trust you have not forgotten what I said after *L'Orfeo*. Keep your mouth shut and your eyes open. I must go and speak with someone; stay here—I will be back as soon as I may.'

She nodded unthinkingly, before remembering that she and William had laid their own plans for the night—but in that case it was better to let Ravenhurst believe her compliant anyway. Out of the corner of her eye, she noticed Lady fitzUrse excusing herself from a conversation and going off in more or less the same direction that Augustus had. Richmond and Bath were nowhere to be seen, and neither was von Orlok himself; Canon Glover had also contrived to vanish.

'Permit me to pay my respects, Miss Redglass,' someone said hoarsely to her left. She started, and turned. It was Horace Dane. A wave of disgust, fear, and hostility broke over her.

'Thank you—Brother Dane,' she replied in a colorless voice.

'What is your opinion of all this?' he asked, waving his hand at the architectural finery about them. 'Frivolous waste, is it not?'

'Oh, yes,' Marie said drily. 'I have always said, the whitewashing and burning of centuries' worth of English religious art by the Protestant Reformers was a decision exhibiting the greatest piety and good taste.'

Dane's eyes narrowed. His fingers twitched slightly. She took a half-step back away from him; he responded with a full step forwards, towering over her.

A clear, hostile tenor rang out, 'Excuse me!' Marie looked to her right, and saw William approaching through the crowd. Dane turned his face toward him, with a contempt amounting to revulsion etched on it; William, to her surprise and secret satisfaction, returned Dane's contempt openly. How could he afford to be so aggressive? Was his status as the Duke's courtesan really as high as that?

'His Grace the Duke has requested a conference with Reverend Tinsmith and his chief assistants, those being Canon Glover and yourself … my lord,' he said, letting the honorific hang unspoken for a moment, as if to underline that it was a mere formality.

'And he has dispatched a common whore as his messenger, has he? He was not always so crass.'

'I dare say. Given that he arranged for this conference by a letter direct to the Oratory two weeks ago, I dare say too that His Grace may have thought you would display more presence of mind. Or perhaps he merely feels that trivial chores like notifying you of a standing obligation are beneath him.'

Marie choked back a laugh, caught between glee and shock. Dane glanced in her direction and then turned back to William. 'It is a great fortune that His Grace's bat wing which curls about you has not been punctured. The arrow would pierce your flesh as easily as another's.'

'Ah. Shattering,' William replied in an idle voice. 'Shall you attend His Grace's pleasure?'

'Not so well as you do,' sneered Dane. 'But mark my words: the night is not far hence when a vampire shall strip you naked and suck you dry. Miss, do excuse me.' He stalked away.

'Thank you,' breathed Marie.

'My lady's service,' answered William, bowing his head. His smile rapidly faded as he looked at her face, and he went all tender and anxious, like a dog that has found one of its puppies in a shivering little heap. He whispered, 'My love, what's wrong? Or no, don't tell me here—come to one of the side rooms and talk with me about it.'

'I can't, Lord Ravenhurst told me to stay here.'

'Well, pretend you want to feed or something. I expect he noticed about the servants and the palace courtesans?'

'He did. … Yes, all right, I'll come.'

She made an imperious motion with her hand, arranging her features into an approximation of undead haughtiness, and went out of the throne room into the corridor, just past the great bronze doors, where there were perpendicular flanking passages, which led to private rooms dedicated to feeding. As they walked, she listened to her *fiancé*'s footsteps fall like drumbeats, and breathed in deeply so as to catch his scent.

They found an unoccupied chamber, papered in vermilion with a mahogany floor. The door closed with a click, and Marie hid her face in her gloved hands; and then William's arms were around her and his warmth was seeping into her body, his touch at once heavy and gentle, his hands resting peacefully on her back. She laid her cheek on his shoulder, just below his chin, and put her hands against his shirt.

'Marie,' he said softly. 'Don't fret, my love. It's going to be all right.'

'God,' she whispered, 'it's just all so—so perfectly ghastly. All those monsters about us—and, high heaven, I'm one too, and—'

'Hush. Your condition is no fault of yours; it is Ravenhurst who should be ashamed. You have done nothing to feel guilty for.'

It came to her that she had never told him about her father, or the Dees. His confidence in her entire innocence scalded her. She lifted her head and tried to formulate words, but her voice would not come out properly, and he hushed her again, laying a hand on the nape of her neck and pressing her close, insisting again that she had nothing to be ashamed of. She submitted to the comfort, resolving privately that he had to know. She would tell him, after she had been to Confession to disburden her soul of those deaths. But not yet.

They stood still together for a few blissful moments. Then Marie raised her head again and said, 'But what are we to do tonight, William? I mean, how exactly are we to escape from the palace? Do you know of secret exits, or will there really be enough of a bedlam to simply walk out?'

'I really think it will be the latter,' he said. 'Once Pandæmonium is unlocked, there's no stuffing the devils back inside; no one will care or even notice where a courtesan and a fledgling vampire are going—except Ravenhurst, and I think we can manage to elude *one*. But I have got two things I want to give you, in case we get separated, just to be safe.'

He reached into an interior pocket, and pulled out a slender silver chain, with diminutive beads carved from mother-of-pearl in the shapes of flower-buds. It was a Rosary. He opened her glove, coiled it in her palm, and closed her fingers around it. 'Father Weld blessed it. It is for after the wedding, chiefly. But if you should find yourself confronted by an unfriendly vampire between then and now, I dare say you'll find a use for it.' He smiled cunningly. 'And secondly, there is this.'

Again William reached into an inner pocket of his jacket, pulling out a small box; he sank to one knee. 'The jeweller was nonplussed when I insisted that it must not be made of gold,' he said merrily. 'He supposed I was being tightfisted. But I feel strongly that Venetian glass is an attractive substitute, especially with these particular stones.'

He opened the box. Within was a glass ring, bearing a single brilliant-cut diamond flanked by minuscule sapphires, which caught the light both in their own right and from the many-faceted prism created by the ring, until the whole glowed like a magic flower.

Marie put a hand to her mouth. William beamed up at her, and quoted from one of the books of poetry they had lingered over together in the old days:

'*The Sun of May descended on their King,*
They gazed on all earth's beauty in their Queen,
Roll'd incense, and there past along the hymns
A voice as of the waters, while the two
Sware at the shrine of Christ a deathless love:
And Arthur said, "Behold, thy doom is mine.
Let chance what will, I love thee to the death!"'

She put out her left hand, and he slid the ring onto her third finger as she answered:

'*To whom the Queen replied with drooping eyes,*
"King and my lord, I love thee to the death!"'

He rose again, and they embraced. They stood so for an æviternal moment, till suddenly he broke the spell: 'Damn! Oh, I am sorry, Marie,' he said, 'but I'm a perfect fool—*all* this time I've been reckoning without telepathy! and how on *earth* are we to circumvent that? I haven't the faintest idea. Look, you know more about it than I do; speed will not suffice, will it?'

She smiled, laying a hand on her bosom over the concealed amulet. 'We won't need speed—not for that purpose. Listen, you go back to Lambeth now. I will follow as soon as I am able.'

'We said we would go together. I cannot leave you here,' he said firmly. 'It would be cowardly.'

'Will, don't—'

'No, it is out of the question. It would be better to die by your side than to leave you alone, with the impending uproar, among these—these *things.* I will not do it.'

'William …'

He crossed his arms. 'Say what you like, Marie darling, it won't happen. And anyway, *how* do you propose to get down to Lambeth alone? Running is scarcely safe enough, after all.'

'I had forgotten that. Well—I assume the palace has stables. I ride well.'

'It does,' he conceded reluctantly, 'but …'

'Will, *listen* to me,' she insisted. 'Every minute you stay here is another minute for Lord Ravenhurst to get suspicious and try to read your mind. If he does, he will discover all our plans.'

'Why my mind? Why not yours?'

'I—' Suddenly she remembered the conditions that Miss Glastenning had made in putting the mysterious object under her care, one of which was that she must not reveal its existence to anyone. She had observed the conditions very imperfectly so far, and an inner prompting suggested that now, with such delicate and dangerous plans at stake, would be a good time to take no chances. 'I am warded against him. I have enough mastery to keep him out.'

'Really?' asked William with interest. 'I understand that that is a remarkable degree—'

'We haven't time for this!' she whispered furiously. 'If you go *now*, and wait for me in Lambeth, our plans are safe. If not, they may not be. *Please*. I'll steal a horse from Duke von Orlok's stables and ride down to find you.'

'How will you avoid detection if you take one of the Duke's horses?'

'Hmm. Quite. All right, I shall ride it down to the Thames and then send it back when I reach the Waterloo Bridge.'

'And the scent you'll leave there?'

'Goodness,' said Marie with a smile, 'you think of everything. Er—oh, of course! I don't need to breathe *or* keep warm: I can walk along the bottom of the river!'

He beamed. 'Brilliant. Brilliant!' He kissed her forehead. 'Very well. I trust you. I'll see you in town before long, beloved. Be swift. Be safe.'

She smiled and clasped him tightly. Then they slipped out of the room again, and William turned to the left to leave, while Marie went to the right, back into the cavernous throne room.

'Your chief duty tonight, *Augusto*, is to keep the Redglass girl out of harm's way.'

'*Si, Madre.*'

The Lady with the Black Fan patted the concealed armillary sphere. 'That degree of power is mesmerizing … She will be valuable in restoring stability, after tonight's furor.'

'How exactly do you mean to dispose of von Orlok?' he asked. 'Out of curiosity.'

'If memory serves, your Irish subjects have a saying: *curiosity killed the cat*. Considering that the House of Fairfax, or your cadet branch of it at any rate, is armed *argento armellino oro leone rampante verde*, I should advise you to be wary of curiosity, *figlio*.'

He shrugged and nodded. 'When?'

'Immediately after the announcement. You will have to be prepared to retreat rapidly, Livilla.'

'*Si, Madre*,' answered Lady Bath. 'Although I still don't see why *I* have had to be embarrassed repeatedly by Augustus' fledgling *slut*, merely for—'

The Black Fan held up her hand to cut off Augustus' murderous retort, as she cut Bath off in mid-sentence. 'She had to learn how the game is played. She'll do now. Your ego is of no importance to me, my darling.'

'Shall I tell Chastelard?' asked Augustus.

'Yes,' said the elder vampire idly. She had taken out and opened her eponymous fan. It was of Japanese workmanship, crafted from ribs and plates of steel and enameled in black, save for the outermost edge, where a razor-thin line had been left bare. 'Go.'

Augustus and Livilla made their courtesies to their mother, and went.

Marie positioned herself as close to her original spot as she could determine, but was not quick enough to prevent Augustus from noticing her absence.

'Absolute obedience,' he hissed.

'I'm sorry,' she told him. 'I was thirsty, I led a courtesan aside.'

'*You abysmal fool.* Did you *completely* forget what—'

'It wasn't a palace courtesan, it was somebody else. Somebody who hasn't been, you know, treated.'

Her sire gave her a contemptuous glare. 'Vavasour, you mean; I *can* smell. Admittedly he probably has not been alchemically poisoned, but don't you recall that he is the Duke's property?'

'Well *that* is hardly going to matter in a few—'

'Whist!' Augustus snarled. Baroness St Sepulchre swept by them, her dark skirts rustling like faraway thunder. When she had passed, he continued, glowering at her. 'Howling idiot. I am going to find Chastelard. This time, *stay here.*'

Marie caught sight of Carmilla, and realized that she had no notion of what was going to happen—nobody would have told *her* anything. She felt a surge of pity, and waved hello to her. Lady Ely looked a little startled by being noticed, and clutched her reticule nervously, but managed a smile and came over to exchange greetings with Marie.

'G-g-g-good evening.'

'Good evening. Lady Ely, listen to me. Something terrible is going to happen tonight.' The pale face began to formulate a question, but Marie forestalled her with a gesture and went on in a low voice. 'There is no time to explain. But if you run, as fast as you can, the moment Duke von Orlok proclaims his edict, you can probably escape.'

Carmilla nodded and spoke faintly. 'Thank you.'

'Of course,' said Marie warmly. 'You are almost my only friend in this underworld.'

Carmilla gave her a grateful smile and clasped her hand, and then went on her way. Marie abruptly remembered another friend: Miss Glastenning. Where was she tonight? Would she be safe? Marie looked about the room, but there was no sign of her, though every other vampire of her acquaintance seemed to be accounted for, save the Duke himself. If she saw her, she would do her best to deliver a warning; Marie owed her that, for the amulet at least.

Augustus appeared at her side again, with Chastelard in tow, just as the customary gale of trumpets announced the imminent arrival of the Duke. As in the ballroom, so here, a torrent of smoke began pouring forth from the floor before the Manticore Throne, belching its way through the air up toward the ceiling.

'Doesn't that stain those lovely carvings?' Marie asked of Augustus.

'Oh, no. There is a pipe concealed in the vaulting, just there, and slaves man a set of bellows beneath that cause it to suck up the smoke.'

A herald cried, 'His Grace the Duke of London, overlord of all English vampires: Julius von Orlok. My lords, ladies, and gentlemen, hail your liege.'

Bows and curtsies went through the massive crowd like a ripple being blown through a piece of silk. 'Hail,' roared the Babelish assembly.

Von Orlok had already seated himself, and was caressing the manticore's sculpted paws lovingly. His eyes drifted about the congregation, lit with triumph.

'As you know,' he began, 'this is a primarily social occasion, though We have an official matter to set before you all as well. But that shall wait. To begin with, We should like to present to you all a copy, which Our Grace commissioned, of one of the latest works of the recent *Spanisch Meister*, Francisco de Goya.' A subdued murmur of appreciation passed through the crowd.

Duke von Orlok lifted an insectile hand and gestured. High on the rear wall behind the throne, where there was an expanse empty of reliefs, from a concealed place over the cornice above which stood the deeply-recessed fundament of the vault, a vast canvas was unfurled by some invisible instrument. Pouring down the wall with a rushing sound, it reached its extremity with a crack like lightning, jolting and swaying for a few moments. Marie gasped.

'*Et cum aperuisset sigillum,*' murmured Chastelard abstractedly from beside her, '*audivi vocem animalis dicentis, Veni et vidi, et ecce, Mors et inferus.*'

She knew the painting, though, when she had heard it was by Goya, she had had in mind his classical compositions, like the cloudy, reddish-golden *The Adoration of the Name of God.* But this had been selected from among the infamous Black Paintings, and was perhaps the most diseased of them all, *Saturn Devouring His Son.* She had seen a facsimile in a book once before, when she was in America, while reading through a text addressing the last century of European art; after a single glance at the picture, she had slammed the book shut, taken it straight back to the Mount Holyoke library, and never touched it again.

The piece was shockingly crude. The titan's limbs careered wildly in shape and proportion, in one place skeletally pinched while another was as malformed as a golem, and all the colors and outlines, especially on Saturn's skin, were smeared. In his hands he held most of a corpse, presumably Neptune's or Pluto's, though in its defiled state it might have been any of the gods: headless, the right arm gone and the left going, gnawed down to the elbow in its father's gaping mouth. The torso of the mutilated body was an olivine-polluted white, except for streaks near the top in a sickly vermilion, and some similar hints on its twisted back, where the sarcophage's knuckley hands bit into it. But worse than all of this were Saturn's eyes. Surrounded by a nimbus of matted grey locks, whereof it was impossible to distinguish the hair of the head from the ragged beard, the god's face was filled with the terror of madness. The wide-stretched eyes pleaded desperately with the viewer to intervene, to stop the cannibal feast, fixed eternally in this enacted nightmare. It looked the very portrait of damnation.

'I wish I could vomit,' whispered Marie.

'I feel the same way,' Augustus whispered back. 'What kind of *animal* has an oil painting copied in gouache?'

'Now,' said the Duke, 'official business. Approach the throne, *Markgräfin* of Bath and Wells, *Frau* Livilla Thackeray.'

Livilla strode forward, her face disfigured with a bestial joy. The other vampires drew apart to make a path for her as she advanced, and she walked up onto the platform and made a deep curtsey to the Duke. He motioned her to the right of the throne, where she turned to face the rest of the vampires.

Von Orlok spoke. 'Owing to various considerations pertaining to the welfare of Our subjects and the beneficent ordering of this Our realm of London, and recalling the great loyalty displayed by Our noble subject Livilla, it is Our settled mind and fixed purpose, here annunciated to you all publicly, to appoint the same Livilla to be *Frau* Chief Justice of London.'

A mutter passed through the crowd. Some looked shocked, others angry, many scornful. Marie noticed Carmilla edging forward, as if missing the support of her newly elevated protectress.

'Approach the throne, *Graf* of Richmond and Kingston-upon-Thames, *Herr* Nigel Carroll,' called the Duke resonantly.

Lord Richmond did not look surprised. He stepped forward; Chastelard, displaying more vigor than usual, muscled his way to the front of the crowd. Richmond's face was a leaden mask. He made the most perfunctory of bows and stood still, awaiting the blow.

A serpentine leer crossed Duke von Orlok's face. '*Herr* Richmond, sometime Chief Justice of this Our realm of London: it has come to Our ears that ye, in the discharge of the office that We committed to you in the year 1789, have been guilty of the grossest negligence, cruelty ...' The chorus of indignant murmurs became a clamor, and the Duke was forced to stop and shout at them all to be silent. They did, and he proceeded, looking murderous. 'The grossest negligence, cruelty, disloyalty, and corruption, being inflated with the dignity of your station, and triumphating in despite of your own native weakness and insapience; and that,' he continued loudly, over another surge of contradictions from a crowd of the younger Chartists, whom Chastelard was waving down, 'not content with this display, secret and open, of your utter unworthiness of the aforesaid office, ye have indeed conspired against Our Grace in sundry ways, of which not the least are the vanities of the so-called Chartist Letters, proposing to do away with the very benignant office of the *Fürstreich*, and procuring thereby the false conviction of our beloved and pleasing child Francis Barrett, sometime *Herr* Arden. Wherefore, mindful of the peacefulness of Our subjects and the dignity of this Our realm, We now declare a blood chastening ...'

But here the noise and affront of the mob boiled over. Von Orlok stood and motioned for silence, shouting furiously, though at this point inaudibly. Livilla gave him a withering look, and stepped a few feet away from the Manticore Throne, which puzzled Marie. Then, sudden and strange, a shining orb flew over the heads of the crowd.

The glass sphere hit the Duke squarely in the face and shattered, and a viscous liquid poured over him, a little too slow and clinging to be water. He stumbled backwards and collapsed onto the throne. Then, he began to howl: a shrill, tearing sound like a screech owl; smoke was rising from his hands and face where the liquid made contact with his skin, which was full of shining fragments of blue glass. He thrashed powerlessly, his screams sickeningly continuous. His flesh was twisting and melting.

'What in God's name—' gasped Marie.

'Sacred chrism,' said Augustus, and, to her alarm, he sounded shocked himself. 'The unholy bitch.'

'Who?'

A stampede for escape from the throne room had begun; but even as they ran, a third of the vampires in the room abruptly collapsed. The alchemically doctored blood had done its work. As the area in front of the throne cleared of vampires, she got a look at the murderess, who was mounting onto the platform.

It was Carmilla.

Marie stood motionless as a statue. She could make no sense of anything. Ravenhurst was pulling at her arm, saying something about leaving at once, but she could not understand him—the din alone might have been enough to confuse her, but the sheer nonsense of Lady Carmilla Borgia, the meek, stammering, harmless—

Ignoring the shrieking corpse dissolving on its throne, Carmilla and Carroll were now circling one another. Carroll's fangs and talons were extended; Carmilla had taken out and opened a dark Japanese war fan, on which a vague white pattern was discernible.

A male nude dancing with a skeleton, in fact, her mind told her. *You saw it at the Yule Masque, in the hands of Death.* She *was that ghastly woman in black on the balcony.*

Carmilla was brandishing the fan, sometimes swiping at Richmond with it, sometimes using it to parry his attacks—apparently it was made of some type of metal. Livilla, meanwhile, was apparently among the stupid ones who had drunk of von Orlok's offerings (perhaps out of a misplaced sense of trust), since she was lying in an unconscious heap to the side of the throne and being ignored by everybody—neither a threat nor, any longer, important enough to be worth killing.

For Carmilla and Carroll were not the only duellists in evidence. Of those who were still on their feet, only a tithe were running now, and of them not many were going unpursued: the throne room was turning to a brawl. Undead blood slicked the marble beneath them. Most of the vampires were armed, formidably enough, with only their talons and fangs; but some had found weapons. Tinsmith in particular had torn a gigantic ceremonial axe from one of the ornaments in the hall, and was prowling through the mob, slicing into the spines of those already engaged in combat.

'Marie!' Augustus bellowed in her ear. 'Out! Now!'

But a howl like that of a wounded animal distracted them both. It was Chastelard. At first she thought he had been wounded, but he was looking forward, toward the Manticore Throne. Marie's gaze followed his, and she saw that Lady Ely had finally triumphed. Her elegant fan was protruding from Lord Carroll's ribcage. He fell to his knees before her with unnatural sharpness, and a carmine spray spattered her bosom. Carmilla reached out and slid the fan out of his body, reopened it, and used it to slice through his throat. Blood bubbled from his mouth as his unblinking eyes stared into hers; she reached out again and placed her hand softly over his lips, like a mother hushing a crying child, and then smeared the wet, hot liquid over her cheeks and throat like spikenard. She raved over the din:

> '*And thus he fell, and as he passed away,*
> *Spirit with body chafed; each dying breath*
> *Flung from his chest swift bubbling jets of gore,*
> *And the dark sprinklings of the rain of blood*
> *Fell upon me; and I was fain to feel*
> *That dew—not sweeter is the rain of heaven*
> *To cornland, when the green sheath teems with grain …*'

She licked a wide patch clean on the back of her hand, the skin showing pale and hideous. Marie felt as if her own entrails would curdle at the sight. Carroll, his eyelids fluttering slightly one more time, wavered on his knees and then fell face downward before Carmilla, who bent down and, it being secured now only by a narrow strip of flesh, twisted off his head and thrust in in the air like a mænad.

Marie finally picked up her skirts and bolted like a panicked foal. Augustus went after her, shouting for her to stop, but she could hardly understand him, and she was lighter and quicker than he and had soon lost sight of him in the chaos. She had made it halfway down the immense throne room when she ran headlong into another vampire.

It was Dane. He grinned at her, a death's-head. Making no attempt to hide her revulsion, she screamed at him to get out of her way.

'Oh no, dearie,' he gloated, 'you have teased me one time too many!' She tried to dart around him, but he seized her by the arm, laughing hideously.

Rage overcame fear, and she fought him. She tore open her gloves by extending her talons, but he was a better brawler than she by far, and managed to grab her left hand and keep it away from him, crushing the glass ring on her finger as he did so. Dane leaned forward, licking his lips. Her brain burning, she reached into her gown and pulled out the Rosary that William had given her, grasping the crucifix through her ripped glove, and swung. The string of beads caught him across the left cheek, and he shrieked in agony and stumbled backward, letting go of her to hold his seared face in his hands.

'You whore!' he bellowed. 'I'll kill you for that!'

He swiped at Marie, and she ducked, but another hand caught his. It was Lord Ravenhurst. Before Dane could recover himself, Augustus levelled him with an uppercut, and Dane slipped and fell onto the floor. Augustus then turned to her and made a wordless, angry gesture to the exit.

They ran. As they came to the doorway, Marie looked back and gasped, just as Chastelard gave out another scream of wrath. Tinsmith, with the unerring accuracy of undead strength and sight, had hurled his axe at Carmilla and severed her gullet. She writhed with her tongue and lips soundlessly for a few seconds; then her head tumbled from her body, which fell down on top of it.

Marie screamed. Augustus seized her arm and got her running again, letting out a terrible leonine roar whenever a slave or a fellow vampire appeared, and gained the main entrance. They rushed down the majestic flight of steps into the dark garden, seeing a few other refugees fleeing through the grounds in the distance. They reached the gate, and he pulled the bars apart bodily, bending them into a gap wide enough for Marie and himself to get through, pausing afterwards to tangle them up again. Before she could escape, he grabbed her arm again and brought her firmly to the landau, shoving their coachman out of his seat, and, with a great deal of cruelty to the horses, carried the two of them away from the pandæmonium and off into the night.

The clock was chiming three when Augustus forced Marie into the hall at Ravenhurst. He slammed the door shut, locked it, and extended a talon, making a shallow gash in his wrist and dripping blood into his other hand, which he then sprinkled on the door, muttering rapid, indistinct words.

'Let me out,' demanded Marie.

'You're mad, child.'

'What are you doing?'

'Revoking every invitation I have ever issued,' he replied. 'Now mother is dead, no one's to be trusted. When I've done, no one will be able to enter Ravenhurst save you and me. Now be quiet so I can concentrate.'

'You can revoke mine as well,' she told him proudly. 'I am leaving.'

'Don't be ridiculous. What would you do, make war against all London? A dragonet would not last nine hours. Now obey me and *shut your mouth*. This is the only way we can be safe.'

'You can be safe if you like. I've finished with you and this whole lunatic asylum you call undead London.' He gave a derisive 'Hah' at this, but did not turn his head. Incensed, she erupted, 'William and I have discovered a way to make me a mortal again. I am going to be married to him.'

At this, he did at last stop—or perhaps he was finished—and turned around and stared at her. Marie tensed herself for a fracas as he seemed to swell slightly; then, he burst into merry peals of laughter.

'Married to … *mortal* … again,' he gasped. 'Discovered a way to … *married!* Priceless …'

She was nonplussed. Anger, arguing, restraining her by force, scorn: all these she had been ready to expect. But not this bubbling gaiety.

There was a loud bang from the library. The poltergeist. To her surprise, Augustus took no notice of it. He laid a hand on her wrist and led her deeper into the castle, his laughter gradually subsiding. They passed through the emerald-hung dining room, where Marie cried out in shock to see Godalming lying on the floor, unconscious.

'What—why—'

'He was one of mother's,' her sire told her simply. 'She has frequently had him under direct control of late, to keep an eye on me; she didn't trust me to make sensible decisions about you. *Ma fleurette*, haven't you worked it out yet?'

'What are you talking about?'

'My mother,' he said tartly. 'Carmilla Borgia. You *really* were gulled by her harmless idiot act, weren't you?'

'But you told me—you—you lied to me!'

'Oh, surely not,' he answered witheringly.

'But why?'

Augustus chuckled to himself again. 'Married! hah! My mother—excuse me, my *late* mother—wanted the kingdom and the power, not the glory, especially since in our world they rarely all go together for long. What better disguise than the kind that begs to be ignored?'

They had come to the forbidden cellar. His hand closed tightly about her wrist, he flung the door open, making it crash against the outer wall.

'Go on.'

'No,' said Marie, beginning to be frightened, 'please—'

'You were ever so curious about it,' he said, spite mixing with his glee.

'Augustus, you're hurting me—'

He forced her down the stairs ahead of him. The roughly cut stone steps jarred her feet, and she extended her free hand so as not to ram into a wall in the dark. When they reached the blind landing, he flung her from him toward the center of the cellar, and the place went pitch-black to a noise like a gunshot from high above them. The upper door had been slammed shut.

After several seconds of dancing, unbalanced footsteps, she managed to steady herself. She listened earnestly for her sire, but he must have been standing unnaturally still, for she could hear nothing.

'Augustus?' she called raggedly.

'*Marie*,' he called to her in a singsong voice far to her left, having gotten somehow to the remote end of the room. She turned her face toward him, but a moment later, behind her and to the right, '*Marie*,' came tauntingly out of the darkness again, followed by a wraithlike laugh and a metallic rattle.

'Stop it,' she sobbed. 'Please stop it.'

'It's all right,' he said quietly from the foot of the stairs. 'It's only the poltergeist.'

He drew closer; she could hear his footsteps on the flagstones. Nearby, he rustled in one of the brackets, pulling out a matchbox, as she had done many weeks before, and lit a torch. His face in the coppery firelight was sober, and sad. He struck her, for the first time, as an old man. Hundreds of years old.

'You know, I was very like you once,' he said. 'Spirited, romantic. Stupid.'

Frowning, Marie waited for him to continue, but he said nothing more. He was not looking at her, she perceived: he was looking down the cellar (or *chantry*, as he had curiously called it) toward the distant alcove with its inscrutable boxes. A faint glimmer showed where the polished brass nameplate of the rightmost one was.

He walked toward the alcove. She followed. As they drew close, she realized that the boxes were coffins. She gave him an inquiring look, but he simply nodded at them and signed that she should begin reading the inscriptions, starting from the left. She hesitated, and complied, wiping the grime off the plaque with her mangled glove. The inscription was in a crabbed type of black-letter, but she was educated enough to decipher it with attention.

'*Richard Fairfax,*' she read aloud, '*born 1ˢᵗ January* anno Domini *1295, Westminster. Wedded to Rosamund Lefebvre, 1313. Issue: Augustus, Gloria, Benedicta. Created Viscount Ravenhurst, 1318. Died 1ˢᵗ November, 1348, Ravenhurst Manor.* In te Domine speravi: non confundar in æternum.'

'Plague,' said Augustus.

'Your father?'

He hummed an affirmation, and indicated the next coffin. The poltergeist chittered in the remoter parts of the cellar, but Marie ignored it.

'*Rosamund Fairfax,* née *Lefebvre, born 25ᵗʰ March* anno Domini *1300, Rouen. Wedded to Mortimer Fairfax, 1313. By the grace of God bore a son, Augustus, 20ᵗʰ December 1314; bore twin girls, Gloria and Benedicta, stillborn, 4ᵗʰ May 1319. Entered religious life in Carmel, 1350, London, and there died in the odor of sanctity, 6ᵗʰ August 1390.* In odorem unguentorum tuorum currimus: adolescentulæ dilexerunt te nimis.'

'She had radiant curls of golden hair,' mused Augustus. 'So unusual for a Frenchwoman. A great pity for them to be shorn.'

'If she became a nun, why is she not interred in the convent? Did you collect her remains when Henry VIII suppressed the monasteries?'

But he simply directed her to the last, and largest, coffin. This was the one with the polished plaque, easier to decipher than the others.

'*Laura Clare Fairfax,* née *Aylesford, born 2ⁿᵈ November* anno Domini *1324, London. Wedded to Augustus Fairfax, 1338. No issue. Died 7ᵗʰ January, 1347, Ravenhurst Manor.*' Marie felt curiously cold, but proceeded to read the epitaph:

'Generatio præterit, et generatio advenit: terra autem in æternum stat: vanitas vanitatum, et omnia vanitas.'

Without warning, the vampire at her side flung the lid from the coffin savagely; it broke clean off its hinges, and banged deafeningly onto the stone floor. The poltergeist began to shriek and to rattle every loose object in the room, making screws squeal in rusted brackets. Marie felt Augustus throw a large ward up about them both. As the cloud of dust raised by his violence dissipated, she beheld within the coffin, lying to one side of it, dressed in a perfectly preserved gown of pure white satin, the greyed and scabrous remains of a female corpse.

'Marie,' said Augustus sharply, 'my widow. Laura, permit me to present my daughter Marie.'

She began to back away, but he said severely, 'Do not leave my ward! She will attack you if you do, she is horribly jealous!'

A light broke on Marie. 'My God—the poltergeist! And you—ugh!—you brought me in to *replace* her, didn't you!'

He spoke, in a voice she had never heard him use before: brittle, even pleading. 'I came back here after Carmilla sired me. She had just come from Sicily, you see, to take refuge from the intrigues and violence of the Italian vampires, and chose to flee to England—I don't know why, she didn't even speak any English at first. She needed someone to be her proxy here, and I had been an assistant to the English ambassador in Venice. So she sired me. And when Carmilla made me understand what had happened, at first, I abandoned her. I came back here, to my Laura, and spent the whole day trying to sleep, only I couldn't, and I was getting thirstier and thirstier, and I couldn't eat either; and finally Laura came up to my room to ask me what was wrong, only she had scraped herself on something or other, and I was so thirsty ...'

She screamed at him to stop, shaking with disgust and horror.

'You will do the same thing to Vavasour if you marry him,' Augustus told her. 'Face facts. You are a predator, your soul is gone, no commerce you have with a mortal can ultimately be for the sake of anything but blood—'

'You're lying!' she shrieked over him, '*I don't believe you!*'

'—no matter how it disguises itself, and you cannot—'

She screamed again, and clapped her hands over her ears, shaking her head violently as if to dislodge the words from it. His fingers were on one of her wrists, trying to pull her hand away, but she savagely thrust him from her before he could establish his grip. Then she turned and bolted, ignoring a few projectiles which the poltergeist—which *Laura*—was able to hurl at her, and ran up the stairs out of the black underbelly of the manor.

'Marie!' Augustus bellowed after her. '*Marie! Come back!*'

The door slammed. He stood still for a moment; then he nodded weakly and crossed to one of the pillars, where he mounted the torch in a bracket. He went back across the emptied chantry and climbed up into his wife's coffin, where the shape of his body had been imprinted in the lining by centuries of use. Augustus settled himself blindly, laying his arm across what had once been Laura's breast, and closed his eyes as if to pray or sleep. The torch guttered and slowly went out.

CHAPTER XVIII

THE PASSAGE OF THE WATERS

I have in all the world
Little to comfort me, few that do name me
With titles of affection, and but one
Who came into my soul at its night-time,
As it hung glistening with starry thoughts
Alone over its still eternity,
And gave it godhead. Thou art younger far,
More fit to be beloved; when thou appearest
All hearts incline to thee, all prouder spirits
Are troubled unto tears and yearn to love thee.

— THOMAS LOVELL BEDDOES, *DEATH'S JEST-BOOK*

Marie did not go back to her room for any of her effects. She had brought little to Ravenhurst, and did not want to take anything out of it; the lovely painting of St Teresa that had beguiled many of her daytime hours did occur to her, but Augustus had painted it, and she wanted nothing of his. She went straight to the front door, realizing that by the rules she had learnt, since she meant to abandon residence there, she would not be *able* to return. Somehow this knowledge elated her even more than a simple departure would have done. Then she remembered, in the nick of time, that, if she left now, she would be barred from getting into the stables for a horse, having already renounced her membership in the household; so she found her way to an inner door to the stables, where she saddled and bridled Foamflower.

It crossed Marie's mind as she went that there might be enemies of Lord Ravenhurst's on their way to the manor, or prowling the streets of London. They would not know or care that she had renounced him: to them, she would simply be another vampire, a competing predator. And they would be faster than the mare even on foot—so would she, come to that. But then, the height advantage of the horse might in that case be helpful. Then, inspired by Chastelard and the rose, an idea struck her. She fetched some cubes of sugar; then, clenching her teeth, she pierced her hand with one of her talons, drawing blood, which she sprinkled on the sugar. She fed this to Foamflower, who, almost immediately, began to champ and whinny, as if she were spoiling for a race. Smiling, Marie threw open the stable doors and then leapt up onto her, and when she whipped the reins, she knew her guess had been right. Augmented by undead blood, Foamflower would be capable of outrunning any vampire.

The midnight sky above her was a cathedral vault, crowded with planets and stars as a mass of votive candles. Saturn shimmered over her just above the horizon in the west, reclining in the sign of Aquarius. She drank in the immense, lonely beauty of the winter heavens, delighting to think that in just a few days she would need a cloak to do so, to shield her from the cold. Or she would forego the opportunity, to sit inside by a fire with her husband, drinking a cup of chocolate or a hot toddy. She urged her mare on, heading south.

Thirty minutes later, after the gallop of their lives, Marie and Foamflower were by the bank of the Thames, the lights of Lambeth and Southwark glittering beyond the water. Marie slipped down from the her back, stroking the horse's neck and speaking soothingly to her, while Foamflower steamed and stamped. Big Ben chimed twelve away to their right. Marie took off the saddle and bridle, removing the bit from the mare's mouth and petting her some more.

'All right. Go on back to Ravenhurst, understand? Go home.'

The horse whickered and nuzzled her. Marie laughed softly and pushed her head aside, and gave her a pat meant as a dismissal. Foamflower hesitated, but Marie gave her a firmer swat, and the mare set off at a slow trot northward again.

A slurred, good-natured snatch of song sprang out from her left as she proceeded down the street toward Waterloo Bridge—some lost soul out of King's College who had had a few too many at a party, probably. She passed onto the many-arched bridge. The odor of the Thames met her nostrils disagreeably, but even this could not dampen her spirits, though she did find herself idly quoting Thomas Hood's melancholy lines aloud to herself:

'Think of her mournfully,
  Gently and humanly;
Not of the stains of her,
All that remains of her
  Now is pure womanly.
Make no deep scrutiny
Into her mutiny
  Rash and undutiful:
Past all dishonor,
Death has left on her
  Only the beautiful.'

Her recitation was interrupted when the bridge seemed to warp beneath her step, and she tumbled down onto the footpath, gashing her forehead painfully and wrecking the remains of her gloves still further. She exerted a little energy to heal the cut, and pulled herself back up by the parapet, looking resentfully backward at the loose paving stone that had tripped her.

She turned to go on, but almost swooned immediately. Her head was horribly light. Of course—she was frightfully thirsty, having had nothing at all to drink that night. Well, good, she would approach the wedding with a clear stomach and a clear palate. She again addressed herself to continue across the bridge, but she stumbled a second time, sprawling on the pavement.

Marie cautiously hoisted herself up again. The boisterous voice was coming closer, apparently bound south of the Thames like herself. Her throat felt like dried-up parchment. Would it be quite safe to meet William like this? Ravenhurst might be the father of lies, but all the same, for her to be so hungry around a cour—a *former* courtesan would be a temptation for them both. She thought of finding some animal on her way; but then she remembered the warning she had been given, that feeding on beasts tended to make the feeder bestial. That would not just be temptation: that would be frankly dangerous.

'Hullo, miss!' said the loud voice cheerily. 'What are you out and about for all alone at this hour?' It was not an intrusive voice, only curious and drunk.

'I ... I'm on my ... way home,' she replied.

'And where's that? May I walk with you, miss? Some nasty folk about, you know.' There was in fact nobody in sight except the young man: a handsome specimen of English dandyism, aside from his overbred chin. He impulsively put forward a hand. 'Strickland-Venables is my name.' He had a rich, heavy smell, like venison. His scarf was disarranged, and he seemed to have misplaced his tie and studs, for his starched collar stood open, exposing a healthy throat.

'Pleased to meet you.' She clenched and unclenched her hands. No protectors; no witnesses. And he would probably remember nothing in any case.

'Oh, dear, look at your gloves! Such a pity, miss, they are fine things, aren't they?' He let loose a ludicrous belch, and guffawed. 'Goodness. Excuse me.' He took her right hand in his, peering at her glove closely.

She looked into his face. 'Mr Strickland-Venables.'

'Yes?' he said, looking into hers; then he was quiet and still.

A cloying mist was beginning to rise as the constable began his patrol, but the streetlamps still penetrated it at first. He strode briskly along the street, hoping to enjoy a surreptitious cigar on Waterloo Bridge before continuing. Further down the bridge, he noticed a pair of figures curiously jammed together. He groaned; it looked like a well-born young man making a nuisance of himself with a woman— a prostitute, probably, which meant he would have to go and break them up and cite them both. He drew closer. The two were carrying on in the most flagrantly indecent fashion. The young man was gasping and pawing at the lady, and as for her behavior! Brazenly kissing his neck with the air of an infant suckling at the breast, out here in the—well, not broad daylight exactly, but in this public place, nevertheless.

'Pardon me,' he called out sharply, 'but—'

The two broke apart. The man seemed to be saying something to the woman, who was looking directly at the constable, fog notwithstanding. Disregarding her paramour, she—good God!—she had climbed up onto the parapet of the bridge. The constable ran towards them. The young man had caught hold of her fingers and was pleading with her to desist, but she shook her hand fiercely from his grasp and stood erect upon the wall, arms extended, a cruciform black shape in the mist. 'Miss, stop!' the constable cried. 'That's not—'

She leapt.

The inebriate and the constable leaned over the parapet at the same time, to see her plunge into the opalescent water of the river. The young man became hysterical, weeping and shouting, and began pulling off his coat to jump in after her, but the constable seized hold of him and kept him from climbing up. Neither had ever seen a suicide before. Shaking, his face tinged with sweat despite the freezing night, the constable marched the pale, lachrymose young fellow back up the bridge to take him to the station, where he could commission a search party and have the man questioned.

Marie screwed her eyes shut and tried to brace herself, but nothing could ready her for her shocking impact on the icy Thames. The river struck her like rock, and she was obliged to heal some minor injuries with a small amount of the blood she had just acquired from the young stranger. Her original plan, temporarily forgotten, had of course been to walk or swim along the bottom of the river, and so eliminate any chance of being tracked by her scent; now that she was actually *in* the river, she felt strongly that she would happily have risked being caught *if it* meant avoiding the Thames' loathsome chill, pressure, and above all its foul taste.

Still. Here she was, and the river wasn't getting any narrower. Swimming down to the bottom, she began to make her tedious way across, muscling through the sluggish liquid, and batting away piscine detritus, bits of rubbish, and broken pieces of dead plant life. It was difficult to see.

William was pacing his study, after midnight, his face knotted with anxiety. He was running his Rosary through his fingers, saying the prayers with perfect absence of mind, more soothed by the feel of the beads against his fingers than by the invocations of the Trinity and the Virgin. The room was a cozy one, crowded with papers and books assorted in that peculiar kind of disorder that suggests amiability more than sloth; but neither sloth nor amiability were evident in William just then.

Desmond came to the doorway, his face uneasy. 'Sorry to disturb you, me lord, but there's a vagrant woman at the door now as wants to see you. I asked her in, but she said she wouldn't cross the step without speaking to you first.' He fiddled with his fingers and went on, 'She seems to be mad.'

William was out of the study in an instant. 'Leave it to me,' he called over his shoulder.

He reached the foyer and re-opened the door. On the step was a black, dripping shape, reeking like a cadaver washed up on a riverbank. Spots of bone-pale skin were visible at the hands and chin, the scarlet mouth almost hidden by the clinging remains of a *crêpe* veil.

'Marie,' he breathed, overwhelmed with relief. 'Come in.'

She stepped into the house, looking utterly woebegone. 'I'm sorry about all this water,' she said stupidly; 'I didn't think—'

He cut her off by taking her tightly in his arms. For a moment she simply stood; then she softened, and returned his embrace; then, weakly, she started to cry. It had been so, so long since she had been touched or spoken to with anything like affection. She clung to William's broad, warm shoulders, burying her face in his chest, her cold brow damp against his throat, and cried for her father, and herself, and her brothers, and her mother, and the months of terror and bewilderment and sacrilege and vast, oppressive loneliness. Every day, every hour, every tick of that ghastly clock in the hall at Ravenhurst, leaked out of her; and then it was gone.

Marie leaned back and looked at him, pushing her ruined veil aside and resting her hands on William's shoulders, and looked him in the face. He smiled gently. Suddenly she laughed, and could not stop.

'You are a dripping mess,' she managed to rasp. 'I've made a complete wreck of your shirt-front.'

He laughed too, and mingled kisses with their laughter. 'A snow-white shirt-front is honored by being made the handkerchief of my lady Snow-White,' he told her. 'Besides, I have plenty of shirt-fronts and only one of you; I call it an excellent trade to secure the one with the other.'

'Quite. You realize I am only marrying you for your shirt-fronts, darling.'

'Naturally,' he replied gravely. 'All the perfumes of Arabia cannot clean this little shirt-front. Therefore, to have an incessant supply is the gentleman's only recourse; and Norfolk's nephew can open all the windows of the world, from brooding Tyre to the contemplative Sphinx to garden-girdled Babylon, all to supply my lady with endless shirt-fronts.'

They laughed again, and he showed her to a room (explaining to Desmond, in a stern voice, that the young lady was his guest and was to be treated accordingly): a peacock-blue fantasy of a thing, with an adjoining bathroom, where she gratefully extracted herself from her mangled gown and washed the river's stench off her body. She lay in the bath for an hour, the hot, soapy water soothing her skin. At last she forced herself to get up out of it and dry herself, and pulled on a pale grey silk chemise that she found in the wardrobe, and went to the bed to lie down and rest. Admittedly sleep was still impossible, for the present, but it was so wonderfully relaxing to lie on the soft coverlet and gaze dreamily at the ceiling that that hardly mattered. For she had, she saw, been telling the truth unawares when Strickland-Venables asked her where she was going. She was home.

'Name?' said the workhouse porter, whose accent made a number of valiant sorties into the Queen's English, but for the most part remained in the Bethnal Green Cockney that was clearly his native tongue.

'Henry Arthur Edmund Redglass.'

'Profession?'

'None.'

'Address?'

'None,' Henry lied.

'Physical condition?'

'Good.'

The porter nodded, flipping over the pages of a voluminous record-book with a pencil in his hand. 'Bit posh for the casual ward, aren't you, sir? Look like a right gen'leman.'

Henry shrugged. 'That's as may be; I've nowhere else to go.' Strictly speaking, he ought not be at a workhouse—they were designed for the truly destitute—but he half-hoped to find Marie there, or someone who had seen her. Besides, he was exhausted, and although he did have enough money for a few nights at an inn, the only one he had yet passed was shut up for the night.

'You, and myriads of myriads, like i' says in the Bible. Are you a Bible-reading man, sir?'

'I am a Catholic.'

'*Are* you naow,' said the porter in a much more clipped voice. 'Well, understand, we don't admit papis' priests and that 'ere, not unless a chap's a-dying, like. Don't 'old wiv i'. Me, I'm a plain, God-fearing *English*man, sir, and I don' need no bishop a' all, and surely not a foreigner for a Pope, see? You ever 'ear of General William Boof, Mr Redglass?'

'Does this have anything to do with whether I can have a bed in the casual ward tonight?' asked Henry curtly.

The porter gave him a sour look. 'Time of entry, twen'y minutes past eleven. Leave your personal effecks 'ere. You can discharge yourself not later than eleven tomorrow morning, so long as you give free 'aours notice firs'. 'Ave a scrub down over there,' he pointed, 'and then they'll issue you your cloving for the night, excep' shoes, seeing as you don' mean to stay, like. And don' make any trouble, if you'd be so kind, sir,' he concluded severely.

'Thank you,' said Henry tonessly, setting his precious knapsack on the counter (from which it was immediately whisked away into the *Ewigkeit*), and walking a little way down the corridor to the room indicated by the misanthropic charity worker. Here his clothes were also taken to be stored, and he was given a few minutes to wash in cloudy water that seemed somehow to be even colder than ice. He was then given a faded cotton shirt, a pair of trousers, a woolen jacket, a sturdy cloth cap, and a thin pair of socks. Though ill-fitting, and in some places repaired with patches stitched on with gross incompetence, the clothes were at least clean. He touched his wounded nose gingerly; it still hurt, but the swelling had gone down, thanks to the cold.

The casual ward for men between the ages of 14 and 60 was a single large room, with a wretched bucket in the middle that received every kind of waste, and a number of large cots covered in straw (most of which had been pushed as far away from the central bucket as was physically possible). There were no sheets or blankets, and no fireplace. Each cot, constructed to accommodate one man, held three or four. The smell was almost audible.

Henry muscled his way onto a cot close to the door, already occupied by two scrawny, squirming youths, and a whiskered man, perhaps in his forties, who snored like one prepared to sleep through the Seven Trumpets. He meditated, looking at the two young men—boys, really—and wondering whether either of of them could have seen Marie.

'Excuse me,' he whispered to the one nearer him, 'may I ask you something?'

'You *'ave* done,' groused the young man, keeping his eyes tightly shut.

'Ask 'im if 'e's got any money, Tom,' said the next.

'Don' be stupid,' sneered the first. 'If 'e did 'ave, 'e wouldn' be a-come to a spike now, would 'e then? Prat.'

Henry propped himself up on his elbow and whispered more urgently. 'Have either one of you, over the last week or so, seen a woman in her early twenties, curly black hair, violet eyes, extremely fair of skin?'

'This is the chaps' side, of course we 'aven' seen a woman.'

'No, I mean out and about in London.'

'Look,' said the nearer young man, opening his eyes angrily, 'we don' go ou', see? 'Tisn' done 'ere. No' permitted. You wan' a tar', like, you eiver ge' religion and give i' up wan'ing, or you find a mandrake and a quie' corner.'

'It's nothing like that!'

'Quiet is to be kept after lights out,' said a warden through a speaking trumpet, making everyone stir unhappily in their cots.

'So bugger off,' muttered the boy beside Henry.

He nodded hopelessly. Then he got into the least uncomfortable position he could find, grateful that the multitude of bodies at least provided a little extra warmth, and worked vainly at falling asleep.

William slept right through most of the day, not waking until a couple of hours before sunset. He sent a telegram to Fr Weld, allusively indicating that Marie had arrived safely, and that they would come up to St John the Divine at nine for the wedding, and had a late tea before going up to Marie's room. He knocked softly.

'My love?'

She bounded up from the bed and flung the door open and threw her arms around him. 'Oh, Will, I am so happy!'

'None of that,' he reproved her mockingly. 'You are to be wedded, Miss Redglass, and ought to comport yourself with appropriate sobriety, in the manner of Isaac Watts' poetry.'

'Oh, I do apologize, Mister Rochester. I shall be only grave and gloomy, if it please you.'

'Please me? Such frivolity!' They laughed, and he kissed her forehead. 'It's about six now; I have sent word to Father Weld, and we shall go up to Saint John's at about half past eight. Is that all right?'

'Yes,' she said. 'But what about a wedding dress? I don't want to be married in black!'

'I thought of that. You remember my Aunt Dolores, who was jilted by that cad Fulbright about eight years ago? Well, she did not want her gown after that—understandably—and set it aside for any of her nieces to use, or any nephews' brides, and in fact she left it here. It's one of those elegant Georgian ones, and it's white. I think it will fit you.'

Marie nodded appreciatively. 'How serendipitous.'

'But come and have a sit for a while before we start to get ready,' he said eagerly, clasping her hands. 'Let's talk for a bit.'

They went down to the drawing room, and sat together before a low, drowsy fire, and spoke hardly at all.

The gown was a bewitching, austere thing, in the Regency style: a short bodice, laced up just beneath the breasts with a royal blue ribbon, and then falling in simple folds to Marie's slippered feet. Long satin gloves and a thick veil attached to a pearl-studded circlet completed the ensemble. Although she still could not see herself, she lingered before the mirror for a moment to enjoy the beauty of the dress in its own right. One of the Vavasours' servants had been dispatched for a bouquet, which sat in a little vase near the door. She picked it up, inhaling the scents: it contained gardenias, white and yellow roses, poppies, and morning glories, with little ornamental lemon blossoms and oxeye daisies.

The two regretfully forebore from the pleasing superstition about the bridegroom not seeing the bride in her glory before the wedding ceremony itself, and took a single landau together out towards Islington. William was looking splendid in his evening dress and silk topper, his waistcoat crossed by a silver watch chain. Usually his preference for going clean-shaven looked a little odd among the bearded, mustachioed, or muttonchopped men of fashionable London, but tonight, it softened the strong, masculine lines of his dress with a touch of youthfulness and innocence, like the beardless pictures of Apollo on ancient Greek pottery. He wore a bright, milk-white sprig of asphodel in his buttonhole. As they drove across the Thames, he suddenly frowned.

'Marie? Are you ... will you be all right? Visiting a church, and during the wedding, I mean.'

'Well, really, we haven't got a lot of choice, have we?'

'True,' William said, and sighed. 'I just wish I could protect you.'

'From God?' she answered with a laugh.

He smiled and said, 'No, of course not. But all the same, it is terrible to see the smallest suffering in a person one loves, however necessary. One cannot suppress one's instincts entirely.'

'Well,' she said, clasping his hand in her glove, 'if it is any comfort to you, though the phrase may have waxed trite, you have the instincts of a perfect gentleman.'

This did not seem greatly to comfort him; but, having grown up with two brothers, to say nothing of her father, she was well acquainted with the male habit of sulking when things are not exactly as desired for a beloved, rather than sensibly making the best of things. But he was at least trying to mask his apprehension, and she was pleased by the effort.

The landau came to the street-side entrance of St John the Divine Catholic Church, and William disembarked and put out his arm for Marie. He instructed the coachman to wait at a nearby coffeehouse, and they went to the neighboring door of the rectory and knocked.

A wiry youth with eyes pointing in different directions opened it. 'Are you Miss Goldsmith and Mister Vavasour?'

'We are,' said William.

'Father said to expect you. Come on inside, then.'

William looked at Marie, and said, 'Actually, young man, would you mind fetching Father for us first?'

The boy shrugged. 'If you like. Father!'

The priest, dressed in cassock and collar, padded up. 'Don't shout, John,' he said, and looked brightly at the pair. 'Miss Goldsmith, Mister Vavasour, I'm delighted to see you.' He said the former name with the slightest hesitation: the pseudonym had been arranged for Marie's safety. Fr Weld asked them both over the threshold, and they stepped inside, Marie's skin tingling faintly with the sensation of being so close to the holy place.

Fr Weld told John to fetch Michael, the other boarder, and for them to vest and get the vessels and candles ready in the church, and that he and the prospective spouses would be along in a moment.

'Well!' The priest's eyes twinkled. 'William has informed me of your, ah, condition, as I expect you know. Are you ready, my daughter?'

'I am,' said Marie. 'It is hard to believe it has been only a little more than three months. I have missed the Mass a great deal.'

'I can scarcely imagine. Would you like to make your confession before we begin the Mass?'

She frowned. 'To be perfectly honest, Father, I am a little afraid of the consequences, given …'

'Yes, of course. And I realize that the two of you are working on a rather constricted schedule. Come.' He led them toward the main body of the church, where John was lighting the candles. The chalice and paten, veiled in a trapezoidal prism of white, were already sitting upon the altar. John and Fr Weld went back into the sacristy to vest, and the bridegroom led his bride into the church, genuflecting to the Blessed Sacrament.

As Marie crossed the threshold into the church proper, the tingling in her flesh increased to pins-and-needles all over. The temperature seemed to rise, and she felt a faint ache in her head whenever she looked at the crucifix, the tabernacle, the statues of St John and the Mother of God ... *It will pass*, she told herself firmly. The pyx and its concealed amulet, which she had half-forgotten, seemed to glow benignly at her breast. She and William went over to the prie-dieux at the edge of the sanctuary and knelt, hand in hand. She could feel his heartbeat in the veins of his palm.

Michael and John, acting as acolytes, came in. Fr Weld was close behind them, dressed in a chasuble of figured white silk, trimmed in gold. They came to the altar and knelt, and the priest began to intone the Introit: '*Deus Israel conjugat vos, et ipse sit vobiscum, qui misertus est duobus unicis: et nunc, Domine, fac eos plenius benedicere te. Beati omnes ...*'

The prayer grated on Marie's ears like a knife dragged across slate. She set her teeth, screwed her eyes shut, and gripped the shelf of the prie-dieu with one hand and William's fingers with the other, as if to break them both; it was a battle not to get up, put her fingers into her ears, and run from the sanctuary. But she held still and waited. Every pause in the prayers and readings was a lungful of fresh air.

After an eternity of shrilling pain, there was a silence. She opened her eyes, wondering whether the Mass was somehow over, though she had no memory of pronouncing vows—but then she saw John picking up the missal stand to move the book to the gospel side, and realized that they were much less than halfway through the liturgy. She almost whimpered with exasperation, but controlled herself. John, with his oddly uncoördinated eyes, gave her a curious look just before he turned around to genuflect, as if he had noticed her strange behavior; but the moment passed and was gone.

'*Alleluia, alleluia*,' sang Fr Weld sonorously. '*Mittat vobis Dominus auxilium de sancto: et de Sion tueatur vos. Alleluia. Continuatio Sancti Evangelii secundum Joannem.*'

Even in the midst of her discomfort, Marie smiled at the twofold fitness of the gospel passage: the wedding at Cana, where the Lord had changed the water into wine. She chanced a look at the statue of the Virgin, and whispered a brief prayer despite the pain.

Fr Weld skipped the customary reading of the Scriptures in English, and also spared Marie a homily; and then, the moment was upon them. He turned around and looked paternally on the pair. A tinge of anxious anticipation was clear in his eyes, and the same unspeakable question was written across all three faces.

'William, do you freely and willingly take Marie, here present, as your lawful wife according to the laws of God and of holy Church?'

'I do,' he declared ringingly.

The priest turned to her. In a moment, they would know. 'Marie, do you freely and willingly take William, here present, as your lawful husband according to the laws of God and of holy Church?'

'I do.'

She winced, anticipating the fiery sting of the sacrament's effect. But there was no pain: no searing of her flesh, no ache, not so much as a pinprick. She gasped, and looked wonderingly first at Fr Weld, then at William. He glowed. The priest put his hand to his mouth, and seemed to be trying not to weep. He shook his head rapidly and went on, his voice shaking a little: 'Now that you are united in holy Matrimony, join your right hands and say …'

They repeated the words as Fr Weld said them, William first, his tenor rich with joy, followed by Marie, her soprano sunk to a whisper. She was transported. She hardly perceived the praying of the Canon and the Secret, though her eyes were drawn upward to the Host at the elevation and stung with tears. She felt a delicious wave of warmth when Fr Weld made the sign of the cross over her, to bless her in lieu of receiving holy Communion, since she was still unshriven.

The postcommunion. The final peace. And then, at last, the priest said, 'You may kiss the bride.'

William reached forward and threw the veil back over Marie's glossy curls, his eyes shining like grey suns.

They left for Calais that night, taking ship from the Grand Surrey Docks. Marie stood at the rail as they sailed out over the English Channel. The thinnest crescent moon was visible, like a tarnished shilling with one polished edge. A salt wind blowing down from the North Sea swept the air clear, so that she could make out faint points of light on the far shore.

The solitude—for of course most passengers preferred the warmth and softness of their beds—was not like the solitude of Ravenhurst. The densely luxuriant manor had had mere isolation, polluted with an unpleasant sense of continuous, unseen movement: the servants, and Augustus, and the poltergeist, all going about their strange sorts of business on the other side of the walls; never there when one looked, yet always and indefinably intruding, providing neither company nor privacy. But here, as she gazed at the rippling sea, there was a wild, enchanted feeling in the loneliness; it made her think of the vast expanses of space in the chasms between great mountains.

A pleasing and familiar scent met her. She smiled as William slid his arms around hers from behind her and placed his chin on her shoulder.

'What are you thinking of, Mistress Vavasour?' he said.

She paused, searching for the right words. 'I am at peace.'

'Are you hungry?'

'Yes. No. Not now. I want to look at the stars.'

'May I join you?'

'Please.'

He kissed her ear. They gazed up at the stars, flaming silver in the blue midnight, like an illuminated Mediæval apocalypse. The sign of the Lion reared in the eastern quarter of the sky, and the head of the Virgin's constellation looked back at them as it cleared the horizon.

'Will?'

'Hmm?'

'What if … what if I cannot have children any longer?'

He placed his right hand on her cheek. 'You are mine. I am yours. That is enough. I did want children, and I do; but let that be. If they come, they come. And if they do not, well, with my wife's permission, it will not be for lack of trying.'

She giggled and pinched him. He laughed, and hugged her more tightly.

They reached France at one in the morning, and quickly made their way to the train station, where William booked them a private compartment on a train bound for Geneva. From there, they would traverse Switzerland, and finish across the Austrian border in Innsbruck. Marie spoke no German yet, but William's was adroit, and they would be able to hire Marie a professional German tutor once they got themselves settled in Austria.

The train rumbled amiably upon the tracks. Their car was not particularly comfortable, but love covereth a multitude of railway accommodations. They talked until sunup of the things they wanted to see: the elegant Hofkirche, with its great statue of King Arthur among the heroes and relatives ranked about the sepulcher of the Emperor Maximilian; the eighteenth-century Church of St James, fantasticated and triumphal, the apex of the Austrian baroque; the lavish Helblinghaus, the Tyrolean Theater, and the immense Hofgarten with its outsize chess sets, so large a man could stand in the squares.

As they climbed into the French side of the Jura, William finally fell asleep, his head in Marie's lap. Grateful to be close to the window, she pulled down the shade, lest the sunlight wake him. Still exulting in her liberation from the winter's nightmare, she was too overjoyed to sleep, and beguiled the time by cautiously extracting one of William's books from his luggage—a pristine copy of *Sir Gawain and the Green Knight*—and reading through it. Its eccentric dialect of Middle English was difficult but rewarding work, and made the time pass easily, until William began to stir again.

'Good day, my chevalier,' she said to him sweetly.

'Good day, my lady. What time is it?'

'Getting on for six o'clock. You've slept all day.'

'Gracious. I *am* an attentive husband, aren't I?'

She leaned down and kissed him. 'You have had as much to do as I have over the last two or three days; I think your sleep was well-earned.'

'You perfect angel. Where are we?'

'Outside Zurich, I think,' replied Marie. 'Perhaps further.'

A terrific thunderclap startled them both, and hail began to beat a tambourine on the windows. William let up the shade; though sunset was not long past, the sky was as black as ink, and distant lightning showed the towering firs and pines about them as flashing silhouettes on the mountainsides. Eager for distraction, she asked him to teach her a few German phrases, and was pleased to master them quickly.

The storm became more severe as they journeyed on. Eventually a member of the staff came to their compartment to inform them that the train would have to halt in a little Alpine town, until the weather abated somewhat. It was a place called Sankt Gallenkirch, in the westernmost reaches of the Austrian Empire. Since they did not have a sleeping car, having expected to arrive in Innsbruck more promptly, they were welcome to leave the train there and seek lodging at an inn if they wished—they need only leave word with the conductor not to depart until their presence had been verified.

The train pulled to a cautious stop, so as not to careen off the steep, slippery tracks. The Imperial officials made rather a meal of checking the foreign couple's passports, but they let them disembark. William wrapped his cloak around Marie as well as her own, and, being advised that Frau Brunner's was just the place for them, they darted as briefly as possible through the cacophonous rain. They found the inn: a drowsy sort of place in the center of the town, run by a matronly, fat woman with a large Rosary at her waist. On learning that the foreign couple were newlyweds, she was suddenly all grins and winks and nods and nudges and chuckles, and showed them to (so she said, at some length) the finest room in the place. They thanked her as politely and briefly as they could, and at last she left, and they shut the door against the whole world.

'Will,' said Marie, shaking her black ringlets loose from her hood, 'you are my heart and soul.'

'Oh, go on,' he said shyly.

'I am serious.' She laid her hands upon his chest, trying to find the words to convey the urgency of her meaning. She could feel the warmth of his body and the music of his heartbeat in her fingers. He must understand, she must tell him. 'You have saved me from hell: from the clutches of that rapacious, murdering—no, I won't talk about Ravenhurst. Not tonight. But you do realize, don't you, my darling—it sounds like melodrama and yet it's the plain truth, that you have stared death itself in the eye to rescue me, and death blinked first?'

He slid his arms around her and kissed her, and then put his forehead against hers. 'I could do no other. It was you who rescued me first; your forgiveness gave me back the hope to live. You are my life, my very body. Oh, Marie …'

Their embrace lingered; their kisses spread, flesh to flesh. Her fingers, freed of gentling gloves, ran over the points of his collar. His empyrean hand cupped her breast over her heart, close to the forgotten circlet of the phylactery. The room, the storm, the past, all Europe receded as they entered into the fire.

The fields that lay about Ravenhurst Manor were cold. Rimbaud had answered the viscount's invitation, and suspected he knew what lay behind it. But, though he delighted in the nomadic, epicurean life of the professional æsthete, he was growing tired of men. Verlaine had long consumed all his energy, bad and good; and his short-lived if pleasant affair with Germain Nouveau had ended in disappointment and desertion. He was not altogether sure that he wanted to become the plaything of Augustus Fairfax now. He went anyway: partly because he was also unsure that he did *not* want to.

The butler met Rimbaud at the door with a weary air. Something seemed to have been taken out of him—some guiding force or purpose. It was strange. Nonetheless, Rimbaud entered and went to the library, where Ravenhurst greeted him formally and sent for some wine.

'*Bonsoir, Vicomte Ferface*,' said Rimbaud. 'A rather quiet night is anticipated, I gather?'

'Yes. Something more intimate.' He spoke with his usual charm, but he too seemed somehow different: tired, or distracted.

'Will Monsieur Chastelard be joining us?'

Augustus winced. 'No.'

Rimbaud nodded and sat down. 'Tell me, Monsieur—what shall we talk about tonight?'

The other also sat. 'I do not mean to be abrupt, *mon ami*. But I also have no desire to waste your time or mine, and so I shall speak frankly. Would you like to come here to Ravenhurst and live with me? I have taken a fancy to your company as well as to your poetry, *chère grande âme*' (the Frenchman stiffened at this echo of Verlaine's first letter to him, but he said nothing), 'and I should be delighted to have you here in style, as long as you like.'

He nodded again. 'And in return?'

'What?'

'In return? What would you have of me?"

Augustus gave a forced smile and gestured elegantly. 'The pleasure of your handsome company.'

'*Alors*. That.' The butler entered, setting glasses before the men. 'It is an exceedingly generous offer, Monsieur. I may need a little time to consider.'

'Naturally, naturally,' said Augustus, not quite managing to conceal his disappointment.

'Tell me,' said Rimbaud, picking up his glass, 'where is the young lady who was staying here, Marie—I think you said she was your niece?'

'Oh, she—'

But Augustus' reply was interrupted by Rimbaud choking violently on his drink. '*Vierge Mère de Dieu!*' The poet coughed. 'This is the foulest vintage I ever have tasted!'

'What!'

'It has the taste of liquefied iron! What is the meaning of this?' he said angrily to his host.

'I—there has been some confusion—'

Rimbaud stood up rapidly, accidentally knocking his wine glass over. Its contents cascaded onto the rug. He opened his mouth to continue his tirade, but the stain stopped him; its hue looked anomalous for wine. He examined it more closely, and sniffed. Augustus sat motionless, watching him. Then Rimbaud straightened again, his face clammy and pale. 'That is blood.'

'Don't be ridiculous, Arthur. Why would I give you blood to drink?'

'It is blood. *Why* does not matter, that is what it is.'

The two regarded one another in silence for a few moments. Augustus could practically see the gears in the poet's head spinning. Rimbaud whispered, adapting Baudelaire's lines: '*Toi qui, forte comme un tropeau de démons, vins, folle et parée, de mon corps humilié faire ton lit et ton domaine—non?*'

Augustus said nothing to this. There was nothing to say.

Rimbaud spoke again, his voice shaking and his eyes moistening with tears of terror. 'I have been to the houses of many English lords and burghers, and many of your sort take great pride in their fine mirrors. You have none at all. Why have you no mirrors, *Vicomte Ferface?*'

Ravenhurst said, 'Rimbaud, listen to me. Impossible though it may seem, I have the power to bestow eternity upon you—beauty that cannot die. Let me show you …'

But he was already backing away toward the door, the tears flowing freely across his cheeks now, his hands up, as if to fend off the nightmare. '*Dieu.* You are a raving madman.' His eyes flickered with nausea for a moment. 'Chastelard, Marie … Murderer. Murderer.'

'Arthur—'

'*Non.* If you would kill me, kill, but do not do this, *mon Dieu*, this thing, this perversion of life and death both. Kill, or else leave me be.'

Augustus stood, and followed the poet, keeping pace with him, the two ever facing each other as Rimbaud fumbled his way backward through the mansion and toward the door, too frightened or too wise to run. 'Please listen to me. Your verse is incomparable. Would you really have it die in a mere fifty years? Your physical beauty is singular; would you have it wither? The secrets, the pleasures and powers I have to offer you, need never perish or fade, and you need never cease from tasting them.'

'*Satan, farceur, tu veux me dissoudre, avec tes charmes*,' Rimbaud answered. 'Keep away from me.'

'*Mon ami—s'il—* '

'*Non.*'

His wandering hand found the front door. Augustus halted, unwilling to leave the manor, his lone sanctuary. 'There are others out there, you know,' he said. 'Their only law is to do as they will. Thus far, only my patronage has kept them from taking you.'

'And if that is true, why have you not taken me by now, by force?' said the other coldly. He opened the door.

'Don't leave me,' said the vampire wretchedly.

Rimbaud pulled the door shut, and fled Ravenhurst forever. Augustus stared mutely at the door and ran a hand through his hair; then he wandered, unseeing, through the labyrinth of rooms that composed his house, until he found himself entering Marie's old room. He sat down on her bed and looked at his copy of *The Holy Communion of Saint Teresa of Ávila*, thinking back to the act of painting it, counting the brushstrokes it had taken. Hours later, he was still at it: six hundred ninety-two ... six hundred ninety-three ... six hundred ninety-four ... six hundred ninety-five ...

CHAPTER XIX

CONSUMMATION

The old constraint of an essential bond
Hath linkt them in my mind: opposed they stare,
Twin silences, that through Time's Otherwhere,
The ruinous past, thus each to each respond,
One with mysterious gaze that sees beyond
The straining suns, calm as the voidness there;
And one with eyes like deserts of despair,
Flameless as granite, clear as diamond.

— CLARK ASHTON SMITH, *SPHINX AND MEDUSA*

Fr Weld, having sent John and Michael to bed for the night, was sitting down to a last cup of tea when there was a knock on the door of the rectory. He sat still for a moment, his eyes shut, gripping the table: Lent had just begun, and he was hungry and tired and short-tempered, and could hardly face a visitor now. But the knock was repeated with vigor, and he sighed and rose to answer it.

To his surprise, he had not one but three guests. One was Archbishop Manning. The other two were Bishop Danell of Southwark, and a man who introduced himself as Mr Tomasz Kowalczyk, evidently the Polish secretary of whom the Archbishop had spoken previously. The priest invited them to sit around the table in the kitchen, and the Archbishop nodded to Kowalczyk to speak.

'I have been translating the text that you furnished His Excellency with recently, Father.'

'Yes, the one about—er—' He flashed a look at Archbishop Manning.

'Vampires, yes, that one. Come, Father: I should hardly have brought them if they did not know,' the Archbishop said.

Kowalczyk spoke. 'I have some regrettable news, Father.'

'What could be more regrettable than the mere fact of these lethal creatures?'

Bishop Danell spoke. 'You performed a clandestine marriage for a Mister William Vavasour and a Miss Marie Redglass, just two days ago—is that correct, Father?'

'I did, Your Excellency. Allowing for some circumlocutions, I outlined the whole matter in my letter to the Archbishop. The young lady was obliged to use a pseudonym in the official record, as they were planning to leave the country in secret, on account of vampire pursuit; but it is the same person. According to young Mister Vavasour's researches—'

'How quickly can you get in contact with them?'

'I can't,' said the priest. 'The Vavasours were going into hiding, on the Continent, I believe. They were afraid to leave a trail.' Manning's face became grey, and the other two exchanged miserable looks with each other. 'Your Excellencies, what is this about?'

Kowalczyk pulled out the volume *Wampiry*, and essayed to speak again, but seemed unable to do so. Archbishop Manning collected himself and told Fr Weld, 'The young couple are dead.'

Marie could feel William's eyelashes upon her cheek, his warm palms running up and down her back. For a single conscious moment of strangeness, the contrast almost took her breath away—the slight callusing on his hands against her petal-smoothness, the keen but yielding hairs on his cheek grazing hers, the vibration of moans in the depths of his chest below her treble murmurs, the vetiver scent of his body commingling with her own lavender and myrrh. The fingers of her left hand were in his golden hair; her right plucked at the buttons of his shirt. His hand stroked the loosened corset-cords between her shoulders, his breathings feathered against her skin as his mouth broke from hers, she kissed his cheek and his eyes and his brow, and found herself whispering a phrase from the Little Office of the Virgin: '*Læva ejus sub capite meo, et dextera illius amplexabitur me.*'

'With my body,' he breathed back to her, 'I thee worship.'

Heat. Sighs like music. Neither was aware of the passage of time. Heartbeat. She was as naked as Eve, and he was her Adam. She kissed his throat, and his right hand pulled her waist in close to his own.

Augustus did not notice how long he remained numb. When he came downstairs again and found Godalming, he gave him a passionless reprimand for mixing up the glass of blood with the glass of wine.

A letter was on Augustus' desk when he retreated to his study. Evidently the butler or young Peter had brought it there and forgotten to tell him. It was from Vivien Glastenning. He opened it.

Though it would have been the obvious thing to do with him, the Duke had apparently not been put to the Second Death. But he most likely wished he had: both his fangs had been pulled out. The rumors were saying, too, that his fingers had been chopped off just above the outermost joint—no growing back talons for him. He'd have to settle for twisting the heads off of birds and animals for blood, if that were true.

She had gone on to write that not only (as Ravenhurst probably knew already) had Lord Richmond, the recently deposed Chief Justice, been killed, but Tinsmith had killed the killer—who, by the way, was the Duchess of Ely, of all people. Apparently she had been quite the dark horse: a number of slaves and servants in several prominent vampires' houses, including several at the palace itself, had come out of telepathic trances after her death. It seemed she had been maintaining an eyes-and-ears network, the likes of which the Duke himself could not have hoped to rival even at the apex of his powers. Well, no longer.

Chastelard, deprived by the Reverend Doctor of revenge upon the murderess of his lover, had disappeared. But somehow Miss Glastenning did not think that he had been killed. After Carroll's death, he was the obvious rallying point for the surviving Chartists. Surely, if he had been murdered as well, it would have been published by whatever enemy had accomplished it. Did Lord Ravenhurst by any chance know where he was? He had been raving with grief and wrath: he was horribly dangerous, and likely to attract attention. Especially if there did happen to be any vampire hunters in England at the moment—perhaps among the refugees from the recent Italian wars.

Augustus looked up from the letter, brooding. The expression on Paul's face when Carroll was killed, and the bestial howl he had let forth, were things not easily forgettable. And however he had posed as a detached ironist, Chastelard's attachment to the Earl of Richmond had plainly run far deeper than he admitted— as Augustus realized, too late, he ought to have foreseen: they had drifted apart as lovers precisely due to Chastelard's passion and his own lack of it. Augustus might have taken thought for the ferocity coming from a love first requited and then snapped in mid-course. Chastelard ought to be found, before he did something really drastic. But the notion that he could draw the attention of modern-day hunters was surely absurd. The last hunter of any importance had been Konstanty Grabowski, a Polish priest who had died sometime around 1760; and as for Great Britain, why, even Catholics like the Redglass family—

Catholics like the Redglass family; and that tomfool courtesan, Vavasour, he came from an old recusant clan of Yorkshire—and if memory served was moreover linked to the notoriously popish Howards, the Dukes of Norfolk. Marie had said they were getting married: that meant a nuptial Mass. Surely a vampire was likely to attract attention at such an event? And Vavasour himself, so famously devout: had he been confessing all those dirty little conferences in the Manticore Palace, the groans and the sighs and the scars on his neck—which would have been less shameful had they been mere whorings in the style of Mrs Berkley? Could some canny or superstitious priest have put two and two together?

Augustus shook himself. There was time for that later. And seeking Chastelard's whereabouts was imperative, but not this instant. The letter. Yes. He returned to the table and picked it up, realizing only as he did so that he had risen and begun to pace through the library, just thinking about the Catholic Church in England mobilizing vampire hunters.

Anyway. Livilla had assumed the Manticore Throne, parlaying her newly assigned office into some notion of being the heir apparent. Yet even she knew, now, how meaningless it was to be the Duchess of London. She clung to the dignity not out of conceit, but from sheer fright—it seemed to her a small shield, especially in the absence of both von Orlok and Carmilla. Even with regard to the palace, she was mistress of only two wings: the rest was under the control of Tinsmith and his lackeys (whose numbers had multiplied substantially in the past few nights). The alliance between the Chartists and the Precisians against the monarchy had proven fraudulent; Tinsmith had never expected Carroll to uphold his end of the deal, and had planned accordingly, so that he had resources to fall back on, which the Chartists had not after the February apocalypse. The Reverend

Doctor might not be the undisputed master of undead London, but he was as powerful as any other single contender.

Dozens of vampires had been massacred before the riot had turned to a stampede. More had been caught and killed later, by one of the factions or over a personal grudge, on their way home. Most vampires were living off their servants for now, having, like Augustus, carefully revoked all their invitations—though it was rumored that the Baron of Monmouth, who had been such great friends with Lady fitzUrse, had granted her refuge in his own manor house and been beheaded by her for his trouble. For the rest, the wardings and revocations, and a greater care in the choice of favors to old friends, would hopefully suffice; though naturally all that would prove useless if anyone should light their houses on fire.

Augustus shuddered. He laid the letter down again, tenting his fingers in thought. *Ubi nunc gloria Babyloniæ?* He did not mind the social collapse in itself; even though, as Carmilla's son, he had theoretically been attached to the monarchist establishment, it was an open secret that he had no real political loyalties; and the recent Ragnarok had the merit of being entertaining when viewed from a safe distance. But the *extent* of it—it was a game, and people (other people) did lose games, but already the number of vampires who had been put to the Second Death was a little frightening. It made him wonder whether lying low was an adequate response. The alternative was to go somewhere else for a while. France was too obvious—anyone who wanted to kill Augustus would be killing him as a rival and a danger, not out of passion, which meant that they would try to track him down—but Scotland might do. Or Spain. Travel might be risky while you were engaged in it, especially toward the beginning, but get more than a score of miles outside London and the danger fell dramatically, whether on the road or off it. It was something to consider.

He licked his lips. Fire. Such a horrible idea.

The aristocrat rose and fetched himself a frock-coat, top hat, scarf, and gloves. Days ago he would have sent a servant for them, but he was feeling ill-disposed toward his staff at the moment. He walked out into the night, alone, ignoring the landau and the horses, and made his way toward the city, murmuring to himself the harmonious desolation of Omar Khayyám:

> '*Lo! some we loved, the loveliest and best*
> *That Time and Fate of all their vintage prest,*
> *Have drunk their Cup a Round or two before,*
> *And one by one crept silently to Rest.*'

And Augustus an immortal, no less. Fire, or sword, or sun. Did it make much difference?

In William and Marie's room there was warm, drowsing dimness. A sudden gasp and moan. A star-silhouetted figure, going over to the sink in the corner of the room. Running water splashed on skin. Outside, the trees shivered as the late winter wind gusted through their branches, and were still.

His breath steaming, Henry Redglass adjusted his knapsack on his shoulder as he walked gingerly on the ice of Gray's Inn Road. His night at the workhouse had been entirely sleepless: he was looking for an inn tonight, but he would sooner find a disused doorway than go back to the workhouse. If a constable objected, Henry was hoping a few gold sovereigns would convince the fellow to let him be. He had had no luck yet in finding news of Marie—God alone knew how long it would take—but, thus far, he had only been through the Temple and High Holborn, and his hopes were not dampened, even if his enthusiasm was.

There was another figure on the road, coming from the general direction of St Pancras. He had an arresting appearance. He seemed to be nearer thirty than forty, though his brown hair was already flecked with grey; his clothing proclaimed him a nobleman, and a sybaritic one, with a malachite-green scarf peeking out of an impeccably tailored, Regency-style frock-coat. His silk hat flashed like a hypnotist's focus in the streetlamps. What on earth was a man of his stature doing wandering about London in the middle of the night?

A few yards away, the stranger stopped and sniffed the air. Then he approached Henry. 'Mister Redglass, I believe.'

Henry was still. 'How do you know my name—sir?'

'You might say that your reputation precedes you. And that of your late father, for whom I offer you my profoundest condolences.' The man had drawn level with Henry now, and lifted his hat in token of respect.

'Thank you. I, er … sir, I don't—'

'Fairfax is my name,' said the stranger, extended a gloved hand and shaking Henry's firmly. 'I am the Viscount of Ravenhurst.'

'Augustus Fairfax? The Spiritualist medium?'

'The same.'

'I see, my lord. Charmed.'

Augustus smiled. 'Everyone is. You are looking for your sister, I suppose; she vanished recently, I saw it in the *Times*.'

'Yes,' said Henry eagerly. 'You two knew each other, I gather; have you any idea where she could be?'

'Alas, no. But yes, I did know her a little myself—such a charming, clever girl, and a lovely one. I should be happy to put what resources I can at your disposal; between ourselves, I have followed the case a little, and I am not at all satisfied that the metropolitan police are doing all that they could be. Of course, no gentleman ever has any money, but even so, I feel sure I can conjure such familiars as will resolve you of all ambiguities.'

'Why, I thank you, Lord Ravenhurst. I hardly know what to say. Will you come and have a drink with me?'

Augustus smiled again. 'I should be delighted, Mister Redglass.'

The bloodless starlight was spilled across the floor of William and Marie's room. It was night. The gas-lamps were unlit. The curtains had been drawn earlier, but now they were open, to let the light in. It distorted the appearance of everything inside, so that silver, blue, and black were the only colors. Marie was sitting on the bed; she had resumed the white gown she had worn for the wedding.

A servant boy knocked and came in, asking cheerfully, '*Mein Herr und meine Frau, ist—*'

Her head shifted, veiling her face with shadow. The irregularly shaped tarn of liquid on the floor had its own proper color, of course, but it looked like a pool of quicksilver—except for the spots where William's arm and crown cast black shades in it, and a sliver where the more natural light from beyond the door stained it red.

The boy gasped, '*Meine Frau?*'

'*Hier raus. Jetzt.*'

The boy was still. The vampire extended her arm and pointed away imperiously, opening her mouth to pronounce no words, but an infernal hiss. He choked on a fearful cry and ran, slamming the door shut behind him.

So. So it had all ended like this. She had become a night-nursery terror. Marie lowered her hand back into her lap. Then she reached up again, compulsively, and dabbed at her lips, though they had already been clean since the wee hours of the preceding morning.

Augustus had foreseen it. He was cruel, thoroughly selfish, and right. Probably he had been telling her the simple truth—for the first time in all their acquaintance, maybe—when he had said that, once, he had been like her.

Could it have turned out any differently? If she had stolen a bottle of blood before leaving Ravenhurst? Or refrained from feeding on that fellow on Waterloo Bridge? Or, or, or … useless speculation. It made her sick to prolong it. No matter what, there lay William's body, motionless and icy as her own. His was still naked, since they had consummated the—the …

She smiled coldly. Of course. That was why the sacrament of marriage had not burned her when she pronounced her wedding vows: not due to a miraculous cure, reversing death, but just because she was dead already and therefore ineligible for the sacrament; hence, no sacrament had been effected. *For in the resurrection they shall neither marry nor be married, but shall be as the angels of God in heaven*, she recollected wryly. *Invalid by defect of matter*—an impediment that could not be dispensed even if they had requested it of the Vicar of Christ. *Till death do us part*, as the Anglican Prayer-Book phrase had it. Death had preëmptively parted them.

The clock struck eight. She had been sitting with the corpse, the exsanguinated body of her widower, for seventeen hours, unmoving. She had considered weeping; but the horror was still too fresh for any deliberately exerted display of that kind.

And what now? She remembered when she had asked Augustus what one did as a vampire, and he had said to her grandly, *Whatever one pleases. We have, quite literally, all the time in the world.*

The thing to do, the honorable thing, was clearly suicide. Less out of remorse for William's death—such a gesture felt meaningless—than to protect others from the monstrosity one had become. This hideous *thing* in human shape had no right to exist. That the human shape did happen to be Marie's own was not important or even interesting. But, at the same time that she saw the honorable thing to do, she realized plainly that she lacked the courage to do it. It did not even occur to her to consult her religious conscience, and if she had, she would have had no way of telling whether it was still a sin to commit suicide when one was already dead. But that metaphysical question was of little consequence. The brute fact was that, faced with the prospect of the Second Death, she could not bring herself to set her flesh aflame, or throw her throat on a blade, or sit outside and wait for the sun to consume her. She was afraid.

It came to her vaguely that she now understood her fellow vampires perfectly. The æstheticism, the *realpolitik*, the decadence: all of it made a costume that concealed or justified their own monstrosity to themselves; nothing more. Tinsmith, she realized, was the only one who looked vampirism squarely in the face and accepted it, and was, correspondingly, the most shambling devil of them all.

Marie's rattling mind suddenly threw up a text from the Catechism: *When oppressed by mortal guilt, nothing can be more salutary, so precarious is human life, than to have immediate recourse to the tribunal of penance; but could we even promise ourselves length of days, yet should not we who are so particular in whatever relates to cleanliness of dress or person, blush to evince less concern in preserving the luster of the soul pure and unsullied from the foul stains of sin.* But that gate was shut to her. No soul; no sacrament that she could both receive and endure; and, if suicide were indeed a sin for her—to say nothing of the sins she had committed since being made into a vampire, which, apart from absolution, themselves assured Marie of her seat among the damned—no repentance seemed logically possible, for to make her confession would presumably kill her, and since she knew it beforehand, would that not be counted suicide? She released a ragged cry of anguish.

Augustus, then, had the right of things, he and Chastelard: accept what one is, and play it to the hilt. It hurts less. Though even Augustus was not quite consistent—she rightly guessed that he hated the Masquerade Ball because it reminded him at once of his own falsity and his happier past. And she suspected that some lingering tincture of conscience was still in him, too: his last warning would have saved William's life, had she heeded it. He even loved her, in his own twisted fashion, as she had realized in the cellar before she left. The notion did still fill her with distaste; but it was now distaste merely, rather than horror and disgust, as it had been when he told her about Laura. Her image of herself was now too sickening for her to feel sickened by the image of any other.

She glanced at the mirror above the sink, and could not help laughing grimly. She and Will had been so preoccupied—or, subconsciously, so unwilling to test their dream—that neither of them had noticed the emptiness of the white bridal gown.

Well then. Back to London, back to Ravenhurst, back to the whole black bloody business. What else was there to do? Besides, it was her own business. She was not, as William had fondly, foolishly called her in one of his letters, a Muse and a Grace. She was a Fate and a Fury.

The vampire rose from the bed and crossed to their heap of luggage. She needed almost none of it, but the money would be useful for train and boat fare, and to keep officials from making difficulties about what they would think her eccentric need for darkness and privacy. There was no need to deal with the corpse. They would be able to give him a decent burial in Sankt Gallenkirch. She noticed the Red Scapular he had worn among the bedclothes, and laid it gently on his body, so that they would know at least that he had been a Catholic, and put him to rest in consecrated ground.

She was not worried about making good her escape, not even with the witness of the servant boy to endanger her. She knew, without pride or enthusiasm, that she was a skilled enough telepath to make herself unremarkable to anyone she passed. Picking up a cloak, if only out of habit, she moved toward the door; but something stopped her. She could not bring herself leave as perfunctorily as that. Standing at the door, she turned back and looked at William's lifeless face, his glassy, sea-grey eyes open. She crossed over to his body again, closed his eyes, and steeled herself to pray.

'*Requiem æternam dona eo, Domine: et lux perpetua luceat eo,*' she pronounced, ignoring the burn. '*Requiescat in pace. Amen.*' She finished by making the sign of the cross, though it made her hand ache and sting. She owed him that.

Marie pulled the door open, slipped out, and closed it again.

'Lord Redglass?' said Harker gently.

James groaned and sat up in bed. 'What is it?'

'Master Henry has come back, my lord.'

'What?' He fumbled for the lamp, and then found his wire-rimmed spectacles and pulled them on. 'When did he arrive?'

'Just a few minutes ago. He is downstairs in the drawing room. He doesn't seem altogether well. He has a badly anæmic look, and will hardly speak. I've given him some cognac; would you like me to fix him something to eat?'

James swung his feet down into his slippers. 'Thank God he's alive. Yes, Harker, thank you—I mean please—scramble him some eggs or something. Thank you for waking me. Where is my dressing gown?'

'Here you are, my lord.' The aged butler helped his master into the silk robe, and led him downstairs. Harker then turned down the servants' stair to the kitchen, and James went into the drawing room, where Henry was sitting before a waxing fire. He was oddly slumped, and his eyes were nearly shut; his left hand lay above them, shielding them from the light. He was breathing rapidly, shallowly, and Harker had been right—he was an ugly white.

James croaked, 'Henry! You're safely home, I'm so glad.'

Henry looked up from under his hand, and muttered something inaudible, though it did not seem to be hostile.

James sat down in an armchair opposite him. 'Your room is as you left it. I shall have Harker take your things back. Are you quite all right?'

Silence.

'Henry, say something, please.'

He inhaled heavily and spoke again, in an obscure, slurred voice. James had to lean forward and ask him to repeat what he had said several times before he made it out; not that that mattered much, for the words made no sense:

'Charmed, charmed. I feel the same way, my lord. Such a leonine physiognomy. Why there? Oh, well, certainly. Nothing at all? Thank you. Next time, perhaps.'

As he spoke, he raised his other hand to his ashen, clammy throat, massaging two reddish spots there as if they pained him.

CHAPTER XX

HOMECOMING

Her skin was as white as leprosy,
The Nightmare Life-in-Death was she,
Who thicks man's blood with cold.

— SAMUEL TAYLOR COLERIDGE, *THE RIME OF THE ANCIENT MARINER*

A few melancholy nights later, Augustus was sitting in his library, a glass of blood in one hand and a copy of *Paradise Lost* in the other. He was reading aloud to himself: he savored the agglutinated cadences of Milton's verse.

'*Thrones, Dominations, Princedomes, Vertues, Powers,*
Hear my Decree, which unrevok't shall stand.
This day I have begot whom I declare
My onely Son, and on this holy Hill—'

He was interrupted by Godalming. 'What?' Augustus snapped.

'You have a visitor, my lord.'

'Who?'

'I do not know, my lord; the lady declined to give her name, and her face was veiled. I offered to show her in, but she refused, saying she had to speak with you personally.'

Livilla, probably, seeking refuge from the consequences of her foolishness. Or Miss Glastenning—it was just possible, if she had news of Chastelard's whereabouts, given how little Augustus had managed to find out. Or it could be a messenger from the Oratory.

'Very well. You may go, Godalming.' He rose and went to the front door, which was shut, and opened it.

On the step, in a Georgian gown of champagne-white satin, her veil now thrown back over her luxuriant ringlets, stood Marie.

They stared at one another. She spoke in a hard voice.

'I'm back, Augustus.'

He nodded, expressionless. Then he took a step backward, opening the door more widely and making a courteous gesture. 'Come in.'

She stepped boldly over the threshold.

APPENDIX A

FOREIGN WORDS AND PHRASES

FRENCH

· *a tout pourquoi il y a un parce que*: 'For every why there is a wherefore, there's a reason for everything.'

· *allemande*: 'German [dance].' A type of dance, originating in the Renaissance, that formed part of the baroque suite.

· *alors*: 'Well then.' A semantic filler word.

· *aperitif*: 'Opener.' A drink, typically alcoholic, served before a meal; comparable to an appetizer.

· *arabesque*: 'In Arabic fashion.' A ballet position in which the dancer stands on one foot and extends the other leg out behind the body, both legs being held straight.

· *assez*: 'Enough.'

· *attendéz*: 'Attend, look, pay attention.'

· *au premier sang*: 'To first blood,' as opposed to *à l'outrance*, to the death.

· *aussi*: 'Also, as well.'

· *béatifique*: 'Beatific.' With reference particularly to the Beatific Vision, the final beholding God in heaven.

· *beau geste*: 'Beautiful deed.' More particularly, a noble or pretty gesture that is basically meaningless.

· *beauté*: 'Beauty.'

· *bien sûr*: 'To be sure, certainly, of course.'

· *bon mot*: 'Good word.' An intelligent remark, usually witty.

· *bon sang toujours ment*: 'Good blood always lies.' A perversion of the actual French proverb *bon sang ne saurait mentir*, 'Good blood doesn't know how to lie.'

· *bonsoir*: 'Good evening.'

· *ça ne fait rien*: 'It doesn't matter.'

· *ça va*: 'How are you?' Highly informal.

· *câlice*: '[[Holy]] chalice!' An oath sworn by the Holy Grail or, more generally, the Eucharistic chalice used in the Mass.

· *çe que l'enfant out au foyer, est bientôt connu jusqu'au Moustier*: 'What the child hears at home is well known to Moustiers [[a city]].' The equivalent English proverb is 'Little pitchers have long ears.'

· *c'est dans l'ordre des choses*: 'It is in the nature of things.'

· *c'est impossible*: 'It is impossible.'

· *c'est le ton qui fait le chanson*: 'It's the tune that makes the song.' The English proverbial equivalent is 'It's not what you do, it's how you do it'; Chastelard is probably being flat-footedly literal here, however.

· *chaise longue*: 'Long chair.' A chair designed for reclining, similar in shape to a couch or divan.

· *charmante*: 'Charming.'

· *chère grande âme*: 'Dear great soul.' This phrase was employed by Verlaine in his famous first letter to Rimbaud, inviting the latter to come and stay with him after becoming acquainted with Rimbaud's poetry; the two (of whom Verlaine was married, with a child on the way) then carried on a tempestuous and sometimes violent affair for some years, chiefly in France and England.

· *chouquettes*: A type of French pastry, consisting of a small roll-like piece of light pastry dough sprinkled with coarse, or "pearl," sugar, and sometimes filled with mousse or custard.

· *comme regardez-vous nôtre père Auguste*: 'What do you think of our father Augustus?'

· *comme vous et le Président de la Haute Cour de Justice*: 'How are you and the Lord Chief Justice?'

· *comme-es tu*: 'How are you?' An informal or familiar greeting.

· *coup d'état*: 'Blow of state.' A sudden seizure of power, usurpation, or overthrow.

· *courante*: 'Running.' A type of fast dance, traditionally the second part of the baroque suite.

· *crêpe*: 'Curled.' A type of fabric (usually silk or wool) with a distinctively crimped appearance, often associated with mourning clothes. Sometimes Anglicized as 'crape.'

· *demimonde*: 'Half-world.' A class of people, especially women, who have lost their full status in high society through promiscuity or otherwise immoral behavior, but who are not regarded as low-class. Violetta of *La Traviata* (who is typologically similar to Satine in *Moulin Rouge*) is an exemplary demimondaine of fiction, and the titular character of *Gigi* is schooled to play the same role by her benefactresses; Madame de Montespan (a mistress of Louis XIV Capet), Barbara Villiers (one of the many mistresses of Charles II Stuart), and Wallis Warfield Simpson (mistress and eventual wife of Edward VIII Windsor) are historical instances.

· *demoiselle*: 'Young lady.'

· *diablette*: 'Little she-devil.'

· *douce/doux*: 'Sweet.'

· *dragonette*: 'Little dragon, dragonet.'

· *Du mécréant saisit à plein, poing les cheveux, / Et dit, le secouant: 'Tu connaî tras la règle*: 'He grabs a fistful of the infidel's hair, / And says, shaking him: "You shall acknowledge rule!"' From *Le Rebelle* ('The Rebel') by Charles Baudelaire.

· *égalitariste*: 'Egalitarian.'

· *élan vital*: 'Life force, vital essence.' This phrase was later used by the French creative evolutionist philosopher Henri Bergson, to identify and explain the tendency of living things to organize themselves for self-preservation and in more and more complex forms. It is not attested before Bergson's work; it is possible that the phrase was used by coincidence, or alternately, that Miss Redglass' memory misled her due to some subsequent acquaintance with Bergson's terminology, projected backward to the relevant conversation due to the essential similarity of the concepts.

· *Enchanté, bien sûr, Mademoiselle de le Manoir de le Nid de Corbeaux. Parlez-vous Français, ma, si je peux me permettre, mignardise?*: 'Charmed, to be sure, Mademoiselle of Ravenhurst Manor. Do you speak French, my—if you will permit me—delight?'

· *enfant terrible*: 'Terrible child.' One who says things that customarily are not said aloud and in public.

· *et puis après?*: 'And what then?, So what?'

· *et votre petit demoiselle, que ç'est tres belle! Votre penchant en la féminité, pour toujours excellent*: 'And your little lady, who is very beautiful! Your taste in women ⟦is⟧ always excellent.'

· *êtes-vous bien*: 'Are you well?, Are you alright?'

· *façade*: 'Frontage, face.' Generally the face of a building, and most often sets the tone for the rest of the structure.

· *fer-face*: 'Iron face.'

· *folie à deux*: 'Madness for two.' A shared psychosis, usually beginning with one person and then being transferred to another; may be extended to more parties, and even become a mass delusion.

· *fouetté*: 'Whipped.' A ballet move in which the dancer spins on one foot, using momentum from the other leg by raising it and swiftly bending it at the knee.

· *garçon*: 'Boy.' A term used to address servants.

· *gaucherie*: 'Clumsiness.'

· *gavotte*: 'Gavotte.' A French dance, originating as a folk dance of the Gavot people (hence the name) in Dauphiné, north of Provence. Was sometimes substituted for the more customary *gigue* or jig that followed the *sarabande* (when that was used) in the baroque suite.

· *il vous plait?*: 'It pleases you?'

· *ingénue*: 'Innocent girl.' Also used as a term for a stock role in theater, opera, and (today) film, for an endearing and wholesome young female, usually a lead character, typically beautiful, kind, gentle, virginal, and unsophisticated; sometimes provided with a *femme fatale* as a foil, or vice versa.

· *la Bible*: 'The Bible.'

· *la vertu*: 'Virtue.'

· *la vérité*: 'Truth.'

· *la volupté*: 'Pleasure.' Specifically, sensual pleasure.

· *Le Léthé*: 'The Lethe.' The river of forgetfulness in the classical concept of the underworld.

· *l'Enfer*: 'Hell.'

· *les chasseurs*: 'Hunters.'

· *Les Fleurs du Mal*: 'The Flowers of Evil.' A collection of poetry by Charles Baudelaire, one of the most influential poets of the Decadent movement.

· *ma belle soeur*: 'My beautiful sister.'

· *ma chérie*: 'My dear, my beloved.'

· *ma fille*: 'My daughter.'

· *ma fleurette*: 'My little flower.'

· *ma mignardise*: 'My delight, my pleasure.'

· *mes gants son en la*: 'My gloves are on the —'

· *mon ami*: 'My friend.'

· *mon amour*: 'My love.'

· *mon petit chou*: 'My little head of cabbage.' An endearment (if, to English-speaking ears, a rather baffling one).

· *née*: 'Born [[as]].' Indicates a maiden name.

· *nous sommes bien*: 'We are well.'

· *nouveau riche*: 'Newly rich.' One whose wealth allows them to mix with the aristocracy, but whose manners or character expose them as being of commoner stock.

· *Nymphes des Bois*: 'Nymphs of the Wood.' A piece written by Josquin des Prez, a composer of the French Renaissance, in memory of his recently deceased teacher John Ockeghem.

· *Ô beauté si ancienne et toujours nouvelle*: 'O beauty so ancient and ever new.' A quotation from the Confessions of St Augustine (X.27), according to a translation dating to 1841 (suggesting that Chastelard had kept abreast of developments in Catholic literature).

· *plaisir*: 'Pleasure.'

· *pour vous*: 'For you.'

· *Quand la pierre, opprimant ta poitrine peureuse / Et tes flancs qu'assouplit un charmant nonchaloir, / Empêchera ton coeur de battre et de vouloir, / Et tes pieds de courir leur course aventureuse, / Le tombeau, confident de mon rêve infini*: 'When the stone, oppressing your frightened breast / And your flanks, now supple with charming nonchalance, / Will keep your heart from beating and from wishing / And your feet from running their adventurous course, / The grave, confidante of my limitless dreams ...' From the poem *Remords Posthume* ('Remorse After Death') by Charles Baudelaire.

· *quand on dîne avec le diable, il faut se munir d'une longue cuilleur*: 'He who sups with the devil needs a long spoon.'

· *rebelle*: 'Rebel.'

· *remords a noyé plus de gens que Neptune*: 'Remorse has drowned more people than the sea.' A perversion of the French proverb *vin a noyé* etc., meaning 'Wine has drowned more than the sea.'

· *saintes putaines*: 'Holy whores.'

· *sarabande*: 'Sarabande,' Gallicization of Spanish *zarabanda*, 'whirl, rush.' A type of dance in triple meter, sometimes included in the baroque suite, but condemned by some observers as sexually indecent. When the dance migrated to France (and thence to present-day Germany, where Bach favored it in his compositions), it became a slow dance.

· *Satan, farceur, tu veux me dissoudre, avec tes charmes*: 'Satan, jester, you would dissolve me with your charms.' A quotation from Rimbaud's own poem *Nuit de L'Enfer* ('Night of Hell') from his first book, *Une Saison en Enfer* ('A Season in Hell').

· *soirée*: 'An evening ⟦party⟧.'

· *solécisme*: 'A solecism; a violation of the rules of grammar.' Metaphorically, any act that is conventionally incorrect.

· *soubrette*: 'Coy; conceited.' An operatic voice-type and role, generally a light soprano in a comedic opera, playing a character who is young, saucy, and clever; sometimes she is overtly sexual. Mozart's Despina from *Così fan Tutte*, Papagena from *The Magic Flute*, and Zerlina from *Don Giovanni* are all *soubrettes*.

· *soupçon*: 'Relish, savor, taste.'

· *sûrement*: 'Certainly, surely, obviously.'

· *thuriféraire*: 'Thurifer, censer.' Metaphorically, a flatterer or sycophant.

· *Toi qui, forte comme un tropeau de démons, vins, folle et parée, de mon corps humilié faire ton lit et ton domaine—non?*: 'Thou who, strong as a troop of demons, came, mad and adorned, to make of my humbled body thy bed and thy domain—no?' An adapted set of lines from Charles Baudelaire's *Le Vampire*, from his influential collection of poems *Les Fleurs du Mal* ('The Flowers of Evil').

· *une moment plus, s'il vous plait, mon coeur*: 'One moment longer, if you please, my heart.'

· *Vicomte Ferface*: 'Viscount Fairfax.'

· *Vierge Mère de Dieu*: 'Virgin Mother of God!'

· *voici*: 'Behold.'

· *zut*: 'Damn, oh my God.' A general (and thus almost untranslatable) expression of surprise.

GERMAN

· *angst*: 'Dread, anxiety, fear.' Used by Kierkegaard (in its Danish cognate *angest*) and some later Existential philosophers, to denote the fearful or vertiginous sense of possessing moral freedom, unique to man among the animals.

· *Burggraf*: 'Burgrave.' An approximate equivalent of the English title *viscount*, but cf. *Markgräfin* below.

· *der Blutsauger ist, was er ißt*: 'The vampire is what he eats.' An allusion to the same phrase, with *Mensch* ('man') instead of *Blutsauger*, from Ludwig Feuerbach, a nineteenth-century German Hegelian philosopher known for his advocacy of Liberalism, atheism, and materialism.

· *Ewigkeit*: 'Eternity.' Approximately equivalent (particularly in the phrase *in alle Ewigkeit*) to the liturgical phrase 'world without end,' but also an ordinary equivalent of English 'forever.'

· *Frau*: 'Lady, ma'am.'

· *Fürstreich*: 'Princedom, princely rule.' Here used as an approximate equivalent of *dukedom* (in the sense of institution rather than territory), owing to differing meanings of the title *duke* in British and Germanic usage.

· *Graf*: 'Earl, count.'

· *Herr*: 'Lord, sir.'

· *hier raus*: 'Get out.'

· *jawohl*: 'Yes indeed, absolutely.' An emphatic form of *ja*, 'yes.'

· *jetzt*: 'Now.'

· *Markgräfin*: 'Marchioness, marquise.' An approximate equivalent; German noble titles, derived from the hierarchy of the Holy Roman Empire, do not correspond at all points to the terms of English peerage.

· *Mein Herr und meine Frau, ist*: 'My lord and my lady, is —'

· *Mein hure*: 'My whore.' Probably intended as a derisive pun on *Mein Herr*, a courteous form of address.

· *Phänomenologie des Geistes*: 'The Phenomenology of Spirit.' The most important philosophical work of Hegel, detailing his theory of the development of human consciousness and its implications for ethics and social history.

· *realpolitik*: 'Practical politics.' Politics based solely upon expediency rather than ethical principles.

· *schnell*: 'Quickly, hurry up.'

· *Spanisch Meister*: 'Spanish Master.' A quasi-technical artistic term as applied to Goya and his predecessors.

· *Weltanschauung*: 'Worldview, perspective, philosophy.' First used by Kant and popularized by Hegel; borrowed into English usage under the academic influence of German philosophy.

ITALIAN

· *a domani sera*: 'Until tomorrow comes.'

· *ahimè*: 'Alas, woe.'

· *amico*: 'Friend.'

· *Augusto*: 'Augustus.'

· *argento armellino oro leone rampante verde*: 'Argent ermined or, a lion rampant vert.' A coat of arms, consisting in a white background patterned with yellow symbols designed to resemble ermine tails in shape, with a rearing green lion superimposed on it. In practice, tawny (a shade of orange rarely used in most heraldry) would probably be substituted for or, yellow being so difficult to see on a white field.

· *avanti*: 'Come in, enter.'

· *basta*: 'Enough.'

· *basso cantante*: 'Singing bass.' A type of bass voice toward the higher end of the range (often equated with the bass-baritone voice), typically displaying a rapid vibrato. Known in opera for such roles as Don Alfonso from *Così fan Tutte* and Don Giovanni from the eponymous work, both by Mozart, and Méphistophélès from Gounod's *Faust*.

· *brava*: 'Bravo, good ⟦work⟧, well ⟦done⟧.' Here made feminine; *bravo* is masculine.

· *bravissimo*: Superlative form of *bravo*.

· *buona notte*: 'Good night.'

· *buona sera*: 'Good evening.'

· *burattinaia*: 'Puppet-mistress, puppeteer.'

· *cazzo*: 'Fuck!'

· *Chiarachioma*: 'Ravenhurst.'

· *cicisbei*: 'Lovers, paramours.' A loose masculine equivalent of a mistress (singular *cicisbeo*).

· *Colombina*: 'Little dove.' A stock character in professional Italian comedic plays (called *Commedia dell'Arte*): an intelligent, tricky, coquettish servant-girl, often paired with the *Arlecchino* or Harlequin (himself a servant apt to thwart his master), and frequently acting as a go-between and aide for her mistress and her mistress' true love.

· *coloratura*: 'Coloring.' In music, ornamentation (or the capacity for it), such as trilling, wide leaps, and the like.

· *come si desidera*: 'As you wish.'

· *cortigiani*: 'Courtiers; courtesans.'

· *Così fan Tutte*: 'Thus do all ⟦women⟧,' or loosely, 'Women are like that.' A comic opera of Mozart's, in which two soldiers lay a bet that their beloveds will be faithful while they are away, then returning in disguise to try (with ultimate success) to seduce one another's respective paramours.

· *dragotte*: 'Dragonets, young dragons.'

· *figlia*: 'Daughter.'

· *figlio*: 'Son.'

· *il passo è periglioso, può nascer qualche imbroglio*: 'The step is perilous, some calamity may ensue.' From Mozart's opera *Don Giovanni*.

· *il ventaglia nera*: 'The black fan.'

· *L'Orfeo*: 'Orpheus.' The tale of Orpheus' tragic attempt to bring his wife Eurydice back from the dead, in operatic form, by Monteverdi.

· *malebolgia*: 'Evil pouch.' A reference to Dante's *Inferno*, in which the Eighth Circle of Hell (where sins of Fraud are punished) is called the *Malebolge* or evil ditches, in the plural; the circle is subdivided into ten rings, each being a singular *malebolgia*. Anglicized by Dorothy Sayers in her translation of the *Divine Comedy* as 'Malbowges,' from the obsolete Middle English word *bowge* or 'pouch.'

· *negarlo*: 'Deny it.'

· *nostra*: 'Our.' Sometimes used in place of 'my' in formal speech.

· *o, poverini, per femmina giocare*: 'Ah, poor fellows, to wager on a woman ⟦a hundred ducats⟧.' The incomplete quotation comes from an arioso in *Così fan Tutte*, in which Don Alfonso predicts the outcome of the opera.

· *Paolo*: 'Paul.'

· *porco Iddio*: 'Pig God!, For God's sake!'

· *primo uomo*: 'First man.' The male equivalent of a *prima donna*.

· *quell'osservazione era fuori luogo*: 'That remark was uncalled for.'

· *scacco matto*: 'Check-mate.'

· *Smanie Implacabili*: 'Torments Implacable.' An aria from *Così fan Tutte*, lamenting loneliness.

· *Una Donna a Quindici Anni*: 'A Lady of Fifteen Years.' An aria (also from *Così fan Tutte*) in which a maid urges the two female leads to surrender to the seductions of two apparently foreign gentlemen (who are in fact their own lovers in disguise, each making an attempt on the virtue of the other's mistress).

· *Una molta bella donna, si, bellissima. Come sta, Signorina?*: 'A very lovely lady, yes, the loveliest. How do you do, mademoiselle?'

· *Vetrosso*: 'Redglass.'

· *vostra*: 'Your.' Courteous plural.

Latin

· *anima enim omnis carnis in sanguine est*: 'The life of all flesh is in the blood.' See Leviticus 17.11.

· *arbiter elegantiæ*: 'Judge of elegance.' A title ascribed by several ancient historians to Petronius, a dissolute courtier of the Emperor Nero, known for his *panache* and wit.

· *contra mundum*: 'Against the world.' From a storied dictum of St Athanasius: when summoned before the Emperor in Constantinople and asked why he would not subscribe to the Semi-Arian heresy, being told, 'The whole world is against you,' the saint calmly replied, 'Then I am against the whole world.'

· *Converte nos, Deus salutaris noster: / Et averte iram tuam a nobis. / Deus, in adjutorium meum intende: / Domine, ad adjuvandum me festina. / Gloria Patri et Filio et Spiritui Sancto: / Sicut erat in principio et nunc et semper*: 'Convert us, God our savior: / And avert thine anger from us. / O God, come to my assistance: / O Lord, make haste to help me. / Glory be to the Father and to the Son and to the Holy Ghost: / As it was in the beginning, is now, and ever shall be …' These lines come from the opening of Compline, the night prayer of the Little Office of the Blessed Virgin Mary.

· *Deus Israel conjugat vos, et ipse sit vobiscum, qui misertus est duobus unicis: et nunc, Domine, fac eos plenius benedicere te. Beati omnes*: 'God weddeth you, Israel, and he himself is with you, who is compassionate unto both singly: and now, O Lord, make these to bless thee more fully. Blessed are all …' The Introit of the matrimonial liturgy, according to the Tridentine form then in use.

· *dixit insipiens in corde suo*: 'The fool hath said in his heart.' From Psalm 14.1 (Psalm 13.1 in the Vulgate).

· *Et cum aperuisset sigillum, audivi vocem animalis dicentis, Veni et vidi, et ecce, Mors et inferus*: 'And when he had opened the seal, I heard the voice of a beast say, "Come and see," and behold, Death and hell.' Adapted from Revelation 6.7-8.

· *generatio præterit, et generatio advenit: terra autem in æternum stat: vanitas vanitatum, et omnia vanitas*: 'A generation goes, a generation comes: but the earth stands forever: vanity of vanities, and all is vanity.' Adapted from Ecclesiastes 1.4, 2.

· *homo natus de muliere brevi vivens tempore*: 'Man that is born of woman hath but a short time to live.' See Job 14.1; this verse is used in the Anglican service for the dead.

· *in odorem unguentorum tuorum currimus: adolescentulæ dilexerunt te nimis*: 'We run unto the scent of thy ointments: the young woman have delighted in thee exceedingly.' Taken from the Song of Solomon 1.2, and used in the Little Office of the Blessed Virgin Mary.

· *in omnibus requiem quæsivi, et nusquam inveni nisi sed in angulo cum libro*: 'In all things I sought rest, and never yet found it but in a corner with a book.' A quote from St Thomas à Kempis, author of *The Imitation of Christ*.

· *in te Domine speravi: non confundar in æternum*: 'In thee, O Lord, I have hoped: let me not forever be confounded.' The last line of the *Te Deum*, a liturgical hymn traditionally attributed to SS Ambrose of Milan and Augustine of Hippo (said to have been sung by them, spontaneously and responsively, when Augustine was baptized). The *Te Deum* is generally sung on Sundays and the greater feasts.

· *læva ejus sub capite meo, et dextera illius amplexabitur me*: 'His left hand is under my hand, and his right hand embraceth me.' From the Song of Solomon 2.6; also used in the Little Office of the Blessed Virgin Mary.

· *lamiæ*: 'Succubi, vampires.' A type of monster hailing originally from a paramour of Zeus in myth, named Lamia, whose children Hera jealously killed (or in some versions kidnapped), so that Lamia went mad with grief and became a monster that destroys the children of other women. One of John Keats' greatest poems is titled *Lamia*.

· *Laus Veneris*: 'The Praise of Venus.' A famous, lengthy poem of Swinburne's, relating a version of the Tannhauser legend, about a knight who lived in sin with the goddess Venus herself.

· *massa damnata*: 'The mass of the damned' ('mass' here being used in the quantitative sense, not the liturgical). Some Catholic theologians, past and present, have been of the opinion that a majority, even an overwhelming majority, of the human race will go to hell, and hence referred to the bulk of humanity as the *massa damnata*. Other Catholic thinkers throughout history have disagreed very strongly with this view, some even being bold to hope for the salvation of all mankind (e.g. St Gregory of Nyssa, St Isaac of Nineveh, and Lady Julian of Norwich), though the doctrine of free will prevents this from being asserted dogmatically.

· *Mittat vobis Dominus auxilium de sancto: et de Sion tueatur vos. Alleluia. Continuatio Sancti Evangelii secundum Joannem*: 'The Lord sends you help out of the holy place: and from Zion he guards you. Alleluia. The continuation of the holy Gospel according to John.'

· *Officium Defunctorum*: 'The Office of the Dead.'

· *omne animal triste post cenam*: 'Every animal is sorrowful after dinner.' A reworking of *omne animal triste post coï tum*, 'every animal is sorrowful after coitus,' attributed to Galen, a prominent Greek physician of the second-century Roman Empire. Exact wording varies.

· *quid autem habetis quod non accepistis*: 'For what have ye that ye did not receive?' From I Corinthians 4.7.

· *quod Moses exaltavit serpens in deserto*: 'Which serpent Moses lifted up in the desert.' A slight rewording of part of the Vulgate text of John 3.14, where Christ compares Himself to the bronze serpent made by Moses as a sympathetic antidote to snakebite (see Numbers 21.4-9.)

· *requiem æternam dona eo, Domine: et lux perpetua luceat eo*: 'Eternal rest grant unto him, O Lord: and let light perpetual shine upon him.' A specified adaptation of the commonest phrase in the Mass for the Dead.

· *requiescat in pace*: 'May he rest in peace.' A common phrase in the Mass for the Dead and in Catholic prayers for the dead.

· *Resurget frater tuus. Dicit eo Martha, Scio quia resurget in resurrectione in novissima die. Dixit ei Jesus, Ego sum resurrectio et vita. Qui credit in me et si mortuus*: 'Thy brother shall rise again. Martha saith to him: I know that he shall rise again, in the resurrection at the last day. Jesus said to her: I am the resurrection and the life: he that believeth in me, although he be dead ...' From the Gospel of John (Vulgate text; the translation here given is taken from the Douai-Rheims, then the standard English Catholic translation), 11.23-25.

· *Sacrificillum Scientiæ*: 'A Small Sacrifice for Knowledge.'

· *Sola vobis relinquimus Templa*: 'We have left you only the Temples.' From the *Plea for Allegiance* of the late second and early third century African Christian apologist and theologian, Tertullian, describing the ubiquity of Christians in the Empire after only two hundred years.

· *Te Lucis ante Terminum*: 'To Thee Before the Close ⟦of Day⟧.' A Latin hymn used for Compline, the prayers recited before bed, in the Roman Breviary. Ascribed by some to St Ambrose of Milan.

· *Theatrum Chemicum*: 'Chemical Theater.' A compendium of alchemical writings, compiled in the first half of the seventeenth century, published in six volumes from 1602 to 1661.

· *ubi nunc gloria Babyloniæ?*: 'Where now is the glory of Babylon?' A slight adaptation of a phrase from a Latin hymn titled *De Contemptu Mundi* ('On the Despising of the World'), sometimes attributed to St Bernard of Clairvaux.

· *usque ad futurum sæculum non desinam, et in habitatione sancta coram ipso minitabar*: 'Even unto the coming age I shall not cease, and in the holy dwelling before his face I threatened.' A corruption of a line from the Vulgate translation of Sirach, used in the Little Office of the Blessed Virgin Mary, which has *ministravi*, 'I have served,' rather than *minitabar*, 'I threatened.'

OTHERS

· *draugar*: 'Revenants.' Old Norse, singular *draugr*. A creature of Scandinavian folklore, extremely similar to the vampire.

· *fakir*: 'Poor man.' Arabic. Originally a type of Sufi ascetic; sometimes used broadly to denote ascetics from the Levant, Persia, and the Indian subcontinent.

· *hoi polloi*: 'The masses, the plebeians.' Greek. Transliterated (and adopted into English usage) from οἱ πολλοί, meaning 'citizens.'

· *Loobly wher he leyde Lytch himself awaken / For to prollen þe pasture of Mars peple. / Euer he eketh lyf endyng anoþeres, / Baryng for þe blood þe bones so whyte. / Swych schall he be swelt, sweuenes troubel, / Lyuen not, and lust, nor may he leue / Til Domes Day and deþes dien, / Except a meke mayde schall amenden his synnes. / Wedded as a widwe to þat whyte deuel / Sche schall grace get him, þe graue to undoen*: 'Loathsome where he laid, the Litch roused himself / To prowl the pasture of Mars' people. / Ever he increases life, ending another's,

/ Baring their bones, so white, for blood. / So shall he be dead, trouble dreams, / Live not, and lust; nor may he leave / Till Doomsday and death's dying; / Unless a meek maiden shall amend for his sins. / Wedded as a widow to that white devil / She shall get grace for him, to undo the grave.' Middle English. Note, both here and in the other selection from *King Arthur the Holy*, the obsolete grammar and spelling *passim*: the use of the letters *þ* (thorn) and *ȝ* (yogh), rather than the later digraphs *th* and *gh*; the orthographic (though not phonemic) identification of *u* and *v*, with *u* always employed in the middle of words for either sound, and *v* at the beginning of words in the same fashion; the preservation of the archaic genitive in *-es*, surviving today only as *-'s*; the use of *y* exclusively as a vowel, frequently in preference to *i*; and the frequent use of *-en* as a verbing suffix appended to adjectives and nouns (still used in Modern English, as in verbs like *darken*).

· *rubáiyát*: 'Collection of quatrains.' Persian. A collection of a particular type of Persian verse called *rubá'i*, of which that of Omar Khayyám is the most famous, first being published in English in 1859.

· *strigoi*: 'Wraiths, specters, ghosts.' Romanian. The spirits of the restless dead, some of them vampiric.

· *upir*: 'Vampire.' Exists, in slightly differing forms, in Belarusian, Czech, Russian, Slovak, and Ukrainian. Of uncertain etymology; may be derived from the Slovak verb *vrepit'sa* ('to stick, to thrust into'), or alternately from a Turkic term for 'witch,' cf. Tatar *убир* (*ubir*).

· *wampir*: 'Vampire.' Serbian. The reason for its use in the journal of a Polish priest (as opposed to a native term such as *wapierz*) is uncertain; it is possible that he learned the word from the villagers of Kisilova, where the purported vampire Petar Blagojevich had lived.

· *Wampiry: Ich Natura i Maniery*: 'Vampires: Their Nature and Habits.' Polish.

· *Wynd out of þe westelond wouen aboute him / As he had ryden riȝt harde vpon rouþeless Badon. / Caliburn clouen hem, crested heddes fellen / In swych scarlet as swete wyne / Flouyng in þe far feldes of fayre Camalot*: 'Wind out of the west land wove about him / As he rode right hard upon ruthless Badon. / Excalibur clove them; crested heads fell / In such scarlet as sweet wine / Flowing in the far fields of fair Camelot.' Middle English. Cf. the above entry under *Looþly wher he leyde*, etc.

APPENDIX B

NAMED PERSONS

This is an index of all of the chief players in undead London in late 1874 and early 1875 who appear in this text, as well as of the historical personages referenced in it. Vampires, whether active, deceased, or missing at the time the *Diaries* were written, are marked with a dagger (†) before the name.

I have not been able to find equally thorough documentation of the histories of all the people noted here: of some, whose lives intersect with better-known history, I have been able to give a modest biographical *précis*, while of others I have hardly been able to verify anything more than a name. Although not all the names appear in full in *Death's Dream Kingdom*, I have listed them alphabetically by surname or its closest equivalent. For vampires, the dates before the semicolon are those of life, and those after it, of undeath (unknown or indeterminate dates being printed as such or left blank); however, I have provided slightly less information on that score than I might have done, so as not to turn the index into a minefield of unmarked "spoilers" for those readers who want only to keep the names and titles straight. References to other entries in the index are set in italics.

Readers will notice that some figures mentioned only in passing in the text are given fairly substantive entries, while conversely some major figures have fairly brief paragraphs here. I have seen fit to address things in this fashion since, while the frequently terse *Diaries* could presume in their readership British and classically liberal education and habits of reading, an intelligent American audience of the twenty-first century can scarcely be expected to be acquainted with the finer points of peculiar matters like the religious risings of sixteenth-century England or the folklore of rural Hungary. Since the full force of many remarks and persons often draws heavily upon this background, I have tried to provide such information as the lay reader would be unlikely to have immediate access to, or would find particularly interesting, or both—hopefully without lading down the text.

†À Tintagel, Stephen. 974?-date unknown; date unknown-1499. Prominent priest in pre-Reformation vampire religion in Britain; exact sphere of influence uncertain, but probably Wales and southern England. Claimed to have been born in the noted date, and to be of pure Cornish-Breton blood; both claims are plausible but unverified. Reputed to be the great-grandsire of von Orlok, Julius through two unknown vampires. Rebelled against *de Ville, Saturninus* and brought about his death; was killed himself shortly thereafter, with about thirty companions, in the St Ives Massacre.

†Barrett, Francis. All dates unknown. Referred to in the text primarily as Lord Arden; it is uncertain whether he is to be identified with the occultist Francis Barrett (fl. ca. 1800). Sired by *von Orlok, Julius*; convicted of writing the seditious Chartist Letters (though historians unanimously regard the verdict as rigged). Was punished by having one fang pulled out. Went into exile, reputedly in Scotland. No further records or activity are known.

†Bath, Lady. See *Thackeray, Livilla*.

†Báthory, Elizabeth. 1560-1600?; 1600?-1614? Countess in the Kingdom of Hungary. She is known to history as one of the most prolific serial killers on record, having tortured and murdered at least 80 victims, though uncertain reports place the number as high as 650. She cannot have been sired as a vampire any earlier than 1598, after the birth of her last child; scholars mostly agree that she was a vampire not later than 1601, when her husband's mysterious illness began, attributable to her depredations. Her career as a serial murderess and sadist had, however, already been going on for about fifteen years, and she carried such practices further than any vampire on record. Her sire is unknown, though it has been conjectured that she was sired by *the Mad Margrave* sired by *à Tintagel, Stephen* in 1453; she is also rumored to have sired *von Orlok, Julius*, but this is unconfirmed. Her eventual fate is also unclear: she was tried in 1610 and condemned to life imprisonment for her murders, and was certainly found dead in her cell in 1614; whether this was merely undeath or the Second Death has never been established. No apotropaics or vampiricides are known to have been in her cell, which had no windows, so vampirologists tend to favor the idea that this was a ruse on Countess Báthory's part, and that she escaped from one of the sites of her burial (she was first interred in modern-day Slovakia, but was moved to the Báthory family crypt in Hungary); the present location of her body, dead or undead, is unknown.

†**BORGIA, CARMILLA**. 1099?-1135; 1135- . Duchess of Ely. May have come originally from Sicily.

BORGIA, GIACOMO GIAMBATTISTA. 1824- . Opera singer (baritone). Born in Tuscany, he became an operatist at a young age, and toured much of the European side of the Mediterranean, including most of Italy, Savoy, southern France, Spain, Portugal, Dalmatia, and southern Greece. He spent a short time as a courtesan in Savoy, but backed out of his arrangement with his patron, and was helped in escaping to Florence by *Fairfax, Augustus* and *Borgia, Carmilla*, who were in Savoy at the time.

†**CARROLL, NIGEL JOHN**. 1655-1685; 1686- . Earl of Richmond and Kingston-upon-Thames from 1745, following the suicide of an unknown predecessor; Lord Chief Justice of undead London from 1792, succeeding *Eyre, Jonathan*. Generally believed, both by his contemporaries and by vampirologists, to have authored the seditious Chartist Letters against *von Orlok, Julius*. Lover of *Chastelard, Paul* from about 1810.

CASSILDA [FORENAME UNKNOWN]. 1850?- . Cook at Ravenhurst Manor. No other facts have proven ascertainable.

†**CHASTELARD, PAUL ALPHONSE**. 1766-1789; 1789- . Sired as a vampire by *Fairfax, Augustus*. Formerly a Cistercian postulant, and then and aspiring vampire-hunter in Paris. Lover of *Fairfax, Augustus* for some time after his siring; after about twenty years, left Ravenhurst (on amiable terms) and became the lover of *Carroll, Nigel*.

†**CULPEPER, GABRIEL THOMAS**. 1693-1709; 1709- . Viscount of Chelmsford; member of the Judiciary Council. Widely thought to be the same person as Gabriel

Culpeper, grandson of an illegitimate son of Nicholas Culpeper (fl. ca. 1640-1650), a prominent English physician, astrologer, and herbalist.

†**DANE, HORACE OLIVER**. 1700-1745; 1745- . Seminarian of the Oratory of the Divine Sovereignty; member of the Judiciary Council. Sired by *Tinsmith, Lazarus*.

DARCY, THOMAS. 1467-1537. Was created first Baron Darcy of Temple Hurst by King Henry VIII in 1509. Was twice married (widowed of both his wives) and had three sons, two daughters, and one stepson. Was a prominent military leader under Henry VIII, particularly in the intermittent conflicts with Scotland. Began to display discomfort with the direction of the court after the downfall of Cardinal Wolsey; he secretly communicated with the Holy Roman Emperor in 1534, asking him to stop the English state's encroachments upon the Church by invasion. When the dissolution of the monasteries provoked a revolt called the Pilgrimage of Grace, Darcy eventually turned over Pontefract Castle to the rebels and was sworn to their cause (though he claimed afterwards that he was attempting to redirect the rebellion because he had no power to stop it). Henry VIII pardoned Darcy for this, and he had a hand in putting down Bigod's Rebellion. However, Darcy was eventually tried for treason on other grounds, and was beheaded in London in 1537. Marie states that the mother of *Redglass, James II*, her paternal grandmother, was descended from the Darcies; the Darcy family had become extinct in the male line in 1635.

DAVIES, HYACINTH. 1859- . Maidservant at Ravenhurst Manor.

DE GOYA Y LUCIENTES, FRANCISCO JOSÉ. 1746-1828. More commonly styled simply *Francisco Goya*. Court painter to the Spanish Crown, 1786-1808. A pivotal figure in European painting; has been called the last of the Old Masters and the first of the Moderns, displaying a mastery of classical and realistic technique, combined frequently with subtle adumbrations of later movements' themes and styles, such as Expressionism. Though a client of the monarchy and a practicing Catholic, he not infrequently criticized corruption in both the state and the Church in Spain in his work, notably in a series of aquatints titled *The Disasters of War*. One of his most famous collections, the *Black Paintings*, were domestic pieces painted onto the walls of his own house, never intended for public exhibition and, so far as is recorded, not spoken of by him while he lived; their subject matter varies considerably, but most exhibit near monochromatic colors, muddied lines, and disturbing subjects: *Atropos* (or *The Fates*), *The Great He-Goat* (also called *The Witches' Sabbath*, though Goya authored another painting of that name), and *Saturn Devouring His Son* are characteristic examples.

†**DE VILLE, SATURNINUS**. 875?-909?; 909?-1499. The dates of de Ville's birth and siring cannot be confirmed by outside testimony, and are reported only by sources traceable to himself. Duke of undead London from an unknown date until his death by burning in 1499, somewhere in the South Downs (probably near Sutton, Sussex). Sired *Eyre, Jonathan* in 1449, appointing him Lord Chief Justice a little over thirty years later.

EDWARD THE CONFESSOR (SAINT). 1003?-1066. King of England, 1042-1066, and second-to-last Anglo-Saxon monarch of the country; generally regarded as the last king of the House of Wessex. Known for his piety and unworldliness. The Redglass family (cf. all *Redglass* entries below) claimed descent from him; *Glastenning, Vivien* was widely believed to have been part of his retinue at one time.

†**ELY, LADY**. See *Borgia, Carmilla*.

†**EYRE, JONATHAN**. 1406-1449; 1449-1792? Lord Chief Justice of undead London, 1480-1792. Sired by *de Ville, Saturninus*, and survived the civil wars of 1499-1563 and 1631-1667. Fate unclear; disappeared from the Pantheon in 1792, and no corpse was ever found. Some historians speculate that he was secretly murdered by or on the orders of *von Orlok, Julius* as a potential rival claimant to the monarchy, but this cannot be confirmed.

†**FAIRFAX, AUGUSTUS**. 1314-1347; 1347- . Second Viscount of Ravenhurst, on the northwestern outskirts of London. One of the exceedingly few to have maintained a noble title that he possessed in life after being made a vampire; kept up a certain cautious involvement in mortal society through frequent trips abroad, and by styling himself as his own son, nephew, or cousin over several generations. (At the time the *Diaries* record, Augustus was putatively the seventeenth Viscount of Ravenhurst.) Sire of *Chastelard, Paul* and *Redglass, Marie*.

FAIRFAX, LAURA AYLESFORD. 1324-1347. Viscountess of Ravenhurst by her marriage to *Fairfax, Augustus* in 1338. Died without issue.

FAIRFAX, RICHARD. 1295-1348. Anglo-Norman; the family name is reputedly derived not from the Anglo-Saxon *fager feax*, meaning *fair hair*, but from the French *fer-face*, meaning *face of iron*, barbarized into its later form perhaps through phonological association with the Fairfaxes of Roxburgh. Married *Fairfax, Rosamund* in 1313; the next year, they had a son, *Fairfax, Augustus*. Created First Viscount of Ravenhurst in 1318 for his service in Wales and Ireland, particularly at the Battle of Faughart. Died when the Black Death came to England.

FAIRFAX, ROSAMUND LEFEBVRE. 1300-1390. Norman French, from Rouen. Married *Fairfax, Richard* in 1313 and became the mother of *Fairfax, Augustus*. Was widowed in 1348, and entered religious life as a Carmelite sister in London two years later. Was made Mistress of Novices about 1370, and remained there until her death.

†**FINCH, JOHN**. 1584-1660; 1660- . Baron of Pontefract; member of the Judiciary Council. Before being sired as a vampire, carried out a political and judicial career, chiefly under King Charles I, and served on the notoriously authoritarian Star Chamber. Was created Baron Finch of Fordwich in 1640, but was impeached by the Long Parliament the same year, and fled to Holland for an indeterminate period of time. Returned to England, probably under Charles II, and took part in the trial of the regicides of Charles I. His barony was extinct with his death; he was appointed Baron of Pontefract by *von Orlok, Julius* in 1722. An outspoken critic of the Chartist Letters, penning two severe pamphlets against them.

†**fitzUrse, FRANCESCA**. 1155?-1209; 1209- . Baroness of St Sepulchre; member of the Judiciary Council. Believed to be the illegitimate daughter of Richard fitzUrse, who also fathered Reginald fitzUrse (one of the assassins of St Thomas à Becket). Her mother's identity is not known; however, fitzUrse visited Italy at least four times—once on a pilgrimage to Rome in 1183 while still alive, three times in the sixteenth century—and it was the belief of *Chastelard, Paul* that her mother was an Italian, hence her name. Her sire is not known.

GAUNT, PETER. 1865?- . Servant at Ravenhurst Manor, primarily an errand-boy. Possibly of Romany descent.

GLASTENNING, VIVIEN. All dates unknown. Friend of *Fairfax, Augustus*.

†**GLOVER, DOMINIC**. 1616-1645; 1645- . Canon of the Oratory of the Divine Sovereignty. Great-uncle of the husband of Ann Glover (the last woman hung as a witch in Boston, in 1688). Sire unknown. Appears to have crossed from Ireland around the same time as *Carroll, Nigel*. Reputed, perhaps due to his experiences as an Irish Catholic under the Anglo-Scottish Protestant monarchy in life, to be a Chartist sympathizer; many historians believe he had a hand in distributing the Chartist letters.

GODALMING, MERVYN TITUS. 1819- . Butler at Ravenhurst Manor. Otherwise unknown.

HELLRIEGEL, JOHN (JOHANN) SEBASTIAN. 1861- . Bavarian Catholic, of Jewish extraction, raised in England. His parents went to London to work (one surviving letter of the Hellriegel family in Germany suggests that their conversion to Catholicism was not well received by the family at large, leading to their decision to emigrate). The parents' further information has proven irrecoverable, except that the mother's name was Susanna. Both died of cholera, in or around 1872; thereafter their son lodged at St John the Divine with *Weld, Francis*.

†**THE LADY WITH THE BLACK FAN**. Sire of *Fairfax, Augustus* and *Thackeray, Livilla*. Claimed to have engineered the ascendancy of *von Orlok, Julius*. If this claim is true, was probably the power behind the throne for at least two centuries of London's vampire history; some vampirological historians speculate that she was mistress of the city for more than four hundred years.

†**THE MAD MARGRAVE**. 1407?-1453; 1453- . A German noble by birth. Sired by *à Tintagel, Stephen* while on a pilgrimage in England, in an attempt to consolidate the power and independence of the vampire cult against *de Ville, Saturninus*, who was rising in influence at that time. After being made to understand he was a vampire, the nobleman went mad, and was loose in England for some time before returning to the Continent, where he disappeared somewhere in eastern Europe.

The identity of this margrave is uncertain, though he was widely said to be Prussian; many scholars identify him with Jacob I of Baden-Baden, which would be inconsistent with this report, but otherwise appears to be a convincing possibility, and it may be that the belief that the Mad Margrave was Prussian came from a confusion between him and his (putative) descendant *von Orlok, Julius*. If true, this would put his birth in 1407; whether true or not, it appears that the Mad Margrave was already a man of substance at the time of his siring, so that he was likely born in the first or second decade of the fifteenth century. Regardless of identity, the Mad Margrave is widely thought to be the grandsire of *von Orlok, Julius*, possibly through *Báthory, Elizabeth*.

MANNING, HENRY EDWARD. 1808-1892. Catholic Archbishop of Westminster (consecrated 1865); later Cardinal (1875). Traditional Anglican cleric and important member of the Anglo-Catholic Oxford Movement in the 1830s and 1840s. Converted to Catholicism in 1851, and was an important figure in the Church, in part for his firm and public support for the doctrine of papal infallibility and for his concern for social and economic justice.

†**MONMOUTH, LORD**. See *Tudor, David*.

†**MOUNTJOY, PETROC**. 1729-1752; 1752-1875?. Secretary to the Lord Chief Justice, 1837-1874. Was involved in the notorious kangaroo court that tried *Barrett, Francis*, and expressed sympathy for sentiments expressed in the Chartist Letters thereafter. Tried and convicted of treasonous trespass upon ducal territories, deposed, and imprisoned in 1874. Was slated for execution in the early months of the following year, and the sentence is believed to have been carried out; however, no record of the execution exists, either legal or witnessed, and he may have escaped.

PHILLIPS, AUGUST. 1857- . Footman at Ravenhurst Manor. Otherwise unknown.

†**PONTEFRACT, LORD**. See *Finch, John*.

†**RAVENHURST, LORD**. See *Fairfax, Augustus*.

REDGLASS, HENRY ARTHUR EDMUND. 1858- . Younger son of *Redglass, James II* and *Savoyard, Rose*. Educated at Stonyhurst in Lancashire.

REDGLASS, JAMES II HOWARD. 1824-1874. Sixth Baron Redglass. Husband of *Savoyard, Rose*, father of *Redglass, James III*, *Redglass, Marie*, and *Redglass, Henry*. The Redglasses were a Catholic recusant family of minor gentry, connected to the Throckmorton and Arundell families, and living chiefly in Cornwall. Traditionally, the Redglass family were fervent legitimists and Jacobites, and several of the six Redglass brothers living at the time participated in the Forty-Five in support of Bonnie Prince Charlie; however, the heir to the barony fought for the Hanoverians, resulting in a lasting estrangement between the two branches of the family: the pro-Hanoverians (who held the title to the barony) and the Jacobites. Unwilling to completely dissolve familial ties, the barons departed to live permanently in London, leaving the enjoyment and management of the Cornish estate to the Jacobite branch. They maintained minimal contact up to the time of Miss Redglass's *Diaries.*

REDGLASS, JAMES III ÉDOUARD. 1848- . Seventh Baron Redglass, succeeding 1874 on the death of his father. Elder son of *Redglass, James II* and *Savoyard, Rose*, brother of *Redglass, Marie* and *Redglass, Henry*. Educated at Stonyhurst and attended Campion Hall, Oxford, where he read History.

†**REDGLASS, MARIE CATHERINE AURORA**. 1851-1874; 1874- . Daughter of *Redglass, James II* and *Savoyard, Rose*, sister of *Redglass, James III* and *Redglass, Henry*. Was sent by her father to Mount Holyoke Female Seminary (now Mount Holyoke College) in Massachusetts, USA, from 1868 to 1871. Engaged to *Vavasour, William* in the spring of 1874. Sired as a vampire by *Fairfax, Augustus*.

†**RICHMOND, LORD**. See *Carroll, Nigel.*

RIMBAUD, JEAN NICOLAS ARTHUR. 1854-1891. French poet of the Decadent movement (cf. Charles Baudelaire, Paul Verlaine, Oscar Wilde, Robert W. Chambers). At the age of 17, was a prolific and talented poet. Carried on a homosexual affair with Verlaine from 1871 to 1873, and traveled back and forth between the Continent and England during that time and until about 1875, when he also entirely ceased writing poetry. He dwelt and traveled largely in eastern Africa and the Arabian peninsula thereafter; in 1891 he was diagnosed with bone cancer after an amputation, and returned to France for treatment. He was hospitalized at Marseilles, and was there reconciled to the Church, received Extreme Unction, and died.

Savoyard, Rose. 1829-1858. Of French extraction and education, but brought up in England. Wife of *Redglass, James II* and mother of his three children. Died in childbirth with *Redglass, Henry*. Cf. all *Redglass* entries.

†**St Sepulchre, Lady**. See *fitzUrse, Francesca*.

Stride, Michael. 1867- . Foundling and boarder at St John the Divine Roman Catholic Church (cf. entries *Weld, Francis* and *Hellriegel, John*). Because he was found near the Poplar Workhouse with a note signifying his name pinned to his chest, scholars have suggested he may have been the illegitimate son of Elizabeth Gustafsdotter and John Thomas Stride: the two married in 1869, but Gustafsdotter was living in London by 1866; she is known to have worked as a prostitute, and may have met Stride in that trade. Gustafsdotter is also known to have gone to the Poplar Workhouse in 1877. (She was killed by Jack the Ripper in 1888.)

†**Thackeray, Livilla Claudine**. 1784-1812; 1812- . Marchioness of Bath and Wells. Had become a mistress and favorite of *von Orlok, Julius* by 1840, and Marchioness by 1848.

Theobald, Howard. 1859- . Footman at Ravenhurst Manor. Generally identified with Howard Theobald of Scarborough, Yorkshire. Otherwise unknown.

†**Tinsmith, Lazarus Ezekiel**. 1608-1649; 1649- . Minister of Ministers to the Oratory of the Divine Sovereignty. DD from Jesus College, Cambridge. Though an extreme Calvinist in life, he was also a staunch Royalist in the English Civil War. Tinsmith had been preparing to go into exile in the Netherlands after Cromwell's triumph and the execution of Charles I; however, he was sired by *von Orlok, Julius* before he could leave. He assumed power over the then-decentralized vampire cult almost immediately, refashioning it into a tightly controlled and ferociously persecutory institution; it was largely due to fear of *Tinsmith's Terror*, as it became known, that the former parliamentary deadlock was resolved in *von Orlok*'s favor.

†**Tudor, David**. 1510-1545; 1545- . Baron of Monmouth. Distantly connected to the Tudor dynasty. Reputedly sired by his mistress, an otherwise unknown English dragonet of the Howard family, who committed suicide a few years later. Became attached to the monarchist establishment after the accession of *von Orlok, Julius.*

Vavasour, William Saint-George. 1846- . Cousin (through his mother, Clementine Clifton, illegitimate daughter of the 14th Duke, b. 1830) of Henry fitzAlan-Howard, 15th Duke of Norfolk. Member of an old and well-known family of English Catholic recusants. Educated at Eton and attended Magdalen College, Oxford.

†**von Orlok, Julius Otto**. 1558?-1605; 1605- . Duke of undead London, 1667- . Reputed to the be great-grandchild of *à Tintagel, Stephen* through an unknown sire (though it has been suggested that his sire may have been *Báthory, Elizabeth*) and unnamed grandsire, widely speculated to have been *the "Mad Margrave."*

Weld, Francis. 1830- . Priest of the Catholic Diocese of Westminster; took Holy Orders 1855.

†**Whitgift, Malcolm**. 1775-1808; 1808- . Secretary to the Lord Chief Justice starting in 1874.

About the Author

Gabriel Blanchard has been published in *Crisis* and *PRISM Magazine*, and is the author of the blog *Mudblood Catholic*. He writes prose fiction, poetry, personal and theological essays, and reviews, and is a regular contributor for Pints & Prose. He currently resides in Baltimore and has lived in California, Scotland, and Japan.

You can find Gabriel on Twitter (@mudblodcatholic) and on Facebook at facebook.com/mudbloodcatholic.